and then life was beautiful

HANSON FAMILY BOOK ONE

ASIA MONIQUE

blurb

Couri Mitchell

August Hanson was the *silent* type, the kind who spoke through his actions and not his words.

He possessed enough power to make me feel safe and secure.

I was ready to open up and share the parts of myself I'd never shared with another, and then I got hit with a truth that changed everything.

There was a slight chance he'd still want me, only he had to accept our baby, too.

August Hanson

Couri Mitchell was *my* type, the kind you married the first chance you got.

She possessed enough power to silence the chaos around me.

I was ready to grab ahold of her and never let go, and then I got hit with a truth that changed everything.

There was a slight chance she'd still want me, only she had to accept my daughter, too.

trigger warnings

Grief
Parental death
Pregnancy
Death during childbirth (off-page)

quote

Sometimes the right place is a person.

PART ONE

where we are

"*Death must exist for life to have meaning.*"
–Neal Shusterman

ONE
couri mitchell

THE PRESENT...

"Shit," I cursed, staring at two bright pink lines before shifting my gaze toward the plus four on the digital test next to it.

Life wasn't shaping out how I'd imagined it would.

If anything, it showed me that not all of our plans were meant to unfold how we wanted. I was living proof of that.

Pregnant.

As I choked on my laughter, I slid the tests into my purse, washed my hands, and left the guest bathroom at my sister's place. There was no time to think about how my life was about to change, not with my cousin barreling at me the moment her watery eyes found mine in the sea of people—all dressed in dark clothing—milling about.

"I'm so sorry, Couri," Nani cried, dramatically falling into my arms. "Auntie was the best; she'll be missed."

I hummed and patted her back, my gaze fixated on the lingering sad eyes of family and friends alike, waiting to repeat the exact words my cousin had. I figured Nani needed to be consoled more than I did, so I let her get it out then stepped away to accept words from the rest of the guests.

I allowed people to apologize for my mother's death for a few minutes.

The more they used the five-letter word in an obscene variation of sentences, the more I became numb to it. My heart didn't ache anymore and my hands had finally stopped shaking since getting the news.

It took one week to plan her funeral.

Seven whole days to follow her carefully laid out instructions, right down to the type of casket and burial outfit.

One hundred and sixty-eight hours of trying to remind myself that we had been prepared for this outcome. That my mother had battled hard and fiercely until the very end.

She was the epitome of strength and the perfect example of accepting when being strong wasn't the answer. My mother was the best and I would never be the same without her.

"Excuse me," I mumbled, pulling away from the man who had lived next door to us when I was a teen.

He still smelled like cigarette smoke and something stale I couldn't quite place.

I gagged a little while I walked through my sister's home, into the kitchen, and out of the backdoor onto the oversized deck her husband had built recently. One side was stained a dark chestnut shade while the other still had the store-bought light tan color.

Grateful for today's crisp air, I sucked in as much as possible then released it a few times. The wind rustled the thick brush of trees around the yard and I watched the leaves shift in that direction as it blew.

"What do you think of the chestnut?" King asked as he stepped beside me and tossed his arm over my shoulder.

I leaned some of my weight into him and sighed.

4

Kingston, Journi, and I grew up together on Detroit's east side. I was five years younger than them but knew they'd been starry-eyed for one another from the day he and his mother moved in next door to us.

At some point during their time at Michigan State University, they'd made things official and married exactly one month after graduation. King was the best chosen big brother a girl could have asked for.

I found a love for the game of basketball because of him.

He'd been the guy who always bounced a ball around the neighborhood, even though he was a star wide receiver at one of the best high schools the Detroit Public School system had to offer.

Kingston had been all legs and arms back then, but these days he had bulked up while looking lean because of his height.

"It's nice," I said, eyeing the stained wood again. "I'm sure Journi is ready for it to be done."

"You know your sister."

I nodded, my lips curling at her particular tastes and how he gave her everything she wanted, no questions asked. Their love was so beautiful.

"You found her."

Journi was on my other side before I could turn, arms around me right after.

King held onto both of us, giving us the protection we needed to feel our emotions freely. I appreciated him deeply for always finding me important enough to protect as he did my sister.

"We'll be okay," she whispered, her voice filled with the tears I knew were falling down her pretty face.

Mine were stuck and viciously burning the back of my eyes, but at least I was feeling *something*, right?

"Yeah," I murmured. "We will be."

I kissed her cheek and pulled away from her and King.

"I think I want to head home..." I shook my head when Journi's lips moved. "Too many people here haven't talked to Momma in years. They left her behind when she was most vulnerable and I just need to breathe away from them."

I hated how packed her funeral was when not one of those who got up to give remarks had visited her once in the hospital.

Fucking hypocrites.

King and Journi shared a similar look, one I would surely have to see for a while. You didn't get over the loss of your mother overnight and the concern from the people around you came with that sad truth.

I had no clue how it worked if we were *all* grieving, though.

Who looked out for who?

"I'll come back and help you clean up when the people are gone."

"No need." Journi shook her head. "We have an eleven-year-old child walking around with a garbage bag as we speak. She's taking a stance."

I frowned.

"A stance?"

King chuckled, clearly proud of his expressive child.

"If she starts cleaning, people may get the hint that they aren't wanted here anymore," Journi elaborated.

I smiled.

"Well, at least she didn't yell for them to get the hell out. I call it progress."

Kali had her father's attitude but her mother's soft voice. That small fact never stopped her from speaking her mind and it was something we encouraged in this family.

We were a speak now or forever hold your peace kinda

crew and our relationships with one another thrived because of it.

"Are you leaving, Te?" Kali asked as I neared the front door where she stood.

Her light brown eyes mirrored my sadness and it broke my heart that she had to endure this kind of pain at this young, innocent age.

Kali loved her grandmother.

I tucked a piece of her straightened hair behind her ear and cupped her chin.

"How you feeling, Buttercup?"

"Not happy," she admitted, her little glossed lips pulling into a deep frown. "I want these people gone, so I can be sad in peace."

I nodded slowly, deciding right then to make her wishes come true.

"Alright, everybody, listen up," I yelled, spinning on my heels to face the silenced crowd. "We appreciate each of you being here for us during this challenging time. Today has been a lot for my family and we need the space to finally process how our lives have changed forever. We need the time to... start the healing process. So, if we could wrap this up, my family and I would greatly appreciate it."

I met the eyes of as many people as I could until they started moving toward the exit, where Kali had opened the door wide for them. We stood side by side while our guests exited, murmurs of more apologies and looks to match as they went.

As the last person stepped over the threshold, Kali slammed the door.

"Thank you, Auntie." She walked into my arms. "You're the best. I love you, and if you ever need to talk, I'm here."

She walked off after that and I stared in the direction she'd gone for a long while.

That girl was something else, but she was a great kid with a big heart and I was so grateful to be a part of her world.

"Oh, thank God," Journi rejoiced as she approached me. "I thought I would have to make King kick them out once you were gone. Kali blinked those big brown eyes at you and you couldn't help yourself."

She lifted her thick brows and I shrugged.

"The girl deserves the world."

"Still heading out?"

I nodded and pulled the door open.

"Yeah, but I'll see y'all at the lawyer's office tomorrow."

"Forgot about that shit," she mumbled to herself but followed quickly with, "I love you."

I popped the lock on my truck and climbed inside, eager to get to my domain.

"I love you more!" I yelled through my lowered window as I backed out of their driveway and drove out of their quiet Bloomfield Hills neighborhood.

I made the forty-minute drive to my townhome in Sterling Heights in complete silence. My shoulders dropped as I pulled into the driveway.

My father was gone.

My mother was gone.

I was pregnant.

Over and over I repeated those things in my head, finding peace in their truth.

Eventually, the truth would be too much to bear, but one day I'd wake up and be able to function again. It was the vicious cycle called life—unpredictable and terrifying.

I hadn't found my happy medium yet, the place in this

world where I could find a reason to smile even when bad things happened.

Kingston, Journi, and Kali had that with one another; they were the standard in my eyes.

"It won't be so bad, Couri," I whispered as I locked myself inside my place. "You'll be a great mom while excelling in your chosen career. You will survive and be happy. You will—"

The hard knock on my front door startled me out of finishing my on-the-spot affirmations.

Still standing by the door, I turned, flipped the bottom lock, and opened it.

My gaze settled on the man who'd become a father if the tests in my purse were confirmed by my doctor.

"Hey..." I held onto the door and watched him watch me. "Do you want to come in?"

I widened the opening and he slipped his muscled frame inside, taking the door from me to close and lock it himself afterward.

August Hanson was the silent type.

I'd learned through observation that he spoke through his movements and inaudible actions first and foremost. He spoke silky smooth words only after showing you what was on his mind through his whiskey-brown eyes.

He kicked off his Nike slides and stashed them next to the black loafers I'd toed out of.

I blinked, and he was on me, securing his large hands around my waist. He tugged my body into his and pushed a hand up my back. Softly, he palmed the back of my head and guided it to his chest.

The smell of his family business emanated from his person and I sighed.

Brown sugar, some type of spice, and honey.

I wondered what concoction he'd been working on earlier

today but chose to stay quiet instead of asking. His silence meant everything to me and I wanted to bask in it for as long as possible.

"What do you need from me?" he asked; his chest vibrated with each syllable.

I leaned back and searched his eyes, feeling a surge of desire spread outward from my core. Eventually, it consumed me, and I said, "Give me what you've been giving since day one."

Something I couldn't quite place passed in his eyes, only to disappear soon after.

It gave me pause, but his reaction to my request shifted my attention back to what was right before me. August lifted me off the floor and I locked my legs around his waist.

"You're being weird," I pointed out, my lips brushing against his ear as he carried me up the stairs.

I couldn't shake why the way he held onto me felt like... *goodbye.*

But that... that couldn't be it.

What we had worked.

There was a system in place.

I quickly met his gaze as he gently laid me on the bed.

The look in his eyes, the disappointment shining through them, told a different story.

We weren't working.

The system we had in place was fucked, but whatever reason he'd decided to end things wouldn't stand. Not when I revealed the truth, told him I was carrying his child.

I didn't want to hold on to him if he didn't want to be held, but I wouldn't take his right to be a father away from him just because he didn't want me anymore. And knowing the pieces of him I did, I knew he'd step up.

AND THEN LIFE WAS BEAUTIFUL

Because August Hanson was the type of man who took care of his responsibilities.

That much I was sure of.

Co-parenting would be a breeze between us.

"Kiss me," I all but begged, tugging him between my legs after he slid my dress pants off my body.

He obliged and dropped his lips atop mine as he worked the buttons apart on my shirt. I could finally forget about the present and future for a while; even if it were only for a minute, I was grateful for the slight reprieve.

TWO

august hanson

ONE HOUR PRIOR…

"I'm looking for—"

"August!" Shondra's mom called, her voice uncharacteristically high.

I turned away from the nurse's station and stuffed my hands into the pockets of my sweats as my ex's mother approached me. Her eyes brimmed with tears and all of the confusion I felt during the phone call that brought me here flooded back.

"What's going on, Mrs. Thomas?" I asked.

She touched her chest and sighed.

"This is not how you should be finding this out, August…" Her voice cracked, but she swallowed down her emotion, seeming determined to get through whatever she needed to tell me. "I told Shondra you needed to know, but she was still hurt from the breakup and not thinking straight."

Nothing she said registered clearly.

I heard her, but I couldn't *hear* her.

What the fuck was she trying to tell me?

"I'd prefer if you ripped the band-aid off."

"Shondra gave birth to a little girl at four this morning," she started, her eyes dancing with mine. "It was a full-term pregnancy and baby girl is doing well."

Not wanting to believe what she'd told me, I stared at the woman in disbelief.

"I know this is probably a lot to take in right now, but your daughter will need you, August," she went on. "More now than ever."

"I'm a father?" I asked, needing to hear her repeat it.

Mrs. Thomas nodded; the tears that had been hanging on for dear life escaped down her cheeks.

"To a little girl?"

Another nod.

I'd never seen that coming and I wasn't prepared for it.

Shondra and I ended things—I had assumed, amicably—almost a year ago.

"Where's Shondra?" I asked, rubbing the fog from my eyes. "We need to talk. I know she's probably exhausted, and I don't want to stress her body further, but I need answers only she can give me."

Whatever I'd said conjured up a broken sob from Mrs. Thomas.

She leaned forward a little and I instinctively reached out to hold her up.

Her sadness felt backward, wrongly placed.

She'd always wanted this and never had problems announcing it to Shondra or me during our four-year relationship. It was the reason we'd broken up, not because it was being asked, but because of *what* was being asked.

Shondra didn't want kids and I did.

She wanted a carefree life for as long as she was alive. I respected her choice but had to make a decision that hurt like hell when I realized I couldn't continue with her.

"Shondra, she—"

I lifted her upright and forced her to look me in the eyes.

"You gotta clue me in."

"She didn't make it," she blurted through sobs.

Her confession stabbed me in the chest and twisted to drive the point home.

Everything around me slowed and I stumbled back, the noise in my head growing by the second. Though Shondra and I hadn't worked out, I had no ill feelings toward her.

She'd been a great girlfriend and an even better friend during our time together; we weren't meant to be. I'd come to terms with that, moved on even, but this... this was a lot to take in.

"Didn't make it?" I repeated aloud, the words bitter on my tongue. "That can't be right. T-That's crazy."

I turned toward the nurse's station and ate up the distance between me and it.

"Can you tell me what room Shondra Thomas is in? She gave birth to our daughter this morning and I'm here to see them."

The nurse typed in the name after I spelled it out and I knew when her eyes shot toward me then back to the screen that Mrs. Thomas hadn't been lying. Shondra was gone and she'd left me a piece of her to take care of all alone.

Life was fucking joke.

"I need some air," I declared, rushing out of the hospital and toward my car with no destination in mind.

I wouldn't abandon my daughter or my responsibilities, but I needed a second to breathe without feeling like I was choking.

Where I'd ended up hadn't registered until the door to the townhome I stood in front of opened and the owner appeared from the other side with the saddest eyes.

It was selfish of me to end up here of all places.

Couri *fucking* Mitchell.

She was the most laid-back woman I'd ever encountered and smart as a whip. Couri loved randomly spouting off facts no one would have ever known. Her randomness pulled me in, then she followed me home and that landed us in bed.

Even with all of the right qualities to help me forget how my life just changed forever, she was dealing with her mother's death; a different kind of change in a person's life.

One look into those deceptively dark eyes and I wanted to be the one to help her forget for a while. Between asking her what she needed from me and her requesting the usual, we ended up in bed with her bare thighs squeezing the sides of my head as I feasted on her.

I was a pussy eating man.

Bald, hairy, or a little bit of both, Couri knew I was diving in every chance I got.

Eating it religiously put hair on your face and separated the men from the boys.

I knew what I was doing was fucked up. That leaving my newborn alone in that hospital without the only parent she had left, as I tried to forget about it for a while, was a horrible start to fatherhood.

But I needed *this* one last moment with the woman I'd grown to appreciate.

This was it between us.

Couri wouldn't go for this, me suddenly being a dad after eight months of knowing me as a childless single man. Shaking my head, I slurped on her clit, swiping the swollen nub with my tongue repeatedly.

"Mmm, shit," she moaned, suffocating me with her thighs.

She rolled her pelvis firmly into my mouth, raising her hips off the bed as a deep ass, guttural moan escaped her. I ate her through the orgasm, only coming up for a rush of air after she sagged deep into the mattress.

"You're being weird," she said for the second time since I'd arrived, her chest heaving.

This time as the words left her lips, her eyes were closed while she caught her breath.

"It's been a weird day so far," I admitted, the confession feeling like sandpaper on the tongue.

She opened her eyes and sat up a little.

"Do you want to talk about it?" she asked, being true to herself.

Couri was a great listener and an even better confidant.

It didn't matter if I was talking or silent; I knew she was listening. That she was storing everything in her memory bank in case we discussed it again, but never to use against me.

"Not yet..." I got out of bed, my mind still back at the hospital. "But soon."

She nodded slowly, watching me reach for my jeans and slide them on.

"Leaving so soon?" she asked, something desperate in her voice made me feel like I was being stretched in two different directions. "You never leave before we..."

Her voice trailed and I wished I could be in both places at once.

"There's something I have to take care of," I told her, pulling my shirt over my head then leaning over the bed until we were nose to nose. "I wanted to... needed to ensure you weren't drowning."

Her shoulders dropped a little as she darted her gaze away from mine.

I knew she was thinking of her mother again and I could feel her despair mixed in with mine. And as bad as I wanted to stay and help her forget, I couldn't.

Never would I ever abandon my daughter again, not even for Couri.

Though, if she'd known about...

I held in a sigh.

If Couri had known about my baby girl, I was sure the woman would've pushed me out the door and demanded I go back where I was most needed.

"Thank you," she murmured, pulling the thick duvet over her body.

"We'll talk soon, alright?"

I started backward while she turned away from me.

"Yeah..." She dipped her head in acknowledgment. "Soon."

I left her place and called the three people I'd need the most to get through this, then went home to shower Couri's scent off me. The last thing I wanted or needed was for sex to be the first thing my daughter smelled on her father.

"Glad to see you're back," the nurse from earlier said as I approached the working station just shy of two and a half hours later.

"Is..."

She set an envelope in front of me.

"She left that for you just in case you returned. Said she'd be back later tonight to check in."

I stared at the white envelope with my name scrawled across it in Shondra's handwriting.

"I'd like to see my daughter." I stuffed the letter in my pocket. "Did she..." After clearing my throat a few times, I tried again. "Did she name her?"

The nurse got up and rounded the large station without responding.

"I'll take you to the nursery."

She moved quickly in her clogs, down a long corridor and through a set of double doors. As I crossed the threshold

17

behind her, the sound of babies crying hit me and I felt this urgency to protect surge through my body.

"Is she okay?" I asked, peering into the glass with eight babies inside transparent bassinets.

Two were crying and the two nurses inside were tending to them.

"She's the quietest one," the nurse pointed out, tapping the glass toward the baby on the end.

She was the only one draped in pink.

I stepped closer to get a look at her.

Her skin was a beautiful shade of brown, which I knew would darken if my genes took over. I couldn't pinpoint who she would look like yet, but she was beautiful and tiny.

So tiny.

She slept peacefully with her fists balled up near her mouth, no knowledge of how her life had changed too. How her mother, who carried her safely to term, was gone.

A burning sensation at the back of my eyes had me looking away but only for a second.

When I turned back, my gaze zeroed in on the tag attached to her bassinet.

Baby Thomas.

"So, she doesn't have a name?" I choked out.

"You have time," the nurse said, her voice soothing. "How about you go in and hold her first?"

She opened the door and gave an encouraging wave for me to enter.

It took a second to find my footing, but once I did, I all but flew through the door.

"I should wash my hands, huh?" I asked, looking between the two nurses who were already inside.

Both had this look that said they knew this baby —*my* baby.

That she'd had a loss in the first hour of her new life.

"Right behind you, Mr. Hanson."

I went over to the sink, washing up to my elbows for a minute straight.

When I turned back, one of the nurses had my daughter in her arms.

"Time to officially meet your daughter, Dad."

Dad.

Blinking a few times, I inched forward and allowed the nurse to place her in my arms.

The second she was tucked close to my chest, my heart constricted.

"So, this is what love at first sight feels like," I murmured, my eyes filling with those burning tears I'd been trying to keep at bay.

I looked down at my baby girl and made a promise, something I'd try my hardest not to break.

"You'll have a good life with me..." Her name came to me right then. "You'll have a good life with me, January Hanson. I won't always get it right, but I promise to forever try, even when you're a teenager and want nothing to do with me. My love for you will be endless. Infinite."

She shifted slightly against me, her fists balling tighter as she got comfortable again.

"You kinda look like your Aunt June," I whispered, gently touching her nose. "She has this same snout but keep that between us."

A few taps on the glass got my attention. Until then, I hadn't realized I'd been left alone by the nurses. Turning, I made eye contact with my sisters, their eyes wide as they stared at me.

"I'm a father," I mouthed, tipping my head down at January.

I'd told them on the phone about Shondra passing but hadn't mentioned the baby.

They came to be a support system, thinking I needed consoling about losing my ex, someone I'd genuinely been in love with. Though we'd broken up, there was still an ache there when I thought of her no longer being here.

The three of them raced to the door; July opened it, but they all stayed on the other side.

"A father," June repeated softly. "You-She—oh my god," she sputtered, covering her mouth.

June was the tallest of the three, not by much. Then there was July who was shorter than both June and September.

"Oh, August," July murmured, shaking her head. "We got you, you know that, right?"

I nodded and looked down at the little girl who wouldn't have her mother but would inherit three aunts immediately. They'd be the sounding boards for everything I saw myself cringing about in the coming years.

She would be safe with them.

"Have you named her?" September asked. "Or did..."

She shook her head, tears filling her eyes.

"So, fucking unfair," she cursed, balling her fists up.

"It is unfair, but I love her already," I said, rocking her even though she was sound asleep and didn't need it. "January Marie Hanson."

Marie had been Shondra's middle name and January was the month she'd been born. I wanted our daughter to have something of hers she could carry for life.

"It's beautiful," they said at once.

"Ma is going to have a heart attack, then she's going to spend a lot of money," June added, shaking her head at the idea.

I chuckled and walked over to January's temporary bed.

Our parents would love this once the shock wore off.

Before placing January back, I kissed her forehead and promised I'd return soon.

My sisters had their arms around me once I entered the hall.

I needed this, needed them.

After a few moments of silent consoling, we turned toward the glass.

"When do *we* get to take her home?" September asked.

It was always a group thing when it came to us Hanson siblings.

We stood in order of birth more often than we cared to admit.

June had come one minute before July, while July had come two before me, then there was September, who'd appeared less than a minute after me.

She'd been a surprise for our parents and the doctors. When they pulled me out, she'd been hiding under me at an angle that a multitude of ultrasounds had missed.

The doctors said I kept her alive.

It wasn't exactly true, but they believed anything could happen in the womb and being close to me kept her going. She'd been the smallest but the strongest.

The three of them weren't *just* my sisters.

They were me, split into three, just as I was to them.

We were one.

If anybody could help me battle this new chapter in my life, it was these three.

"Two days," I finally said. "We can take her in two days."

"We better get to it then," June chirped, ready to play the big sister role as always. "You need *everything*."

July and September clapped at once.

"Get Mom on the phone," July requested. "We'll tell her

together and start getting your place in order. Thank God you splurged on the four-bedroom townhome over the two."

"Time to work, people," September bellowed.

She covered her mouth seconds later when a nurse gave her an amused brow lift.

They walked off, each talking over the other.

I stayed a little longer, watching January do what babies do, in awe.

When I stuffed my hand into my hoodie pocket, it grazed the envelope I'd forgotten was there. I stared at it briefly and slipped the single piece of paper out.

Dear August,

If you're reading this, I'm not here to explain why I didn't tell you face to face.

I had a weird dream a few months back, right after I found out I was pregnant.

I can't remember it entirely, but at some point, my life flashed before my eyes, and when I woke, I knew I wouldn't make it past giving birth to this little girl growing inside of me. Calling you should have been the first thing on my mind; it should have been the first thing I did when I learned I was pregnant, but for some reason, I couldn't bring myself to do it.

This is me we're talking about, the girl you know through and through.

I was scared shitless that you'd think I did it on purpose.

My love for you was so goddamn deep and strong, and because you knew that, facing you felt... wrong. It didn't feel fair to either of us because I knew we were still hurting early in our breakup.

Breaking up had always been in the cards for us; I know that more now than before. You and I have similar mindsets and I'm confident enough to believe you'll agree with me on this. We did the right thing, August.

To be clear, I was going to tell you after I had her.

I would never keep your child from you, ever.

I planned to give her to you and let the two of you live the beautiful life I knew you'd provide her. Because when I said I didn't want children, I'd meant that with every fiber of being.

Maybe it sounds selfish, but this is my truth.

It's just...

When I found out, this ridiculous feeling filled me.

Something said I needed to do this for you.

To prepare you for your future.

I don't know why, but I think life has something great in store for you, August Hanson.

Something's brewing and it's big.

As one final goodbye, I present to you, your daughter. The one thing in the world you wanted more than being a master distiller at your family's company.

Name her as you see fit; you'll do great because you are amazing.

All my love, Shon.

Damn.

couri

YOU WERE RIGHT, *Couri*.

I couldn't stop thinking about the appointment with my doctor. She'd fit me in last minute before her first patient and it took less than twenty minutes for my pregnancy to be confirmed.

You're six and a half weeks along.

I blinked the echo of her words out of my head and tried focusing on our long-time family lawyer as he read our mother's last will and testament. We were privy to her final wishes already. The overly prepared woman made us read it and add things we wanted to prevent fighting.

Journi and I wouldn't fight, but the only way for her to rest peacefully was to be absolutely sure. God, I was going to miss that woman.

"Did Nana leave me her pearls?" Kali asked, grabbing my attention. "She said she would when I asked." She rolled her eyes. "After she *made me* ask."

"Kali..."

"Well, if she did, I don't want them," she went on, ignoring the tone of Journi's voice. "All it means is she's gone."

She crossed her arms and looked away afterward.

My poor baby was hurting and I wished I knew how to make her pain go away, even if it meant I had to hurt a little more for the both of us.

King pulled her chair closer and draped his arm around Kali.

"She did leave them," Jacob said, a sad smile drifting across his face. "But she put a two-year hold on them. When that time passes, they'll be yours."

My heart tugged a little at how in tune my mother had been with people and their feelings. The woman knew how to read the room well.

"She did?" Kali asked, lifting her head.

When Jacob nodded, she wiped her eyes and sighed in relief.

"Good. I think I'll be ready for them by then."

"I think you will be, too," he said. "She told me you all are aware of what's here, but there is one thing she added recently that we need to discuss."

"Aw, hell," King grumbled.

I covered my mouth to keep from laughing but as I cut my eyes in Journi's direction and found her trying to hold in laughter, I burst. We fell into one another dramatically, both of us thinking the same thing.

"She said you two would get a good laugh out of this."

We sobered immediately at that.

It was her attempt at giving us a last laugh; now that we saw it as the last one straight from her, nothing felt funny anymore.

"Go ahead..." I nodded. "Tell us."

"She left each of you one point two million dollars in stocks and bonds. You have the option to reinvest or cash out. The estate will pay the taxes, meaning you can take home the exact amount she left. What's left of her money will be donated to any charity of Kali's choice."

He flipped the printed and stapled pages shut.

"What the fuck?" I cursed. "Mama had enough money to give us each over a million and still donate?"

Oh, that crazy ass lady really had something up her sleeve.

"She'd been investing since before either of you was born. Never touched it and now it's yours. Her last gift to you."

He slid thick packets of paper in front of us.

"I need you each to sign, and once I file them, you'll get your deposits..." He glanced at Journi, Kali, and Kingston. "I know the three of you have joint accounts. The deposits will be made to the main one, leaving you the room to distribute as you want."

"She left me money, too?" King asked, his brows pinched.

Jacob shuffled around some of the papers in front of him before finding the one he needed.

"Her exact words for you are, *'Kingston, thank you for caring for and loving my baby the way you do. Take this money as my appreciation and love for you.'*"

I cut my eyes at Kingston and watched a barrage of emotions cross his face.

Our mother loved him very much; thus, it didn't surprise me that she left him something.

"Myka just won't stop, huh?" King mumbled as he tugged Kali closer.

"So, we just sign and we're done?" I asked, picking up my pen.

Jacob nodded and I scribbled my name on a few pages and initialed the others.

When finished, we stood together and shook Jacob's hand one by one.

"I know sorry isn't sufficient enough, but I am. Myka was a great woman."

I dipped out of the room and rushed up the long hall until I made it outside.

After a few good deep breaths, the sick feeling in my stomach went away. I knew it'd be back sooner rather than later and I wasn't looking forward to it.

This baby wasn't going to be nice to me.

"Hey, are you okay?" Journi asked, rubbing my back.

"Mmhm," I hummed, turning my head to look at her. "How about you?"

She smiled, but it didn't reach her eyes.

"It'll get better."

It was her go-to response.

For a second, I wanted to blurt that I was pregnant. That Mama had maybe left us another present by way of my womb, but it didn't feel like the right moment. Not when August didn't know and telling him had to be my first priority.

At the thought of him, I checked my phone.

I'd sent him a text before my appointment this morning but received no response yet and he always responded. August was an early riser, not hearing from him took my mind back to his weird behavior yesterday.

My stomach flipped and the insides of my mouth got all slick. Before I could stop myself, I leaned over and released the contents of my breakfast.

"Ah, fuck," I growled, spitting whatever was on my tongue out.

"Te, are you okay?" Kali asked, dropping down into a squat to talk to me. "Is it the week we've had or your stomach? Have you eaten?"

I groaned and shook my head.

"I'm fine..."

I stood tall and reached into my bag for the water bottle I'd stashed there. After a few sips and spits, I capped it and grabbed two pieces of Doublemint gum.

"...been holding that in for a while."

Kali eyed me closely like she had me figured out, but thanks to her mother, I didn't have to fake my expression.

"Kali, stop all the questions," Journi ordered with a smile. "It's been a rough week."

"I need to get home and brush my teeth..." I walked toward my truck while avoiding eye contact. "I love you guys. Later."

"I'll check on you, Te," Kali called, warming my heart.

After getting into my truck and starting it, I rolled my window down.

"I know you will, Buttercup."

King ushered her into the back of their SUV while Journi stared at me from the passenger side door. She tipped her head then nodded.

"We'll check on you later. Get some sleep and electrolytes in your body; you'll feel brand new."

I ignored the knowing expression in her eyes, rolled my window up, and backed my truck out of the parking spot. I only wanted to get home as quickly as possible until I spotted the red circle with the matching filled dot in the middle of it on a large post a few blocks from the lawyer's office.

I flipped my blinker on without much thought and turned right, straight into the parking lot. It was packed as usual, but I found a decent spot amid the chaos of afternoon shoppers.

"Electrolytes, new coffee mug..." I grabbed a cart and continued to mentally tick off the things I needed and wanted. "...decaf coffee pods and—"

My eyes roved over all the options available in the baby section. I stopped my cart in front of a rack of footed onesies. The one in front looked like one Kali had when she was a baby and I picked it up, smiling at the elephant and giraffe stitched into the thick fabric.

The urge to put it in my cart danced inside me, but I forced myself to hang it back and walked away, focusing my attention on the things I'd come for instead. But once everything on my list was accounted for and in my cart, the urge to return to the baby section became too strong to ignore.

I maneuvered my cart into an aisle stocked with boxes and bags of diapers.

You don't need these yet, Couri.

I reached up anyway and pulled a box of newborn Pampers from the top shelf. I wasn't sure what brand I'd settle on by the time the little one got here, but it felt nostalgic to grab this one. There was a time when using anything other than Pampers or Huggies was a crime.

"Times have changed," I mumbled, putting the box back.

"Is that really necessary?" a deep rumble I recognized questioned.

I spun around, but August wasn't there.

"It'll come in handy, I swear," a soft female voice responded a few seconds later.

My heart staggered and I frowned at the half-empty shelves before me.

The voices were coming from the aisle to my right.

I pushed my cart to the end of mine and turned it until it was lined up with the end cap. I poked my head around first then stepped into his aisle.

August had his head ducked with hers while they looked at the baby Keurig.

The girl looked over first, her big brown eyes the same shade as August's.

"Couri," he said after following the woman's gaze to where I stood.

He walked over to me, and I waved, feeling weird about spotting him here, and in this aisle of all places.

"Hi," I muttered, meeting his questioning eyes.

He surprised me and wrapped an arm around my waist. As he tugged me close, I dropped my head to avoid the expression in his eyes.

What the fuck are you doing, Couri?

"What are you doing on this side of town?" he asked, releasing me after a few gentle squeezes.

I glanced at the woman he was with, taking note of her watchful gaze.

"Um... I..." I cleared my throat. "The... lawyer's office is a few blocks from here. He..."

I felt the weight of my emotions in my throat and it became hard for me to speak. August nodded when I met his gaze and I felt a sense of relief wash over me.

He understood and glanced over into my cart, his eyes lingering on the Gatorade and Pedialyte for a short while.

"You sick?" he asked, returning his attention to me.

I shook my head faster than I'd meant to.

"No," I said, keeping the lie going. "The week is just catching up to me. I emptied my breakfast out on the sidewalk not too long ago and... my sister suggested electrolytes and rest. Needed to get the former first."

August lifted his hand and placed two fingers on my forehead.

He didn't believe me and it was a bold implication on his part.

We stared at one another accusingly, but eventually he dropped his hand from my face.

"June, please, you know August isn't spending all that money on a—"

He stepped to the side as he turned and revealed two more

women standing behind him now, making three total. Each had their brown eyes pinned on me and I realized then that they had to be his family.

The similarities were uncanny.

"Who's the cutie?" the shortest one asked, stepping closer.

I reached out and took the hand she pushed in my direction.

"I'm Couri," I said, unintentionally grazing the single daffodil flower on the fleshy part between her thumb and index finger.

August had the same tattoo.

"Couri and I know each other through Kingston," August explained, his gaze perusing my frame.

I met August at Journi and Kingston's one random day toward the end of summer the year before. He'd been introduced as an old friend, but I'd been able to put some of the unspoken pieces together.

Kingston owned a construction company with his half-brother Primo and they'd won a bid to be head contractors working on the new additions to the Hanson Distillery. When I learned that August was a Hanson, their friendship made sense.

It also made sense that August had tossed the opportunity his old friend's way.

"He's my brother-in-law," I elaborated.

"These are my sisters June, July, and September," he said, nodding toward them.

We'd never talked about our families; he only knew about Journi and Kali by default. August and I had great conversations about any and everything but that.

I eyed his sisters one by one, really taking them in.

June was lanky, all legs and arms. Her hair was larger than life and in thick ringlets that looked to have come from a perfectly done rod set. She was dressed in sweats and a hoodie, makeup-free except for the fiercely dark-winged eyeliner and shimmery-coated lips. Her eyes were much more guarded than her sisters.

July was the shortest, with more defined curves; she had an athlete's body. Her hair was silky straight and hung down the side of her arms. I noticed her brushing it away more than once in the few seconds I had my eyes in her direction. She had a knowing gleam in her gaze as she watched August and me interact.

September was taller than July but shorter than June, her body thicker than her sisters. Her hair was cut into a cute little tightly coiled fro. September's eyes weren't guarded but curious as they darted back and forth as if they'd missed something.

They were all different but shared the same face as their brother.

Same dark skin, whiskey-brown eyes, and the ability to capture your attention with a simple glance.

I had to get away fast.

"It's nice to meet y'all…" I pulled my basket to me. "It was good seeing you, August."

I walked off and turned my cart into the first available line I saw at the front of the store. The cashier took her sweet time ringing me up, and while I'd never been an impatient person, she was working on every nerve I had left.

When I spotted August and his sisters in the lane next to mine, two carts filled with baby shit galore, I wanted to ask who it was for. None of them were pregnant, but that didn't mean anything in this day and age.

There could be a surrogate.

Maybe one of them had the baby already but hadn't prepared properly from stress.

Or they were donating it to a mother in need.

There were many scenarios, but one thing stood out to me, and it wouldn't stop playing in my head as I pushed my cart out of the store into much colder air than when I'd arrived.

"You know August isn't spending that much money on a—"

On a what?

What wouldn't he be spending too much money on? And why was it solely his decision?

I popped my trunk from a distance and shook my head.

It wasn't any of my business, but fuck if I wasn't curious.

"Couri!"

August caught up to me before I turned. He grabbed the five bags from my cart in one fell swoop and stashed them in the carrier hanging off the back of my second-row seats.

"All of these months..." I waved my hand while gathering my thoughts as he moved the cart to the side. "I never imagined you having siblings."

"It's a lot we don't know about the other," he said, shutting the trunk and leaning against it. "But, I think we know enough to understand one another."

"True..." I tugged on my sleeves. "The four of you look a lot alike. It's kinda creepy even for siblings."

He chuckled, his eyes dancing as they met mine.

"Does it make it less creepy that we shared a womb too?"

I slanted my head while I processed what he told me.

"Oh... like y'all are quadruplets?"

He nodded and a new fear unlocked inside of me.

"Did you know that fraternal twins are hereditary and not identical?"

It'd be just my luck birthing a handful of Hansons the first time around.

The smile on August's face disappeared, but I could still see it lingering in his eyes as he said, "I enjoy learning about the random things you have swimming in that head of yours."

He pushed off my truck and quickly closed the distance between us.

"I like you, Couri," he said softly, his eyes searching mine.

"You didn't respond to my text," I said, speaking the first thought on my mind.

A flicker of understanding flashed, but it was gone just as quickly as it'd been there.

"Been preoccupied with life today," he told me, shoulders dropping a little. "I had every intention of ending my night with a response."

I dipped my head once because I believed him.

"I like you too, August."

Someone laid on the horn from beside us and we glanced over to see his truck rolling to a stop. He let out a little chuckle and turned back to me when whichever sister was driving flickered the lights at us repeatedly.

"Do you have time to meet up tomorrow?" he asked, backing away. "We can grab breakfast and talk."

"O-Okay..." I cleared my throat. "Yeah, we can do that."

August stopped at the passenger door and waved his hand toward my truck.

"Get in, then I'll go."

He waited with the door halfway open until I slid into my truck and started it up. I watched his truck pull away until another car started to back out of a spot and blocked my view.

I brushed my fingers across my abdomen and sighed.

What a week.

august

"THAT'S THE GIRL, RIGHT?" June asked as she merged onto the freeway. "The one that got you out of your Shondra funk after the breakup?"

I cut my eyes at her and frowned.

"What?"

"You were broody one day, then you weren't the next," September elaborated from behind my seat. "We all noticed and figured it was some woman."

I didn't care to have this conversation with any of them, but I knew my sisters well enough to comprehend that I didn't have a choice.

Not with June at the wheel of my favorite truck.

"Yeah," I said, looking out my window. "That's her."

"She's pretty," July said, poking her head between the seats. "Kinda looked sad, though. Is it because you told her about the baby?"

"You didn't break it off, did you?" June questioned as September said, "Don't be an idiot, August."

They were talking over one another and I let them, grateful for once that this was a thing they did.

I'd been thinking about sitting down with Couri for months to talk about starting something more serious than our current situationship.

My priorities had changed overnight.

My daughter was the most important thing to me right now, and even with that, I couldn't get Couri out of my head. Truthfully, she'd been a staple in my mind since we met.

"It doesn't matter what I plan to do," I said, cutting into my sisters' bickering. "Right now, I need help figuring out how to be a good father. I don't want or need advice about my love life."

"But, August—"

I cut my eyes at June; she rolled her lips together and focused on the road again.

"Sorry about the bass in my voice…" I brushed my hand down my face, more frustrated with my predicament than I wanted to admit. "I love y'all and I'm grateful that I have you. Can we leave the conversations about who I'm dating for another day?"

"Of course," June murmured, reaching over to grab my hand. "Your plate is already full. We're here to help with that."

She laced our fingers together and squeezed.

"We're reworking the schedule to give you the time off you need," July chimed in after a few seconds of silence. "It's a good thing we have paternity leave already. You've got twelve weeks to get into a groove, longer if needed."

I hadn't planned on taking time off, but I sensed the argument that would come from mentioning my plans and decided against telling them.

"They've descended upon your place and you'll never get rid of them now."

September's words echoed as we pulled into the driveway

of my townhome to find my mother waving delivery men through the front door.

I almost regretted giving them an emergency key, but this was a damn emergency.

My home wasn't prepared for a newborn baby.

It felt unfair that this was how I'd been introduced to fatherhood. Shondra had known all this time; she got to process her feelings and make peace with her dreams about death but decided I needed to be left in the dark.

I had a right to know, a right to be there.

It was taken away from me and I was upset with Shondra.

She wasn't here to defend herself, but the letter was enough to evoke a lot of emotions.

This was supposed to be a joyous occasion, but my chest ached.

The walls were closing inside of my head. I hadn't brought my girl home, yet experienced the highs and lows of parenthood and was already tired.

Confused.

Hurt.

But ultimately, I was just tired.

"Don't ever stop feeling, son," my father said as I approached him in my garage.

He pulled me into an embrace I loved.

My father was a strong hugger. He gave everything he had in them and people noticed.

"I don't know what you mean…"

He grabbed my forearms and held me at arm's length.

We'd inherited his brown eyes and they stared at me with concern.

"I'm fine," I lied.

"This is what I mean, August. Pretending like you're okay.

It'll catch up to you eventually. It's only been a day and you're already compartmentalizing. Can your old man give you some advice?"

I nodded, though I wanted more than anything to say no.

"The only way to make this work is to care for yourself as much as you want to care for your child. Mentally and emotionally. Physically, too."

"I don't know what to do," I admitted.

"And that's alright." He squeezed my arms and released me. "Be honest with yourself and ask for help. You aren't in this alone."

But wasn't I?

My family would be here, they'd see me through, but I had to man my new life alone at some point. I had to be a father when they wouldn't be here. On the days that they were living their own lives without me.

"I'll keep that in mind."

My father didn't look convinced, but I'd heard him loud and clear regardless.

We walked into the house together, and before I could make it to the stairwell and up to the bedroom I'd picked for January, my mother came halfway down.

"Why are there people I don't know moving about freely?" I asked, meeting her in the middle.

"Because I can make this part easy for you. They're setting up the big pieces of furniture and your sisters will handle the small stuff."

"I can handle the small stuff. The large stuff, too."

I needed something to do, anything to keep me occupied.

"You need to take a moment to breathe. Go do that but not in the baby's room." She patted my face and started back up the stairs. "Stay out of our way, August."

My dad stopped beside me and gripped my shoulder. I gazed at him to find a small smile on his face.

"She's something else when she gets all sassy."

I retreated down the stairs, disgusted with the twinkle in his eyes for my mother.

"What are you doing?" I asked September after finding her opening and closing kitchen drawers.

She held something up, but I missed what it was.

"It silences the drawers when they close..." She gave me a pointed look I understood while holding up one to show me. "You tend to slam them. This will eliminate unnecessary noise when trying to keep as quiet as possible."

She rolled her eyes and I couldn't help but smile.

My sisters complained about how loud I was a lot growing up. They didn't know that a lot of annoying shit I did was always on purpose. Anything to get back at them for hogging the bathroom we shared.

"I did that on purpose, you know?"

She smirked.

"Duh. That's why we stayed in the bathroom longer and longer."

I chuckled and looked around.

My kitchen had just been redone a few months ago by Kingston and his brother. It had all-new stainless steel appliances, onyx-plated countertops, and cabinets with gold hardware.

It was currently overrun with bottles soaking in the sink, cans of milk, bottle warmers, and a bunch of other baby shit that cost me an arm and a leg.

"Maybe you should take a drive and clear your head."

I blinked a few times and turned my attention to September.

"I'm good. I need to be here and—"

"You aren't fine," she cut in. "I can feel it. We know you want to be strong about all this. So, go take a drive. Get it out and then come back ready to tackle tomorrow."

"Only tomorrow?"

She nodded and walked over to me.

"One day at a time, big bro."

She wrapped her arms around me and squeezed tightly.

"You only call me that when you want me to follow your orders," I pointed out, returning the squeeze. "But I'll take a ride."

September returned to what she'd been doing and I picked up my keys from the counter and left.

When I was a kid, I played youth football. After every game, my dad would drive me around for hours. I was always wired after a win and too in my head after a loss.

Riding around silently had easily become my favorite pastime and it stuck into adulthood. I couldn't think with noise, let alone process my feelings.

So, I didn't think about anything as I merged onto M-59 toward Rochester Hills.

I arrived at the hospital and sat in the parking lot for a while, staring at the entrance doors as they slid open and closed and people went in and out.

Every second I stayed put, my chest tightened.

I could turn around and leave, telling my family I wasn't strong enough for this, but I cut my truck off instead and ambled inside until I made it to the labor and delivery unit.

I bypassed the nurse's station and went straight to the nursery.

"I'm sure she loves having visitors," the nurse standing in front of the nursery with a computer tray said as I approached.

"Is she okay?" I asked, peeking through the glass to see Shondra's mom in with her. "Still good to come home?"

"She's healthy and eating well."

I nodded and sighed in relief, the tightness in my chest lifting.

"I-I never asked..." I cut my eyes at the nurse. "How much does she weigh?"

"Seven pounds, eight ounces, and nineteen inches long. You'll get her chart during discharge."

Satisfied with what I'd been told, I pushed into the nursery and drew Helen's attention in my direction.

She looked up and the smile on her face disappeared.

"I, um..." I stepped a little closer. "I got the letter you left for me."

Helen looked down and stared at January.

"All I see is Hanson written all over this little girl so far," she murmured. "I thought maybe..."

"She'll probably have all of her mother's personality," I reasoned.

"I'm sorry she didn't tell you."

I shrugged, but it felt heavy, like the wrong thing to do.

Thinking about Shondra put me in a bad space, but I couldn't tell her mother that.

"What's done is done. I wish she would've let me be there, but I can't harp on that, not when I have such a big responsibility to our daughter now."

Helen stood and nodded toward the chair she'd been occupying.

"Sit. You need to bond with her."

I did as I was told after washing my hands.

She set my little angel in my arms and I saw her eyes pried open for the first time.

41

"Big and brown, just like yours," Helen whispered, stepping back.

"True," I agreed. "It's a Hanson staple, I guess."

"I hope one day you can forgive Shondra."

I didn't respond because I wasn't sure when that would be. Maybe when the guilt of being angry with her disappeared I could work through how this all made me feel. Especially her moves leading up to this bittersweet ending.

"I also hope you'll allow me to be a part of January's life."

I slowly moved my attention to Helen.

"Helen, I wouldn't dare keep her away from you. January is a part of you, too."

She was all alone with Shondra gone and I felt her pain from where I sat, the anguish in her eyes growing by the second.

"If you'd like to stop by tomorrow after I pick her up, we can have dinner. You can help me get her settled in."

Her eyes flickered with hope.

"I would love to feel a part of something again." She chuckled wearily. "It's been a rough nine months."

"I'm sorry this is how your debut as a first-time grandmother went. Do you have a date for the..."

I dropped my gaze as the right words eluded me.

I knew what I needed to say, but they were stuck on the tip of my tongue.

"She asked to be cremated," Helen told me. "No funeral."

I guess that was it.

No proper goodbye, *nothing*.

That hurt enough to burn the back of my eyelids with tears. A deep sadness worked its way into my spirit, then the anger I'd been feeling sprouted.

"Dinner tomorrow," I repeated, my voice rough. "My

parents and sisters will be there. Getting rid of them will be impossible these days."

I never looked up again.

She resembled her daughter too much and it would be unfair to expose her to my pain when she'd suffered a loss this big.

"I will be there."

The door opened after she confirmed our plans, and when it shut, I lifted my gaze just in time to see her passing the glass without a backward glance.

January squirmed and let out a little wail that startled me a few seconds later. I looked down and her eyes were shut tightly as she moved again and raised her fists in what looked like a protest.

A nurse came in with a bright smile on her face.

"Someone's ready to eat," she announced. "Would you like to feed her?"

I nodded, my gaze still pinned on my little girl.

Her cries didn't scare me like I'd thought they would, but they stirred emotions in my gut that I couldn't decipher. A small bottle was thrust into my free hand and I did what I'd been doing since I was old enough to babysit for money.

"You're natural," the nurse complimented. "Not your first time?"

"My sisters and I were the resident babysitters in my family."

I'd never held a baby this new before, but new or old, they all had the same ticks.

Eat, shit, sleep, and repeat.

The nurse left with a promise to return shortly and I nestled back in the rocking chair, the bottle tipped just right while January dined on her five-star meal.

"You won't be this easy on me when I get you home, will you?"

Her fingers curled around the end of my sleeve and I smiled.

"I figured that'd be the case. I'm up for the challenge."

I had no choice but to be ready, my daughter's life depended on it.

FIVE

AUGUST and I stared at one another from across the small wooden table. His eyes were apologetic, sad even.

I had so much to say, but I couldn't shake how tired he looked.

"Are you okay?" I asked, breaking the silence. "You look so tired like you haven't slept in days."

He rubbed his eyes as if to wipe away what I'd already seen and sighed. The barista yelled out his name and he jumped up to grab the coffees we'd ordered.

We opted to sit down at a coffee shop halfway between our places instead of breakfast.

I didn't have an appetite and he'd sounded preoccupied when he called this morning, like meeting with me wasn't the most important thing he had to do today. Because I didn't want to hold him up, a quick conversation over coffee made more sense for us both.

As August made his way back, I watched him closely. Those sure steps I'd grown accustomed to weren't so sure at the moment. He even slouched his shoulders as he slid into his seat and passed my frozen decaf with extra caramel to me.

"I'm not okay," he said, pushing the paper cup filled with his coffee away from himself.

"Are you ready to talk about it?"

He shook his head and I nodded.

"That's okay; I think I understand, but—"

"I don't want to talk about it, but I have to," he cut in, observing me.

"This is a safe space, August. I'm listening."

"I've been thinking about you a lot lately, about us and what we have going on." He glanced away. "I meant it when I said I liked you last night but..." He brought his apologetic eyes to me again. "I learned over the weekend that my ex hid a pregnancy from me."

I pulled my hands from the table and clasped them together in my lap.

"Oh."

He sat back while shaking his head.

"She carried her to term and gave birth early Friday."

Her.

He had a daughter—a newborn.

The day my mother had been lowered into the ground, his ex-girlfriend gave birth to his first child. I'd been carrying around pregnancy tests all weekend, trying to muster up the nerve to tell him and...

I blinked it all away.

"She didn't make it, and now everything has changed, Couri."

His revelation hit me and I sat up a little.

"What do you mean she didn't make it?"

"Shondra," he mumbled. "My ex. She didn't make it."

My heart constricted, and suddenly, his sad eyes made sense. The baby shopping at the store last night and his sisters being with him. He'd been the one who wasn't prepared.

46

Goodness.

"August..." I leaned forward and placed my hands atop his. "I'm... if this weekend taught me anything, sorry doesn't cut it. No words can, but I feel for you. I feel your pain."

He leaned in and flipped our hands to hold mine.

"We had bad timing, you and I."

I nodded, my heart breaking for this man.

"We did," I agreed. "Did you... have you met her?"

His lips curved a little and I had my answer. The gentle smile had even reached his eyes.

This man was already in love with his daughter, and though the circumstances were heartbreaking, it was nice to see.

"She's beautiful and healthy," he said, brushing his thumb over my knuckles. "I'm bringing her home after I leave here."

"I think you'll be a great dad."

He leaned back a little.

"Are you sure you've learned enough about me to believe your words?"

I shrugged.

"I've learned more about you than you think. It's enough to confidently make this assumption."

"I think I needed to hear it from someone else," he mumbled.

I squeezed his hands then took mine back.

"You're lucky to have your family. It's nothing like having a solid support system."

The news of our baby felt... insignificant all of a sudden. He had the world on his shoulders and I was about to add more.

My stomach rolled and I bit my lip.

I could wait, give him time to settle in as a newly single dad then break the news.

There were so many things that could happen in the first trimester.

Why put him through that?

"I know you're here to break this off and I understand," I said, meeting his gaze. "You have to take care of your daughter, first and foremost, but I want you to know I'm here if you ever need to talk. To get away. To think in the quiet. I'm just a phone call away."

He got up and held his hand out. I allowed him to pull me up and drag my body into his for a hug. It felt so safe in his arms, in the way he hugged me tight but gently at the same time.

"I meant it," I said, pulling back to see his eyes.

Right person, wrong time, I thought as I stared into those pretty browns.

"Never doubted that." He laced his fingers with mine. "Let me walk you to your truck."

Because my bag was already around me, I picked up my coffee with my free hand.

August led us from the coffee shop to my truck, parked directly beside his. He'd gotten here after me this morning.

"I can make it to my door from here."

I tugged my fingers from his and walked the rest of the way alone.

I needed the courage to leave here without telling him the news.

It didn't feel right but burdening him even more with an unborn baby didn't either.

I opened my door and turned to find him watching me.

"How are you feeling?" he asked out of nowhere.

"I'm... with everything you have going on, you're worried about me being sick?"

August frowned.

"What I have going on doesn't change me caring for you, Couri. In case you didn't know, I do..." He inched closer to me. "...care for you."

I looked off and blinked my tears away.

"I wasn't asking because you mentioned being sick yesterday. You have a lot going on too. I'm checking in on that."

Of course he was.

This fucking man.

I stashed my coffee cup in the empty holder then turned to close the distance between us.

"August, I need to tell you something," I began as I stopped in front of him. "I was about to do something stupid just now and leave you in the dark because, for a brief second, it felt like the right thing to do..." I shook my head. "You deserve to know. To—"

"Couri," he called out, gently gripping my chin. "Take a breath, then tell me."

I pulled in a rush of air through my nostrils and released it the same way.

"I'm pregnant," I said, opening my eyes. "I took a test on Friday, my doctor confirmed yesterday, and..."

I stepped back to give us both some space.

He had this faraway look in his eyes that I understood.

"I know you need time to process and get your daughter settled in. We can figure this all out lat—"

"Is that why you were sick yesterday?" he asked, looking me over.

"Could be, but I don't know. I'd been sick to my stomach since finding out about my mom."

"And you're taking care of yourself?"

I shrugged.

"I'm still processing it."

"Fuck, Couri..." He walked up and grabbed my face. "I'm

sorry I have to leave like this. You don't deserve that after what you told me. I want to talk to you, figure this out, but—"

"You have to go, and I understand, I promise."

He leaned in and kissed my cheek.

"We'll talk soon, alright? Please don't go to another appointment without me. I want to be there..." He searched my eyes. "That's if you decide that doing this is what you want."

"I won't go to another appointment without you," I said.

Relief filled his eyes and mine.

I backed away and waved.

"Don't be the dad who starts his relationship with his daughter by picking her up late. You're supposed to save that for her teenage years."

He opened his door at the same time I opened mine. With my truck backed into my spot, we stood between our vehicles.

"Hey, Couri," he called, drawing my attention over my shoulder.

"Yeah?"

"Thank you."

I turned a little more.

"For what?"

"Not leaving me in the dark. I didn't get the same courtesy the first time and it feels good to be included."

I nodded.

"Feels good to include you, August."

And that had been the truth.

It felt good to share, to see his reaction.

His immediate concern then acceptance.

But it hadn't settled me like I'd hoped. I was more terrified now than before he arrived at the coffee shop.

How the fuck were we going to get through this?

The answers eluded me, making me sicker than I already felt.

Shaking my head, I tapped a button on my steering wheel and answered Kali's incoming call.

"What can I do for you, Buttercup?"

"Te, where are you? Your place is empty and Mom brought me over so I could check on you and make breakfast. Well, she's making breakfast. I haven't perfected the right crisp in my bacon yet."

I smiled.

"I'm fifteen minutes away," I told her. "Tell Mom I don't want a heavy breakfast."

I could feel Kali's frown through the phone.

She was a perceptive kid, always picking up on the small things.

"Are you still sick?" she asked softly. "Maybe you need a doctor like Nana."

"No, baby..." I shook my head as if she could see me. "I don't need a doctor like Nana. But I have something to tell you and your mom, so sit tight, okay?"

She sighed into the phone.

"Okay. I'll go tell Mom that you don't want a heavy breakfast. Maybe some toast and tea?"

"With butter and jelly."

Kali giggled but ended the call without saying anything.

I got to my place soon after, and when I entered, she rushed me. Her arms were around my torso before I could process her quick movements.

"You okay, Buttercup?"

She nodded against my chest and lifted her head.

"Yes. I'm okay. Just happy to see you."

Her eyes told another story, but I knew she'd open up when she was ready.

Journi and Kingston had done a fantastic job teaching her how to communicate about anything and everything with them. I think there were some days they regretted it because Kali told it all and held no qualms about it.

The smell of bacon hit me, and I gagged, jerking hard enough to get Kali's attention.

"Excuse me," I murmured, sidestepping her to get to the guest bathroom on the lower level.

I arrived just in time to empty my stomach into the toilet. Remnants of my coffee were present, but I'd only taken a few sips before giving up on the taste. That was tragic because I loved a frozen caramel coffee, though decaf hadn't hit like I needed it to.

"Is there something you need to tell me?" Journi asked, shutting the door as she came into the bathroom.

"I'm sure your nose has already figured it out. You're like a damn hound dog."

She chuckled, and I flushed the toilet, dropping the lid and sitting right after.

Journi handed me a bottle of water and leaned against the sink.

"I'm pregnant," I said, glancing over at her. "Almost seven weeks."

"This has Mama written all over it," she muttered with a smile. "Can't believe my baby is having a baby."

I rolled my eyes.

"The only baby you have is that eleven-year-old eavesdropping on the other side of the door."

Kali thought she was slick, but she wasn't slicker than us. We'd written the manual.

Journi pulled the door open, and sure enough, Kali stumbled inside.

Her big eyes moved from me to her mother.

"Uh... can I eat?" she asked.

"When have you ever needed to ask to eat?" Journi questioned, tipping her head. "Go on with yourself, Kali Rain."

I smiled at the wide-eyed look that crossed her face. She took off and Journi shut the door.

"I can't believe I still haven't had to use her entire government. Who knew Kingston and I would birth such a good kid?"

I snorted.

I didn't have enough fingers to count how many times I'd been called Couri Lee Mitchell growing up by our mom. I wasn't a troublemaker, only a finisher. Folks started with me and I took it further. You went low, and I was dragging us both to hell.

My mouth had gotten me into many fistfights, but I could always back it up.

"Couri Lee Mitchell," Journi mocked, sounding just like Mama. "Why'd you put a knot upside that girl's head? How would you like it if—"

"I put a knot upside your big ass head," I finished.

We burst into laughter.

"That lady knew exactly why I bopped that little ugly ass girl every time I saw her."

In fact, if I saw her all these years later, I'd make her square up for old times' sake.

"Have you..." Journi sat on the end of the bathtub in front of me. "Are you planning to keep it?"

I nodded.

There had never been a doubt in my mind about the baby itself. I wanted to be a mother no matter how it happened.

"And the father?" she prodded, resting her elbows on her knees. "Is he... have you told him? Do you think he'll be in the picture?"

She looked hurt that I hadn't told her I was dealing with someone. I never wanted to talk about August because all we were doing was fucking around. Eventually, I would have revealed it all, but it didn't seem appropriate.

My sister was my best friend, but I only wanted her to meet and know about the man I wanted to spend my life with. Not a late-night booty call.

Though August had never felt like one of those.

"He's a good guy..." I took a few swigs of water and set it aside. "You know him; Kingston does too."

She stared at me, her eyes thoughtful.

"I'm drawing a blank here."

"August," I said, twisting my fingers.

"As in August Hanson. Kingston's childhood friend?"

I nodded.

She whistled.

"Damn, girl. That's a beautiful man you've let knock you up."

"Isn't he?"

I sighed.

"He knows?" she asked.

"That's where I was this morning. I know he'll be around, you know? He's the kind of guy who shows up and takes care of business, but Journi, he has so much going on. I can't... I don't want to put more on him."

She frowned, her brows pinched close together.

"I don't know what he has going on, but this baby is important. You can't suppress your needs to make his life easier, Couri."

"You don't understand—"

"No," she cut in, shaking her head. "I do understand. You're so selfless. You think of everyone else and never yourself. I need you to stop it now because if you continue down this path, your life will revolve around that baby once he or she gets here."

"He just found out he has a daughter," I blurted. "You can't tell Kingston this because I don't know how August plans to tell everyone but I'm talking right out of the cooker. The mother didn't make it. She hadn't told him a thing and he became a single dad overnight."

Her eyes bucked.

It was the knee-jerk reaction I should've had to his news, but instead, I only felt concerned for him and all that came with his newfound life.

"Well, fuck," she grumbled. "That is a lot, but I stand by what I said. The baby you two created is important, too."

I scoffed.

"That's if it's only one baby in here. Did you know that man is a quadruplet? Fraternal twins are hereditary, Journi!"

My eyes twitched at the thought of multiple babies.

"Had you told me you two were knocking boots, I could have warned you." She rolled her eyes. "I would ask why you know fraternal twins are inherited, but it doesn't matter."

"Technically..." I swayed from side to side. "I might be in the clear because there's more than two of them. I need to find out if triplets and quads are hereditary too."

"One baby or six—"

I gasped.

"Too far?" she asked, smiling.

"Too fucking far."

"Your baby or babies will be loved. I've got your back and you know Kingston does."

"So do I!" Kali yelled from the other side of the door.

She pushed it open slowly and poked her head inside.

"I called Dad," she said, looking between us with a bottle of Vernors dangling between her fingers. "He brought ginger ale. Nana always said it was the best medicine."

It was indeed the best medicine, but it only worked if you were lying down and not looking at your phone.

"You heard, huh?" I asked, accepting the ginger ale.

"There's a baby in there..." She grimaced, pointing to my stomach. "Can I touch it?"

I laughed and slid my shirt up a little, showing off my flat abdomen.

"Sure, go for it."

She reached out and brushed her fingers across my stomach.

"When do you get bigger?"

"Slowly, but now that I know it'll probably start to sprout overnight."

Kali tugged her hand away and I dropped my shirt.

"You'll be a great big cousin."

"I know. I mean, it's me we're talking about."

Journi rolled her eyes and I laughed.

"Give your mom and me a few seconds and we'll be right out."

Kali ducked out of the bathroom and left the door open.

"She's special, that kid."

"She is. That's my pride and joy right there. And now you'll experience the feeling I've been talking about all these years."

I let the tears I'd been holding onto fall.

"I'm so scared, Journi."

"It's okay to be scared." She hugged me tightly. "I was scared. I'm sure Mama was too. We'll get through every step of this together, okay?"

I nodded and held onto her for dear life.

And so it begins.

august

"WHERE WERE YOU?" June asked as I approached with the book bag I'd settled with as my diaper bag hanging off my right shoulder. "Thought you were coming straight here."

I ignored her and walked over to July, who was fawning over January.

A soft chuckle escaped at the fucked up way I was using calendar months to keep the Hanson tradition going.

"She has June's nose," July muttered, looking up at me with adoration dancing in her irises. "I'm in love."

"Didn't believe in love at first sight 'til I met her," I said, kneeling before them.

I set the backpack on the floor beside me and stared at my daughter.

There was no way to explain what I felt inside for this little girl already. She was tiny with chubby cheeks, a bald head, barely their eyebrows, and small lips.

My heart recognized her as someone important and she was. The most important.

I started digging inside the book bag for the outfit I'd picked to change her into.

"Have the nurses been in yet?"

"Mmhm," June hummed from behind us. "She should be back with paperwork soon."

Once I had everything I needed from the bag, I stood and set it all on the changing table on the left side of the room.

I turned to grab her, but July was up and heading over. She sidestepped me and laid January on the table.

"I can help if—"

I shook my head and she moved to the side.

"I got it," I said, walking to the sink to wash my hands. "Can you check the car seat base for me? I know we did it last night, but I want to be sure she'll be secure on the ride."

"Of course, I'll pull it around to the front too."

I turned.

"Hey!" I called.

July stopped and glanced over her shoulder.

"Thank you for everything."

She smiled and walked off, then June came over and leaned against the wall near me.

"I've wanted to say this, but it didn't feel right. Honestly, it probably never will, but congratulations, August."

I cut my eyes at her.

"I know the circumstances are fucked, but you've always wanted to be a dad. And now you get to be that while also honoring what Shondra wanted when she decided to keep our girl."

After drying my hands, I walked over to the changing table and she angled her body in that direction.

"Never wanted to be a single dad."

June nodded.

"I know. You want love and family and rings and shit. We all do, but sometimes God has other plans for us."

Now that I believed wholeheartedly.

My faith hadn't wavered, not even with all the news I'd been given this weekend.

"I guess it's true when they say if you want to make God laugh, tell him about your plans."

She smiled.

"That's why I move in silence."

"June..."

She laughed and rested her head against the wall.

"He knows all and sees all, I know. I guess I mean I have things I want, but I don't have precise plans for them. My heart and mind are open to the endless options there are."

As I gently changed January from the hospital-provided attire into something a little more colorful—a purple onesie, to be exact, with yellow daffodils on the front—I thought about Couri. About how we hadn't planned to have a baby together. Neither of us had ever mentioned kids to the other, but sharing a human being with her didn't turn me off.

I fucked with Couri heavily.

I liked her *a lot*.

Now I had to hold on to those things while I got to know her in ways that didn't involve entering her body. The more intimate and personal details, like if I had to choose between her and our baby in a life or death situation. What would she want me to do? I would always make sure she had a choice, even if she couldn't verbally make it herself.

It was the only way to be a proper partner, in my opinion. Asking the hard questions and being a standby advocate, strapped with the knowledge you acquired.

"Can't believe you're dressing her in a tutu," June mumbled as I slipped it on over the onesie. "I mean, she's adorable, but I'm shocked it wasn't something that said *daddy's girl* on it."

I grabbed her little zip-up jacket and slipped her arms inside. As I pulled the zipper up, I glanced at my sister.

"Knew it!" she exclaimed after catching the wording on the front.

Daddy's little princess, it read.

We'd spent a grip on clothes, knowing half the shit wouldn't fit by the time she turned a month old.

I didn't care.

I wanted her to have it all, and when it was time to buy more, I'd happily pull out my platinum card.

"I'll grab the car seat," June announced, there and back with it seconds later.

I placed January into the unnecessarily expensive carrier. She whined a little, but eventually, she was sound asleep again, and I could adjust the straps to her body better once I'd snapped her in.

"You're a natural."

"It's all those times I snapped JJ in. He was a wiggler, too, so I'm prepared for that phase."

"And now he's running the streets," she said. "I never thought about how the kids we watched growing up would turn out as adults."

JJ was still young.

He didn't need to have it all figured out right now, but I did wonder if where he was in life was a phase. Running the streets of Detroit wasn't for the weak.

JJ grew up in the suburbs and went to private school his whole life.

None of it made sense, but it wasn't my business and I wouldn't make it mine either.

"Oh great!" a nurse chirped, stealing our attention. "You guys are ready to go, I see."

She came over and checked the car seat, nodding her approval.

"Perfect fit." She handed over a folder. "All of the paperwork for your records are in there." She lifted a clear bag. "I took the liberty of making you a care package. Some diapers, formula, baby wraps, and a few other things are in there. I would slowly wean her off the formula she's been drinking here then implement your preference."

I took the bag and handed it to June, who had the diaper bag draped over her shoulder.

"Thank you for taking care of her," I said, picking up the car seat after I laid a blanket over it. "Is there anything I should know? Or... I..."

The nurse smiled at my loss for words.

"I think you've got this handled."

She walked over to the door and opened it.

June walked out first and I followed.

"You'll want to follow up with a pediatrician."

I nodded, already a step ahead on that front.

There was only one pediatrician in the state of Michigan I trusted to take care of my daughter and she bore the last name Hanson.

"Thank you again."

The hallway had more nurses standing around than when I had arrived. I knew they were lingering because we were taking the baby with the dead mom home.

Once we were out of the building, June said, "Way to make that shit awkward."

"I know," I agreed, watching July pull my truck to the entrance.

"The base is secure," she said, walking around to open the back door. "I'll drive so you can sit in the back with her."

"Didn't think of that, thanks."

She nodded and turned to June, tossing her a set of keys.

"I'll be right behind you guys," June said, catching them as she walked by.

I lifted the carrier into the backseat and set it on top of the base it came with. A loud snap sounded, indicating it was locked in. I tightened the seatbelt around it and got inside.

"You ready?" July asked from the driver's seat as I buckled myself in.

"Yeah..." I pulled the blanket from over January's carrier and leaned back, my eyes pinned to her sleeping frame. "Let's go home."

I thought about Couri the entire drive.

Was she okay? Still sick?

Did she need anything? Maybe me?

Another hug and some reassurance that I would have her back.

My mind played a loop of her words until it was all I could hear.

I'm pregnant.

I almost laughed, but July's voice dulled the urge.

"Are you okay?" she asked. "You look zoned out back there."

I hadn't realized I'd been gazing out the window until I blinked and saw flashes of greenery.

"Yeah, just thinking. I'm good."

I adjusted the blanket over January and laid my head back. With my eyes on the upholstery, the first time I met Couri clouded my mental.

"Who's the unknown?" she'd asked Kingston, referring to me.

She'd already stolen my attention when she hopped out of her eighty-thousand-dollar truck in a pair of oversized sweats and a matching hoodie. It swallowed her little frame whole.

Kingston told her who I was, then she instructed the man to tell me her name.

She amused me.

Everything out of her mouth was a contradiction to her soft voice. She was somehow loud without actually raising her voice and direct without sounding harsh.

"You smell like brown sugar and honey," she'd said after we had an exchange about handshakes and sweat. "Molasses gives it that distinctive brown color, making it healthier than its white cousin."

She made no sense to me; I could tell she knew and enjoyed my confusion.

That encounter was the first impression she'd left on me. And every moment after got better and better, each embedded in my mind forever.

PART TWO

where we began

> *"His eyes were my new favorite brand of whiskey."*
> — **Couri Mitchell**

couri

THE PAST...

"Of course he found a way to get that old ass hoop up on the garage," I mumbled as I pulled into the driveway of my sister and her family's new home.

Kingston stepped to the side and revealed a face I'd never seen before.

He was shirtless, his dark skin littered with tattoos. I wanted to know who his artist was because they deserved my money. There weren't many who could perfect visible art on darker complexions. But this man, he was a walking art gallery.

Our gazes met and I admired his full lips, unkempt brows, and nigga nose. I even found his barely there facial and chin hair sexy.

It was his brown eyes that stole the show.

I felt like I was staring into a bottle of Woodford Reserve.

Damn.

When Journi invited me over for wine and gossip, I got my lazy ass off the sofa and dashed out to buy our favorite dry red.

She hadn't mentioned that there'd be someone else here other than family.

If she had, I might've spritzed some water into my dry ass curls and found a more flattering pair of sweats.

"I'll never understand how you were an all-American football star at one point, but somehow you love basketball more," I mused as I exited my vehicle with plastic bags in hand.

"You don't need to understand as long as you respect it," Kington quipped, repeating his usual spiel.

I rolled my eyes but smiled and started to walk past them.

A mixture of brown sugar and honey wafted in my direction, and I stopped, turning my attention to the newbie.

"Kingston, who's the unknown?"

Mr. No Name tipped his head, his eyes wistful.

I was intrigued.

"The unknown is August. We grew up together before I moved around y'all way back in the day."

I tipped my head forward.

"Tell him my name," I requested, never breaking eye contact with the silent August.

He hadn't spoken one word, not verbally anyway, but his body spoke to me in many languages.

"August," Kingston drawled slowly. "This is Couri."

I pushed my free hand toward him, but he shook his head, declining it.

"Sweaty," he said, revealing a voice reminiscent of an after-dark radio show from my era.

I shrugged and dropped my hand.

"Builds character..."

He raised a bushy eyebrow.

"...sweat builds character," I went on.

His brows dipped into a mean furrow and I wanted to laugh.

I'd just made that up for the hell of it.

"You smell like brown sugar and honey," I said, turning toward the front door. "Molasses is what gives it that distinctive brown color. It's actually way healthier than its white cousin."

"She spontaneously spouts random facts all the time," Kingston said, a swoosh sound following.

All net, I thought.

I glanced over my shoulder with my hand on the door handle and August's eyes were on me, a twinkle in them. The tiniest smirk played on his lips and I looked away with a smile.

Yeah, you see me.

I pushed the front door open and went inside.

"Finally!" Journi exclaimed as she jogged down the stairs and followed me into the kitchen. "We got an hour, maybe two, of drinking time. Kali is up in her room setting up that damn old-school Nintendo you had shipped here. Where did you even find it?"

My niece loved all the nostalgic shit Journi and I grew up on. She'd already been a fan of video games, so it was only right I introduced her to the game systems we played on.

"Got it from eBay." I set the hefty wine bottle on the counter. "The seller restores and sells them. It has over fifty games built inside. I couldn't pass it up."

She hummed and poured us two full glasses of red.

"What's up with you?" I asked, narrowing my eyes at her.

I should've known there was more to her need for a drink.

"I'm thinking about finally quitting the firm," she exclaimed, gulping down half the glass.

She took a breath then swallowed the rest.

"Crazy, right?"

It wasn't crazy, but she wouldn't believe me no matter what I said. Journi had worked hard to make partner before thirty. She'd voiced her desire to work with companies directly a few years into that role.

Instead of working for a firm and taking clients as they were handed to her, she'd be brought in by a company directly to handle their affairs as their in-house counsel but with stipulations that she could work with other companies who weren't a direct conflict of interest.

Kingston promised to fund her private practice after signing two big contracting deals. He'd met those qualifications two years ago.

Money wasn't an issue, but Journi's fear of failure was.

"Nothing beats a failure but a try," I said, tipping my glass to my lips afterward.

"Kingston said I didn't have a choice anymore," she grumbled. "He bought me a fucking office building."

"And you're upset?"

"What?" She looked at me. "Upset? No way, I'm so appreciative. He kept every promise he's ever made, and I... I'm frustrated that I'm scared to keep mine."

She took more gentle sips from the second glass of wine.

"You have a good rapport with your clients. Even if you can't legally steal them, they have friends who have friends."

"The guy in the driveway..." She sipped.

"August?" I asked, eager to hear more about the mystery man.

Journi nodded, oblivious to my interest.

I wouldn't have gotten away with it if she hadn't been freaking out about the change.

"He's a Hanson," she went on. "His family owns that big ass distillery tucked in the cut downtown. The one Kingston worked on."

The Hanson Distillery had been around since we were kids, probably even before that.

Over the years, they'd expanded, opening tasting rooms and bars throughout the city. I'd been to a few, but nothing beat the experience you got at the distillery.

They took you on a tour where you tried whiskey, gin, and vodka straight from the barrels. The expansion included an updated tasting room, an inside wedding venue, and an on-site restaurant.

Kingston had been the one to draw up all the designs and implement them with his team.

"What about it?" I asked, giving her my undivided attention again.

"He offered me an in-house counsel contract."

"You have your first client, and a big one might I add, but you're standing over there like it'll be snatched from you at any moment. Get out of your damn head!"

I lifted my glass and she rolled her eyes, but I saw the relief in them. All she needed was a sisterly nod only I could give. It was all shaping out for her.

"Let's toast."

"To what?"

"Yung Miami being single," I deadpanned. "Girl, lift your damn glass so we can toast to your success. To you being a fine ass, big booty, Black female attorney who just landed her first in-house client."

Journi lifted her glass, a glimmer of happiness in her eyes.

"To me, being a badass bitch," she declared. "And to the start of a successful career venture."

We tapped glasses and sipped, both taking large gulps for extra luck.

"Baby..." Kingston walked past the kitchen, his strides swift. "Meet me upstairs for a second."

She moved a little too quickly and I scoffed.

"Be back, Sis."

"So much for sister time!" I yelled to her retreating frame.

Nasty asses.

I downed the rest of my wine and stood to leave, refusing to stick around and wait for them to emerge from their bedroom.

Once I cleaned our mess, I picked up my keys and phone and walked outside. The door slammed behind me as I moved down the stairs with my eyes on August.

He stood in front of his matte black Land Rover, eyes on me.

"So, you're a Hanson, huh?" I asked, walking down the driveway to get to my midnight blue Lexus LX truck.

"And you're a Mitchell," August returned as if my name held the same weight that his did in the city.

He shut his trunk and turned his body in my direction. I was slightly disappointed he'd put a shirt on, but his black basketball shorts gave a nice peek at the muscle between his legs.

Thick.

But, is it long too? I thought, licking my lips.

"That's why you smell like brown sugar and honey," I continued, ignoring his sarcasm and my wild ass thoughts. "It's a nice scent."

I opened my driver's door but didn't move to get inside; instead, I kept my eyes locked with his.

"You know about my profession, am I allowed to inquire about yours?" he asked.

"Technically, I don't know what you do at your family's company. Everyone has a job description, right?"

He blessed me with a full smile, straight white teeth and all. I knew good dental work when I saw it. He'd been a brace face like me.

"Master Distiller," he informed me.

Mmm, a hands-on man.

His title would have him in the thick of it with his employees regularly and for some odd reason, I liked that.

"Your turn." He inched up the driveway. "What's your chosen profession?"

"What makes you think I'm not working a dead-end job I hate?"

He chuckled, but it sounded more like a rumble from deep inside his chest.

"I don't take you as the settling type and that truck ain't cheap."

I sniffed and raised my head in a regal manner.

He was right; the thought of settling gave me hives.

"Good eye," I complimented. "I'm a zoologist. I currently work closely with the penguins at the Detroit Zoo."

"Currently? That changing anytime soon?"

I shrugged.

"Maybe. Maybe not."

I went wherever my animal-loving heart wanted me. Right now, it was with the penguins. A few years prior, it had been a wildlife sanctuary in Indiana where I worked with big cats. Some years before that, I'd been hoofing it with the elephants —who happen to have my heart more than any animal I'd ever worked with.

"I'll see you around, August the Master Distiller."

He took a step back, his eyes filled with intrigue.

"See you around, Couri the Zoologist."

I settled in my seat and started to back out the driveway but stopped before making it onto the street. Through my left mirror, I saw August move from where he stood. He approached after I rolled down my window and ducked my head out of It.

"Forgot how to reverse?" he asked, stopping so close I was forced to pull my head in.

"My reverse game is fine, thank you."

As soon as the words left my mouth, I wanted to hide, but I played it off like a G and asked, "Got somewhere you need to be?"

He didn't respond right away, only stared with his eyes narrowed.

Not in a glaring way but more thoughtfully, like he needed a moment to feel me out. I had a lot of patience and rested my head on the seat with my gaze still pinned on his.

"Only place I need to be is in my shower," he finally said, his eyebrow rising slowly.

Was that a challenge?

No... that had been an invitation.

I wanted to join.

It was the craziest thought I had had all week, but I knew he'd be a good fuck and I needed one of those. The last time I'd let a man crack my back evaded me and that was a problem I needed to remedy.

Was getting fucked by your brother-in-law's childhood friend on the day you met him—a Sunday, to be exact—a sin? Probably but...

Fuck it.

"What kind of man are you, August Hanson?"

He licked his lips then let out a soft chuckle.

"Talking about the kind of man I am is too far outside my purview," he said silkily. "I can show you, though."

"Yeah?"

He nodded and I leaned forward to put my truck in reverse.

"Your place or mine?"

He backed up as I slowly lifted my foot off the brake and the truck began to roll.

"Follow me," he said as he turned away and slid into his truck.

And I followed him to a cul-de-sac of townhomes in Troy, into his home, and let him strip me bare.

"You good with this?" he asked, backing into the massive shower encased in glass.

The tip of his dick bounced off my stomach repeatedly as he moved us.

It was thick, long, and heavy.

Way better than I'd hoped for.

"I'm good with it," I said, lowering myself onto the shower floor. "Are you good with this?"

I slid my fingers down his length, admiring its slight curve.

The thick flesh was smooth to the touch and I stroked it a few times to get my fill.

"Yeah," August groaned, resting his hands against the shower wall as he stared down at me.

I'd never let a man get me on my knees before he buried his dome between my thighs. August made me want to break all of my rules and I was horny enough to let it slide this one time.

His dick was too pretty not to swallow at least once in this lifetime.

I angled my head underneath his shaft and licked it from tip to base, my eyes locked with his.

He thrust forward as I parted my lips for him.

"Mmhm," I hummed, encouraging him to fill my mouth.

The deeper he went, the more saliva I accumulated. I slurped it all up when it became too much by dragging my lips along his smooth and thick flesh.

I spat it all out on my hands and enclosed them around him.

"Shit," he moaned softly, jerking forward. "Get up."

He lifted me and I stumbled into him.

75

August gripped my waist and held me in place.

"You're trouble, Couri Mitchell."

The tips of his fingers danced against my flesh as he backed into the shower wall and pinned my body against it. I'd never felt so alive before, not like this.

"Just now figuring that out, huh?"

I slid my leg up his and wrapped it around his waist, tugging him closer.

"Knew it the first moment I heard you speak."

Slowly, he enclosed his fingers around my throat.

I leaned into the pressure and he adjusted his grip, slipping his hand to the back of my neck. He caressed the length of my throat with his thumb and I got lost in him.

"Can't get over how fucking pretty you are," he murmured, brushing his lips gently against mine.

He stroked the inside of my thigh before cupping my entire pussy and grinding the heel of his palm into my clit.

"Oh my—please," I begged, holding onto his shoulder to lift myself higher.

"Never took you for the begging type," he taunted, pulling his hand away as I was on the verge of coming undone.

I dropped my head against the shower wall and took deep breaths.

"You've caught me in your web, August Hanson."

Our eyes met.

"You enticed me first," he quipped, slipping his fingers between my pussy lips.

My body hadn't been prepared for this kind of pleasure.

I hadn't been prepared.

"Fuck me," I demanded.

August spun me around, pressing my body into the shower wall with his.

"Ask nicely first."

He dug his fingers into the meat of my thighs as he pushed them apart.

My pussy dripped with anticipation; I could barely breathe.

"Please," I begged, backing my ass into his erection until it poked at my entrance. "Please, fuck me, August."

He released me instead of giving in and I slapped the wall, my frustration seeping through without my permission.

"Someone has a temper..."

His voice serenaded my ears from afar as a cold drift from the shower door opening tickled my back.

"Don't worry," he went on, closer now. "I know how to remedy that attitude."

"W-What are you doing?"

I turned to find him entering the shower again, his dick sheathed.

"Protecting us."

My God, that was sexy.

He commanded me through his touch, moving my body toward the corner where the built-in bench was. I bent over and August tapped the back of my thigh. He maneuvered it onto the bench as I lifted it, forcing my body into a deadly arch.

"Damn, this view is breathtaking."

I wanted so badly to see things from his perspective—a chance to admire how he stroked my pussy with his shaft over and over, engaging my clit along the way.

"Mm shit," I whimpered, slapping the shower wall with one hand while gripping the small groove in the side of the bench as he entered me.

The first stroke was always the best.

My pussy pulsed around him, grateful for the thickness he was working with.

I rocked back and rolled my hips, guiding my pussy along his dick.

August's fingers dug into the arch of my ass as he met me halfway, connecting our bodies in a fluid back-and-forth motion.

I could feel him all up and through me.

My skin vibrated with pleasure I'd never experienced before, not by my hand or another man.

"Knew you'd fuck my head up," August growled, quickening his thrusts.

The faster he fucked me, the deeper I felt him, and the harder it became to keep up.

I was holding on for dear life, gasping for air as my body chased the high rushing at us.

"Breathe," August coached after he tugged me back by my throat, his lips against my ear. "Take a breath and let it go."

I took that breath, pulling the steamy shower air into my lungs and releasing it.

As my chest deflated, that orgasm I'd been chasing rolled through my body in deep waves.

"Fuck. Fuck. Fuck," I screeched, taking the powerful strokes that followed like a champ.

Soon after I drifted down from my high, August reached his peak and blessed me with the most beautiful moan I'd ever heard come from a man.

His breath tickled the inside of my ear and I wanted him again.

It was an odd way to get turned on by a man, but everything he did was sexy.

What the fuck was he doing to me?

August lifted and spun me around. Our lips collided moments later.

I wanted more of him, and from the feel of him stiffening against me, so did he.

"Hold up." He stepped back and carefully pulled the condom off.

After stepping out of the shower to dispose of it, he returned with different plans than me.

"Come here," he beckoned from the shower door, a towel opened wide for me to step into.

I couldn't resist following his command.

There was something about this man that called to me and made me feel safe and protected.

He turned the shower off after wrapping me in the towel then dried me off, only doing the same for himself after he finished with me.

"You have a daffodil tattoo." I reached for his hand and caressed the smallest piece of art he had on him.

"I like the meaning. I'm all about new beginnings."

I lifted my gaze and met his whiskey browns.

"Yeah?"

"Mmhm..."

August led me in his bedroom, ushered me into what had to be high thread count sheets, and exhaustion hit me. He'd drained me of all my energy.

I wanted more of him, but my eyes drooped as he guided my head to a fluffy pillow and covered me in a soft duvet.

"I'll never be the same," he murmured in my ear as he wrapped his arms around me from behind. "Not after tonight."

I'd never admit it, but the feeling was mutual.

August Hanson had fucked my world up.

Big time.

At three in the morning I woke with my body still wrapped in August's arms.

I didn't remember falling asleep, but *damn* had that been

the best rest I'd gotten since my mother started her radiation treatments.

Slowly, I maneuvered from his hold and slipped out of bed. I cursed myself for falling asleep at his place and tiptoed around while I dressed. With my sweats and hoodie on, I stuffed my thong into my pocket and stuck my feet in my Crocs.

Halfway out his bedroom door, August's voice startled me to a stop.

"Let me walk you out," he said, the words vibrating up my spine.

That sleepy raspiness paired with his deep baritone was the best kind of music to my ears.

"Walk me out?" I asked, looking over my shoulder to find him standing in nothing but black boxer briefs.

I perused his frame in awe of how beautiful this man was.

My pussy ached from that one good fuck, but I would let him have me again if he asked.

"It's three in the morning." He pulled on a pair of basketball shorts with his eyes pinned on mine. "I can't let you walk out alone at this time."

Why'd he have to be a gentleman?

Those were the kind of guys you cuffed, not fucked and dipped on.

"Do you walk all of your one night stands out?" I asked as we approached the front door.

He turned to look at me instead of opening it.

"I don't do one-night stands."

"Well, that's what this is." I gestured between us, not believing a word that left my mouth.

August didn't respond; he turned, opened the door, and waved for me to take my leave. I took his silence as us agreeing, but when I angled my body out the door past him, he tugged me into his chest.

"What are you—"

He lowered his head and brought his lips close to mine.

"I don't do one-night stands," he reiterated, kissing the corner of my mouth.

He pulled back and I knew the expression in my eyes showed the disappointment I felt about that half-ass kiss he'd given.

"Drive safe, Couri."

"First, you're walking me to the door..." I backed onto the top step and twisted my body in the opposite direction of the morning chill. "And now you want me to drive safe. If you wanted to be my man, you could have started with that."

Really, Couri?

He only chuckled and I appreciated his silent nature, especially at three in the morning when the sky lacked light. But mostly because if he'd spoken, I'd have to keep embarrassing myself.

"Later, August."

I waved and slid into my truck with one question on my mind.

What the fuck have you gotten yourself into?

EIGHT

THREE SHOT GLASSES FILLED with the first batch of a new Hanson brand whiskey lined the bar in our on-site tasting room. It had the perfect amber shading, not too dark or light but smack in the middle.

My sisters stood on the other side, eager to try what I'd produced. We were going for a richer taste, something that went down smoothly but had a silent burn.

"Still can't believe you changed your mind," June said, leaning into the bar and flaring her nostrils.

They'd been waiting to taste for four weeks and two days. I'd lost count of how many times they asked, including last Friday when I'd told them it still needed more time.

It hadn't been a complete lie; the longer whiskey could age, the better it tasted, but checking the progress along the way was part of my process.

We could've tried it a month ago but I hadn't been ready. Being fresh off a breakup had my confidence lacking as of late.

"Felt like it was time," I said, wanting to move past the coming conversation.

June looked over at July and September; a silent conversation commenced between the three and I sighed.

"No, I didn't get back with Shondra," I said, answering the question they were arguing with their eyes over. "I'm good. Friday it wasn't ready and today it is."

"Don't know what happened over the weekend, but I like it," July said, clutching one of the shot glasses.

I waved for June and September to do the same, ignoring July's assumption that something had transpired to change my mind.

This specific bourbon whiskey had aged about three and half years thus far. The liquid sat in ten previously used American oak casks.

Matured barrels were the best whiskey makers.

The more the barrel had been used over time, the better.

Our whiskey should have rich woodsy notes from the cask and hints of honey and vanilla. The richer, the better.

"I want honest opinions only," I told them.

June sipped first; she held the liquid in her mouth for a few seconds then swallowed.

I observed her closely, but she managed to keep a straight face.

July and September went next, following the steps June had.

They looked at one another and I stepped closer to the bar.

"What's wrong with it?"

September leaned her elbows on the bar top, her eyes pinned on me.

"What makes you think something's wrong?"

I learned the process of making whiskey at nine years old, the same age my father and his had been introduced to it. Neither of them had created their own, making this a Hanson first.

I had to get it right, but I wasn't against failing a few times first.

"Something is always wrong the first time around," I pointed out. "The three of you know it just as I do."

I wasn't the only Master Distiller, my sisters and I had followed the same path.

June's specialty was gin.

July leaned more toward vodkas, while September had taken a liking to wine.

"Hate to break it to you," June started with a smirk curling the left side of her mouth. "But what I just tried is damn near perfect, August."

"The notes are rich like we talked about," July added. "I can taste the aged American oak, but it's not overpowering the subtle notes of vanilla and honey."

"I know you were on the fence about using a multi-grain base, but it was a smart move," September said, smiling. "Few more months in the barrels and we can start talking about packaging." She reached for the decanter I'd filled three-fourths of the way. "Try it."

She poured the last of it into the shot glass she'd used and slid it across the bar.

I typically didn't try my experiments until I had a handful of test dummies to do it first. But, I valued my sisters' opinions the most, so I downed the shot.

I held the liquid in my mouth, drowning my taste buds in flavor, then swallowed.

"Smooth," I mumbled, nodding at how it went down. "Rich. I can taste the honey and vanilla like you said, July."

Damn.

"He has that look," June said, excitedly smacking the bar. "The confidence is back."

I looked between the three of them and shook my head.

Just as I'd read their silent conversations easily, they'd been able to pick up my lack of confidence the last few weeks.

"Finally," September muttered. "I was ready to knock ol' girl upside the head for breaking your heart."

I picked up the empty decanter and walked away.

"Appreciate y'all," I said over my shoulder.

Talking about my ex hadn't been on the agenda.

Shondra didn't deserve to be knocked upside the head. We ended amicably, but a part of me did wish she'd been more honest about not wanting children earlier in our relationship. Maybe it could've saved us the four years we'd spent planning our lives together.

I guess we had her mother to thank for that.

"August!" June shouted just as I'd made it across the room.

I cut my eyes over my shoulder.

"You are deserving," she said and turned away.

Mmph.

I pushed through the doors and walked down a long corridor toward my office.

Whether I deserved anything wasn't on my mind at the moment.

It was *her*.

Couri Lee Mitchell.

She said what was on her mind, and while I didn't know it to be true about her yet, I had a feeling she would never waver from who she presented herself to be. I wanted to explore that and see what she was about outside the bedroom.

I came in this morning ready to sample the whiskey with my sisters because of her.

That woman was a breath of fresh air I needed to breathe in more.

I let her leave my place this morning without exchanging numbers, but only because I knew I could find her when I was ready to. Had I thought it would be shy of twelve hours when the urge hit? No, but that didn't stop me from searching the Penguin Conservatory website, where I purchased a ticket.

"Leaving already?" July asked, walking into my office as I gathered my things.

I tucked my phone in my pocket and reached for my keys.

"Got an appointment I can't miss," I told her. "Then, I'm heading over to the tasting room in Royal Oak for a couple of hours."

"You know it's okay if you and Shondra decided that you want to try again. People change their minds about not wanting to have kids all the time."

I sighed and lifted my laptop bag onto my shoulder.

"She isn't changing her mind. I'm not changing mine. We aren't getting back together."

I'd been repeating those three statements to everyone around me for weeks.

They were dull on my tongue now.

"I need you to believe me and convince your sisters and parents."

She chuckled.

"You make it sound like you aren't part of this family."

"I'm a proud Hanson," I said, briefly inflating my chest. "I swear I'm good."

It wasn't a lie.

Shondra and I ending our relationship had been for the best. If she hadn't figured it out by now, she would. Our life goals had never been aligned. We were only two people biding our time together.

The lack of confidence I felt didn't come from Shondra directly. Our breakup ignited thoughts of starting over, finding and loving someone new. That fueled insecurities about work and the direction my family and I were taking the business in.

We were starting over.

Re-branding.

It was all new, and the weight of it, the weight of everything, felt like too much to bear.

June had been right, though, my confidence was back and I felt good.

"I actually believe you," July mused.

She followed me until we got to her office and I continued to our private entrance at the back of the building. The expansion of the distillery has been the best investment we'd made thus far.

It had taken a lot of work to convince the more senior Hansons, who had a stake in the company, that expanding was for the greater good. Now that we had tasting rooms all over the city and an upgraded main location with more amenities for guests and events, business had been booming, checks were cut, and everybody was happy.

We were taking the Hanson name and likeness to the next level.

As the large Detroit Zoo sign came into view, my mind shifted to a memory from my childhood.

The last time I'd set foot on the one hundred twenty-five acres of land in Royal Oak, my sisters and I were turning seven. The day's memory was embedded because it had been a disaster.

June cried after not being able to touch the lions and didn't stop until cake was shoved in her face hours later.

July slapped another kid for standing too close to her. She'd always been a little violent and that day proved it.

September and I had been unbothered by the entire experience and every picture from the day showed the bored expression on our faces.

Our parents never took us back.

The penguin conservation center sat near the zoo's entrance and it took me no time to get to the abstract-shaped white building. From the research I'd done on the website, it was the largest center for penguins in the world at thirty-three thousand square feet with a three hundred twenty-six thousand gallon, twenty-five-foot deep aquatic area.

The second I walked through the doors, I was immersed in the lives of penguins. Through a wide floor-to-ceiling window, there was a glimpse into the rocky side of their habitat.

I walked closer, more interested in the webbed foot animal than I cared to admit.

To the left of me was a gift store, and on the right, a ramp led me down to another level.

I moved in the direction of the latter, taking the ramp into what I learned was an underwater gallery. Inside the curved tunnel, I got a better view of the penguins swimming below the surface.

Monitors lined the walls with little facts about the kinds of penguins that lived in the habitat. Another wide floor-to-ceiling picturesque window sat at the end of the tunnel, but it was all ice and snow instead of dry, rocky terrain.

I'd been so enthralled by what I had in front of me, I missed her approach.

"I think you like them," Couri said, startling me but not enough that I reacted.

She stopped beside me, and I glanced over, my gaze lowered to the rubber boots on her feet, and then slowly, I took her in.

Her oversized overalls and long-sleeved shirt blocked my view of everything I found sexy about her, but I was still somehow turned on.

"I think I might like them, too," I agreed, gaze lingering on her side profile.

She was hard to look away from. I'd cataloged all of her features last night, right down to the smooth curve of her jawline, the widespread in her nose that resembled the top half of a heart, and the deep arch in her cupid's bow. It was perfection slathered onto rich brown skin.

Couri looked over and asked, "Did you come here to see the penguins or me?"

"You," I answered without pause.

She dipped her head in reply, sending her curly topknot tumbling to the side.

"Can I show you something?" she asked as we turned to completely face one another.

I felt the urge to tug her into me but stuffed my hands into the pockets of my jeans instead.

The fuck is wrong with me?

"Only if I can take you somewhere afterward," I said, ignoring what I couldn't decipher.

Couri smiled, spun on her heels, and started in the direction she must've come from.

I took that as a yes and followed her, my eyes glued to how her ass managed to sit up perfectly in her baggy clothing.

"How'd you know I was here?"

She laughed but never answered.

couri

I DIDN'T THINK he'd come to my job, but I knew August would find me.

He'd made it clear he didn't do one-night stands and I believed him.

I led him through an employee-only door and down a curved corridor toward the zookeeper's entrance. We passed a security room along the way, and Bea, the guard inside, whistled.

It was because of her that I knew he was here.

On the days that our schedules aligned, I fed us both and ate with her in the control room.

August had walked inside while I was chowing down on some authentic ramen.

"Damn," Bea had mumbled. "They don't make 'em like that anymore."

She hadn't been lying.

They didn't make 'em like August anymore.

Men weren't fucking like him. They damn sure weren't getting you off properly *and* walking you to the door after you slept your sex high off.

He was a different kind of man.

My kind of man.

I shook my head and turned, my entire body colliding with August's solid frame. He caught me by my arms and our gazes clashed.

I felt flush all of a sudden and looked away.

"Sorry," I muttered, shifting my weight to get loose.

"All good," August said softly, freeing one of his arms but only to wrap it around my torso. "Is it okay if I hug you?"

We were one step away from me being tucked deeper in his hold, but he still asked if it was okay and I melted.

"Yes." I looked up and enclosed my arms around his waist. "But I'm working, so don't grab on my ass."

He chuckled and his chest vibrated against the side of my face. It felt like shockwaves throughout my body. My clit thumped and I quickly pulled away.

"In here..." I pushed the door we stood in front of open and waved him inside.

One side of my office was encased in thick wall-to-wall glass similar to those around the exhibit. I had a view of one of the many blind spots inside the aquatic tank.

"It's my favorite place to be when I'm not working directly with the penguins."

I kept the lights off, the same as I did when it was only me inside. Enough came from the tank to keep my office from being pitch black.

"You find it peaceful?" he asked, staring at the underwater rocky terrain.

His voice dripped sex without trying.

I leaned against the edge of my desk to quell the ache between my thighs.

"The most peaceful," I said softly.

My thoughts drifted to my mother; she was getting sicker by the day and I hated it.

The only time I didn't think about her declining health was in my office, where the noise in my head and heart didn't exist.

August turned and walked over to me; he lifted my chin and stared into my eyes for a while. It was like he heard the sadness in my voice and needed to be sure.

I closed my eyes to hide my feelings and he kissed me.

His lips were extremely gentle against mine and I couldn't understand why he was handling me with this much care. We didn't know one another; no connection other than a long-lost friend who happened to be married to my sister.

I wanted to be handled gently and with care like this, though.

With soft caresses in the form of kisses.

"The lock," I muttered into his mouth, my hands finding their way into his cotton shirt.

August pulled me back and searched my eyes with his, a question lingering.

"I'm sure," I told him and he reached over to flip the lock.

He pulled at the only done strap on my overalls and unclipped it. The baggy material fell to my ankles, and I stepped out of it, my boots still secured to my feet. Underneath I wore black boy shorts that kept everything tucked in.

"Hands on my shoulders," he ordered, tightening his fingers around my waist and lifting me after I obliged.

He sat me down on the desk and I pushed my legs further apart to give him room to stand between them. His fingers traced the inside of my thigh while we stared at one another for an infinite amount of time.

I could get lost in his eyes for ages and never get bored.

I didn't know how to handle the kind of intensity that came with being intimate with him.

August tugged at my panties and got down far enough that his lips were inches from my clit. I squirmed and he hooked his arms around my waist to hold me in place.

"I've been craving this since last night, so hold still and let me eat."

His lips connected with my pussy lips and I jerked back, surprised by the gentle move but so goddamn turned on.

"Soft," he whispered, sliding his tongue over and between the wet flesh.

Needing more, I cupped his head and rolled my pussy against his tongue, thankful that he allowed me to do my thing for a minute before taking control again.

He pinned my arms against my stomach and lifted, dragging my body mid-air while he feasted on me.

August had turned me into a lightweight with the rapid tongue flicks.

I came undone way too soon.

"Oh my... fuck," I cried out, uncaring of the way my voice might've carried.

Slowly, August lowered my body, his eyes on mine.

He stood after I showed promise of holding myself up, lapping my essence from the corners of his mouth with the tip of his tongue on the way. I had no energy and appreciated him wiping me clean with a paper towel from my shelf, sliding my panties back into place, *and* pulling my overalls over my legs.

"I'm sure you have some work shit to handle before I can steal you away, so how about you meet me at *The Quad Room* a few blocks from here when you're available?"

His eyes were on the penguins swimming by as he spoke.

"I won't be long," I said, having already finished my work for the day.

Mondays were always short for me; he'd picked the right

day to show up and steal me away. But I couldn't let him take me when I wasn't dressed in the clothes I'd arrived in.

"Good," he said, turning to me. "Next time we part, it won't be without me having a way to contact you."

He lowered his head close to mine, then pulled back and walked to the door. I was disappointed at his abrupt change of heart to kissing me.

August left and I quickly cleaned myself up with the things I always kept in my desk.

Bea came barging in not a minute after I'd changed out of my overalls and into my high-waisted blue jeans. I set my rubber boots aside and put my black and white Nike AirMax on while she stared at me from the door's opening.

"You nasty witch," she accused, her voice low to avoid anyone hearing.

"I have no idea what you're talking about."

She snorted and I bit my lip to hide my smile.

Bea and I were good friends outside of work. It helped that I'd known her since we were seventeen years old. She'd moved to Detroit from New York with her father to live with her grandmother around that time.

"Girl, that man walked by licking his lips as if he were savoring his favorite meal."

"Bea..." I stood and grabbed my Nike windbreaker. "There's nothing to tell."

Was it weird that I wanted to keep what I had going on with August to myself for a while? It felt good doing something as outrageous as I was and I wanted to bask in it without other people's opinions.

August and I were only having a little fun; nothing would come of this.

"Just be careful," she mused, following me up the hall until we reached her stop. "I know his kind and they're hard to let go."

Bea dipped into the control room and I took my leave, heading straight for *The Quad Room;* one of the three tasting room locations August and his family had opened up in the last three years.

It sat on East Third Street, one of the busiest in Royal Oak. There were bars and restaurants that lined the street; no matter what day of the week, there was always a crowd after six.

Thankfully, it was still early afternoon and the streets were clear. I found a parking spot near the tasting room and walked less than half a block to the front door. They'd somehow snagged a corner location with outside seating that wrapped the building.

I stepped inside and was immediately hit with a rustic feel. No matter how many times I'd met Bea here after a shift over the last few months, walking into this building still felt like an out-of-body experience.

A few tables were filled with groups of people, each with a flight tray in front of them as they talked and tasted their orders.

I walked to the bar and slid onto one of the oak stools and a bartender with shoulder-length faux locs came over and set a napkin before me.

"Ever been here before?" she asked, her brown eyes staring deep into mine.

"I'm here to meet—"

I spotted August as he entered the enclosed bar space from a room beside the liquor shelf. The bartender turned as he said, "I got her, Mia."

She gave me a curious glance but left without saying anything.

I wondered if August was the kind of man who mixed business with pleasure. Did he sleep with the women he employed or was it true that most of the Hanson-owned locations in and out of the city were staffed by family?

As he approached, it was on my tongue to ask, but I managed to keep it in.

"Have you ever been here?" he asked, resting his forearms on the bar.

His eyes were so damn descriptive. I could see everything he was thinking, maybe even some of his feelings. What kind of man laid himself bare in this way?

"A couple of times after work," I said, resting my elbows on the bar and placing my chin in my hands. "Never been treated like a VIP guest before, though."

"What's your poison?"

"Anything that burns good. Has to be dark."

He looked to be thinking up brands to pour as he stared at me.

He nodded after a few seconds then turned to the liquor shelf.

August retrieved three bottles, two from the shelf and one from under the bar.

He lined them up in front of me, grabbed a flight tray and three glasses, and filled each with the contents of the bottles.

"Tell me which is your favorite."

He reached under the bar and returned with a pack of thin crackers. While he ripped it open, I grabbed the first glass and sniffed.

Inside was the lightest shade of brown liquid he'd poured. I could smell honey in the mixture and something woodsy.

I sipped and August tucked his hand under my chin, catching me off guard.

Our eyes met while he stroked my jaw with his thumb.

"Hold it in your mouth until all you can taste is the liquor," he instructed, softly tipping the glass back after I filled my mouth.

I held the light-tasting bourbon in until his thumb dropped to the center of my neck. The expression in his eyes encouraged me to swallow and I let the now slightly bitter whiskey coat my throat.

"What do you think?" he asked, pulling his hand away.

I followed it until he cleared his throat and forced me to look into his eyes.

"I can smell and taste the honey," I told him, following his every movement. "It felt nice on my tongue, but it was bitter going down."

"That happens when you age bourbon in a newer cask instead of one that's been broken in a few times."

He brought a cracker to my mouth and I opened it without thinking.

August had me under a spell.

I didn't need to hear his commands or questions; I saw and felt them instead. My body reacted with a response before my mouth ever could.

"I prefer fresh bread as a palate cleanser, but crackers fit a bar situation better," he said, breaking the cracker off in my mouth.

My goodness.

Did he not feel how goddamn erotic this was?

People were around us, but he fed me while stroking my jaw and throat anyway.

And not once did I think to stop him, nor would I.

I liked the way he moved at his own pace, in his own way, without much thought of who might be uncomfortable.

The second glass of whiskey had caramel notes that fit

nicely on my tongue. It went down smoothly and burned afterward, setting my inside ablaze.

"I like that one," I told him, biting down on my bottom lip. "What kind of…"

I looked to him for help and he smirked.

"Cask or barrel, same difference. It was aged in white oak. Did you taste the caramel?"

I nodded.

"That last bottle doesn't have a label on it," I pointed out.

He glanced at it and nodded.

"Try that for me," he urged, nodding toward the last filled glass.

I picked it up and eyed him over the rim while I filled my mouth with the richest whiskey I think I'd ever tasted. The sweet and woodsy notes tap danced on my taste buds as I swallowed it down. I emptied the rest of the glass to be sure I liked it and nodded.

"Very smooth," I said, thinking of my father. He loved whiskey and cheese. "I think I tasted vanilla."

"Is it something you'd buy?" he asked, observing me closely while he cleaned the glasses and bottles off the bar.

"Absolutely. My father always said the smoother the whiskey, the better the burn."

"He sounds like a smart man."

I shifted a little at that, dropping my gaze.

"He was," I muttered.

I never meant to bring him up but it was hard not to think of the man who'd introduced me to quality liquor when I hit twenty-five. My father had been my favorite drinking buddy and I was grateful to have spent my last moment with him sharing three fingers each of a thousand-dollar bottle of Scottish whisky.

"It's a tester for a Hanson-made whiskey," he revealed,

pulling me out of a funk I hadn't realized I'd fallen into. "It's been aging for three and a half years."

My eyes widened a little when it finally registered what he was telling me.

"That's your blend?" I asked for clarity.

He tossed a sheepish smile my way and nodded.

"Yeah. You're one of five people who've tried it so far."

"I feel honored, first and foremost..." I pressed my hand to my chest and he chuckled. "August, that whiskey is good."

"It has six more months in the aging process," he said, ignoring my compliment.

I hoisted myself a little by digging my elbows into the bar and beckoned him closer. If he was okay with public displays of affection, so was I.

"Your whiskey is amazing," I told him again, smiling as he leaned in. "Can I have a kiss?"

He touched his forehead to mine.

"You may," he murmured, covering my mouth with his.

Bea had been right.

August was exactly the kind of man you had a hard time letting go.

august

"IF I WIN, you have to give me a signed bottle of your whiskey when it's ready for distribution," Couri challenged, bouncing a basketball between her legs in my driveway. "Deal?"

We'd been kicking it for a few weeks now, in and out of each other's personal space more often than two people only *having fun* should be. In that timeframe, she religiously mentioned the batch of whiskey I'd let her try.

"What do I get if I win?" I asked, stealing the ball and pulling up for a layup.

"I'll name a penguin after you," she offered, nudging my body back with her shoulder.

To be so small in stature compared to me, Couri had strength.

I palmed her forehead and held her in place at arm's length.

She shifted and I lowered my eyes to her nipples. They were poking through the thin cotton fabric of her bodysuit and I stared far longer than I should have.

"Can you do that?" I asked, looking into her eyes.

"People always adopt animals at the zoo," she confirmed. "Naming them is one of the perks."

A silly idea filled my head.

"What if I wanted to adopt a lion?"

She stopped struggling against my hand and lifted an eyebrow.

"It's a long story."

A part of me wanted to tell her about my sisters, about the memory of our last visit to the zoo, but I chose to keep it to myself.

"Okay," she said, nodding. "You can adopt lions. Not at our zoo currently, but there are wildlife habitats worldwide doing adoptions."

Couri slapped the ball out of my hand while I focused on adopting a fucking lion for my sister's inner seven-year-old.

She went up for a jump shot and I wrapped an arm around her waist to stop her.

"Cheater!" she exclaimed, kicking one leg out with enough force that it jolted us back a step or two.

I sat her on the hood of my truck and took the ball from her hands.

She leaned back on her elbows and propped one leg up.

"Thank you for helping keep my mind off my mom."

I wasn't certain she'd have told me, but because Kingston and I were real friends, he felt comfortable mentioning Journi struggling with their mother's illness.

She'd decided recently to forgo the rest of her treatments for lung cancer, and while I had tried my best to be there for an upset Kingston, I couldn't stop thinking about Couri.

Her resilience was unmatched.

Not once had she indicated that she was grieving what was to come.

"I'm only doing what we've been doing for weeks."

She shrugged and looked away, her eyes taking in the contents of my garage.

"It's different now," she murmured, turning her attention to me. "I wasn't having that great of a day until you called."

"Well, it's a good thing you were on my mind."

"Good thing..." She smiled and shook her head. "I don't know what to make of you."

"I think you and I both know that isn't true. I am exactly as I present myself to be, and so are you."

Our eyes met and lingered.

She was so damn pretty that I noticed something different whenever we were together.

Maybe it was because she happened to be staring deep into my soul but today her eyes were the star of my new obsession.

"I like the way you handle me," she said, rising into a seated position.

Her gaze flickered up and down my frame as I leaned into the opening of the garage, the basketball we'd been playing with tucked underneath my right foot.

"Yeah, that's how you feel?"

"Mmhm," she hummed, her eyes fixated on mine.

Her lashes were longer and thicker than usual, and she wasn't wearing any makeup, so they had to be extensions. I liked the way they framed the curvature of her eyes, the way she peeked at me from under them when waiting for a response.

"I like handling you, Couri."

Fucking you, too.

She smiled, hopped off the hood, and sashayed her fine ass over to me.

"Then why am I sweating from a basketball game and not from riding your dick?" she asked, kicking the basketball from under my foot.

Couri pressed her body against mine and I secured my arm around her waist. The move felt natural, but I shook that off and stared down at her.

I fucking liked this woman and it was an intense feeling, one that I could see growing with a little time and care, and effort. If she'd let me.

Would she?

I wanted to know the answer, but we were on a time restraint, and I needed my fix.

A few weeks in, Couri was my new favorite drug.

"You can ride my dick another day," I muttered into her ear. "Go bend over the sofa and I'll be right in."

She turned without a fight, slapping and grabbing her ass cheeks for me a few times along the way. Couri was too goddamn sexy for her own good and nasty as hell, just how I liked my women.

I grabbed my shirt and the basketball from the yard before following her inside and dropping it all by the door with my mind solely on getting to her.

"August," Couri whimpered, calling out to me.

I found myself moving toward the living room more urgently as her moans grew louder.

She'd known exactly how to pull me in and the sight before was one to behold.

Couri's legs were propped up on the sofa, wide open, with her fingers buried deep in her pussy.

"Damn," I mumbled, closing a little of the distance between us.

"A-August," she moaned, her head back and eyes shut. "F-Feels so good."

I wanted to engage, but the show Couri was putting on looked too good to stop. She was so fucking wet I could hear her from where I stood.

"Don't make me do this alone, August... Mm, *shit*, stroke yourself for me."

Our gazes collided, and I decided to oblige, dropping my basketball shorts and briefs without question. I used my precum as a lubricant and slowly worked it up and down my shaft.

"You look so... words can't even describe..." I stroked myself faster, wanting so badly to catch up with her. "Fuck, Couri."

"I love the way you-u say my name. Always so p-passionate."

She slapped her clit and I couldn't hold off anymore.

I opened a drawer on my coffee table and grabbed a condom from inside, sheathing myself quickly before allowing my body to propel forward in her direction.

Couri moved her hand to give me access and I thrusted into her; immediately she consumed me in ways I didn't under-stand. This hadn't been what I'd invited her over for but this addiction I'd conjured for her wasn't letting up any time soon.

Fuck.

This was more than two people having fun.

So much more.

PART THREE

where we left off

"ALL OF MY GOOD DAYS, INCLUDE HER."

– August Hanson

ELEVEN

THE PRESENT...

"You up for grabbing drinks after we get off?" Bea asked, poking her head into my office. "It's been a minute since we kicked it."

I felt terrible about ducking and dodging her lately.

My stomach had started to harden suddenly; one minute, I had a flat tummy, and the next, there was a little bulge poking out.

"Can't," I said, glancing over at her. "I'm taking my niece to her first guitar lesson."

She nodded, assessing me closely.

I hadn't lied about taking Kali to her lesson; she preferred me because I could hold a note or two. We wrote a few songs together that she's been practicing for her YouTube debut before summer started.

The girl had every video pre-planned and the first three ready for upload.

She took it seriously and I had no choice but to give the same effort.

"Okay, but you and I need to talk," she said. "We're

supposed to be homegirls, so if something is happening in your life, I want to know about it."

She left before I could respond and I promised myself to make it up to her.

Bea was a good friend but I was having a hard time expressing what was happening to me. I needed time to figure it all out but I knew she'd understand when we finally got to talk.

My phone vibrated on the desk and I knew it was August without looking.

He texted around the same time every day to check in, but this morning I'd gotten to him first with the time, day, and place of my first prenatal care appointment.

We hadn't seen one another physically since our conversation at the coffee shop. I wanted to give him time to focus on being a dad to his now two-week-old baby.

Can you talk?

August only asked to talk when he wanted to FaceTime.

I glanced at the mini-mirror on my desk, checking my bun and edges for flyaways. They were there from being out in the penguin enclosure administering medicine, but I texted back yes anyway.

My phone rang a second later and I answered just as quickly, propping the iPhone against my laptop screen as he came into view.

August had the phone angled low and some distance from his face while lying in bed with no shirt on. I rested my arm at an angle on the desk and placed my head against it.

"Still got that headache?" he asked, raising his phone slightly.

"It's not as bad, but my doctor moved the appointment up to be cautious. I know it's the same day you take Jan—"

"I'll be there, Couri," he cut in, voice firm. "The pediatrician appointment got moved to Saturday and won't interfere with me being there for you on Friday. Let me man up, alright?"

I sat up, then back in my chair, needing to shield my eyes from the camera for a second. He read me too well and responded to my silent cues too often.

"Okay." I nodded. "I'm sorry."

It was easier to focus on him and his needs than mine, but August shut it down at every turn. He knew what I was doing and never verbally called me out.

He was the kind of man who held himself accountable and I adored that trait now more than ever.

"I appreciate you; now, come back to the camera."

I lowered my head on my arm again and a soft hum rolled out of him.

He was pleased with me; it was written all over his face.

"Your day is starting later than usual."

"June stayed over." He sat up. "I fell asleep after a shower and she never woke me."

With his face closer to the lens, I noticed the bags he'd accumulated under his eyes were less puffy. I hated that he wasn't sleeping and wanted to offer my help, but it didn't feel appropriate. Not when we hadn't hashed our own shit out.

There was also the possibility that he wouldn't want me in his daughter's life. And he had every right to make whatever decision he felt was best for his child.

I just...

I wanted to see if we could be a family, if maybe we fit together.

"I think I'm ready to tackle the day now," he added, standing.

My chest ached at the thought of him ending our call.

It was so fucking ridiculous, but I craved his conversation.

"Okay, well, I'll let you go," I said while he moved around his bedroom. "I'm sure you have things to do."

August came to a stop and looked into the camera.

"I'd like to feed you on Friday if you have time after the appointment," he said, his head tipped to the side.

I nodded.

"Yeah, I'll have time."

And if I hadn't, I would've made it happen regardless.

The baby I was carrying was much more important than my fleeting hormones for August. We had to figure that out first and foremost, but I missed him.

I think I needed him.

Everything was different and much more complicated than either of us had wanted. I didn't want to lean on him too hard for emotional support, but inside I was falling apart.

Nothing had color anymore; the more I thought about it, the sadder I became.

It wasn't one thing making me feel this way, it was *everything*.

My mother.

This baby.

Every-fucking-thing.

I made up a reason to get off the phone.

August could decipher my inner thoughts by staring into my damn soul sometimes and I wasn't in the mood to be read like a children's book.

"I have to make a few rounds," I said, grimacing.

My head throbbed and my stomach turned at once, but I managed to keep it together until we ended the call with promises to talk again.

"Oh, fuck," I groaned, leaning over to empty my stomach into the trash.

I hadn't exactly been eating, but it wasn't my fault, and the clear liquid spilling from my lips attested to it. Nothing was working and my head had been hurting for a week straight.

I was tired.

Extremely fucking tired.

How did women do this? Sharing their bodies, energy, and nutrition with the life inside of them.

Little parasite.

There was a living being inside of me stealing everything my body had to offer to grow, sounded like a goddamn parasite to me.

Throwing up had become such a staple in my life since learning about the baby that I carried around a travel-size bag filled with toiletries. I grabbed the small black pouch covered in yellow daffodils and left my office to find an unoccupied single bathroom.

I eventually found one and quickly did my thing, stuffing a piece of gum into my mouth after brushing my teeth and gargling. Then I cleaned up using the mini-pack of Clorox wipes I kept.

The idea of entering a bathroom at work or a public place after someone brushed their teeth and spit in the sink made me sick. I looked up in the mirror and didn't recognize the person staring back at me.

"Time to call it a day," I mumbled, leaving the bathroom sadder than when I went inside.

It took me about thirty minutes to clear my desk of work and change back into my overalls. My stomach rolled as I stepped into the hall but thankfully nothing came of it.

This would be the last trip into the enclosure of my shift and I needed to keep it together.

"Hey, Bea..." I ducked my head into the security room and she spun in her chair to face me. "You know that kale salad you're good at making?"

She nodded, her eyes filled with curiosity.

"Want to come by Sunday with a bowl of that and I'll make some salmon?"

"And we can talk?" she asked.

"Yeah, we can talk."

"I'll bring wine, too. Seems like you need a glass or two."

She had no idea how bad, which made me feel worse.

Here I was, growing a human being and craving wine.

Ugh.

"Sure, yeah," I agreed, deciding to tell her later about the baby. "I'm heading into the enclosure if anyone stops by looking for me."

Bea nodded and turned back to the sea of monitors before her.

On my way into the enclosure, my phone lit up with a text from Kali.

> How are you feeling, Te? Mom is making you some homemade ginger tea for your all-day sickness.

I smiled and sent back a quick reply.

> I feel okay, Buttercup. Tell Mom I said thank you and I'll see the both of you after work.

Kali loved me with all of her heart and I needed that kind of love in my life now more than ever. I could only hope the baby growing inside me would feel the same as his or her big cousin.

Wishful thinking, right?

An hour later, I'd successfully escaped work without

puking my lungs up but the second I got to Journi's my luck ran out.

"Hey, Te—uh oh!"

Kali ducked out of the way as I rushed past her to the guest bathroom.

"I'm sorry you have to experience this," Journi murmured from somewhere behind me.

She gently caressed my back and I found comfort in having my sister near.

"I think I'm okay now," I whispered, leaning back into her legs.

"Have you eaten at all?" Journi asked. "There's nothing in there."

I sighed.

"Can't keep anything down, not even water."

"Get up and brush your teeth," she ordered, looping her arms under mine to assist. "The tea is done brewing, come have a cup before I decide if I should take Kali to her lesson or not."

I clenched the edges of the sink and shook my head.

"I can still take her." I grabbed my toothbrush and cut the water on. "I'm sure the tea will work."

Journi watched me brush my teeth through the mirror, her gaze so intense I was forced to break eye contact before she did.

"It'll get easier," she said softly before leaving the bathroom.

Would it though?

I wasn't so sure.

"You should rest, TeTe," Kali said from the doorway. "Mom can take me and we can try again next week."

"Buttercup..." I turned to face her after rinsing my mouth. "I promised to take you."

She nodded. "Yeah and you never break promises but this

isn't you breaking a promise," she said, sounding way too old for her age. "I can see you don't feel good and I don't like it."

Her big eyes filled with tears and I held my arms open for her.

"It's just morning sickness." I tugged her close to my chest. "I'll be over it in no time."

God, please let that be true.

TWELVE

"WHAT TO DO NOW?" I mumbled, rubbing my eyes.

January wasn't just crying anymore, she was having a full-on meltdown and I had no clue what to do. I stood in her bedroom doorway and did nothing for a short moment.

The strained cries coming from her were unbearable, too much for my heart to take.

She was clean and fed. I'd walked around the house with her in my arms since June left.

I hated to admit it, but I had jumped at the chance of peace and quiet, and now that June was gone, it was only January and me.

She wasn't happy with that.

It hurt my heart but I was almost certain my daughter didn't like me.

"Does something hurt?" I asked, inching over to the crib.

I'd only left her for a few minutes to use the bathroom, and now that she was in shambles because of it, a slither of guilt filled me.

I leaned in to find her little round face balled up and streaked with tears.

"You don't like me, I get it," I said softly, reaching in to pick her up. "We're strangers."

The last two weeks had been hard.

I maneuvered myself into the reclining chair my mother had delivered the day after January came home. The remote it came with sat beside me on the arm of the chair and I held down the recline button with my elbow until it was at the angle I wanted.

Thankfully, babygirl had begun to calm down now that she was against my bare chest. After I started the built-in massage function and the chair vibrated—shaking my body and, by default, January's—she went completely silent.

"I'm here," I murmured, stroking her back. "I'm sorry for leaving you."

Both times.

She deserved more than me, more than a single dad.

Her mother was gone; she had to feel that, right?

January hadn't even known my voice until two weeks ago.

I missed bonding with her while she was in the womb. It wasn't either of our fault, but we were suffering the consequences.

My insecurities about becoming a father this way weighed so heavy on me that I couldn't comprehend what was what. Nothing I did felt like enough; it may not ever be.

January fussed a little here and there, but eventually, the vibrations from the chair put her to sleep. I closed my eyes, wanting a few moments of sleep myself.

I'd only been settled in for about fifteen minutes when the handheld monitor on the dresser across from where I sat dinged. The screen switched to the camera outside my front door and Kingston looked into the lens.

He and his brother Primo had helped get it up there and wired the rest of the house.

Earlier in the week, I'd cut the line to the doorbell, anything to keep January from fussing.

My security system had motion detection, which would double as my doorbell for now. All alerts came to my phone and the security monitor I paid extra for.

I rose slowly and approached the crib with a changing table attached. I debated taking her with me for a second but decided to take my chances with her bed. Once she was down and safely on her back, I waited a short time to be sure she wouldn't wake up then went to let Kingston in.

"Wassup," I greeted, pulling the door open and widening it enough for him to walk through.

"Needed to come by and rap with you for a minute," he said as we migrated into the kitchen he and his team remodeled.

I eyed him for a second and opened the fridge.

"Water?"

I pulled an extra bottle out before he could respond, already knowing the answer.

Kingston was a clean eater and drinker, had been since I'd known him. He was the only kid in our neighborhood whose mother paid for him to have a nutritionist. Back then, he'd had his heart set on an athletic scholarship to pay for college and his mother did everything she could to make that happen.

I slid him the bottled water and he uncapped it, his eyes on me as he drank.

"Alright, what's up?" I asked, feeling a little tension coming from him.

He set the bottle down and leaned into the counter.

"Couri," he said.

Right.

She was another part of my life that needed to be reworked.

117

I hadn't forgotten that Kingston was her brother-in-law or that we were friends.

Truthfully, it didn't matter one way or another.

I was a grown-ass man who didn't ask other grown-ass men for their permission on my life choices. Furthermore, Couri was a grown woman who made her own decisions and I happened to be one she made over and over again for eight months straight. We were locked in for life because of that; it didn't matter what Kingston or anyone else felt about it.

"You feeling a way about it?"

He scoffed a little.

"I'm not her man or her father," he said, crossing his arms. "But she is family and she's lost a lot recently."

I nodded, agreeing with him on that front.

"Journi is quieter," he added, gaze drifting off briefly. "Couri's been quiet."

That got my attention.

"Quiet how?" I asked.

He gave me a once over as if contemplating if he should tell me.

It bothered me, but I kept that to myself, needing to know how Couri was doing more than why it seemed my childhood friend didn't trust me.

She took priority over all of it, especially when I noticed that spark in her eyes I'd grown used to wasn't there anymore.

"Sad," he finally told me. "She's pregnant and grieving."

The look in his eyes said enough.

I had to step up and ensure she was taking care of herself.

More guilt ate at my insides.

How the fuck was I supposed to do this?

"You good?" Kingston asked, drawing my attention to him.

After checking the time, I shrugged and started making a bottle for January.

"Got a lot going on, but I'm good."

Baby girl would start fussing soon and I wanted to avoid another meltdown. If she got to that point, she refused to eat until I could calm her down, which was more frustrating than anything.

She was on three ounces of milk every two and a half hours on the dot. It was the only real routine we had so far besides her needing to be changed twenty minutes after every bottle and sporadically throughout our day.

I filled the baby Keurig—worth every penny thus far—with distilled water and set a six-ounce bottle inside. Once it was finished, I would split them into two and refrigerate one for the next feeding.

"You got a baby around here somewhere?" Kingston asked.

I frowned and turned in his direction.

"Is that a joke?"

He didn't respond and I realized I hadn't told him directly, only Couri.

Though I hadn't asked her to keep it to herself, I liked that my business hadn't drifted from ear to ear on her part.

"Damn." I shook my head and tipped it toward the stair-well. "Let me show you."

Kingston followed me up—albeit wary—into January's bedroom.

When I leaned into her crib, her eyes were wide open.

"Caught you," I murmured, lifting her into my arms with my hand at the back of her neck for support.

I turned to Kingston, who held a perplexed expression on his face.

"Became a father and then a single one in a matter of two weeks."

He looked from me to her and asked, "Shondra?"

"Yeah... Shondra."

"When you said you had a lot going on, I didn't think you meant this."

January started to squirm and whine and I nodded for Kingston to follow me.

We returned to the kitchen, and with babygirl in one arm, I split the bottle, put one up, then adjusted her so she could eat.

"Seems like you got it under control."

I chuckled because it felt the complete opposite.

"I wish," I mumbled, staring down at the little girl who'd changed my life in the blink of an eye. "She's good for a while and then—"

"She's screaming and inconsolable?" he finished for me, speaking the exact words on the tip of my tongue.

I glanced at him, feeling like someone had gotten it for once.

My parents said my sisters and I were quiet babies who barely cried. There was a point where they both thought something might be wrong with us because of it.

"When Journi brought Kali home, we walked the house in shifts every night for the first three weeks."

"Same with her..." I moved January from one arm to the other and stretched the one she'd been in to relieve the strain. "It's around the same time every night."

"Has she seen a pediatrician yet?"

I shook my head.

"First appointment is this Saturday. Hopefully I can be schooled on what I need to be doing differently."

My cousin squeezed us in on the only half-day her office had a week. It was allergy season, and she was busy, but we were family and I was concerned about January, which meant she was concerned.

It was either squeezing me in or making a house visit and Leslie hated those.

"You said after three weeks she stopped," I pointed out, thinking about something I'd read online. "So she wasn't a colicky baby?"

It felt weird having this conversation with him, but I brushed it off.

"She was and when we learned what it meant, Couri had just finished college and moved in with us."

I stared at him, waiting for some kind of explanation.

"Couri will never admit this but she's some kind of baby whisperer. Kali was a fussy mess one day, Couri moved in the next, and then she wasn't."

Mmph.

"A bit of advice." He pushed off the counter. "Sometimes a colicky baby is that way because they feel the parent's stress. If it happens at the same time every night, maybe think about what's on your mind and then work the problem."

Work the problem.

It was a phrase our youth football coach used back in the day. No matter what, you can always work the problem until there wasn't one anymore. I still believed it with all my heart but I was man enough to admit I had no clue where to start.

"I gotta bounce but August?"

I glanced his way.

"Congrats. She's beautiful," he said, nodding. "I haven't had to take care of an infant in a long time but if you need anything, my people and I got you. Kali loves babies, so if you want to get an eleven-year-old off me and her mother's back about having one, I'll appreciate it."

"No more for you?" I asked, curious.

He chuckled and shook his head.

"Nah. Journi and I aren't on that type of time right now. We like having a kid that doesn't need her diaper changed or to be bottle fed..." His gaze dropped to January and he pointed. "No offense."

I nodded.

"None taken."

"I mean it," he called from the opened front door. "Don't hesitate to ask for help, August."

I didn't respond because lying wasn't my thing and asking for help was just as hard. I could admit that Kingston got the wheels inside my head turning.

"Do you not like me or is it how I feel inside that has you in distress?" I questioned, taking the bottle from her mouth. "I hope it isn't the latter. I'd rather you hate me than feel this way."

I felt a little bit of everything in waves throughout the day, mainly about Couri and a little anxiety about fucking up with her and my daughter. And from my conversation with Kingston, she needed me more than she wanted to admit.

I looked down at a half-sleep January and sighed.

Maybe I needed Couri too.

THIRTEEN

couri

FRIDAY CAME QUICKER than I'd expected.

"Are you sure you don't want me to meet you there?" Journi asked, her concern evident.

I sat back in my seat, my eyes trained in the only direction cars could get in and out of this parking lot. He said he'd be here and I couldn't bring myself to go in without him.

"I'm sure," I told her truthfully.

I didn't need or want to be fussed over by my sister; if I let her come, that was precisely what I'd get.

"It's your first appointment," she muttered. "August will be there, right?"

I swiped her face away from my screen and glanced at the texts coming through from August.

> Down the road.

> Are you inside?

He was typing something else and I quickly responded to stop him.

> Please, don't text and drive. I'm waiting in the parking lot for you.

"Couri, are you listening?" Journi questioned, her voice raised an octave.

I swiped the screen back to our FaceTime call and she wasn't even there. Instead, she had her back to me as she reached for files behind her desk.

"I have to go," I said, spotting my baby daddy pulling into the parking lot. "August just got here. I'll call you back when it's over."

"Fine but send texts, too."

"I'll send one text. Later, sis."

I watched August back his truck into the spot next to mine, my heart racing dramatically at his presence.

We opened our doors at the same time.

"Hi," I greeted softly, poking my head out and turning my body.

August looked me over as I got out, his eyes dropping and rising slowly.

"Come here," he beckoned but stepped toward me instead.

I closed the space between us and he wrapped me in a hug that I needed more than he'd ever know.

"How you feeling, Angel face?"

He tipped my head back with two fingers and searched my eyes.

"Angel face?"

The man had never called me anything but Couri and now we were on a nickname basis.

I hated how much I loved it.

"Face of an angel," he elaborated. "Been calling you that in my head since I met you."

124

"Oh," I muttered, dropping my gaze. "I'm okay," I added. "My headache is nonexistent today."

He nodded slowly and opened his mouth to speak, but then a loud, shrill cry came from inside his truck and he cursed.

August backed me up and opened the back door, revealing a black and purple car seat.

I didn't think he'd bring her though I'd wanted him to.

"You brought her," I whispered, more to myself than him but he glanced at me as he removed the carrier from its base.

"You cool with that?" he asked. "I can—"

"No!" I shouted louder than I'd meant. "I'm glad you did. I thought—" I shook my head. "Wc should get inside."

He pulled the seat out and I waited for him to move before grabbing my purse, keys from the ignition, and phone.

I checked the time as we walked toward the entrance.

"We made good time," I said, slipping past him as he held the door open.

I went straight to the nurse's window and checked in.

August and I were the only ones in the waiting area and I was grateful for that.

"Can I meet her?" I asked, squatting in front of them.

He hadn't removed the blanket and reached down to peel it back for me.

I spotted her little round face and chubby cheeks first. Her eyes were open; of course, those large orbs were the perfect shade of brown, just like her father's. It had to be a Hanson staple and I wondered if our child would inherit them or my charcoal irises.

January stared at me, one balled fist near her mouth and the other at the side of her body. She was dressed in a light pink long-sleeved shirt and cute little overalls that reminded me of the few pairs I owned for work.

I sighed, a smile on my face.

"August, she's beautiful," I said, glancing at him out of the corner of my eye.

His gaze moved between January and me. I couldn't pinpoint where his mind was, but it was far away.

"Hey..." I used his knee to help myself up and sat in the chair beside him. "How are you feeling?"

He slowly moved his attention to where I'd sat.

"Overwhelmed," he admitted. "Got no idea what the fuck I'm doing, Couri."

I smiled a little, despite his statement.

His honesty made me feel special, like he trusted me with parts of himself I hadn't uncovered yet. I wanted him to feel as safe as he made me, because for this to work we both needed that sense of security.

"I feel that maybe you're being hard on yourself."

He didn't respond to that but said, "Kingston paid me a visit this week."

"Playing big brother?" I asked, rolling my eyes.

He nodded, his lips curled at the corners.

"I'm not mad at it. I like you being protected by people who have your back no matter what."

"I like you having that, too."

I laid my head on his shoulder and August draped an arm around me, then brought his hand up to cup my chin. He tipped my head back and I stared up at him.

This man always regarded me with a gentleness that fed my soft soul. I only ever wanted a man to look at me like he did. I hadn't known it was possible that another person could give me this kind of intimacy.

"You say so much with your eyes," I whispered.

They were silent words that my heart understood, even if occasionally I didn't.

"Sometimes I have a lot on my heart," he said, his voice just above a murmur. "Even when I don't realize it."

"And—"

January released a tiny wail that sent August into a slight frenzy. He sat up and untangled us, focusing on the precious cargo he'd come with.

I watched him unbuckle and scoop her from the car seat. She squirmed and kicked her feet out in protest. Of what? I wasn't sure, but from my experience with Kali, I knew what was coming next.

I felt August's frustration and concern as her cries grew louder and more frantic.

"Can I?" I asked, sliding to the edge of my seat.

He glanced over and the disappointment staring back at me broke my heart.

Did he think he was doing it wrong? I wondered.

God, I hoped that wasn't it.

"Only if you're comfortable with..."

I cradled my arms so he could easily place her into them and he turned to do it.

"It's okay, Snowflake," I sang, rocking her against me while gently massaging her temples.

It was an old trick my mother tried teaching Journi, who could never quite get the temple rub down. For me, it came with ease and because I loved my sister, I used the method to calm Kali who would spend night after night crying her little heart out.

Slowly but surely, January calmed, her little watery eyes opened, and she stared up at me.

"You made that look easy," August said. "Kingston said you were a baby whisperer."

I scoffed, hating they had put that on me.

"I'm no such thing..." I lifted my gaze and met his. "Babies and I just get one another."

"You called her Snowflake," he pointed out, changing the subject.

"Felt right for a girl named after one of the snowiest months in Michigan."

"Snowflake it is," he agreed, lips twitching.

A nurse appeared from behind a door a few seconds after he'd said it, calling my name as if I wasn't the only person waiting to be seen. If my choice of doctor wasn't non-negotiable, the long waits wouldn't fly.

"I got her," I told August when he tried reaching for January.

She felt right in my arms and I didn't want to lose that feeling yet.

I stood and followed the nurse through the door, feeling August as he trailed closely behind. Was this what having a family of my own would feel like?

Focus, girl.

"She's adorable," my usual nurse, Lina, complimented as she turned the corner and relieved her coworker. "Getting some practice in, huh?"

"Mmhm," I hummed, finally handing her over so I could be weighed. "Just so happens her father popped this one inside of me."

Lina laughed, used to my blunt nature already.

"Alright." She pulled my chart out and scribbled on it. "Is it okay to speak candidly?"

I nodded and avoided eye contact with August.

"You lost two pounds," she said. "It happens, especially if you're experiencing morning sickness, so don't be alarmed."

"I'm suffering from it."

She tsked.

"I'll let the doctor know."

I didn't want August to worry, but I couldn't lie about either. Not here, of all places.

Lina led us to exam room three and after I changed into a gown, she took my blood pressure and temperature, noting the numbers on my chart. She left soon after with a promise that the doctor would be in soon.

"Stop staring at me like that," I grumbled, looking everywhere but at the man to my left. "I'm fine."

"You aren't though."

His tone held no room for argument, but I was sure mine wouldn't either when I responded. If we were calling one another out, then so be it.

"Well..." I shrugged and glanced at him. "Neither are you."

He looked down at January, who was spread out against his chest, sound asleep, his hand cupping her overall-covered butt.

"Touché," he agreed, unsurprisingly.

Lina returned with a tray that had tubes and a syringe on it.

I shook my head and frowned.

"I know you hate needles but Dr. Bowman requested a blood withdrawal."

"But she did that when I came to confirm that I was pregnant."

Lina smiled, her eyes gentle as she said, "That is correct but we need to recheck your iron levels. It's important we regulate them during the gestation period."

I sighed and curled my arm in.

"Are you anemic?" August asked out of nowhere.

"Yes and no," I informed him, focusing on the needle in Lina's hand. "Not enough that I need to be prescribed an iron supplement."

It had never been that big of a deal to me but now I was a

little worried and made a mental note to research anemia in pregnant women.

Lina cleared her throat and raised an eyebrow.

"Fine..." I unbent my arm and gave it to her. "But be gentle. I'm more sensitive than usual."

I squeezed my eyes closed and squeaked when August unexpectedly took my hand while Lina poked me.

"Learning a lot about you in this room right now," he said, pressing his thumb into my wrist and stroking.

The anxiety coursing through me at the thought of my blood being pumped into little test tubes evaporated as I opened my eyes and stared into his.

You're so beautiful, August Hanson.

"All done," Lina announced as she cleaned and covered the prick, giving me a reason to break out of the trance August had quickly put me into. "Dr. Bowman will be in soon."

She took her leave and I sighed in relief.

"I really hate needles."

He flipped my hand and slipped his fingers through mine.

"Your pulse was erratic."

"Thank you for being here."

August's thick brow rose and I rolled my eyes.

"I know this is where you're supposed to be," I added. "But I'm allowed to be thankful, right?"

Dr. Bowman entered, cutting our conversation short at the perfect time; August had been gearing up to ask me questions galore.

"Ms. Mitchell," the doc greeted her eyes on August and the baby. "You must be Dad."

I sighed.

"Auntie..."

She cut her cat-like eyes my way and squinted.

My aunt was a young fifty-two with fierce eyes, a sleek bob

she finally decided to let gray, and a stacked body—wide hips, thick thighs, homegrown booty, and a little belly she said my uncle loved. *Yuck.*

She and my dad looked a lot alike.

"I know you want to be professional, but please, stop calling me Ms. Mitchell."

Renee Bowman was one of my father's eight siblings but the only one he liked. She held no qualms about not caring for the *other* Mitchells, as she and my dad called them growing up.

The woman was no joke and I loved her dearly.

"August, this is my Aunt Renee…"

I waved between them. "Auntie, this is August, and yes, he's the dad."

She gave a curt nod and I applauded her for not blatantly asking about January.

"How are you feeling?" she asked while washing and gloving her hands. "Headaches still bothering you?"

"I feel tired," I admitted, closing my eyes while she prodded at the glands in my neck. "My headache went away sometime last night but I don't know if it's gone forever. And I can't keep any food down."

I heard August shift in his chair after I said it.

"Nurse Lina mentioned the morning sickness."

I opened my eyes and groaned.

"All-day sickness sometimes. When does it end?"

She smiled and brushed my cheek like when I was a kid.

It had always soothed me on the spot and even at my big age of thirty, I melted.

"For most women, it ends after the first trimester," she told me. "But, sometimes, it can last longer."

"What can she do?" August asked, drawing her attention to him.

"Eat light but as frequently as needed. Less on the grease intake. Go for more protein-packed snacks and meals. Sometimes more bland foods help." She cut her eyes at me. "You need rest, Couri."

"I'm sleeping," I defended and huffed, embarrassed by her chastising tone in front of August. "I have plenty of tea. That helps with the queasiness."

"My recipe?"

I nodded.

It didn't matter that she'd learned it from her mother and who learned it from hers and so forth. Whoever possessed the ingredients called it theirs, even Journi.

"Your other niece and her mini-me hooked me up with a big supply this week."

"Good." She nodded, pulled her gloves off, and tossed them in the trash for a new pair. "Ready for the ultrasound?"

I nodded and laid back, rolling my head to the side to see August and a now wide-awake January. Her eyes were on me like her father's, evaluating me like only a baby could.

"Ready?" I asked.

He rose a little and slid his chair closer.

I lifted my feet into the stirrups and pulled my gown up a little, while watching my aunt cover the vaginal transducer with something condom-like. She slowly inserted it, on my cue, and a loud whooshing sound filled the exam room.

"Oh wow," I whispered, my heart racing with joy.

Mommy hears you, baby.

"That would be the heartbeat," Aunt Renee said. "It's strong."

She clicked around on the monitor then turned it.

"At ten and a half weeks, your baby is the size of a kumquat—"

I giggled and could hear August's soft chuckle follow.

"Please don't say that again."

"Their eyes are fully formed, teeth are hardening," she went on, ignoring our snickers. "Here, you can make out the outline of the ears forming."

The grainy black and white image was kind of freaky. Yet, somehow beautiful, too.

"Would you like me to print off a few ultrasound pictures?" she asked.

August pulled his phone out and started to record.

"Don't know about you but I want to hear that heartbeat after we leave," he said, cutting his eyes at me. "I'll send it to you."

I looked away and right into my aunt's questioning gaze.

"We'll take them printed," I told her.

She angled her head—too curious for her own good—then looked back at the monitor.

"Everything looks good," she said, wiping down the transducer and hanging it from the ultrasound machine. "If there's anything abnormal with your bloodwork, you'll hear from me personally next week."

"And if everything is good?" August asked.

I loved him opening his mouth and asking questions if he had them, made my pussy wet.

"Then I'll see the both of you at the next prenatal appointment," Aunt Renee stated. "The desk nurse will schedule that."

The machine printed the ultrasound pictures and she handed them to August before helping me clean up.

I tugged on my aunt's white coat until she leaned in close enough for me to whisper in her ear.

"It's not what you think. He's one of the good ones."

She pulled back and stared into my eyes like my dad did when he was still alive.

"I'll take your word for it."

"My word is bond."

"This I know..." She nodded with a smile. "Don't forget to stop by the nurse's station to schedule your next appointment before leaving."

She left the room and I got dressed while watching August as he secured January in her car seat. He stood after tugging on the straps to make sure they were snug against her and placed the seat in the chair.

"Are you hungry?" he asked, picking up my jean jacket and opening it for me.

I turned and pushed my arms through.

As I twisted to face him, August wrapped his arms around me from behind and held me in place against him.

"I missed you," he murmured, placing one hand against the tiny bulge of my stomach and rubbing it. "I want to be a part of this and all it entails—good and bad—with you."

He turned me and lifted my head with two fingers.

I believed him because his actions spoke to that but it felt good to hear.

"I can try and eat."

He caressed my cheek for a few seconds then released me.

"It's still early enough to sit down at a brunch spot. Maybe you'll find something you can keep down."

He picked up the carrier and reached for the door handle.

"August?"

He glanced over his shoulder.

"Yeah?"

Two weeks and five days had felt like a lifetime. The texts and phone calls, where he could fit them in, didn't ease the ache I had to see him.

"I missed you too."

So goddamn bad.

FOURTEEN

august

"MAYBE POTATOES?" Couri muttered to herself from across the table. "Or scrambled eggs."

I studied her closely, wondering if she'd spend the rest of the day with me if I asked.

"How about on two different plates?" I suggested. "You might like one more than the other, but if they're touching, you might not want either."

Couri looked up from the menu and nodded.

"Toast too."

"Whatever you want," I agreed, nodding to the server waiting for her order.

Couri lifted the menu and hid her face behind it.

I glanced at January who was sucking down a bottle, her eyes shut tight and fingers curled around my right index. There was a tiny sliver of hope that maybe I was doing this right whenever she held onto me that way.

I pushed the menu from Couri's face and said, "Never took you as the shy type, Angel face. Why now?"

"Because now this is more serious than it started out," she confessed softly. "You got me pregnant."

135

"To be fair..." My lips curved on one side without my permission. "We used protection each time."

Couri sighed.

"Don't remind me," she groused. "I'm upset we've been careful when I could've had you..." She looked away with a tiny smile playing on her lips. "You know... bare. Clearly, this was our destiny."

I lifted an eyebrow.

"There is time to rectify that if you want."

"I do." She licked her lips and pulled her hands from the table. "I want that."

"That means allowing me to be around you even when there isn't a doctor's appointment. Going from seeing you every other day to whatever this was supposed to be is a crime."

Couri snorted then covered her mouth and nose.

"You're scared of needles, you snort, and suddenly you're shy. What else don't I know about you?"

"I have an oversized elephant portrait that I hide when you're at my place."

I slanted my head to the left and regarded her.

"You don't have a coffee machine," she blurted out of nowhere. "But you drink it with me."

"Can't let you drink it alone." I shrugged, deciding to play along. "I wanted to share a space with you and experience it how you did. That meant drinking coffee at an obscene time in the morning, so I did it."

"Did you figure out why I love it so much?"

"You thrive in peace and quiet. The silence is most heavy at four in the morning in any time zone."

Couri's chest heaved as she sighed.

She'd been much easier to learn because I liked the quiet as much as she did.

At four in the morning, Couri was her most transparent. She wore her emotions on her sleeve, making them easily exposed.

I never took what I learned as a "gotcha" moment, only an opportunity to figure one thing out. Was she worth a lifetime of silent mornings with coffee?

I hadn't figured it out yet, but something about how life tangled us tighter together without our permission felt like the answer I'd been searching for.

"Why'd you believe me?"

"Believe yo—how do you mean?"

She sat back and I did the same, wanting to give her the space it seemed she needed.

"You know we've always used protection, so why did you believe this baby was yours without question?"

"I believed it because *you* told me."

"You have that much faith in my character?"

"I know you, Couri Mitchell. Maybe not everything, but I know who you are at the core; there was no conversation or big revelations needed for me to figure you out."

She leaned forward and I followed her lead, bringing myself back to the table.

"Can I ask you something?"

She nodded. "Anything."

"How are you really feeling? That includes the things you're hiding in an attempt to protect me."

I took a moment to remove the mostly emptied bottle from January and saddle her up against the right side of my chest.

"Every day is different," Couri finally answered after I had babygirl settled. "I don't know how to describe it."

"I think I understand, not your grief per se, but not being about to describe how I feel on a daily."

"Are you sharing this with me to get me to talk?"

"Nah." I shook my head. "You shared what you felt you could and I'm doing the same."

January burped and Couri giggled.

"That was a big one," she said, smiling. "You might think you aren't doing a good job, but August, fatherhood looks good on you."

"I need more time to see what you do," I admitted, grateful for the server returning with our food.

We were at my sisters' favorite brunch spot in Sterling Heights, *First Watch*.

I'd ordered a frittata rustica—an Italian-style omelet with kale, mushrooms, onions, and tomatoes topped with mozzarella and parmesan cheese.

Couri gagged a little and my gaze shot to her.

"No to the eggs," she groaned, sucking on a lemon to lose the taste of it. "Okay." She nodded slowly. "Okay, I think that worked."

I looked at my plate and decided to get it boxed.

"What about the potatoes?" I asked, pushing my food away.

"Better. I think it's the salt," she replied, forking another bite. "You were right about separate plates."

She pointed to my plate with her fork while chewing slowly.

"I smell the Parmesan in that. Aren't you going to eat?"

"Don't want to move her."

"You don't want to enjoy it in front of me, you mean."

"That, too," I confirmed. "Shit feels wrong."

Couri slid closer to the wall and pointed to the empty space she created on her side of the booth.

"Come sit next to me," she beckoned, sliding my plate toward her with the fork in her hand.

I obliged, sliding out my side and into hers with January still in my arms.

"Do you want to know what I like about you, August?" she asked, cutting into the frittata and bringing a hefty portion to my lips. "Eat, please. I promise I'll finish my potatoes."

I opened for her and she smiled.

"I like that you're always a gentleman," she continued, watching me chew. "Is it good?"

"Might like the part where you're feeding more, but it's good."

"I appreciate the smell."

"I appreciate it not making you sick."

"See..." She brought the fork to my mouth again. "If I'd said the smell was bothering me, it wouldn't be on the table anymore. Even though *you* like it."

She slid closer and angled her body to face me.

"I want you to be comfortable," I told her, trying to understand where she was going with this.

"That is something I've figured out already but here's the thing." She tugged on my chin a little, forcing me to tip my head down at her. "I want you to be comfortable, too."

Ah.

"I want you to eat what you like even if I can't hold down my food."

"Yeah?"

She nodded.

"Do I get to say what else I want?" I asked.

"And like, I have to actually follow through?"

I chuckled as she beamed up at me, that spark she'd been missing returning to her dark hue.

"Yeah, I need you to follow through for me."

"I can do that."

"I haven't told you what it is."

"But, I know whatever *it is*, I'll try my best to give it to you."

"Let it be," I said. "Don't hide the bad from me; just let it be. I want you to exist openly, without fear of putting too much on my shoulders."

She looked away, but I was grateful she respected me enough to turn back and look me in the eyes.

"August, it's not that I fear putting too much on your shoulders. I admittedly don't want you stressed but I just... I'm afraid that the more time I spend with you, letting you take care of me while you dote on that beautiful baby, might fill my head with unrealistic ideas."

"It can only be unrealistic if we both agree on that."

I knew what she was trying to convey, but it wouldn't change my plans.

Taking care of Couri while she baked our kid was the right thing to do and something I *wanted* to do.

"I don't want you feeling stuck with me because of this baby."

"And if I wanted to be stuck with you before all this?" I asked, wrapping my fingers around her hand. "Don't answer that. Let me show you, alright?"

She made a noise that sounded like a mix of a huff and laughter.

"The last time you said that..." She leaned in closer, pulling my face down. "We ended up in bed more times than I planned."

"I'm failing to understand the problem."

She gently kissed my lips in response.

"August Hanson, I don't know what to do with you."

I took that as my chance.

"Start with spending the rest of the day with me." I tipped my head at January. "With us."

I knew I wanted her, that she wanted me, but trying to

grasp onto that when life made part of that decision for you wasn't easy.

All I had were my thoughts from before now, wanting to know and be with her while contemplating how to ask for more. Or that nauseating feeling when I realized I had to pull back and the relief after she told me she was pregnant.

"I can do that," Couri said, resting her head on my arm like at the doctor's office. "But I have to go home to grab something then I'll come to you."

"Eat a little more of the potatoes for me first."

She sighed and grumbled something but picked up her fork to eat as requested.

"Thank you."

I leaned over and kissed her temple before sliding out of the booth. Her eyes shot dead in my direction, wide with curiosity and something else I couldn't quite place.

"Gotta change the kid; I'll be back."

She nodded but the expression in her eyes gave me pause.

"Do you promise?" she asked softly when I didn't move to leave.

"Will I be back?" I asked, wanting to be sure that was what she meant.

She looked away and while I didn't know what was happening in her head, leaving and never returning wasn't happening.

"I'll be back to walk you to your car like always."

Couri started to eat again and waved me off.

Definitely need to get to the bottom of that, I thought.

"ARE YOU MOVING IN?" August asked, taking recyclable bags from my hands as he ushered me inside.

My gaze lingered on the amount of shit I'd accumulated for him and January since he'd told me about her. I'd possibly gone a little overboard, but I really loved babies and wanted to do this for August.

"Just a few things for the baby," I said, bypassing him. "Where is she?"

I heard the bags dropping behind me and turned.

"What are you—*mm*."

August kissed and tugged me against him, stealing words from my mouth. Following his lead was as natural as breathing, so I lifted myself up and deepened the kiss, needing more from him.

"I guess my daughter is the star of our connection now," he muttered into my mouth.

I tried to kiss him again and he gently pushed me away, picking up the bags instead.

"That isn't fair," I complained, poking my bottom lip out.

He maneuvered past me with a smirk on his face.

"Greet me like I mean something to you next time," he said.

I chewed on my lip and turned to face where he stood in his living room. There were already gift bags and unopened toys piled up near the edge of his sectional.

"She's upstairs sleeping," he went on, answering my question as he sat on the sofa. "I want you to come here, though."

Eager to be near him again, I went.

"Is that a motorized car?"

He nodded without looking and pulled me down. I positioned my ass in his lap and twisted my legs around to rest on the couch. He engulfed me in his arms as I wrapped mine around his neck and settled my head on his shoulder.

"Don't know what the fuck she's gonna do with it but it's appreciated, nonetheless."

"Well, I don't want the things I purchased left in the *do not want* pile."

He chuckled into my skin and tightened his hold on me.

"Anything you bring here, including yourself, is always in the *want* pile. I'll unpack them before you leave," he said, angling his head to look at me. "It means a lot that you thought enough of her to do it."

"I thought of you, too," I confessed, feeling the weight of his words. "You're never too far from my mind these days."

"Me or my situation?"

I caressed the side of his face while he gazed at me.

God, I love the way this man looks me in my eyes.

"Always you first."

He kissed me like I knew he would.

If August and I had anything I was certain about, it was our innate connection. He was the bee to my honey, buzzing around my mind and body like never before.

"August, where are—*oh!*"

I jerked away from him and almost fell but August tugged me back by the collar of my jacket.

June looked between the two of us and shrugged.

"Glad you didn't dump her," she said, turning to enter the kitchen with a large box in her hands. "Thought I'd have to knock some sense into you."

I tried to move so he could get up, but August sagged deeper into the sofa and held on to me, not a care in the world.

"I told you to stop bringing me shit from those people," August replied, ignoring what she'd said.

"Those people are your family, August."

"Barely," he mumbled.

I stifled the laughter bubbling inside when June turned with her eyes narrowed.

The open floor plan was currently working in her favor.

"I know you said something smart," she surmised, sounding like the oldest of the two.

It made me wonder where he fell within their ranks.

"Everyone says you're being mean and leaving them outside but taking their gifts."

I snorted.

It kinda sounded like something he'd do.

"He put them in a 'do not want' pile, too," I chimed in, earning a sideways glance from August. "Even threw mine over there."

"I told you I would unpack the—" He squinted. "You're fucking with me."

June tsked, a smirk on her face.

"Serves you right. Our family is only being supportive."

He shrugged.

"No, they're being nosy and my daughter isn't a fucking clown show for them to stare at."

Oh, I see.

Every family had a few gossipers in the mix. The aunties or cousins that had nothing better to do but be in your business instead of worrying about their own.

My family had a slew of those.

"Okay," June conceded. "I know it's true for some of the Hanson crew but what about Lola?"

With the straightest face, August said, "She brought a motorized car for my three-week-old child, who at the time had only been home for a week."

June threw her hands into the air and spun her body away from us to rifle through the cabinets.

"Lola really messed up my whole point with that. The fuck was she even thinking?"

"Why are you here, June?"

"Making you dinner..." She nodded and pulled a wok from under the counter. "Your other sisters are headed this way too."

She went on about her business and August turned his attention to me.

"I can go and—"

"I'd rather you stay," he cut in, pushing his fingers through the curls at the nape of my neck. "I want you here but only if you want to be."

There was some doubt in his voice like maybe he thought I *didn't* want to be here.

Goodness.

These babies had really made us insecure in such a short time.

I felt so not like myself and it was the worst feeling, thinking you weren't enough anymore because life decided to blow in and mix up your world.

"Couri, do you eat meat?" June asked, facing the stove. "I'm

145

making stir-fry but I can do a separate helping for you with just the veggies."

So they were all considerate.

It wasn't just an August thing, but a Hanson one.

August watched me, waiting for my answer.

"I eat meat," I told her, my stomach flipping in disgust at the thought of doing it.

"You don't have to," August said, low enough for only me to hear. "Not if it'll make you sick. I'll make you a baked potato."

"Can you turn it into home fries?"

Now that I knew potatoes were my friend, I wouldn't sway from them.

"I can do whatever you need, Angel face."

I ducked my head and he chuckled.

"Kinda like this shy version of you. It's doing wonders for my ego, baby."

My heart staggered a little at his use of *that* term of endearment, but I didn't have time to think on it for too long because January's soft whines filtered through the monitor on the coffee table and August tapped my thigh for me to rise.

"You can come talk to me," June offered as August disappeared up the stairwell. "I don't bite."

"Are you the oldest?" I asked, taking her up on the offer.

I entered the kitchen and sat on a barstool at the island.

"Do I give off that vibe?"

"Very much so."

Her pretty browns sparkled as she tossed her head back in laughter.

"Loving the honesty," she mused. "I am the oldest. Our names give away the order of birth."

I tapped my forehead.

"It didn't even register until you said it."

"It's so obvious that no one ever notices."

After washing them, June started to slice red, orange, and yellow peppers. Every few slices, she'd look in my direction.

"You can say whatever you're thinking."

"Are you sure?" she asked, slowing her hand movements then stopping. "Because—"

"I couldn't find shallots, so I got you the adult version," September announced as she entered the kitchen with July on her heels.

"I told her—"

July's eyes met mine before she finished and widened in curiosity.

"Oh, great," September said, dropping the grocery bags on the counter. "He didn't break up with you."

"That's what she said." I pointed to June. "But August and I aren't in a relationship. Kinda hard to break up."

They glanced at each other, having a silent conversation that, for some reason, I could read.

"He's hard to stay away from," I admitted. "Kid in tow now and all."

All three of their heads snapped in my direction. It was kind of creepy how in sync they were.

"Were you eavesdropping on us?" September accused, her eyes narrowed. "More importantly, how'd you do it?"

I laughed before I could stop myself.

"Sorry," I managed to get out. "I honestly didn't mean to but it was kinda easy."

"No one can do that," July said, eyes perceptive.

"Not even August?"

June smacked her lips.

"It's his fault we're like this," she revealed. "He's never been a big talker, but he would always speak through his eyes."

"Still does," I murmured.

It wasn't supposed to be heard but I knew they caught it by the quick glances they shared. I missed the conversation this time and felt they'd done that on purpose.

June pushed the bowl with the fresh-cut peppers aside and began to pat her cleaned chicken dry.

The smell of the raw chicken became more potent after it left her vinegar, water, and lemon solution. I turned my head for a second to slow the bile rising in my throat.

Breathe, Couri.

Breathe.

I could feel August's energy and when our eyes finally met, he knew.

"Come here," he beckoned, his hand out.

I went to him and he led me upstairs to his bedroom.

"I'm okay," I said, stopping our pursuit to his bathroom. "Just got nauseous for a second."

He turned to me and tipped my head back with his index finger.

"I can send them away," he offered.

I shook my head.

"No, I like them."

His lips twitched then spread into a smile.

"You like that," I surmised.

"Yeah, I do."

My stomach settled and I dropped my head against his chest.

"Can I stay with you tonight?"

The question slipped before I could stop it.

I tried to pull away but he trapped me in a bear hug and slung us both onto the bed.

"August!" I screeched, bursting into laughter as he kissed all over my face. "You're a madman."

At some point in our tussle, August ended up between my legs with his hands on either side of my face.

His head hovered over mine, our eyes lingering on one another before he lowered himself to my stomach and kissed it several times. The desire to have him inside me grew and spread like wildfire; it was a feeling I'd become all too familiar with while dealing with this man.

"What are you afraid of?" he asked.

Everything.

"I'm not sure I know what you mean."

"At brunch, you asked me to promise you I'd return. Why?"

His question put a cap on that fire inside of me.

I didn't want to talk about this.

"It didn't mean anything, I—"

August shook his head, his eyes knowing.

I couldn't even lie in peace around him.

"We don't have to talk about it right now but if I'm doing something to make you feel like I'm about to disappear, tell me and I'll fix it."

I wanted to scream for him to shut up, but I wiggled instead, hoping he'd understand.

He lifted up and I scurried away to the other side of the bed.

"It's not you," I admitted, needing him to know that.

I sat at the edge and stared at my socked feet, kicking them back and forth to calm my nerves.

"Are you sure about that?" he asked from behind me.

It's me.

"Everyone always leaves when I need them the most," I whispered, letting my tears fall.

First, it was my dad.

His death had been unexpected.

The man was as healthy as an ox; at least, he had been in my eyes.

One moment I was getting my heart broken by the man I thought I'd be with for the rest of my life and the next I was told that my father had suffered a massive heartache.

None of us saw it coming.

A part of me broke that day.

But after losing my mother, I felt completely shattered inside.

How was I supposed to be a mother without mine?

"I can't promise you that something won't happen to me," August said as he stooped and kneeled before me. "It would be selfish to do so, but as long as I have breath in my body, I'll be here, Couri."

"You asked me how I was feeling earlier and..."

It was hard for me to say it out loud. The words felt like sandpaper on my tongue.

I didn't want him or anyone else to worry, but I was slightly worried for myself.

"I'm really sad," I told him, twisting my fingers. "I don't know how not to be and I'm scared it won't ever stop hurting."

My chest tightened at the thought of my mother.

"Just be," he said, standing and pulling me with him. "Stop pressuring yourself to be happy when you aren't. You don't need to pretend to smile or put on a front for the world."

He hugged me so tightly, I almost thought he was breathing for me.

Our bodies were in perfect sync as he inhaled and exhaled, slow and deep while stroking my back.

"I can see it in your eyes, how sad you are," he muttered, gently gripping my neck. "I got this urge to make it all go away."

August brushed his thumb across my bottom lip, his eyes

dancing with mine as he held onto me like my mental health depended on it.

"I wish I could make it all go away, but we both know grief doesn't work like that. You can lean on me, though, Couri. Doesn't matter what I have going on; I'll always make time for you."

"Would you have said that if I wasn't pregnant?"

"There's no doubt in my heart about it," he replied without pause.

"Can I stay with you?" I decided to ask again, this time without hiding behind my words.

"January is a crying night owl."

I shrugged and he kissed me.

"You can stay, but I won't feel a way if you decide in the middle of the night you need peace and quiet."

I nodded, though I knew I wouldn't leave him.

Crying babies were my forte.

"I brought a bag just in case."

He smirked.

"I'll get it after my sisters leave." He pulled me into another long and beautifully suffocating embrace. "Come on and I'll start your potatoes."

He led me out of the bedroom and this time as we passed the second bedroom on this floor, I peeked inside.

The room had been completely changed from the halfway bare guest bedroom it'd been before. The floor was covered in a large, light purple, fluffy rug that softened the stark white crib, drawer, and changing table set. A bookcase filled with old and new books was in the corner near a microfiber reclining chair.

"Are some of these handed down through your family?" I asked, walking further into the room after he released my hand.

"A lot of them are from when I was kid, yeah," August

confirmed. "July kept them all and gifted some to January for her shelf."

I hummed and ran the tips of my fingers down the thin spines of a collection of slightly tattered Dr. Seuss books.

I turned and peered into the crib, finding January with her eyes wide open.

"She's awake," I said. "Can I pick her up?"

"You don't have to ask."

I gathered her up, not needing to be told twice.

January was now dressed in a white, long-sleeved, footed onesie. Her eyes stayed pinned on me as I cradled her in my arms.

"You, my sweet little snowflake, are precious," I cooed, stroking her cheek. "Your dad got lucky but so did you."

I reached for one of the folded receiving blankets on the changing table, laid it on my shoulder, and rested her over it.

"Okay..." I turned to August, who had propped himself against the door frame. "Let's go."

He didn't move right away, his eyes bouncing from me to January like they had at the hospital.

"What?"

He shook his head and left my question open for interpretation. I had no idea what the look meant and wanted to know, but his sister yelling that dinner was ready and a burst of cries from January shifted my focus.

August hesitated when I waved him away but let me keep her after she started to settle.

"Aw, look, one big happy family," July cooed from her spot on the sofa as we came into view.

August looked at me again, his eyes offering me an escape I didn't need or want to take.

When I turned away from him and dashed into the living room, he went into the kitchen.

"Are you really okay with this?" July asked softly as I sat on the other end of the sectional. "My brother is a good man but a newborn baby is a lot for two people who weren't in a relationship."

It sounded like she didn't know about my pregnancy, which likely meant no one knew.

"He's hard—"

"Yeah, I got that the first time you said it," she cut in, eyes meeting mine. "But, and I mean this in the most respectful way, I'm calling bullshit. Maybe it's partly true, but something else has got you here."

What was I supposed to say to that?

"Why are you cutting potatoes?" September asked, loud enough for me and July to hear.

"It doesn't even go," June chimed in.

I kept my eyes on January, hopeful this conversation wouldn't become a pregnancy announcement.

"For Couri," August responded nonchalantly. "Preheat a clean pan with butter for me."

I could hear him chopping as he spoke.

"What's wrong with your arms?" June asked.

"Nothing," he said. "But, the request stands."

"You're being weird," I heard June mumble as what could only be a pan hit the stove.

"You're being weird," he threw back, sounding exactly like a younger brother would.

Seeing him like this with his sisters made me smile, even if they were picking up on something that was definitely there.

July hadn't taken her eyes off the side of my face, and if it were possible, there'd be a hole there.

"I'll take her," September said, walking into the living room. "Time for some auntie love before the other two hog her."

I handed January off but now that my hands were empty, I couldn't pretend I was focused on them.

I got up and went into the kitchen, capturing August's attention. He tipped his head for me to come to him and I did, though reluctantly.

"I can eat the stir-fry," I said softly as I stopped beside him.

"Then, why is he making you potatoes?" June asked, one hand on her hip while the other clutched a spatula.

She reminded me so much of Journi.

There was just something about big sisters and their need to know everything, but it wasn't my place to tell her, so I looked to August for help.

Did he want them to know?

Was it something he'd rather keep secret for now?

I wasn't sure how I'd feel if that were true, but it was his family. He'd earned that right to tell them when he was ready, as I did with mine.

"She needs to eat and it's the only thing she's able to hold down right now," he finally said after a long while of us staring at one another. "That cool with you?"

He glanced over his shoulder at June, who looked more confused than before.

"Are you sick?" she asked, looking me over. "I know a good soup recipe that'll knock a stomach bug right out."

"Technically, it's Ma's recipe but whatever," July tossed in as she entered the kitchen and leaned against the other side of the counter. "She's right. It'll fix you right up."

They went from questioning me to wanting to take care of me.

August and his sisters were something else.

Kind of all over the place but organized at the same time.

"I don't exactly have a stomach bug, but maybe it'll help my situation."

"Without the spices," August said, his lips pulled into a small smile.

"No, August Hanson!" June exclaimed. "That's what gives the soup its purpose. If I can't put the spices in, I refuse to make it."

"I'll take the spices."

August cut his eyes at me with a raised eyebrow.

"That look doesn't work on me."

His sisters ooooohed in unison, making me want to duck my head.

August chuckled and dropped the perfectly diced potatoes into the buttered pan June had prepared. The sizzle was loud and satisfying to my ears.

"Can I tell them?" he asked, his eyes pinned solely on me.

He didn't need my permission, yet he asked anyway.

And here I'd thought he wanted to keep it a secret.

"If that's what you want to do."

"Tell us what?" June asked, her brows lifted.

August and I stared at one another for a moment longer then he said, "Couri is pregnant."

"With your baby?"

August shot a glare July's way and she threw her free hand up.

"I'm only getting the facts," she said. "I didn't mean it like that."

Her eyes were on me as she said it and I appreciated her not wanting to offend me. Because I'd had the same question just a few hours ago.

"I didn't take it any kind of way," I told July. "Yes, he's the father."

September whistled as she joined us in the kitchen.

"I knew something was up," she said.

"Same," June and July agreed at once.

"I'll make you a batch of my soup and go light on the spices," June added with a nod.

"Don't be such a mom, June," September grumbled, rolling her eyes. "I'm sure she has her own mom to do that stuff for her."

I didn't, I thought.

Everything I'd been trying to keep in came out in a strangled sob. I turned away from them and covered my mouth but couldn't stop the noises coming from me.

"What did I say?" I heard September ask as August lifted and carried me up the stairs.

It wasn't fair that I had to do this without her wisdom or those unique recipes Journi and I hadn't been able to perfect before she passed.

All I had were memories and those didn't feel like enough. I needed more time with her, more pictures so I didn't forget her face, and videos to store the sound of her voice.

"I know it hurts," August murmured as he laid me gently on the bed and spooned me. "Let it out for as long as you need."

Forever!

I needed forever to get over it.

SIXTEEN

IT TOOK Couri a while to settle, but eventually, she fell asleep and I laid with her for a while, not wanting to leave her alone.

Losing her mother was fresh, but how she'd sobbed made me wonder if she had cried since finding out.

It pained me to see her that way because I had deep feelings for this woman. On the other hand, my sisters didn't know her from Adam, but I could feel them chomping at the bit while they waited for one or both of us to emerge.

I slipped out of bed and covered Couri with a throw blanket I kept lying around.

When I got downstairs, July had January strapped into her baby sofa bed while she sucked on a bottle.

September came and stood in front of me, her eyes filled with concern.

"What did I say?"

I shook my head.

"It ain't your fault," I reassured her.

I glanced at June, who had found all of our mother's soup ingredients and was focused on chopping the vegetables.

"She'll need to eat," she said, dicing faster than I'd ever seen.

"It's appreciated. Couri has a lot going on right now. Her mother passed away a couple weeks back and she's still processing it."

June's knife clattered and September gasped, her eyes wide.

"It is my fault. I should've never assumed—" She shook her head. "That was so careless of me. I'm sorry, August."

"She wouldn't want you to apologize and neither do I. Honestly, she needed that moment. I'm kinda worried about her."

"Do you think she's depressed?" July asked.

"I don't know. I think she's grieving and confused and pregnant."

"Whole lotta hormones," July muttered, shaking her head.

"I shouldn't have pushed about the potatoes," June blurted, her chopping resumed. "You weren't ready to tell us and it should've stayed that way until you were."

"I need all of y'all to chill out with the self-blame game. None of you are at fault, alright?"

"I never said I was," July pointed out with a shrug.

"I'm trying to create a stress-free environment for her," I continued, ignoring my sister's witty remark. "Keep Ma and Dad out of the loop for now."

They nodded.

"You've got a lot on your plate," June said.

"I know but it is what it is."

"Maybe you should take more time off work," September suggested. "We know you weren't going to take the full twelve weeks of paternity leave, but maybe you should."

I shook my head.

"Nah, I need work. It's the only thing in my life that hasn't changed unless I wanted it to."

It would keep me afloat while I figured out how to get all the moving pieces of my life back in order.

"Okay, but if you get overwhelmed or need a break to think by yourself or anything. It doesn't matter, August, we're here," July said.

"I know. Which is why I need one of you to stay tonight with—"

"I'll do it!" September offered before I could finish. "It's my off day tomorrow. I've got time."

"Just until morning—"

"However long you need," she cut in, eager to help because she still felt bad.

"Until morning," I reiterated.

I reached down and unbuckled January. As I lifted her, I noticed the tiny grin on her face.

"Are you smiling at me, Snowflake?"

"Probably gassy," July muttered.

"Snowflake?" June questioned as she stepped up beside me with a bowl of stir-fry.

"Couri gave her the nickname." I kissed her cheek a few times. "I think it's fitting."

"You're smitten," June mused.

"I'm more than smitten," I declared. "I love this little girl."

"Wasn't talking about January."

I cut my eyes at June.

"Is that for me?"

I nodded toward the bowl in her hand.

"Yes, you need to eat."

I put baby girl back and took the bowl.

"I saved those potatoes for Couri in case the soup doesn't work out. I'll finish it before I leave for the night."

"Appreciate you, Ju."

She smiled.

"You haven't called me that in a long time."

"You miss it?" I asked as I speared some of everything in the bowl to maximize the first bite.

June shrugged but that only meant she had.

I kissed her forehead before stuffing my mouth.

My sister could cook her ass off and she knew it.

In a matter of minutes, I scarfed down the whole bowl.

"Clearly, you aren't eating," she fussed, taking the bowl and fork. "Do better, August."

"And she's back," July murmured under her breath.

I angled my head.

"Chill for me."

She rolled her eyes but nodded.

"Fine but only because I get to love on this munchkin for a little while longer..." She turned the little bed chair to her and started making faces. "Can't believe she smiled for your ugly mug."

"You share a similar looking face with this ugly mug," I reminded her.

"Mine is more feminine, thank you."

"Before you two leave..." I backed away. "...send me a text and I'll walk you out."

"We don't need you escorting us," June fussed as I walked up the steps.

"Yeah, alright. Do as I said."

I jogged the rest of the way up and slipped back into my room. Couri had her back against the headboard, her knees pulled up with her cheek against her arm.

"I'm sorry I ruined dinner with your sisters," she whispered, eyes on me as I approached.

"You didn't ruin shit, Couri."

She sat up a little and I realized my tone had been harsher than I'd meant.

"I'm sorry, Angel face. My sisters are remorseful."

She shook her head.

"They shouldn't be."

"I told them the same." I got into bed and backed myself into the headboard next to her. "They'd tell you that dinner wasn't ruined."

"Are you using reverse psychology on me?" she asked.

"Is it working?"

"Sort of, yeah."

She turned her body toward me and I reached for her, dragging her over my legs until she settled in a straddle position in my lap.

"First time really crying?" I asked, gathering her hair.

She handed me the ponytail holder from around her wrist and I did my best imitation of what she called a messy bun.

"That intensely, yes."

Her eyes were puffy and red-rimmed still. I cupped her face and brushed the pads of my thumbs over the slightly raised skin.

"You're beautiful," I told her as our eyes met.

"I know I look crazy, don't lie to me."

"I've never lied to you; why would I start now?"

She shrugged.

"Do you have doubts about me?" she asked.

I didn't understand what she meant by *doubts*.

And my face more than likely revealed that because she started to talk again before I could respond.

"Do you doubt I would be here if I wasn't pregnant?"

"We fucked around for eight months, no kids or serious responsibilities. I wouldn't fault you for wanting to keep that going with someone else."

"Someone else isn't you," she murmured, dropping her gaze.

"Repeat that for me."

"You heard me just fine." She looked up, exasperated.

I waited for her to give me what I wanted.

"Someone isn't you, August," she repeated more forcefully. "I want you."

"I come with a small package now."

"She's the prettiest little package ever," Couri said, doubling down. "This is what I mean."

She untangled herself from me and went into the bathroom. I followed her like a fucking puppy trying to understand.

"I'm not understanding."

The fucking harlot started to remove her bodysuit, peeling it from her frame without regard for where my mind would go.

"It doesn't matter," she mumbled, turning toward the shower.

Her ass was eating up the thong she wore and I couldn't help but to reach out and smack the firm flesh.

"August!" she yelped, pushing my hand away.

I turned the shower on for her and waited until she was fully undressed and inside to speak again.

"It matters to me," I said, addressing her previous comment.

I leaned against the sink and watched her through the glass door.

"You question whether I want to be here even after I've said I do. I've confided in you, cried myself to sleep in your arms, and I'm certain it won't be the last time. I just told you I want you, twice at your request, but there's still doubt in your tone."

"Not on purpose."

"Maybe not. This is new for you, just like it is for me. I guess... never mind."

She started lathering up with the soap she'd left, which reminded me of her bag.

"I'll go grab your bag," I told her, needing a second to process what she said.

"August," she called before I could exit.

"Yeah?"

"Can you bring me something to eat?" She cut her eyes at me while rubbing the washcloth across her chest and shoulders. "Maybe June's soup if it's done. But the potatoes just in case."

I nodded, more confused than before about what she wanted from me.

After grabbing her bag, I stayed downstairs to help June and July load the gifts people bought into their cars to donate.

I appreciated everything but another kid could use it more than mine.

January was set and always would be.

"Why are you dragging your feet?" September asked as she changed January on the sofa.

"Don't give her a bath; I'll do it in the morning."

She rolled her eyes.

"I know the routine you've set for her. Why are you still down here, August?"

"Giving Couri time to herself."

"Did she ask for time?"

I shook my head and went into the kitchen.

"Then stop assuming you know what she needs. It'll never work out if you do."

I grabbed a glass container with a top and scooped some of the potatoes into it, since the soup was still simmering.

"If you were in her shoes, would you stick it out?"

"With a man that wasn't mine to start?" she asked, eyebrows raised. "I don't know how I would handle a situation like this one, but I'm not her. She seems to be really into you and January."

Couri's actions said she wanted us to figure it out together, maybe even be a family if it shaped out that way. For some reason, I couldn't wrap my head around what was in front of me.

"You suddenly think you aren't worthy of the love she's probably been offering from the moment y'all met. I don't know what to tell you other than to figure it out before it's too late."

"She's carrying my child."

"What does that have to do with her finding someone who won't make her feel like her decision to be with them isn't the right one?"

It had nothing to do with it, nothing at all.

I'd been grasping for straws when I needed to go tell the mother of my unborn child that I wanted her too.

"Thanks, Tem."

She smiled and nodded.

"June was right," she said as I gathered all the shit that had to go up the stairs with me. "It's been a while since we heard our childhood nicknames from you."

"We grew up," I pointed out.

"Doesn't change that we're all kids at heart."

I thought about what she said on my way back to Couri. We were all kids at heart, looking for that sense of family we either had or didn't have growing up.

I wanted a family of my own.

I wanted my daughter to have a mother figure that didn't consist of only my sisters.

I wanted the baby I'd created with Couri to have that

family dynamic we had growing up.

More importantly, I wanted Couri.

She was the star of this show and I needed her to know before I lost her and the family I've always wanted for myself.

"You okay?" I asked, entering the bedroom.

Couri sat on the edge of the bed in one of my shirts with her phone in her hand.

"Kali is checking on me," she said, fingers gliding across her keyboard.

"I'm checking on you right now."

She sighed and looked at me as I emptied my hands of the shit I'd been carrying. I handed her the bottle of ginger ale and bowl of potatoes.

"How are *you*, August? You keep asking about me but won't tell me what's happening in your head."

She popped the top of the container and sniffed.

"Smells good," she said softly, almost in relief. "I was afraid being able to eat these was a one-off thing. I'm so hungry."

Her stomach growled right after and she laughed a little.

"I want to be with you, Couri," I confessed, deciding to do it right then.

I sat beside her on the bed and watched as she filled her fork and stuffed it in her mouth.

"Then, be with me, August..." she groaned. "I feel dramatic saying this but I can almost taste a juicy steak."

"I'm just glad you're holding something down."

"Are you afraid?" she asked, taking our conversation back.

"I'm terrified I'll fuck up what's in front of me," I admitted. "My daughter needs me. You need me. Our child will need us."

More people were depending on me today than three weeks ago.

"But what do you need?"

"You."

She set the bowl down and adjusted her body to face me.

"Do you need me or do you only want me?"

"I need *and* want you."

Couri's eyes danced with mine and I only hoped she saw the truth in them.

"You're already embedded in my heart. I want to explore that with you."

She moved to stand in front of me.

"I'm only going to tell you this one more time," she said, cupping my face with both hands while gazing at me with nothing but adoration. "I want to be here with you because it's *you*. Not because I'm pregnant and feel obligated to do so. I couldn't have asked for a better person to go through this with. Maybe we'll end up a family or maybe we'll decide that co-parenting is best, but right now, August Hanson, it's you for me."

The weight of her words did me in and I closed my eyes, but nothing stopped them from leaking.

Fuck.

"Oh, August," she whispered, brushing my tears away. "I know it's been a lot and you're holding it all in for everyone else, but you don't have to do that with me. Let it be. Whatever you're feeling, just let it be."

I wrapped my arms around her and buried my face in her neck.

"I'm angry," I said, all of what I'd been feeling consuming me. "And sad as fuck. I have a daughter who won't ever know her mother. She's gonna have so many questions that I won't know how to answer. All I have is a letter Shondra left and I can't ever let January see it."

How could I give my baby a letter where her mother, in so many words, said she wouldn't have been in her life had she lived? That she'd planned to give her to me and move on like nothing happened.

"You have time to plan for that. I'll help you and so will your sisters and parents. What about Shondra's parents?"

"Her mom will be around. She's still grieving and I think it's hard for her to process that January is all she has left of her daughter."

"A bad hand was dealt, but you have such an amazing support system. It's going to work out."

I pulled back and looked her in those sweet dark eyes.

"Thank you for listening and understanding," I murmured.

"Thank you for trusting me enough to share."

Something shifted between us at that moment.

I could never deny wanting Couri on a physical level; she was intoxicating in the best kind of way.

"Are your sisters still here?" she asked, pushing her hands into my shirt.

"Only one."

"Does that mean you're free to scratch this itch I've been struggling with?"

"Mmhm," I hummed, standing and laying her against the bed. "Free 'til morning."

"There's a lot we can do."

She spread her legs, revealing what I knew was beneath the shirt. Nothing but bare ass and pussy.

"I need you to do me a favor first."

She sat up on her elbows.

"What's that?"

"Finish that food while I shower."

"But—"

I shook my head and backed away.

"You want to get fucked?"

She nodded, her eyes on fire with need.

"Feed my baby and I'll give you what you want."

Couri let out this obnoxious ass laughter that made me smile. She crawled to the edge of the bed where she'd started and picked up her bowl.

"You better make me cum a few times."

"Is that a challenge?"

She smirked and shoveled potatoes in her mouth.

Challenge accepted, Angel face.

I moved toward the bathroom but stopped and turned to face Couri again.

Talking about Shondra left me with a lot of questions I needed answered.

"Hey, I need to know something."

Couri turned, her eyebrows lifted as she devoured what was left in her bowl.

"What's up?" she asked, setting it aside. "You look worried suddenly."

She stood and moved around the bed to get to me.

"What if something happens to you?"

It made me sick to my stomach and fearful of the future.

Losing Couri, having to choose, or worse, raising another kid alone...

"Hey..." She walked into my arms and secured hers tightly around my waist. "I'm so sorry you have to deal with that kind of fear and I know it won't just go away, but we can't predict the future. All we have are these moments right here."

"But we can be prepared..."

She leaned back and looked up at me, her gaze thoughtful.

"How so?"

"I just need to know one thing right now."

"Whatever I can do to ease your mind. Talk to me."

Couri had no idea how badly I needed her to do just that.

"If something happens—God forbid—do I choose you or the baby?"

Her grip on me loosened and I regretted asking immediately.

"I..." She took a small step back, pushing her fingers through her hair. "That's a lot to think about. It's not a question I can answer right now."

We *needed* to talk about it but not exactly at this moment.

"You're right," I agreed, taking a step back. "Another day."

"I realize I've done nothing to ease your mind and I'm sorry, August."

"Don't be sorry for needing time to process. We're good. I'm good."

She didn't believe me; it was written all over her face.

Truthfully, I didn't believe my fucking self.

I wasn't okay and it was eating me up inside. Putting my shit on her wasn't cool and when I got my head together I would apologize properly.

"August—"

"I still need to shower," I cut in, turning toward the bathroom. "Eat. There's more downstairs if you want it."

My fear was clouding my judgment.

Nothing good could ever come from that.

SEVENTEEN

couri

I WAS TUCKED deep under his thick duvet when August emerged from the bathroom.

I felt sick about our conversation because I couldn't give him the answer he needed. At least not as quickly as he'd needed it.

The idea of making him choose felt so unfair after what he'd been through and part of me wanted to pretend tragedy couldn't strike again. But life had hit too hard lately and I couldn't push away his concern.

I'd known my answer the minute he asked.

August moved around the room briefly before the blanket flipped back.

I watched him drop his cell on the dresser, ogling his tatted chest until he cut the bedside lamp off and slipped under the blanket with me, covering our heads just as I'd had it before.

"I'm sorry," I whispered as he slid over and our noses touched. "All of this is unfair."

He was so close I could taste that he'd brushed his teeth.

"To the both of us," he murmured, resting his hand on my face. "It's unfair to both of us."

"It breaks my heart thinking of you having to choose."

Though darkness surrounded us, I felt his gaze staring through my soul as he caressed my cheek slowly. It had been so long since we shared a bed like this, and I pressed my body closer, wanting to be in his skin if possible.

"No matter how I feel, the decision you want will be the one I make. I respect that it's your body and life, and I hope you know that, Couri."

I kissed him with urgency, my fingers finding their way to the back of his neck.

"Choose me," I blurted, pulling my lips from his in a hurry. "You have to choose me, August."

He flipped the comforter off our bodies and lifted up, pulling me into his lap simultaneously. After tapping the base of the bedside lamp, which illuminated the bedroom, August turned his attention to me.

"You said you needed to think about it."

"It was so sudden, you asked that and I couldn't wrap my head around it fast enough to give you a response. I pray it never comes to it..." I cupped his face and gazed into those whiskey browns I was falling in love with. "I pray you and I never have to endure that kind of trauma. With all my heart, I believe we'll be okay."

He touched his forehead to mine and took a deep breath.

"There's this scripture I would hear my mother say in times like this. When all you're searching for is peace of mind," he said softly, stealing a piece of my heart. "Can I recite it to you?"

I nodded and dropped my fingers to his shoulders, closing my eyes but never removing my forehead from his. My heart raced, thumping wildly in my chest as he gathered himself. I recognized him as the man meant to be my husband and that realization gave me butterflies.

Did he know this was fate, God's plan?

"Peace I leave with you, my peace I give to you—"

"John 14:27," I finished for him, understanding the power of that scripture more than he'd know.

August pulled me flush against him and wrapped his arms around me as our gazes met.

We stayed like that for a while, our hearts eventually finding themselves in sync.

"I'm glad you stayed," he told me. "I needed you and wasn't sure how much until now."

I pulled my body from his to get a better look at him.

"You need me?"

He nodded slowly and tucked his fingers beneath my chin.

"You calm the chaos," he murmured, sliding his thumb over my bottom lip. "And right now, everything is in shambles, but when I'm near you, I don't feel the weight of it as much."

The vulnerability it took to speak that aloud had the floodgates opening between my thighs.

"I think you're doing a beautiful job figuring some heavy shit out."

Slowly, and I felt every second of it, August hardened beneath me. I pulled the shirt I'd stolen from him over my head and revealed my naked body. Every part of me craved this moment with him.

August attacked my mouth with vigor, his fingers digging into the curve of my back unlike any other time before. He bit my lip, and I hissed, but refused to let it break our stride.

I lifted up and tugged at his basketball shorts, sliding them halfway down his legs. Just enough room for me to sit on that beautiful piece he was blessed with.

"Need you," I breathed, pulling my lips from his in haste. "So bad, August."

With my fingers wrapped around the base of his dick, I slid down on it.

"Goddamn," August groaned, gripping my hips as I began to ride him. "I missed you..." He dropped his head back. "So fucking much."

"I missed you." I rolled my hips, using his shoulders to balance myself. "I missed this dick too."

He chuckled, but it was mixed with a soft moan that drove me wild.

"Fucking love the way you ride my dick."

His eyes flashed as he watched me lift to the tip and drop slowly.

It felt amazing; the way he filled me... *fit me.*

My body hummed from the connection.

"I'm pregnant," I whispered, really feeling it suddenly. "Can't believe—"

August flipped us, his dick still buried deep inside of me.

"With my baby." His voice was thick with emotion as he worked his hips in deep thrusts. "I'm glad it's you."

I dug the heel of my foot into his calves, taking his strokes like a champ. They were swift and hard, filled with whatever was going on in his head.

Forehead to forehead, his fingers through mine and pinned to the bed, he made love to me. It was invigorating and exactly what I... *we* needed.

"Yes," I cried softly against his collarbone. "J-Just like that."

Tears pricked my eyes and I let them fall, allowing my mind and body to drown in August. It was all about him and how he made me feel inside.

Beautiful.

Understood.

Safe.

I was safe with him—my heart, mind, and body.

"Shit, Couri..."

My core tightened and I let out a small whimper, grasping for the orgasm I was on the brink of. I tightened my fingers in his, needing more of him.

"I need you too," I murmured as I began to tip over the edge.

"I feel that shit," August growled, releasing a hand to slip his under my body, lifting it slightly. "Give it to me."

His command had been all I needed to let go.

I sniffed as August came inside me, everything hitting me all at once.

Before I knew it, I was in a full-blown breakdown that caught us both off guard. Even so, August didn't miss a beat. He rolled off me and tugged my body into his, his voice just above a whisper as he consoled me.

"You aren't alone," he murmured softly, his fingers caressing the length of my arm. "I'm here. I got you."

I burrowed deeper into him and allowed the grief wracking my system to consume me. The fear of what that could do to me had been so intense I'd kept my tears under lock and key for too long.

August brought it out of me.

His gentleness had given me the space to let it go without judgment, only support.

"I hate crying," I grumbled, wiping my tears from his chest.

He chuckled and kissed the top of my head, tangling his fingers in my hair.

"You need to do it more often. Stop holding it all in."

"I want to be strong..."

"But you don't *need* to be," he countered in a no-nonsense tone. "It's okay, not to be okay. Remember that the next time you feel the urge to hold back how you're feeling in the name of being strong."

It was the last thing I'd heard him say before falling asleep and the words stuck.

Fuck being strong.

I woke later to the screams of January as August untangled us to get out of bed.

Slowly, I lifted while rubbing my eyes.

"Go back to sleep, baby," he said, his voice tinged with a rasp I could get used to.

I ignored him and got out of bed, stretching my naked body until parts of me popped. When I straightened, August had his gaze pinned on my breasts.

"Stop being a creep," I mumbled, lips curling into a smile.

"Can't help how attracted I am to you." He rounded the bed and kissed my lips. "Rest, okay? I'll be back after I check on Tem and baby girl."

"I could help," I said, picking up the shirt of his I'd been wearing, then grabbing a pair of leggings from my bag.

He turned, his eyebrows raised.

"Only if you want."

When he opened the bedroom door without responding, I took that as a no, but then he glanced over his shoulder and summoned me with a simple head tilt.

Before he changed his mind, I followed him down the stairwell to find September walking back and forth with a fussy January.

"No." September shook her head and backed away before August could lift his hands. "I'm here to be of assistance. Why are you two down here?"

Her whiskey browns were wide.

"Because we can't sleep while she screams like someone is hurting her," August explained, taking another step forward as she took one back, ready to bolt. "My heart can't take that shit,

Tem. I know you're here to help, and I love you for it, but let me have my baby."

September's gaze softened, her shoulders drooping slightly as she handed January over.

"I know," he whispered, placing her little frame against his chest. "Daddy's got you."

He moved toward the kitchen and his sister's eyes met mine.

"He doesn't know it yet, but he's such a good dad," she murmured, closing the distance between us. "I hope you aren't worried about that because August was meant to be a father."

I shook my head, my heart swelling at her words.

"I'm not worried."

She smiled and it broadened after silence filled the space around us.

"Hear that?" she asked.

No more crying.

We migrated into the kitchen and the sight before me tugged at my heartstrings again.

August had managed to get January into one of those body wraps and was standing at the baby Keurig making a bottle. Her little body was tucked inside, silent as ever.

I padded toward them, and he looked up, his eyes filled with pride.

"I guess you didn't need me after all."

He turned and gently tugged me against him. Even with a baby between us, I'd never felt closer to someone.

"I need you," he said softly. "And I'll keep telling you until you believe me."

That was the thing, I believed him the first time he'd said it, but it felt good to hear it again.

"Can I have my niece back now?" September asked. "I was doing just fine on my own."

August made a noise before kissing my forehead and turning back to finish the bottle he'd been making.

"Go home, Tem," he said, no real bass in his voice. "We have an appointment with Leslie at seven, so I got it from here."

I glanced at the clock on the stove, noting it was five in the morning.

We'd slept longer than I thought, and suddenly, I was wide awake.

His sister huffed a little, but I caught the slight smile on her face as she gathered her things.

"Fine, but text the group chat and tell us how little mama is doing, okay?"

He nodded and followed her to the door, something she complained about the whole way.

August was very protective of the women in his life—reminding me of our first night together.

"You can stay as long as you want," he said, returning to the kitchen. "Or..."

I lifted my gaze to meet his.

"Or what?"

"You could come to the appointment." His eyes searched mine. "Only if you want."

I walked toward him, a sense of urgency in my steps that carried my short legs faster than usual. And as if he'd known what I wanted, August leaned forward and pressed his mouth to mine.

"I'll take that as a yes."

I nodded and he smiled into my lips.

"Absolutely, yes."

EIGHTEEN

august

A LITTLE AFTER SIX, a hard knock at the front door, followed by an attempt to ring the doorbell, stopped me in my tracks. I set January—who was secured in her car seat—on the counter and headed for the door.

Couri hadn't come down yet, but we were making good time.

"Hold up," I called when the visitor knocked again.

Annoyed with their impatience, I snatched the door open with a little more force than I'd meant. On the other side, Shondra's mother jerked back.

"Mrs. Thomas," I greeted, brow raised. "I wasn't expecting you."

She hadn't shown up the day I brought January home as planned and my messages had gone unanswered. After the third phone call to ensure she was okay wasn't returned, I chalked it up to her needing time to grieve.

"Sorry," she rushed out, taking a step forward.

I wasn't sure if she'd expected me to invite her in or if she was inviting herself inside, but suddenly, my mood had shifted. Something about her unannounced visit rubbed me the wrong way.

Our gazes met, and she sighed, her disheveled appearance standing out.

"I was hoping to see January," she said, adjusting her purse. "If that's okay with you."

It took me a moment, but I stepped back to allow her inside.

"We were about to head out," I let her know. "Today is her first pediatrician appointment."

"I won't be long."

She followed as I led us into the kitchen.

I thought she might bolt for a second after I removed the blanket from January's carrier and revealed her sleeping frame. She stepped forward and peered inside, her eyes filling with tears.

"Goodness," she whispered. "She's already getting big."

I nodded and busied myself re-checking the diaper bag, but the more I tried to ignore my annoyance, the harder it became to hold my tongue.

"Can I ask why you've been ignoring me? I thought you wanted to be in her life."

I needed to know if she didn't before my child could feel her absence.

"I understand that you're grieving," I went on. "But coming in and out of her life won't fly. We need to establish that early."

"I'm glad you feel that way." She stood tall and slowly turned her attention to me, reaching into her purse simultaneously. "I think it's best we get this out of the way."

She set a large manila envelope on the counter and pushed it toward me.

"What's that?"

I refused to pick it up.

"I thought it'd be best if I delivered those before you were officially served." She glanced at January again, reaching in to caress her cheek. "I'll leave and give you time to go over it."

She sauntered off, and as the front door shut, I picked up the envelope and pulled the documents out.

"The fuck..."

I dropped the petition for custody of *my* fucking child and jogged to the door, damn near snatching it off the hinges to get it open.

Mrs. Thomas was already backing out of the driveway when I stepped outside.

She'd known exactly what the fuck she was doing showing up here in that way.

I watched until her car disappeared up the street and stormed into the house, searching for my phone with shaky fingers.

"I'm ready," Couri announced halfway down the steps. "Sorry it took so long. My hair is—hey! What's that face? What's wrong?"

She approached as I scrolled through my phone, looking for a specific contact.

"August—"

I lifted my phone to my ear after finding the one I'd been looking for.

"Hey, cousin, what's u—"

"Lola..." I covered my face and took a breath. "I think I need a lawyer."

"Okay," she drawled. "Well, we can discuss why after I check my calendar. One second."

I moved toward the kitchen, Couri hot on my heels.

"I have an opening this afternoon at three, but I can always stop by after I'm done in the office."

"Can you stop by afterward?"

I stared into January's car seat, watching her sleep.

"Of course. Are you okay?"

"I will be. Thanks, Lo."

I ended the call and dropped my phone on the counter.

"What did I miss?" Couri asked, her tone soft.

I took a deep breath and handed her the papers from Mrs. Thomas.

She gasped and our gazes met.

"She's trying to take my baby from me." My eyes burned and I looked away. "I'll go to jail before allowing it."

"No court in Michigan would go for this, August." Couri took a step toward me and rested her forehead against my chest. "You aren't the kind of parent they take a child away from. I think she knows this. Grief can make you do stupid things, like hurt people who don't deserve it."

I wasn't trying to hear any of that but kept my thoughts to myself.

Couri didn't deserve the anger I was feeling.

"But just so you know..." She lifted her head and stared deeply into my eyes. "I'll beat her ass for you, on sight."

I chuckled, the tension in my shoulders rolling off just a tad.

"I appreciate that, but no fighting." I glanced at the papers again. "I don't understand. Custody?"

It didn't make sense, but maybe Couri was right. Grief had convinced Shondra's mother this was what she needed to do.

"Is she under the impression you don't want her around?"

I shook my head.

"Nah. I clarified where I stood on her being in January's life. As long as she wanted that, then the door was open. I guess this is what she'd been doing while I was reaching out."

Plotting against me like I was a fucking bum or something.

Had she forgotten her daughter planned to drop our kid off and never look back?

"We have to go or we'll miss the appointment," Couri reminded me, placing her fingers under my chin. "Keep this lifted. You're doing a great job, especially given the circumstances."

She was right... wasn't she?

I shook away the direction my mind was headed in and picked up the car seat after covering it again.

"Yeah." I nodded. "Let's go."

We made it to Leslie's practice in record time, signing in and being called back almost immediately. We were her first appointment of the day.

The nurse had undressed January and laid her on the table that doubled as a scale.

"We've gained a pound," she said, her lips curving into a genuine smile. "Don't be alarmed. Most babies lose a little weight right after leaving the hospital. Little Miss January is eating well."

Couri leaned into me and I glanced down to find her staring up at me. Her gentle gaze was the reassurance I needed... I craved it.

I love you, I thought.

Shit.

I looked away and watched the nurse do a few more checks. She nodded and wrote things down as she moved through her checklist.

"Alright," she announced, flipping the chart shut. "The doctor will be in soon to discuss any concerns, go over my notes, and do her own checks."

The door closed behind her and I tugged Couri from her seat, guiding her to stand between my legs.

282

"What are you doing?" she asked, placing her hands on my shoulders.

"Looking at you," I told her, never breaking eye contact. "Thank you for being part of my support system."

She dropped her gaze, but I sensed the smile she forced herself to keep at bay.

"Thank you for allowing it."

I enclosed my arms around her waist and dropped my forehead against her stomach, pressing light kisses against it. Part of me was still wrapping my mind around becoming a father of two in less than a year but deep down, I was fucking happy.

Being a dad had been a life goal of mine, and I was being rewarded two times over, just not in the way I'd expected.

January made a little whining noise and Couri turned, pulling away to tend to her.

I observed how she stroked her exposed belly and lifted her carefully from the table, cradling January in the crook of her arm. It was a sight to behold, Couri accepting my daughter without qualms.

Would she be here if we weren't expecting?

Though I wasn't sure I'd ever get the answer to that question, it didn't matter.

A knock at the door drew my attention in that direction.

Leslie Hanson entered, her white coat brightening the room.

"Hey," she said, smiling. "Let's—"

She halted her steps after spotting Couri, her eyes widening slightly.

"Dr. Hanson," I greeted, smirking as she narrowed her eyes at me. "This is Couri and January. Couri, this is Leslie. Unfortunately, we're related."

"If I didn't have to be professional, I'd beat you with this clipboard."

She turned her attention back to Couri and smiled.

"It's nice to meet you, Couri. I'm the smart one in the family."

"Don't let your sister hear that."

Leslie and Lola were sisters and part of the plethora of Hanson kids my father and his siblings produced. They'd both opted out of working for the family business, Leslie becoming a doctor while Lola went into family law.

Landon—their older brother—had chosen a career in STEM, working for one of the top engineering firms in Michigan.

"She won't hear it because you won't tell her." She stepped over to the sink and started to wash her hands. "How's our girl doing?"

"Still fussy most nights. It's breaking my heart."

Leslie turned, and our gazes met; hers softening after staring into mine briefly.

"Let me look at her and we'll figure out a course of action, okay?"

I nodded, and she stepped toward Couri, who hadn't let January go yet, but did so when Leslie reached for her.

"So, Couri, how did that guy get you here?" she asked as she laid January down and started probing around. "I guess he's kinda handsome." She gagged and I chuckled. "Kind of nice."

I knew what she was getting at.

How did I get her *here,* of all places, with a newborn baby, at her first appointment?

Couri cut her eyes at me and I nodded.

"He basically tricked me," she said, going a route I hadn't expected. "Promised me free bourbon for life and I couldn't pass that up."

Leslie tossed her head back and cackled, startling January awake.

"So sorry, cutie pie," she cooed, gently brushing her thumbs over her eyebrows.

To my surprise, babygirl settled right away.

"Do you think it's me?" I asked, changing topics. "The reason she's damn near inconsolable at times?"

"Except for this morning," Couri pointed out.

Leslie's gaze drifted between us before she said, "Elaborate."

"September had her last night, but the crying woke... *us*, and when I went for her, she calmed almost instantly," I explained.

"You're stressed, and considering how all of this came about if you weren't, I'd be concerned. What I'm *not* concerned about is little Miss January here. She's healthy and clearly loved." She looked at Couri briefly. "Don't be so hard on yourself, August. If anyone in this family was made to be a dad, it's you."

"Everyone keeps saying that," I grumbled.

"Because it's true." Leslie smiled and removed her gloves. "He was the best babysitter growing up. The babies loved him and the toddlers only ever listened to his commands."

"So, I'm not doing anything wrong."

"You are a new parent. It's okay to feel like you aren't getting it right, but from what I see, you're doing just fine. Keep a record of her crying spells if they continue. Pair it up with feeding and diaper changes. If you need a house visit, I'm at your disposal, but something tells me you won't."

Her certainty in my ability to be a good parent gave me a confidence boost.

"I'm going to recommend a therapist for you," she said, eyeing me closely. "It's not uncommon for fathers to also develop postpartum depression. And with the circumstances, I think you may feel a little guilty and angry, and it could be what she's feeling."

My chest tightened, but I nodded.

"Just remember that you have a family who will help guide you as best we can, but you can't properly care for her if you don't take care of yourself first."

"Come on." Leslie took a step forward and held her arms open. "Like old times."

I stood, and she closed the distance, wrapping her arms around me the minute she could.

As she squeezed, I felt myself getting a little emotional.

When we were kids, she would dish out hugs, somehow knowing the other person needed it. They were tight, full of understanding, and, most importantly, love. So, like old times I hugged my cousin—the empath—and allowed it to heal a tiny part of me.

I really couldn't do this without my family.

NINETEEN

couri

"YOU SURE YOU can't stay a little longer?" August asked as he walked me to my truck, my overnight bag in hand. "I sound like I'm whining, but I like you being here."

I couldn't help the smile that spread across my face.

The look in his eyes tugged at my heartstrings. I wanted to stay but seeing him with his family made me miss mine and I needed a good dose of their love.

"I like being here." I watched him toss my bag in the back seat and open the driver's door. "My place is a mess and Kali sent a text requesting my presence."

He nodded and guided me into the front seat, leaning his body in as I settled.

"Promise me you'll be safe."

"I promise I'll be safe."

"And that you'll eat something," he went on, eyes following my movements. "I should've fed you."

"It's okay." I smiled and brushed my fingers over his shirt to smooth the wrinkles. "You had a hectic morning and my stomach is finally settled for once. I don't want to jinx it by stuffing my face."

He frowned.

"You need to eat, baby."

"I really like it when you call me baby."

That flipped his frown right side up and I preferred him this way, smiling.

"Before you go..." He knelt down and I turned my body as he took my hands. "I told you this, but I've been thinking about us a lot, even before January." He looked up. "We talked about giving this a chance, but I don't want to leave room for your mind to wander especially after our conversation last night. My intentions are for us to be together. I want to be with you, in a relationship, a real one."

I wasn't sure if it was his heart I heard racing or my own.

"You have to be one hundred percent sure," I said, lacing my fingers with his. "Because, for the first time in my life, I see my future clear as day. It includes a family of four to start, so I *really* need you to be sure, August. If you can say that without—"

"I'm sure," he cut in. "No doubt in my mind that I want to be the face you see while picturing that family and January, too."

I think I loved his daughter already, but I was indubitably in love with her father.

"It won't be easy."

"Nothing leading up to this has been easy except meeting and befriending you."

I pulled my hands from his and cupped his face.

"Okay but ask me right."

August's lips spread.

"Will you be my girlfriend, Couri Lee Mitchell?"

"Aww," I whined teasingly. "And here I thought you were asking me to be your wife."

It was supposed to be a joke, but August's eyes took on an

expression I didn't understand. Why would I even joke that way?

Wife?

Marriage?

I knew in my heart he'd been explicitly crafted for me, but what the fuck had I been thinking?

"I didn't mean—"

"We could do that," he said, standing and pulling me from the truck. "Make you a wife. *My* wife."

I shook my head and took a step back.

"It was a stupid joke. I don't even know why I said it."

He smiled and took a step forward.

"Because deep down, that's what you want, to be married."

I blinked and stared up at him.

"To you?"

August chuckled and dropped his hands against the hood of my truck, angling his body forward to block me in.

"I fucking hope so," he hissed, though he wasn't angry. "You're mine, Couri. *Mine.*"

I loved how he said my name and how his voice dropped an octave or two as he emphasized me being his.

"We should think about it..." I rested my palms against his chest and bunched his shirt between my fingers. "I really hadn't meant—"

He pressed his lips to mine, silencing me in one way but awakening me in others.

Goddamn, this man.

"Don't tell me what you didn't mean to say. Just remember my response after you said it and we'll talk when the time is right."

I took a deep breath and released him as he began to step backward.

"How will we know when the time's right?"

He glanced up at the clear sky and, after a few seconds, returned his gaze to mine with a smile plastered on his handsome face.

"The way you felt when we first met. That gut feeling telling you to come home with me." He smirked and I knew he was thinking about that first meeting. "When you feel like that again, no matter where we are or what we're doing, tell me yes, and I'll know to buy a ring."

It was crazy, but I nodded without much thought.

"Okay."

"Get in your truck and go be with your family, Angel face." He helped me inside again. "Be safe like promised and eat something; I don't care what it is."

"Will you call once you and Snowflake settle in tonight? I want to know what your cousin says about the petition for custody."

His shoulders dropped a little, and I hated that I'd ruined his mood.

"Hate this shit," he mumbled. "It's fucked up what she's trying to do to me, but I'll handle it accordingly. I'll call you tonight."

He kissed my forehead and closed me inside before I could respond.

I leveled my foot with the brake and hit the push to start while watching August walk to the front door. He turned and waited for me to back out before going inside.

For some silly reason, it almost felt like he'd shut me out, not wanting me involved with that part of his life. The logical part of me knew better and I chose to follow that feeling instead of the other one working hard to cloud my judgment.

August was under an immense amount of stress and I wanted so badly to make it all go away.

To keep my mind from stupidly wandering when I got

home, I cleaned my entire place from top to bottom, took a long hot shower, then dressed in baggy sweats with a hoodie to match.

After I finished braiding my hair into two large plaits, Journi called.

"I was just about to start heading that way," I said upon picking up. "Did you cook?"

My stomach grumbled and a deep sense of shame hit me. I had to care for myself better than starving my baby to keep from throwing it all up.

Ugh.

"I made you a fresh batch of tea," Journi said. "And we have an assortment of bread for your choosing; plus, Kingston just mentioned something about potatoes before stepping out with Primo."

I smiled.

"He must've talked to August. We figured out that I can keep them down."

"Figured it out together, huh?" she questioned, a knowing lilt in her tone.

I grabbed my keys and purse and headed for the front door. "I'll tell you all about it when I get there."

"Can't wait," she sang while ending the call.

When I arrived, Kali was standing on the porch with her phone clutched tightly in her hands.

"Te, I have to show you something!" she exclaimed, rushing over to slide in the front seat before I got out. "Look."

She shoved her phone in my direction, and I took in the screen, a squeal leaving my lips after registering what she was showing me.

"You uploaded your first video, Buttercup!"

I glanced over, thinking she'd be smiling, only to find a look of horror stretched across her face.

"What's the matter? You nervous?"

"It's only been up for eighteen hours," she said shakily, pointing at the screen. "So many views."

Frowning, I searched for what she meant, and the moment I saw it, I knew.

"Whoa," I murmured. "That is a lot of views."

Five hundred thousand, to be exact.

"Did you look at the comments?"

She shook her head, eyes still stretched wide.

"Too nervous. I... I didn't expect my video to do that."

I hadn't either, but Kali was talented. She had the voice of an angel and played three instruments fluently while taking on the task of learning another.

Eleven-year-old Couri could never.

To relieve some of the stress, I scrolled through the comments, my smile widening with each compliment my gaze roved over.

Such a talent.

We want more!

Wow! What a cover.

There were hundreds of them and she needed to see them.

"Take a look, Buttercup," I handed the phone over after pressing play on the video. "You're an overnight sensation."

We'd written three original songs thus far, but she'd chosen to cover her grandmother's favorite as tribute. Tears pricked the corners of my eyes as I listened to Kali belt the lyrics of "Unforgettable" by Nat "King" Cole in a smooth throaty cadence while playing it on her keyboard.

Goodness.

I could feel my mother hovering, her spirit filling the space as she enjoyed this moment with us. My chest tightened, but I didn't force the sadness away; I needed to feel it or I'd drive myself crazy again.

"I miss her," Kali whispered, drawing my attention to her. "Mom cries in the bathroom at night. Dad always pulls her out, but he's sad, too."

I sighed and took her hand.

"We are all trying our best to be okay, but it'll take time."

"I know." She flashed those big brown eyes at me and my heart broke. "Do you think Nana is proud of me?"

"Nana is smiling down on you, beaming as we speak. I think those five hundred thousand views in less than twenty-four hours is a sign that she's watching over you."

Kali threw herself over the center console and wrapped her arms around my neck.

"I love you," she whispered. "Please don't ever leave me."

Fuck.

It was a promise I couldn't make, but Kali was smart enough to know that, so I gave her the best possible answer.

"I adore you, and as long as God sees fit, I'll be here in the physical form. Just trust that whenever I have to leave, I'll be in your heart, always."

She sniffled and I held onto her until she was ready to let go.

"Okay." Kali pulled away and wiped her eyes. "I feel better."

"And whenever that sadness hits again, you know where to find me."

She smiled and slid out of my truck, bouncing off into the house like nothing had happened. I could only hope she kept that innocence for a bit longer.

After gathering myself, I made my grand entrance and immediately spotted one of my favorite people in the world.

"Oh, Shiloah!" I screeched in excitement as we rushed one another. "I feel like I haven't seen you in ages."

Shiloah had recently married Kingston's brother Primo but

had been around for years before they finally decided to tie the knot.

"Work has been so hectic, but when Primo said he was coming over to take Kingston somewhere I tagged along for some much-needed girl time. Now that you're here, we can finally crack open this big ass bottle of wine I brought along."

Journi and I glanced at one another and Shiloah caught the exchange.

"Okay... spill. What have I missed?"

"Well..." I dropped down in the reclining chair across from them, pulling the latch on the side to release the footrest. "I'm pregnant as fuck to start."

Her eyes widened.

"Tell her by who," Journi mused, her lips curling mischievously as Shiloah opened the wine bottle.

"Hold on. Let me get a hefty amount of this first."

She filled two glasses, handing one off to Journi before taking her seat.

"Alright, I'm ready now."

"August Hanson," I revealed, knowing she'd recognize the name.

Shiloah gulped half her glass and said, "Start from the beginning and don't leave out any details."

I told them *everything* except the part about marriage being on the table now.

Just say yes and I'll know when to buy a ring.

Life had a way of coming at you fast and hard.

Had August and I always been destined to end up here? It sure as hell felt like it, so then why was I so afraid to say yes?

"How are you two *really* doing?" Shiloah asked, looking between Journi and me.

"Ah, you know..." Journi stood and went into the kitchen. "Doing the best I can, I guess."

I shrugged and closed my eyes, not wanting to be sad.

It only made me sick to my stomach and I couldn't keep doing that to myself.

"Okay... I'm picking up vibes here, and because I'm smart, let's talk about something else."

"I'm glad Primo chose you," I told her, popping one eye to see her face.

"I'm glad I chose her too," Primo chimed in, scaring the hell out of me.

I knelt in my chair and peered at him over the genuine leather.

"Why are you always so light on your feet?"

He smirked but didn't respond.

Instead, he moved his solidly built frame to where Shiloah sat.

I watched him relax and beckon her to him with a little chin lift I might've missed had I not been all in their business.

Primo and Kingston looked a lot alike but were two completely different people.

I guess they'd inherited the physical features from the father they shared, though neither had ever met him.

Kingston was the definition of cool, calm, and collected. He carried a gun and had a no-nonsense demeanor, but Primo had a different type of edge to him, and sometimes I wondered if he used to be into some illegal shit.

When they found one another about ten years ago and started piecing together the truth about their past, it bonded them.

Those two were best friends, and because they both loved designing, drawing, and building shit, going into business felt like the best move.

It worked out.

"You good, Couri?" Primo asked, those syrupy brown eyes pinned to me.

"Y-yeah." I cleared my throat. "Just thinking about how you and Kingston came about."

He nodded but narrowed his eyes to let me know he knew there was more.

"I just enjoy the underdogs coming out on top, that's all."

"Sounds like someone feels like an underdog right now," Kingston chimed in, entering the house with two reusable grocery bags in hand. "Your man requested I stop by and bring this to you."

I frowned, confused by why everyone was looking at me.

"Whose man?"

Journi smacked her lips.

"Girl, our men are right here, so who else's?"

I pushed up into a standing position to see what Kingston was talking about.

He pulled two large food containers from the bags and popped the top on one.

"Oh," I whispered as I approached the island with a smile. "You were talking about August."

"He made you soup?" Shiloah asked, stopping to stand beside me. "Mmm. That smells good."

"His sister made it for me, actually, but I never got around to trying it."

Damn.

In the middle of everything he had going on, the man still found time to show he was taking care of me.

I really meant something to him, huh?

TWENTY

WHEN LOLA ARRIVED, she came with an entourage that I'd expected.

"Hey, cousin," she greeted, bumping my chest with her forehead as she passed.

I greeted Leslie next, who went in for another hug like this morning, sensing I might've needed it.

Landon came hobbling in on a crutch and I shook my head.

"What kinda life-threatening stunt did you pull to end up with a crutch?"

He opened his mouth to respond but his sisters beat him to it, yelling from the kitchen, "He fell down a flight of stairs at work!"

I lifted an eyebrow and Landon smirked.

"Technically," he murmured, only for us to hear. "The love of my life bumped me on purpose after I said something not so nice in a work meeting and I stumbled down a stair or two. She's very sorry and I might be pretending like it's more serious than it is to keep her attention. I think she hates me."

"Yet she's the love of your life?"

"She doesn't know it yet." He adjusted his crutch. "But yes."

It didn't sound like a joke but you never knew with Landon.

"And you decided to keep this charade going around family, too?"

He smiled and I turned away from him.

Landon enjoyed anything that gave him an adrenaline rush. A woman hating him? Yeah, that was right up his alley.

"Hey..." Landon caught up to me, no longer pretending to be hurt. "Lola didn't say what was going on but I'm here for moral support. Whatever you need."

"Appreciate that."

He stepped in front of me to stop my strides, dipping his head to force me to look at him.

We were the same height, and shared the same brown eyes Couri said reminded her of whiskey, but that was where the similarities ended.

Leslie, Lola, and Landon had their mother's reddish-brown skin and the smattering of freckles on her nose too.

"Don't start shutting us out. I know you."

The Hanson cousins were raised like siblings; we got one another, and confided in each other, but sometimes like our parents, we pulled away when shit was too much.

"I'm not," I told him, truthfully. "I'm adjusting, not shutting anybody out."

He regarded me closely then went in for a hug.

"Love you, Aug."

I enclosed my arms around him.

"Love you back, Lan."

"When you two are done with your little bromance moment, August, I need to see you in the kitchen," Lola interrupted.

It was enough to catch my attention.

"I don't like the tone of your voice."

She was focused on the petition, flipping pages slowly, while the frown on her face deepened by the second.

"I figured this is why I'm here. Have you read through it completely?"

I shook my head.

"I wasn't in the right headspace after seeing what it was."

Lola sighed, her brows furrowed.

"Michigan is one of those states that believes in grandparents having rights," she explained. "But, not to the extent that they'd take custody from a parent who isn't a danger to the child. Especially not one with a stable career and supportive family."

I toyed with the baby monitor on the counter, my heart upstairs with January who was sound asleep.

"Have you ever considered that January might not be yours?" she asked, stabbing me in the chest with her question. "And before you start glowering at me, I'm your attorney and not your cousin right now."

I took a deep breath, reminding myself that she was right.

"It hasn't crossed my mind."

She flipped back two pages and tapped a section.

"Helen Thomas is requesting a paternity test. Here it states that you may not be the biological father and on those grounds, the custody of the child should be awarded to the maternal grandmother."

The fuck.

Before I knew it, laughter sputtered from my lips.

I was a respectful man; my mother would have my head if I even thought of disrespecting a woman—young or old.

But Helen had me on edge, ready to spazz the fuck out on

her and anybody else who threatened the livelihood of my child.

She had called *me*.

I hadn't come looking for a child I didn't know I was having.

And as pissed as I was with how Shondra handled her pregnancy, she wouldn't put a kid off on me just for the hell of it.

Not after that letter she'd written.

She was a lot of things but a liar wasn't one of them.

"Okay... are we laughing because we aren't worried or are we about to have a mental breakdown? I'm not good with those. I'll call your sisters, they'll know what to do."

I didn't have a chance to stop her but it was probably best I had them here.

My sisters were my lifelines; I would always need them.

"So, listen," Lola started again after ending her call with June. "I know you believe you're sure but the court is ordering you to take a DNA test."

I nodded.

"Whatever I have to do."

"We'll start there and then I'm gonna do my job. If you want she'll never see our girl again..." She looked around. "Speaking of, can we meet her now?"

Landon's head shot up from his phone.

"That's the other reason why I'm here," he said. "I want to meet the new member of our family. You've been holding out for weeks."

I felt a tinge of remorse for being so anal about visitors but the feeling dissipated quickly.

"I was waiting until after he was done with that diabolical laughter to ask for another peek," Leslie chimed from in front of the coffee maker. "I didn't get to really take her in this morning."

I waved them off and started toward the stairwell. When no one followed, I turned.

"Are y'all coming or not?"

The three of them jumped up in tandem and I chuckled, though deep down inside I was losing my fucking mind.

First custody and now I was being led to believe I'd taken in a baby that wasn't even mine.

I knew in my heart that January belonged to me. The feeling I'd gotten after seeing her for the first time was that of a father. The need to protect and provide, to guide through life.

Helen wasn't taking that from me to quell her grief. *Fuck that shit.*

"Such a beauty," Leslie cooed, leaning into the crib. "Look at that snout."

I couldn't help the smile that spread across my face; everyone noticed that nose.

"Wow," Lola mumbled. "This is a Hanson baby. I know it with all my heart."

It was as if she'd read my mind.

When we Hansons believed something with our hearts, it was always true.

"So..." Leslie turned to face me. "The girl you brought with you to the appointment this morning... Couri, right?"

I sighed when suddenly all eyes were on me.

"A girl?" Lola asked, gaze bright.

Landon was too busy staring into the crib in awe but I knew he was half-listening.

"Yeah..." I nodded. "Couri is her name. My girlfriend."

Or soon-to-be wife if she'll have me.

"So, you have a baby and a girlfriend who isn't freaked out by it," Lola mused softly.

"I'd like to know when you got a girlfriend and why we haven't officially met her yet?" Leslie asked.

"You met her today."

She rolled her eyes and I shrugged, taking a step forward after January started to fuss, but Landon beat me to it. He lifted and cradled the back of her head gently.

"That's right, little mama, come to cousuncle."

Lola rolled her eyes but that smile was apparent.

"Couri and I aren't new but our relationship is," I told them, deciding to be honest. "We get one another."

"She's pretty," Leslie said, looking at Lola. "Like drop-dead gorgeous."

"And she's with him," Lola teased. "Mmph."

"I think I'm in love," Landon sang, staring down at January like he'd caught a case of baby fever.

"Me too," I murmured, glancing at Lola. "Which is why I need you to make sure no one can ever take her from me."

She nodded.

"I got your back but to ease your mind, no court will take this petition seriously."

"Us Hansons stick together," Landon added. "I'll help you smuggle her out the country before that old hag gets her way."

From the look in his eyes, he was dead serious.

I wondered if Couri would come with us then shook the thought away.

January and I weren't leaving the country; it wouldn't come to that.

"Oh..." I turned and walked up the hall to my bedroom and into the closet where I'd hidden Shondra's letter. "You might need this," I told Lola, handing it to her after I returned.

She pulled the piece of paper from the envelope and read over it, her eyes widening before a frown marred her face.

"The fuck," she mumbled, meeting my gaze. "She wrote this?"

I nodded.

"And her mother made sure I received it."

"That dumb bitch." She nodded slowly. "She better hope the judge throws this shit out because I plan to eat her alive."

I smiled.

There she was.

Lola was a beast of an advocate for her clients and I trusted her with my life and that of my kid.

Knowing that, I had this urge to tell them about the baby with Couri. It was time everyone knew what was coming.

I leaned my shoulder against the doorframe and crossed my arms, watching them fuss over who got to hold January next.

"Before I announce this to my parents, I wanted y'all to know that Couri is pregnant."

Three sets of eyes darted in my direction at my confession.

"It wasn't planned but we're happy about it."

"Well, shit." Landon shook his head. "Let the rest of us catch up why don't you."

"Not me," Lola blurted, sounding disgusted by the idea of having her own kids. "I'm still in my prime."

"You're thirty-one," Leslie pointed out, earning a glare from her younger sister.

"Exactly..." Lola shoved her. "My prime!"

I watched them bicker and all I could think about was January having a slew of cousins and siblings to do this with later in life.

There was nothing like family, especially ours.

Later that night, after my sisters came to crash the party, and made their exit with everyone else a few hours later, I called Couri.

She answered right away and I immediately noticed the head on her chest, sleeping soundly.

"Hey, Angel face," I greeted, earning a megawatt smile from her. "Sleeping beauty wouldn't let you leave her presence, huh?"

Couri brushed her fingers through Kali's hair.

"Practically threw herself at me when I announced I was heading home. I couldn't leave after that."

I nodded, understanding that her family was still grieving and probably would continue to for a while.

"You should know that June's soup was a hit. Thank you."

"Don't thank me. I know I got shit going on but you're always on my mind." I closed my eyes briefly. "I miss you."

Our gazes met and I knew she missed me too without ever having to hear the words.

"I miss you back." She dropped her gaze. "How'd everything go with Lola?"

I sighed.

"The court is ordering I take a paternity test," I told her. "Helen is basically saying that January isn't mine but I know she is."

Couri dropped her head back, bottom lip tucked between her teeth.

"You know what I hope for?" she asked, still looking away from the camera.

"What's that?"

"I hope that a year from now the dark clouds hovering over us are long gone. I hope we get to be happy and in love with ourselves, each other, and the family we're building. I want to wake up and smile first thing in the morning because I'm grateful for the life God has afforded me."

She pulled the phone to her face, revealing teary eyes.

"I'm not there yet but I figured speaking it aloud wouldn't hurt."

Fuck. She was breaking my heart but giving me a sense of hope all at once.

I rolled over in bed and turned the camera so she could see who was sharing the space with me.

"Oh hey, Snowflake," she cooed softly. "Seems like she's settling in much better."

"Yeah..." I rested my finger in her little palm and she squeezed it. "Seems so."

I flipped the camera back and stared at Couri, missing her even more now that we were on the phone.

"Do you want to know what I hope for?" I asked, finally finding the words I'd been searching for.

"Sharing is caring."

"A year from now I hope to be married to my soulmate. I hope she sees every day how much I adore her through my actions and that our children see it too. I want to wake up looking forward to her smiling face because it'll be the highlight of my day. I want peace and calm but with the chaos two kids will bring, maybe more if it's in the cards. I hope to have that with you. I want that with *you*, no one else."

We stared at one another, no words needed to express how in sync we were with our wants.

She was it for me and I had proof; her actions since the day I told her about January were all I'd needed to figure it out.

"I love you, August," she whispered. "I wish I had the patience to tell you that to your face, but I can't hold it in anymore. I'm in love with you."

Nothing could have prepared me for those three words.

This had been a long time coming; our feelings weren't new but our circumstances sped up the process.

I knew what being in love felt like, at least I'd thought so until she came along and showed me what I'd been missing out on all these years.

This was a different kind of love, the all-consuming kind.

I wasn't pouring from an empty cup anymore.

She filled me up without having to take from herself.

"I love you, Couri," I murmured back, admiring the smile lifting the corners of her mouth. "You have no idea how much I love your smile, especially when it reaches your eyes."

We sat in our feelings for a moment and I realized I'd gotten my answer.

Couri Mitchell was absolutely worth standing in the silence at four in the morning while sharing a cup of coffee. Even the mornings I couldn't help but make her whimper my name.

She was worth a thousand of those, more if I have my way.

TWENTY-ONE

couri

"YOU'RE HERE!"

I couldn't believe who was sitting on my doorstep when I arrived, but it made me unabashedly happy.

"We missed you." August pointed to January, who was wide awake in her carrier, eyes moving rapidly as she took in her surroundings. "I'm actually off to see my parents, but when you said you were on your way home, I decided to stop by and wait for you."

I walked up to him with my arms out, and he stood, allowing me to bury myself in his warmth.

I was full with him around.

He filled me up in ways no man ever had.

"I'm so happy to see you." I looked up, my fingers digging into his back. "Last night I—"

"You told me you were in love with me."

Our eyes danced.

"I'm so in love with you, August Hanson. You have no idea."

My heart raced in anticipation.

He'd reciprocated his love last night, but something about

hearing it with his arms wrapped around me was different. It made me giddy inside.

"I have an idea. I feel what you feel."

He guided my head to his chest and squeezed me tight.

"I'm head over heels in love with you, Couri Mitchell..." He dropped his hand from the back of my head and slipped it between us, placing it against my hardened stomach. "We created something beautiful together, and whether planned or not, I'm grateful."

Little gurgling noises from January startled me before I could respond and August laughed.

"Yo, she started doing that shit this morning and I almost had a heart attack. Leslie won't let me live that frantic call down. She had to remind me that it wasn't the first time I'd dealt with a baby and should know the sound by heart."

I pulled away and smiled up at him.

"She's happy. Content."

He nodded.

"Yeah, apparently so."

August leaned in and I met him halfway, eager to feel his lips on mine.

His confidence had skyrocketed and I loved that for him. August had no reason to be insecure about his parenting skills because no new parent miraculously got it right the first time. He was doing an amazing job.

"Come inside for a minute," I suggested after pulling away to catch my breath but not wanting them to leave yet. "It's getting a little cold out. I want to warm you two up before you go."

Michigan hadn't gotten the memo that spring had sprung; the winds were stronger than ever, with some of that winter chill lingering.

"We have a little time to spare," he said, picking up the car seat as I started toward the front door. "Even if we didn't, I still wouldn't have said no."

I chuckled and stepped into my place after unlocking the door. As I silenced the alarm, August maneuvered himself past me, grazing my ass with the tips of his fingers along the way.

"You did that on purpose," I accused, smirking in his direction.

August kept moving down the hall into the living room, ignoring my accusation.

He set the carrier on the coffee table, unbuckled January, and placed her against his chest.

"Kinda hard to keep my hands off you when you're wearing those leggings," he said, slowly dropping his gaze. "I want to take you on a date."

Our eyes met and I tipped my head.

"You went from talking about my leggings to asking me on a date."

He smiled.

"Only spoke what came to mind."

"I see..." I walked toward him and balanced myself on the tips of my toes. "What do you have in mind?"

I kissed January's cheek and played the staring game while she got acclimated to my face. I'd read a long time ago that babies liked to make eye contact with people more than random objects at a month old.

"I want you for an entire day."

"A whole day of adventures?" I asked, glancing up at him.

"A whole day," he confirmed.

I nodded and met January's wandering eyes again. Her face was filling out, cheeks protruding in the cutest way as she grew into her chubbiness.

"I'd love to spend a day with you."

"Next Saturday. We'll start with breakfast and work our way to dinner."

I brushed my nose against January's then adjusted her cotton zip-up jacket with a unicorn on the front. She had a pair of matching bottoms with a horn stitched into the butt.

"I won't keep you any longer." I took a step back and leveled my feet to the floor. "I'm sure your parents are excited to see her and I'm having dinner with my friend Bea here in a few hours. Lately, I've been distant, so we have to talk."

It was time for me to open up to someone other than family.

Plus, I trusted Bea.

"I guess we're both making announcements today." He fastened January in her seat and pulled me into him. "I'm telling my parents about us and the baby. I told Leslie and her siblings, Lola and Landon, last night."

I pressed my forehead against his chest as he stroked my back.

"We're making it more real now," I whispered. "I'm scared."

He tightened his hold on me.

"I don't know if it'll make you feel better, but I'm scared too."

It felt nice to hear him express it to me openly.

"Okay..." I backed away and swiped my clammy hands down my leggings. "You have to go or I'll beg you to stay."

He chuckled a little and shook his head.

"I'm not opposed to hearing you beg, but we'll discuss that later."

I crossed my legs to stop the insistent thumping coming from my pussy.

He turned me on without doing much.

"I'll go, but we'll talk later, okay?"

I nodded and followed him to the door, watching from the top step as he neared his truck parked on the street and strapped January's seat in.

"FaceTime like always," I called, earning a wink and nod.

He walked to the driver's side door but stood there, eyeing me over the hood.

"I love you," August said, his voice carrying.

"And I love you."

We stared at one another for a while before he slipped into the driver's seat and drove away. I missed him already and he likely hadn't hit the stop sign at the end of the block yet.

He was part of me now... I touched my stomach and smiled.

In so many ways.

* * *

"So..." Bea eyed me from across the counter, a glass of wine in hand. "You aren't drinking."

I removed the fresh salmon filets from the pan, grateful the smell hadn't sent me under. As I laid them atop the kale salad Bea made, my mouth watered.

August would be happy to hear that I'd eaten something of substance.

Shaking thoughts of him away, I glanced at my friend.

"Not for another seven-ish month," I confessed. "Or more if I decide to breastfeed."

Her eyes widened while my mind started on a journey, reminding me of the benefits of breastfeeding. But did I really want my nipples raw or the pain that could come from clogged ducts?

Nope!

"Are you saying you're pregnant?"

I nodded and turned toward the stove.

"Very much so." I spun back with my homemade garlic butter and smiled. "I'm happy but nervous and scared and so fucking unprepared."

I picked up our plates and moved toward the nook in my kitchen.

"Well, first, congratulations," she said, eyes still bright with surprise. "You've been through a lot recently, so I'm happy to hear you're happy about something."

Bea slid into a chair and I set a plate in front of her before doing the same for myself.

"I'm starving," I mumbled, closing my eyes to say a prayer and forking a good amount of salmon and Kale. "Mmm..." I nodded. "So. Damn. Good."

As silence loomed around us, I looked up with a mouthful to find Bea watching me curiously.

"What?" I set my fork down and touched my mouth. "Is there something on my face?"

Bea shook her head.

"Sorry. No, that isn't it."

I watched the expression on her face go from stoic to shock then sadness right before my eyes. She blinked rapidly, but nothing stopped the tears she'd been trying to keep inside from falling.

Bea covered her mouth and looked away.

"Bea, honey..." I slid my chair back to get to her. "What's going on? What happened?"

I turned her chair toward me and kneeled, my eyes burning with tears as Bea's sobs grew louder. She leaned into me and I held her as tight as possible while softly praying for her peace of mind.

Had I been so wrapped up in my own shit that I missed being there for my friend when she needed someone? The thought of that broke my heart because she'd been there for me when my mother passed, offering more than just her condolences.

Slowly, her shoulders ceased their shaking and the sobs stopped.

I waited until she was ready to speak, and eventually, she found her voice.

"I'm so sorry," she apologized, pulling away to wipe her face. "This isn't about me. Let's eat and forget this happened."

I stood and entered the living room to grab the new box of Kleenex I'd placed there right before she arrived. Once Bea had the box, I slid into the seat beside her.

"There's no way I can forget that," I told her gently. "You can talk to me, you know? I'm so sorry I missed the signs that you were struggling."

"I'm really good at hiding how I'm feeling," she said, red-rimmed eyes meeting mine. "Don't apologize. I chose to suffer alone. You had so much going on already and I needed time to process what happened to me."

She looked away and sighed.

"Your news brought the tears out of me. I hadn't cried until now. This is so fucked up because I'm happy..." Her eyes found mine again. "I'm happy for you, genuinely."

I nodded because it never crossed my mind that she wasn't.

My chest tightened a little after a few seconds of silence, something deep inside me understanding where this was going.

"Do you remember the car accident from high school?"

It wasn't an event I could forget.

Bea and her parents were on their way from visiting her maternal grandparents in Ohio in the middle of winter. Though her father had been driving as carefully as possible, their car hit a patch of black ice and flipped four times.

"You had emergency surgery to stop internal bleeding in your pelvis."

She gave me a watery smile.

"Your memory has always been on point. That surgery changed my life, and because of it, keeping a pregnancy to term has been impossible. Brian and I broke up after the third miscarriage recently. He doesn't want someone..." Her shoulders shook, but she recovered quickly. "...someone broken."

"Oh, Bea." I reached for her hands. "You aren't broken and fuck Brian Sylvester. I'll chop him in the throat the next time I see him for putting that on you. There's always a method to the madness, and I know saying that doesn't help what you're feeling right now, but God has a plan."

I stroked her fingers with my thumbs.

"Jesus, Bea. Don't deal with this alone anymore. I'm here."

She wrapped her fingers around mine and squeezed.

"I really need a friend, so thank you for that."

I stood and pulled her into my arms.

"You're special, Bea Richardson, and I'm grateful to have you as my friend."

"So grateful to have you," she muttered back.

We found an easy rhythm again after that emotional moment, filling one another in on the happenings of our lives recently. I scraped my plate clean, then went for more kale salad.

"You're definitely pregnant. I've never seen you eat so fast before."

I chuckled and stuffed my mouth, chewing slowly to savor the taste.

"I haven't been able to keep anything down," I told her after swallowing. "August was getting a little worried, so I'm happy to regain my appetite, even if it's only for a little while."

Bea regarded me closely then gasped.

"Oh my God," she exclaimed, lips spreading into a knowing grin. "August is the guy who came to see you at the conservatory last year."

My skin heated at her realization.

"Mmhm," I hummed. "We've been under each other since, and now this." I pointed my fork at my stomach. "He also has a daughter."

"Really? How old?"

"She hit the month-old mark recently."

Bea's eyes widened, but the frown on her face spoke volumes.

"Were you two..."

I shook my head.

"We weren't exclusive, but he hasn't dealt with anyone else since we met."

I didn't actually know if that was true but something told me it was.

Bea's frown deepened.

"His ex didn't tell him she was pregnant," I explained, probably sounding like I was being manipulated by a fuckboy. "It's been kinda crazy in my life lately."

I omitted the part about Shondra being gone and her mother fighting for custody. We'd had enough emotional conversations for the day.

"But you're happy with August and everything else? That's all that matters here."

I nodded without needing to think about it.

"He's everything, Bea. I want you to meet him soon to see for yourself."

As if he'd known I was talking about him, my phone vibrated on the counter with a text from August.

My parents are officially inviting you and your family to Sunday dinner next week. You down?

"Any plans for next Sunday?" I asked Bea while typing my reply.

I'm down.

TWENTY-TWO

I HADN'T TOLD Couri I'd officially been served Saturday after she left, making Helen's petition valid.

The hired processor had been confused when I asked why I needed to be served twice. After explaining that the person petitioning the court brought them herself, he schooled me on something that left me angrier than before.

Helen hadn't needed to come and drop off those papers; she wanted to. In fact, because she was the reason for the custody hearing, she couldn't serve me at all.

"I'll have a word with that hussy soon," my mother barked, tossing the papers on the coffee table. "Real soon."

My father sat silently beside her, trying to get January to stand on his thighs. Instead of stretching her legs, she kept them bent inward but kicked every now and again in glee.

"Ma, do you really want to end up in front of the honorable Judge Paula Hanson again?" June asked, her lips curling into a smile. "Last time you got a little rowdy and ended up in custody, she threatened to lock you up for a week if she ever saw you again."

June was playing with fire and knew it.

Our mother had no qualms about giving somebody a piece of her mind and sometimes fists. It hadn't happened in a while, but she wasn't against making it happen.

She was fierce, especially about the girls and me.

"June Hanson, now isn't the time," she warned, her fiery gaze giving me chills. "Furthermore, Judge Hanson can kiss my ass too. She knows what's up."

Dad snorted and said, "My sister already doesn't like coming to events because she's scared of you. Ending up in her courtroom will only give her ideas, like using her power to send you to jail."

"Aunt Paula is a little snooty," Tem murmured as she entered the living room with a warmed bottle in hand. "But she's not like that with us. Ma just likes to intimidate people for fun."

There had always been bad blood between our mom and dad's oldest sister, Paula.

She'd been protective of him, their other six siblings, and the family business growing up.

Once my mother entered the picture, Aunt Paula quickly learned that not everybody would take her shit. Something about a fight and thirteen stitches put her in her place once and for all.

"We're getting off track," I cut in. "This is happening whether you put hands on her or not, and for the record, I'd rather you not. After everything is settled, feel free to do as you please, but I can't put January at risk."

My mother's eyes softened as she nodded.

"All I need from you five..." I met eyes with my sisters then my parents. "...is your support. That's it."

"You have that without ever having to ask," Dad chimed in, his gaze on January as she sucked down her bottle in his arms.

"There's something else I need to talk to the both of you

about," I continued, snatching my eyes away from my little girl. "I've been dating someone."

They glanced at one another, sharing an intimate conversation between husband and wife. I could feel my sisters' gazes lingering on me but refused to take my eyes off our parents.

"Is it serious?" Dad asked as they gave me their undivided attention again. "You would only be telling us if it were serious."

I nodded.

"She went to January's first appointment with me."

My mother leaned in, regarding me closely.

"There's still something missing from this confession, spill it."

I smiled and my sisters chuckled.

There hadn't been a chance of me getting one over on Adrina Hanson.

"In about seven months, you'll be a grandmother of two."

She frowned, but I knew it was because my words weren't fully registering.

"The person you've been dating," she said, more to herself than me. "Is pregnant with your baby. About two months along."

July whistled and said, "Okay, Mom with the math skills."

It earned her a death glare, but she looked proud of herself regardless.

"Yeah, you got it right." I nodded. "And I want y'all to accept her openly because she means a lot to me. More than a lot."

"You love her," my father stated.

It wasn't a question, he knew it to be true without needing my confirmation, but I answered anyway.

"Deeply."

For a while, no one spoke, but then Mom did a weird squeal and jumped up.

"Oh, August," she cooed, pulling me up from my seat to hug me. "You have no idea how happy I am to hear this."

She was talking like I'd announced an engagement, but the joy seeping from her made me smile.

"Ma, don't—"

"Tell me about her," she cut in, leaving me no room to finish my statement. "From the look on your sisters' faces, I know they've met her already."

"On accident," I mumbled, dropping down in the reclining chair after she released me. "Her name is Couri and she's a Zoologist."

She was brilliant.

And beautiful.

Soft but never a pushover.

Couri was so many things and I adored her for them.

"We didn't know that," June chimed in. "What animal does she work with?"

"Not lions..." I smirked in her direction, thinking about the big cat I'd adopted on her behalf for our birthday in a few months. "Penguins."

That still seemed to pique her interest and I wouldn't put it past June to visit the conservatory soon.

"How about you invite her to Sunday dinner?" Dad suggested, earning nods all around.

It was an easy yes for me but with stipulations.

"Kingston is her brother-in-law," I told them. "That's how we met. His wife, Journi, is her sister and they recently lost their mother. It's still fresh, so if you're cool with it, I'd like to extend that invitation to the entire family."

Mom's eyes were watery by the time I finished my request. She was a badass softie.

"I'm sure they could use some love from you, Ma," I added, needing her to understand.

"Of course, August." She wiped the free-falling tears away and took Dad's hand after he reached for her in support. "We'll eat in the big dining room."

I saw her mentally planning the menu and grabbed my phone to text Couri.

She wrote back immediately, accepting the invitation.

For a short moment, I was happy.

Life was starting to take shape, and I needed that, but eventually, my eyes landed on the custody petition and reality set in. Nothing would be okay until Helen was taken care of.

"Pops, do you mind keeping January for an hour? I need to make a run."

He gave me an odd look but nodded.

"Thanks." I stood. "I won't be long."

Before anyone could question me, I got out of dodge and drove across town to Helen Thomas's home. She and I needed to talk face to face and it would be the first and only time I tried to appeal to her.

When I arrived, she stood outside talking to Shondra's godsister, Monique. Both turned as I exited my truck.

"Monique," I greeted as I approached. "You good?"

She shrugged, her dark eyes taking me in.

"Good as I can be," she replied. "What are you doing here?"

"I'm not here for you." I stopped in front of Helen and she took a step back. "I need to know why you're trying to take my daughter from me."

Her gaze moved past me, then she looked down.

"What is he talking about, Auntie?" Monique asked, moving around me to stand next to Helen.

"You need to leave," she said, ignoring our questions. "Whatever you got to say can be done in court."

I stared at her for a minute, taking in her puffy eyes, barely combed hair, and baggy clothes. She looked as if she'd lost a lot of weight, too.

"Are you eating?" I asked, lifting my gaze to meet hers. "Taking care of yourself?"

She didn't respond, but it was all the answer I needed.

"Do you think taking January from me will suddenly make the pain go away? You think she'll make you want to get out of bed in the morning?" I leaned forward and dropped my head to be eye-to-eye with her. "Helen, nothing will bring Shondra back. Doing the exact opposite of her wishes won't bring her back. The only thing you'll accomplish is losing a chance to be part of January's life."

"Auntie—"

"Leave!" Helen shouted, stumbling backward before stepping toward the front door. "The both of you!"

She slammed the door and Monique sighed.

"I'm sorry, August," she said, turning to me. "I knew she was struggling, but I didn't think it was this bad."

I glanced at Monique, irritated with her presence.

"Shondra made it clear to us that she wanted you to have January. Didn't you get the papers she signed? At least, I think she got around to signing them."

I brushed a hand down my face, frustrated all over again.

"What papers?"

"She had papers drawn up to give up her parental rights." She released a shaky breath. "I don't know how it works or if she had to wait until after the baby was born to make it official, but she's been unequivocal about you taking custody."

I frowned.

"All I got was a letter she'd written."

Monique's eyes widened, then she glanced at the front door.

"I don't think Helen will let me in to look through some of Shondra's things, but here's the lawyer she used to do it..." She pulled her phone out and scrolled through her contacts. "Barton Brown. I don't know if he'll be allowed to talk to you, but his office is in Royal Oak."

I felt my phone vibrate in my pocket and knew it was her.

"What else did she say during her pregnancy?"

Monique tipped her head toward the driveway, and I followed, noticing a shift in the blinds as we migrated away from the front of the house.

"I begged her to tell you, but she had her mind made up."

"Made up about what? Not wanting me to be there?"

"No." She shook her head. "About not wanting you to see life leaving her eyes every day. I didn't want to believe she wouldn't make it, but she'd been convinced."

Shondra had been selfish and there wasn't anything anyone could say to change my mind. All she had to do was make one phone call, and instead, she left me to pick up the pieces without time to prepare, not once thinking of what it would do to me and our daughter—especially when she was old enough to ask questions.

"I have to go, but I really am sorry about Helen," Monique said, walking between our cars. "Everything will work out. I'll even give a statement if you need it."

I nodded and moved around my truck to the driver's side.

"I'd appreciate that."

I opened my door just as Monique called out to me.

"I know Shondra didn't want to be a mother, and that might've meant none of us could be in January's life if she were here..." She sighed. "But she isn't here and I want to be part of that little girl's life. Only if it's alright with you. There won't be no love lost if it isn't, just as long as you tell her about me when she's old enough to decide who she wants in her life."

I took a second to think about what she was saying, though I knew my answer to her request.

None of them had asked for this.

"You need to be consistent," I said. "Either you're in her life or you aren't. There's no in-between."

"I'm all the way in. Thank you, August."

She gave me one last look and slid into her car, which prompted me to do the same.

As I drove away, I thought about how I hadn't accomplished anything.

Thanks a fucking lot, Shondra.

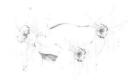

couri

"LOOK." I lifted my shirt after August closed his bedroom door. "This happened fast. I looked it up; it's apparently normal."

He took measured steps toward me, his eyes on my stomach.

It had rounded out in the last five days.

We'd seen one another every day this week but today... Today we were alone.

January was with her grandparents until Sunday, giving August and me the weekend to have a date and then some.

"It's beautiful," he murmured, lowering himself in front of me. "How do you feel?"

He caressed the bump while placing soft kisses all over that went straight to my pussy.

I was so goddamn horny my bones ached.

"I feel..." I rested my hands atop his head as he slowly began to peel my cotton shorts from my body. "Like I might be in heat."

He chuckled against my skin and looked up at me, his fingers dancing along my inner thigh.

"I've been neglectful," he mused, eyes turning molten right before mine. "Never again."

August wrapped his arms around me and pulled my pussy into his mouth. With his gaze lifted and on me, he slid his tongue along my slit until it connected with my clit.

I threw my head back, grateful for his tight hold on me.

"Yes, baby."

I shuddered against him as he feasted on me like no other time before.

My mouth began to water, and suddenly, I wanted nothing more than to devour him whole, to feel his dick tapping the back of my throat while I took it like a big girl.

"Uh uhn," he grumbled, teeth grazing my clit.

Sparks shot up my back and I tried pulling away again, needing so badly to taste him on my tongue.

He lifted my left leg on his shoulder instead of giving in to my silent request.

I couldn't fight the feeling spreading throughout my core, so I stayed put, chasing the high only he could provide.

Grabbing the back of his head, I rolled my pussy into his mouth.

"Bite it," I begged, wanting to feel those sparks and let them take me over the edge.

August gave me what I wanted, scraping my clit gently with his teeth before rolling it between them with more pressure.

My body lit up from the friction.

"Oh, fuck..."

He must've taken that as a good sign because the most delicious mixture of pain and pleasure surged through me as he bit down harder on the sensitive nub.

My body careened forward as I came, leaving me unsteady on my feet.

August caught me as he laughed.

Cocky bastard.

Rightfully so.

Once I caught just enough breath to make a move on him, I went for it.

August didn't question my motives as I led him to the bed and pushed his body down.

He fell back and watched me through low lids as I dropped to the floor between his thighs.

"Love you down there," he murmured, pushing his fingers into my mane.

I smirked and pulled at his basketball shorts while admiring the way his dick stood up in them.

"You can't keep it from me for so long anymore." I marveled at its length, brushing my fingers down the underside as I swiped the pre-cum away with my tongue. "You just can't."

He hissed as I engulfed his penis until my mouth was full.

I looked into his eyes then went to work, never breaking eye contact and appreciating his sheer determination to keep his eyes on me.

"F-fuck, woman." He thrust his hips forward, connecting the tip of his dick with the back of my throat. "Mmhm."

I loved the way he looked at me as I took him a little further down my throat without gagging. He pushed up and cupped my face before fucking it slowly.

"You look beautiful like this."

My eyes watered and my pussy wouldn't stop thumping.

Goodness. I love this man.

"Open up, Angel face."

I opened wide while playing with my pussy, and he lost it, stroking my slick mouth with vigor.

My chest burned with need. I couldn't get enough of him.

With my face still in his hands, dick buried in my mouth, August stood and leaned my body backward.

"I want it right down your throat," he groaned, hardening as he came.

His moans drove me through a wall and over the edge into pure bliss.

I'd been so far gone that I missed him lifting me from the floor until his lips were against mine, uncaring of the mess we'd made covering my mouth and chin.

"I fucking love you."

"I love you so much." I dropped my forehead to his chest and took deep breaths. "I need more."

This baby had heightened my sex drive by astronomical numbers. There wasn't anything I could do but beg for the dick.

And I had no qualms about it.

"Please..." I lifted my head to find him staring down at me, lust and love and something unrecognizable dancing in his whiskey browns. "I need you to fuck me."

He chuckled and I'd been so focused on how it dripped seduction that him spinning and bending me over right where we stood caught me off guard.

The shock lasted for only a second before my pussy gushed in excitement.

"Hold your ankles," he demanded, slipping his dick between my wet pussy lips while gripping my ass. "Spread 'em."

He kicked my legs until I was just as he wanted me.

Everything felt exposed, but I didn't mind because I knew the look in his eyes would have me blushing.

"Hold on tight." He slammed into me and I shook from the impact, propelling forward but not getting far. "No running..."

He withdrew and surged forward again. "Take it like the slut I know you are."

"Your slut," I whimpered, rocking back to meet his relentless strokes. "Don't stop!"

He fucked me like I was a *nasty* slut to be exact, slapping and gripping my ass as he tugged me deeper into him.

I could feel him in my stomach and chest, filling me up just like I needed.

"Good ass pussy," he growled, pressing his thumb into my ass.

I shuddered, allowing myself to succumb, to submit to his every whim.

August could fuck me every which way from Sunday, call me all kinds of sluts while stroking my pussy, and would still go back to treating me with care after.

I trusted him wholeheartedly.

"August, I can't," I cried. "I can't. I can't."

It was too much.

My entire body buzzed, echoing loudly in my ears as I did exactly what I thought I couldn't.

"That's my good girl," August praised, slowing his strokes but keeping the pace steady. "Use this time wisely; I'm not finished yet."

God yes.

Hours later, we were both thoroughly fucked but wide awake.

I was positioned vertically in the middle of the bed, while August was horizontal with his head in my lap.

His arms were in the air with a family-sized bag of Skittles between his fingers.

"Red is the best color," I mused, popping three in my mouth. "Unless it's the sour kind, then blue."

"I'll take all the reds from the new bag I bought and put them in this one for you after we empty it."

I wasn't surprised.

He would literally do anything for me, even without me having to ask.

"What if we're having a boy? Do you want a junior?"

He lifted up on his elbows and glanced at me.

"Haven't thought about it," he said honestly. "I think I'd want our son to have his own identity."

He laid back again and dug in the Skittles bag.

"What do you think?"

"That he'd be proud to have his dad's name."

I caught the curve in his lips before he schooled it.

"What about if it's a girl?" he asked, throwing the question back at me. "I wouldn't be surprised if that's the outcome; my family is run by women. The men are outnumbered."

"Have I ever told you my favorite holiday?"

"Nah but tell me now."

I smiled, thinking about pumpkins, fall weather, scary movies, and candy galore.

Trick or treating, which I only stopped doing at twenty-one but resumed when Kali was old enough to go and really enjoy it.

"Halloween."

It was kind of funny that our baby's due date fell close to the spooky holiday.

"You know..." He chuckled. "That doesn't surprise me for some reason."

"If we have a daughter," I mused, feeling wistful. "I want to name her October."

He was silent for a while but eventually filled the space around us with his deep baritone again.

"You want to keep the tradition going?" he asked softly.

"My sisters decided a long time ago they wouldn't give their kids calendar names. I understand why but I always wanted it for mine."

"I want to inherit your traditions, August. I want to mix them with mine while we create our own."

"So, you want to do life with me."

"Yeah..." Our eyes met, and we smiled at one another. "I want to do life with you."

"January will grow up thinking you're her mother."

I nodded.

"How do we approach that when she's old enough to know? Do you want her to know about Shondra?"

He sighed.

"I don't have a choice, but I wouldn't keep that from her even if I did. What's done in the dark always comes to light and I couldn't stomach her finding out then hating me for it."

I moved to lay beside him.

He cuddled me, dragging my body damn near atop his.

"She didn't want her. How am I supposed to explain that?"

"You'll follow her lead and answer her questions honestly. She'll appreciate you more, even if the truth hurts her a little. My mom was big on honesty. I want us to be that way with our girls."

Our girls had a nice ring to it; I was team girl.

August dropped his chin atop my head and held me tighter.

"Thank you for accepting her," he said, voice thick with emotion. "I almost walked away from you because I didn't think you'd be able to."

I thought of the day I buried my mother, how he'd shown up at my place afterward and wasn't like himself.

"I knew it when you came to me that day. You were being—"

"Weird," he finished, making me laugh.

"Yeah, but I hadn't foreseen the reason behind it."

Nothing could have prepared me for that news.

His fingers drifted to my stomach.

"Do you think this happened so we couldn't push each other away?"

"I think I would've given you space then found a way to invade your privacy," I told him. "My obsession with you started well before you got me pregnant; I don't regret any of this."

August didn't need to respond because the way he curled his body into mine was response enough.

He appreciated my words and I prayed he believed me.

We were tangled in silence for a while, breathing in sync until my stomach growled and startled me.

"We need to rectify that," August declared, pulling us apart. "I just stocked up on groceries."

He climbed out of bed, pulled his shirt off, and tossed it to me.

I brought it to my nose and sighed in contentment.

Though he'd been off work for a couple of weeks, he still smelled of honey, brown sugar, and bourbon.

"I'm keeping this." I slipped it on my body. "Love how good you smell all the time."

He winked and pulled a pair of basketball shorts on, sans his briefs.

"Come on, Angel face," he beckoned. "Let me feed you and my baby."

He pulled me from the room with him and down into the kitchen.

"What do you want now that you can stomach more?"

"Bacon!"

I leaned against the counter as he busied himself, grabbing pans and ingredients from the fridge.

The bacon came only after he grabbed eggs, a container of diced green onions, shredded cheese, and mushrooms.

He moved with ease and the comfort of being in the kitchen more often than not. And his was state of the art from the flooring to the appliances.

"What are we doing tomorrow?" I asked, mind suddenly on our all-day date.

August glanced at me, smirked, then returned to slicing open the packet of center-cut bacon.

I guess that meant I had to wait and find out.

TWENTY-FOUR

"WERE you able to get ahold of the lawyer?" I asked Lola after sneaking out of my bedroom while Couri slept.

We'd been up all night, just living in one another's skin, and I knew she was tired.

"No one answered the phone number you were given, but after a quick Google search, I was able to find his office information and drove over there yesterday."

I chuckled, shaking my head.

After Monique had sent over Barton Brown's information, I sent it directly to Lola. She would have had my head if I tried doing her job by contacting him myself.

That was last Sunday and she'd only been able to get in touch with the man on Thursday.

"What did he say?"

"Shondra never got around to signing the papers, and because of that, no court will validate them," she said, her tone cautious. "But, she did have a will, and in it, you were named. Barton stated that you were next on his list of people to get in contact with about her estate."

I leaned against the counter, needing something to hold me up while I listened.

"I don't want anything from her."

"That isn't up to us lawyers, August. You need to meet with him and see what she had to say. It could stop this custody bullshit once and for all."

I took a deep breath and rubbed my temples.

"I know this is a lot," Lola went on, going from lawyer to cousin. "I hate it for you, but the quicker you handle it, the faster I can end this. This is why I scheduled you to meet with Barton on Monday afternoon."

"Alright," I agreed, though I had no choice. "Just send over where the office is."

"Will do." Lola chuckled. "I have to go but be prepared for dinner tomorrow. Your mom just sent virtual invites."

I growled and the last thing I heard from Lola was hearty laughter before the call ended.

"Are you okay?" Couri asked from behind me as she rested her head on my back.

I hadn't heard her come down, but her presence helped to quell my irritation.

"That was Lola," I told her. "Shondra had a will and I guess I was in it. Also, my mother made an invitation for dinner tomorrow. I'm sorry in advance."

Her face vibrated against my back as she laughed.

"I didn't realize this until now..." She moved to stand beside me and leaned into the counter. "But you are such a grump."

I had no idea why but I smiled.

"Have I ever been grumpy with you?"

She shook her head, eyes peering into mine.

"No, but I bet if I asked some of your family tomorrow, they'd agree."

I straightened and grabbed her waist, lifting her on the counter and stepping between her legs.

"If you engage them, they'll never leave you alone," I warned. "Every event, you'll be on their radar."

Couri eyes lit up and I laughed.

"That's right up your alley, huh?"

She tipped her head in thought while securing her fingers at the base of my neck.

"Do you think I can garner enough support for a trivia night if I pretend not to mind being on their radar at future events?" she asked, looking determined. "There has to be someone in that big ol' family of yours who knows random things. Like how a flock of birds is called a colony."

I kissed her nose then her lips.

"You can play trivia with me," I offered, stepping back after mentally deciding to start our day with French toast.

I could feel Couri's gaze as I moved around the kitchen.

"What random things do you know? Something you think I wouldn't."

I had my answer right away.

"Whiskey is Gaelic for water of life. Different versions of whiskey are called expressions."

"Okay, baby daddy! You've earned yourself a place in my trivia brigade."

"Who else is in it?"

"Me and you." She laughed. "I made it up just now."

"My cousin Landon..." I turned toward the counter after accumulating all the ingredients I'd need. "He's an engineer. I vote him in."

Couri nodded.

"I'll test his skills tomorrow," she murmured to herself. "Hey..."

I glanced at her.

"You are okay with this, right? Me meeting your people?"

I frowned.

"Yeah. I asked because I want you there."

She threw her hands up in surrender, a sultry smile pulling at her lips.

"Don't go all macho man on me," she teased, batting her lashes. "Actually, no, keep it up."

I stared, trying to figure out what was different about her today.

"You're happy," I said once it hit me. "I don't think I've heard you spout a random fact or show interest in trivia since—"

"Today I feel more like myself than I have in weeks," she admitted. "I woke up and smiled and I hope it lasts."

I set the whisk in my hand down and went to her, pushing her thighs apart to fill the space between them.

"It's you and me," I murmured into her mouth before taking her lips.

"Mmhm," she moaned, wrapping one leg around my waist. "You and me."

I pulled away before shit could get too hot and heavy.

"We have an agenda," I said, ignoring the pout on her face. "I'm going to feed us then fuck you in the shower nice and slow."

Her pout disappeared immediately.

"And after that?"

"You'll see when we get there but dress comfortably and pack something for dinner."

"Pack?"

I tossed her a look.

"That's what I said."

She smirked and looked away while mumbling, "Keep talking to me like that, and I'll—"

"You'll what?" I challenged.

Her dark gaze slid in my direction, lust dripping from it.

"I'll beg you to stay in bed and fuck all day," she replied silkily. "I know how much you can't resist me when I beg."

Mm, busted.

She could have her way without begging, but I wouldn't tell her that, not when it was my favorite reason for giving in to her.

Instead of responding, I continued making our breakfast.

We had all day to circle back.

* * *

"My ankles are swelling a little." Couri propped her socked feet on the dashboard as I merged onto I-94 going east. "*Ugh.* I'm gonna look like a blowfish soon."

"The cutest fucking blowfish," I mused, smiling as she swatted at me playfully.

"You aren't one of those types who suddenly become unattracted to his woman after she has his baby, because she doesn't look like the woman he met, right?"

She knew the fucking answer to that question.

My actions always spoke louder than my words.

In fact, the most I ever talked had been with Couri.

She brought a version of me out that only the person God had intended for me could.

"You don't take me as that kind of man, act like you know," I said, gently squeezing her knee before settling my hand between her warm thighs. "But, to reassure you, I'm not the type. I was raised by a gentleman. I have a mother, aunts, cousins, and sisters I adore. If any of them ever came to me about their significant other complaining of their body after they'd carried that nigga's baby, I'd make him disappear.

Holding another man's actions to that standard but not my own would make me the worst kind of man."

She was silent for a while, and I let her be, hoping she believed me.

Her body was beautiful and I was in awe of her every time I saw a difference from the pregnancy. Women were magical creatures, but this woman... she was *my* magical creature.

"I know," she murmured after a while. "I don't know what made me ask that."

"You asked because you're a human being with feelings and insecurities, the same as me. Whether aware or not, I'll validate them when asked *and* even when you don't. That's how important you are to me."

She had me wrapped around her finger, but more than that, Couri had my heart.

I took her hand and laced our fingers together.

"We're taking a behind-the-scenes tour at Sea Life," I told her, glancing over just in time to watch her eyes widen.

"You listen to me." She brought our hands to her mouth and kissed my fingers. "Thank you for always hearing me."

Couri acted as if she had no clue how obsessed I was with her.

I heard everything she said to me, no matter what she was saying.

There wasn't a detail I couldn't remember, including her love for all kinds of animals.

Elephants, first.

Penguins and big cats, second.

She liked the water and had spent endless hours telling me about the species no one had ever heard of.

Sea Life was the largest aquarium in the state of Michigan and it happened to be less than an hour's drive away. With over ten exhibits and more than two hundred and fifty species housed in the one hundred and fifty gallons of water, we had a lot of ground to cover.

I had my heart set on the interactive touch pool; my inner child bounced on his toes in anticipation of touching a starfish.

"Oh my goodness," Couri gasped, drawing my eyes off the road briefly to see her knowing smirk trained in my direction. "You're excited about being here too."

I smirked and focused forward.

"Guilty," I admitted. "You bring the kid in me out."

"Does the kid you keep buried most days want to eat at Rainforest Café for lunch after the aquarium?"

She squeezed my hand as I laughed.

"Already part of the plans, Angel face."

Sea Life was tucked inside the Great Lakes Crossing Outlet mall, the perfect place to entertain ourselves, eat, and shop.

Couri had no idea, but I planned to drop a bag on her today.

We made it to the crowded mall and into the aquarium in record time.

Couri craned her neck to see further inside the tank, eager to take everything in at once. Our behind-the-scenes tour would start when we reached the end, but there was much to do before we got there.

We were currently standing inside the underwater ocean tunnel.

There were turtles—my personal favorite—but the sharks had my attention.

I peered up as one moved above my head, swimming like people weren't gawking at it.

"This is *amazing!*" Couri exclaimed.

She took my hand and pulled me along.

"Let's find the stingray beach."

We moved through the exhibits with measured steps, but

everything slowed as we reached the schooling fish. They moved in sync, coordinating their movements and stilling ours to watch.

"I've seen videos, but this is way cooler in person." She turned to me, her eyes wide. "No one has ever done something like this with me before. Not someone interested in me *sexually*."

She'd murmured that last part, but a woman passing with her two kids glared at us, and I knew she heard. With a lifted brow, I waited for the lady to turn and mind some business that wasn't ours.

Once she got the hint, I gave Couri my attention.

"I want to do the things you enjoy," I confessed, pulling her body against mine. "Making you happy makes me happy."

She beamed and I vowed to keep this look on her face for the rest of our lives.

"I love you."

"I love yo—"

"August," a voice behind us called, pissing me off. "Hey..." Monique moved around to make herself known. "I thought that was you."

"Wassup, Monique."

I spotted her son with his face pressed against the glass and frowned.

"You should tell him not to do that," I said, pointing.

She gave me a weird expression I couldn't decipher, her gaze bouncing from me to Couri, who rested leisurely against me, unbothered by Monique's presence.

"Jasper, pull your face back," she instructed without glancing in his direction. "Where's January?"

"With my parents."

I pushed my fingers into Couri's curls, and she moaned a little, drawing a smile out of me.

"This is Couri, by the way. My girlfriend."

Monique blinked slowly then smiled.

"Nice to meet you, Couri. I'm Monique." She tossed me an incredulous look. "I...Um..."

She didn't know that my baby was well aware of who she was.

I told her everything about my visit to Helen.

"You're Shondra's godsister," Couri assisted, no malice in her cadence. "I'm praying for your peace of mind. Grief is a hard to pill to swallow."

Monique's eyes widened before the tears appeared.

"Oh no." Couri removed herself from me and gave this woman she'd never met before a tight hug. "I probably cracked a locked box you weren't ready to open yet. I'm sorry."

She took a step back, returning to my side where she belonged.

"Thank you," Monique told her before looking at me. "I meant what I said before. If you need a statement from me, I'll do it."

I nodded, appreciative.

"Well, I'll leave you guys..." Her eyes danced between me and Couri. "This looks good on you."

She walked away and I glanced down at my woman, who had her gaze lifted.

"I look good on you."

I smirked.

"You really fucking do."

Couri and I took our time exploring the rest of the exhibits, but the interactive touch pool was hands down the best part.

We debated about the stingrays.

I personally had a bone to pick with their kind for killing our man Steve Irwin.

Couri, on the other hand, defended them. Arguing that it was probably scared.

My animal-loving woman.

Our tour started as we neared the end and that was when Couri came to life.

She asked questions only someone with her job could. The guide—who happened to be a Zoologist—took an interest in her after the fifth detailed inquiry.

"What do you do for a living?" the girl asked, smiling.

"I'm a zoologist like you," she replied proudly. "I work with penguins."

Our guide clapped.

"At the Detroit Zoo?"

Couri nodded. "This place is way cooler, though."

They began to talk animatedly with one another, and I stood back, allowing them to have their moment while admiring Couri.

I'd said to dress comfortably and she wore jeans with a black long-sleeved bodysuit tucked inside. On her feet were a pair of black and white Converse.

She looked good with her stomach poking a little.

I moved to stand at her back and wrapped an arm around her waist, settling my fingers on the bulge.

She leaned into me without breaking stride in her conversation.

"I've worked with elephants, big cats, and now penguins. I would love to switch to another animal after a while, but we'll see."

The guide gushed over her then went on to finish her job with the next group.

Couri smiled and tipped her head back to look at me, happiness shining through her pretty irises.

"Ready for lunch?" she asked. "I worked up an appetite."

I smirked.

"I could eat, but I don't think that's what you meant."

Her eyes went from happy to lustful and I smirked.

"Come on, woman." I pulled her through the exit and started toward Rainforest Café. "I need to fatten you up; give my baby all the nutrients he or she will need to be one of those super athletes."

She giggled, elongating her strides to keep up with mine.

"Sounds like you want me to birth a linebacker, but I think we're having a girl. She's gonna dance. January is gonna play the piano or some kind of instrument. They'll team up and win the hearts of the world, making us famous."

January would probably find a love for ballet like her mother. Part of me thought that was the reason Shondra never wanted kids. Her career was important to her and being a Black ballerina in a white-dominated industry weighed heavy.

"Your niece plays instruments, right?"

She nodded as we moved into the restaurant, prepared for there to be a wait, but because it was only the two of us, we were directed to a two-person table near the back.

Rainforest Café looked precisely as you'd expect, considering the name.

"I can't believe I lived here most of my life and never came to the outlet mall," she mused, sipping water through a straw. "I usually hate big crowds, but I'm enjoying this."

She gazed at me from across the table.

"I love you," I told her, feeling a strong urge to say the words especially after being interrupted by Monique. "Can I spend some money on you after we eat?"

Her eyes widened, and for a second, I thought she'd decline or argue with me about it, but nah, that wasn't Couri.

"How much money are we talking?" she inquired, brows

raised. "Because you don't take a girl with a full stomach on a shopping spree. I can go for hours."

Don't think dirty thoughts.

Don't think dirty thoughts.

"Oh, I know," I mused, ignoring the chants in my head. "You've proven how long you can go on countless occasions."

The waiter cleared his throat and we slowly turned to give him our attention.

We ordered our food, adding an appetizer in case our main courses took long.

"When did they say you'd get the results from the DNA test?" she asked after our spinach and artichoke dip arrived. "Actually, don't answer that. I'd rather focus on other things today."

Because the court had ordered me to take a paternity test, I got it done midweek.

I'd felt sick watching them swab my baby's mouth, all because her grandmother couldn't handle the grief of losing her daughter.

I shook my head.

"We can talk about it for a second..." I leaned across the table and opened my mouth for the chip with dip she wanted to feed me. After chewing it down, I said, "I should have the results in a week, two at the latest."

Maybe sooner if my insistence on them being rushed was heard.

I knew January was mine but having to do this weighed heavily on my shoulders.

"My offer to smack some sense into her still stands."

I chuckled.

"Get in line behind my mother."

Couri's eyes sparkled with mischief.

"Mama Hanson is not to be played with, huh?"

I shook my head and accepted another chip.

"She once slapped fire from a prominent judge's mouth."

Amused, Couri threw her head back in laughter.

"Sounds like our mothers would've gotten along," she murmured, sobering at the thought. "I won't get all emotional about it, though."

I reached across the table and took her hand.

"You're with me," I reminded her. "Feel however you want; it's safe here."

The tears she'd been fighting sprang into action, and I stood, moving to sit beside her, to hide her from the world around us.

She buried her face in my shirt and cried softly.

I could only hope Couri knew I would protect her heart and soul with my life.

And I believed wholeheartedly that she'd do the same for me.

TWENTY-FIVE

couri

AFTER I WAS able to get myself together, we ate our food and talked about whatever was on our hearts.

True to his word, but only after covering our bill, August dropped a bag on me.

Great Lakes Crossing had one hundred eighty-five stores, restaurants, and attractions—including Sea Life, Peppa Pig World, and Legoland, plus a few more attractions like a bowling alley.

I was obsessed with shoes and made August record me trying on different sneakers in FootLocker, heels in Nordstrom, and Crocs at the Crocs store.

I somehow ended up with two new Coach purses and wallets to match after walking out of UGG with a black and brown pair of the classics—the kind that stopped just below the calf.

In the Converse outlet, I managed to snag the last size seven high-top platform in Deep Sleep—a dark turquoise.

As we walked toward Carter's, my hands free of bags, I spotted a jewelry store and slipped inside. My gaze zeroed in on the engagement rings and I ambled up the glass case.

Diamonds sparkled at me, calling my name.

Wear me.

I wanted to tell him *yes* right that instant but held my tongue. Now wasn't the "right time" and when I felt it I'd know.

"Hello," a saleswoman greeted, making her way over as August sidled up beside me. "I'm Gena. Are you looking for anything particular today?"

"Whatever the lady wants," he murmured, his gaze on the rings. "Before she tells you, can you size her ring finger for me?"

Gena's eyes slid over, slightly wide until she noticed I wasn't shocked by his request.

I hadn't known he'd ask it but we'd talked about marriage and expressed that eventually we would take that leap. He couldn't do that without knowing my ring size and since I'd never owned a ring that couldn't be resized I was of no help.

"Sure." She nodded and reached under the counter, grabbing a contraption filled with plastic sizing rings. "Let's see that left hand."

I held it out and she slipped one on but tsked when it was slightly too big. She moved down a size and because there was still a little wiggle room, we went with a five.

It fit snugly but wasn't suffocating.

August nodded, mentally storing that information.

"If you could have the ring of your dreams what would it be?" she asked.

I glanced at August who was watching me intently.

"Pear-shaped halo diamond," I started, eyes on his. "With a thin diamond encrusted gold band."

"Timeless," our sales lady murmured, seemingly in awe of my preference.

"And the size?" August queried.

248

I leaned in and gently pressed my lips to his.

"Surprise me."

He nudged my head and deepened the kiss, uncaring of the woman standing awkwardly behind the counter.

"Baby," I mumbled into his mouth. "You're scaring the poor woman."

"Buy something that'll double her commission for the day."

Gena perked up and I smiled.

"I'm due for a new watch, something yellow-gold with a black face."

Her eyes sparkled as she led us over to the watch case.

"We just got in a Movado I think you'll love."

And I absolutely loved it, more so when August swiped his American Express for the twelve hundred dollar price tag without blinking.

Ugh.

I felt like a princess.

Maybe I could do this for him in return, allow him to buy things he liked on my dime.

His birthday was coming up in four or so months and I'd been wracking my brain for gift ideas. Eventually, I'd figure it out.

"We can peruse children's clothing stores another day," I told August, yawning. "I need a nap before dinner."

He led us to his truck, bags hanging off his arms.

"I want to show you something," he said, storing my things in the trunk. "And then, I'll let you sleep for a little."

I nodded and moved around the passenger side but stopped and turned back after a question nagged at me.

"Where am I taking this nap?"

He smiled and slowly walked toward me, forcing me back a few steps.

As he reached for my door and pulled it open, he said, "That's what I want to show you."

August got low and kissed my stomach while staring into my eyes, something he'd been doing more and more lately. I really enjoyed his way of bonding with our baby.

"Get in before I do things to you in this parking lot."

I shifted but made no move to do as he asked.

August chuckled and leaned in, pressing his lips against the shell of my ear.

"Bad girl," he murmured, biting my earlobe.

I whimpered, wanting so badly to let this man have me in this big ass parking lot but knowing he wouldn't risk exposing me. Not like this at least, in broad daylight.

"I really..." I bit my lip as he pushed his fingers between my legs, cupping my pussy through my jeans. "...want to be bad for you."

"I know you do and the faster you get in the truck, the faster we can make that happen."

I slid into the seat before he finished his statement and he chuckled.

"I thought that might get you moving."

He shut me in and slid into his side a few seconds later.

"My sisters and I are always looking for shit to invest in," he began as we merged onto I-94 going west. "After we revamped the distillery and got the tasting bars off the ground, we thought real estate could be a good next step. We bought a few places, flipped them, and made a decent profit."

I twisted my body to face him, adjusting my seatbelt to give me the room to do so.

"Really?"

He nodded, cutting his eyes at me briefly.

"But there's this one house..." He chuckled a little. "I'd been eyeing it for a while, so we bought it and renovated it. Now I'm debating on if I want to keep it for myself or sell it like planned."

Ah.

"You decided to keep it."

"I'll decide after my future wife sees it."

My cheeks warmed and I turned away.

"How will your sisters feel about that?" I asked. "Their money is wrapped in it too, right?"

"They know I might want it for myself..." He paused. "For our family."

"So, how would that work?"

"The house is under our LLC," he explained. "We'd do a transfer of owner and that's that."

"What about the bank?"

I knew I was asking a lot of questions but he answered each without thinking twice about it and that was the kind of man I needed, one who didn't mind me wanting to be included in all the details.

"No bank involvement. It's been paid for with cash."

I blinked and frowned as we exited the freeway and entered a neighborhood less than twenty minutes from my sister's place.

This wasn't a flip, revamp, and sell kind of area.

"August..."

He pulled into the driveway of a massive brick home with a large tree in front and a swing hanging from it.

My eyes widened at the sight of it and tears sprang free.

How did he know?

I'd never told him the story of the swing in front of my childhood home. In fact, Journi and I never talked about that fucking swing.

Our father had hung it when I was seven, adding another

soon after so the neighborhood kids could take turns swinging too.

When he passed, we couldn't even look at them without getting emotional.

It had gotten so bad that our mother paid someone to take them down, along with the tree that sat in the yard. Once it was gone, I felt empty inside but never had the guts to admit that we'd probably made a mistake.

"Whoa," August muttered, getting out and coming around to my side. "Why the tears?"

He gripped my face and forced me to look him in the eyes. I could barely see through my watery gaze but I felt his concern.

"I..." I took a deep breath and tried my best to gather myself. "The swing."

He frowned and glanced at it.

"June put it up," he explained, tone cautious as he wiped my stray tears away. "There's one in front of my parents' house and she thought it was a nice touch. We can take it down if—"

"No, it's just..." I shook my head and grabbed his face. "Journi and I had a swing too because of our dad and after he passed it was hard to look at, so Mom took it down and had the tree cut. We regretted it immediately but none of us had the guts to admit it. Seeing that one brought back memories is all."

He nodded slowly and pulled me out of the truck.

"So, you're okay with it staying?" he asked, encasing me into a warm embrace.

I nodded against his chest.

"Yes, please. It feels like home here already."

August took a deep breath and I felt his shoulders sag in relief, like he'd been hoping I wanted to live here with him.

We continued to stand in the driveway, holding onto one another for support.

"Needed that," he murmured as he eventually pulled away. "Don't know why but I needed it."

I nodded, understanding.

"Me too." I gazed at the home he wanted to call ours and smiled. "Show me."

He moved around me and reached into the truck for his keys, shut my door, then led us up the driveway that curved into an L.

The garage door was attached to the side of the house and as it lifted, I could see it doubled as a mudroom with a door that led into a short hallway.

"The laundry room is the first door to our right," he explained, pushing it open to reveal a brand new washer and dryer set inside with the plastic still attached. "It has a lot of space and storage but across the hall is another closet we can stash shit in."

I nodded, peeking into the large closet as we left the laundry room, noting that it could be used for coats and shoes as well.

"Up ahead is a half bath, nothing special, besides the new hardware." He moved into the kitchen and it mirrored the one in his townhome. "I'm sure this looks familiar, only difference is the size and the nook right there with the bay windows. No appliances yet but we can pick those together."

It was beautiful; the dark marble countertops and matte black cabinets with gold hardware all around really stood out, especially with the light funneling in from the large windows.

August continued to show me the three thousand square foot home with five bedrooms and four and a half baths. It was perfect for having guests and kids.

"When we found this place it had that old wooden look, so gutting it and starting over felt like the best plan. There's still a few things I want to do before we can officially move in, so if you have any preferences let me know."

He had good taste and didn't need my input on the design itself, but the idea of putting my own decorative spin on the foundation he created for us sounded good.

The main floor had the master suite with its own bath, while the upstairs housed three more bedrooms, one with an ensuite bath and another that could be shared between the other two bedrooms.

Once we made it to the basement I couldn't believe what I was seeing.

There was a smaller kitchenette with a high-top bar I had a vision for, a living room and dining room space, half-bath, and a bedroom that could double as a recreation room depending on our preference.

"Wow," I gushed, taking in the space with wide eyes. "This is beautiful."

"Yeah," August murmured. "It is."

His eyes were on me as he said it and I looked away, hiding my smile.

"I want to see the master suite now."

"How about the backyard first?"

I sighed and his lips curled into a smile.

"Fine, but—"

August pressed his lips to mine then led us up the stairs toward the sliding doors leading to a wraparound deck. It sorta looked like the one at Kingston and Journi's place but a little larger.

The yard was spacious and I immediately wanted a dog or two.

I wanted a full house with lots of noise except at four in the morning when I was having coffee with my husband.

"You know..." I turned and leaned against the railing,

drawing August to stand in front of me. "I think everything is falling into place soon."

He moved in close and dropped his forehead against mine.

"It's already in place, just a few kinks to straighten out."

I bumped his head so I could see his face better.

"How are you feeling, really?"

Our eyes danced for a little before he sighed and shook his head.

"I want to take you to bed and hold you until it's time for dinner," he said, his gaze begging me to let it go for now. "Is that okay?"

The urge to ask again slipped away.

He needed time to process what he was feeling and I understood that.

When he was ready to talk I'd be here.

"Okay, baby," I agreed, nodding. "Let's go cuddle."

He took my hand and led me inside, into the master suite. It was the only room in the home fully furnished and my goodness it took my breath away.

There was lavender in the air, blowing from a diffuser sitting on the nightstand next to the California King bed. The wall behind the bed had three gold and black abstract canvases but when I looked closer I could see the outline of a couple holding onto one another.

On the left side of the room there was a little lounge area with a small sectional sofa, empty bookshelf, and round coffee table.

It was homey and felt like the perfect retreat for two people in love.

I didn't care to see the bathroom or the his and her walk-in closets because I knew they were up to par. All I wanted in this moment was to be held and to hold the man I loved.

I walked over to the bed and began to undress.

August watched me from his spot near the bedroom entrance until I was in my bra and panties.

"You coming?" I asked, smirking in his direction as I pulled the thick duvet back.

He started removing clothes as he approached, eyes on me as I slid in and buried myself underneath. The bed dipped after a few seconds then he joined me beneath the blanket, sliding close until our foreheads touched.

"I love you," he murmured, brushing his nose and lips against mine. "Feels good to say that whenever I feel like it."

"You've felt it for a long time?"

"I knew I wanted to live in your skin the moment I got you to follow me home with a look." He chuckled. "Don't think I realized until now that I fell for you right then."

I smiled and tried to slide closer but we were already touching, our limbs tangled together in perfect harmony.

"I love the way you make me feel," I murmured, caressing his cheek. "The way you handle me with the utmost care at all times. Your eyes when you're turned on but especially when the sun hits them at the right angle. I love that even if we drift away from one another in the middle of the night you find me and pull me back. I just... I love *you* and I know with all my heart none of this would feel okay if it was with anyone else. We were meant to find each other."

He was my person.

My heart.

The gentlest protective soul who deserved to be loved and cherished by everyone around him, but most importantly, by me.

"You and me," he whispered against the shell of my ear.

I closed my eyes and sighed.

"You and me," I murmured back before falling into a deep sleep.

TWENTY-SIX

"DAMN," I mumbled, watching Couri saunter toward me in a little black minidress that stopped high up on her thigh.

The fabric clung to her frame, showing off her little bump.

She stopped halfway to me and twirled in her heels.

"What do you think?"

I loved when she sought compliments from me.

"I think we might miss our reservation," I mused, beckoning her to me with two fingers. "Let me feel on you right quick."

She giggled but walked her fine ass to me like I knew she would.

With the limited products she'd brought, Couri managed to define and magnify the thickness of her curls. I couldn't get over the way her hair grew from her scalp.

"You look good, mama," I murmured, pulling her into me by the back of her thigh.

Her gaze slid up, darker than usual because of the heavy black eyeliner she wore.

"So do you," she complimented, hands on my chest as she sniffed the air. "You smell amazing."

"You can't sniff me and think it won't make my dick hard."

I pushed my hand inside her dress and gripped her bare ass.

"August..."

As I glanced at my watch, I said, "If I didn't have to call in a favor to get this reservation I'd bend you over and say fuck dinner."

"I'll decide if it's worth it," she declared, her lips curling. "Where's dinner?"

"Grey Ghost."

"Ooh!" she squeaked, stepping back. "The executive chef is Black there. Some of my coworkers have bragged about the food..." She nodded, her decision clear. "Let's go."

I picked up the bags we'd repacked and left by the front door after showering and waved for her to walk out first.

Couri moved on command and I admired that sexy ass confident walk of hers.

She was so goddamn fine and I was overly obsessed.

I followed her but turned to lock up first, making a mental note to talk to my sisters about officially taking the house for myself.

"This neighborhood is so nice," Couri murmured as I approached her from behind.

She stood at the end of the driveway, peering from left to right.

The sun was on the verge of setting, leaving the sky a bright orange-purplish color.

"Black families live there..." I pointed to the house across the street. "Next door and at the end of the block."

"Have you met them?" she asked, turning to face me.

I nodded and began to guide her back toward my truck.

"We wanted them to know it might be a little noisy during

the day back when renovations were happening. Everyone was cool with it and friendly."

"Even the..." She pointed to her palm as I helped her into the front seat and I chuckled.

"Even them," I confirmed, leaning in to kiss her cheek. "Buckle up for me."

She pulled the belt and glanced over.

"Must you watch me while I do it?"

"It's imperative."

With her gaze pinned to mine, she snapped the seatbelt into place and sat back.

"Come on, baby daddy, I'm getting hangry."

Shaking my head, I shut her door and ambled around to the driver's side.

We drove in a comfortable silence, hand in hand while SZA's SOS album played softly in the background. I could live in silence with her for a lifetime and never get tired of it.

"So much traffic," I groused.

Grey Ghost sat in the Cass Corridor in downtown Detroit.

With it being a Saturday night, the city was alive. Cars lined the streets and music blasted as residents drove around to show off their cars but most importantly pick up girls.

Couri leaned forward and smiled.

"I love downtown at night aside from the people. The lights, the music... *everything*."

"It's a vibe," I agreed, taking a breath after we finally made it down Woodward through traffic and turned onto Watson street.

I slowed in front of the building and watched as a valet attendant approached my window.

"Dining at Grey Ghost?" he asked, smiling.

I nodded, handed him a twenty, and took the ticket before getting out.

Couri had her door open before I got to it and I lifted an eyebrow.

"You want to fight with me or something?" I queried, earning a sheepish smile from her.

"Sorry, I did it before I realized it."

She placed her soft hand in mine and I led us toward the entrance.

"As long as you know I'm the only door opener around here, I'll let it slide."

Upon entry we were greeted by the host.

"Welcome to Grey Ghost, do you have a reservation with us today?"

I pulled Couri into my side, draping my arm over her shoulder.

"Under Hanson."

"Ah, there you are," the host confirmed after sliding a finger across the screen of her iPad. "You have the best seats in the house tonight, courtesy of the owner."

I could feel Couri's gaze on me as we followed the host toward a private seating area in the back.

"You know the owner?" Couri asked the moment we were seated and the host excused herself.

"I know a lot of people," I said, smirking. "And yeah, I know the owners. One of them got married at the distillery and owed me a favor for fitting them in last minute."

She smiled and glanced around before bringing that dark gaze back to me.

"I feel like there's still so much I don't know about you."

I nodded because it was true.

"We have a lifetime of figuring each other out."

"Do you think..." She shook her head and looked away. "Never mind."

"Nah." I reached across the table for her hand, waiting

patiently for her attention until she gave it. "Tell me what's happening in that head of yours."

"Everything is happening so fast," she murmured. "Love and babies and homes."

"We said we're scared but leaping out on faith, right?"

She nodded.

"I'm still jumping with you. I guess I like hearing that you aren't having second thoughts about us."

"Nah, I'm all in, Angel face. I told my parents about you. Tomorrow you're meeting my big ass family, at least some of them. It's me and you, remember?"

"Yeah, me and you..." She looked up and smiled. "We should probably include the kiddos in that saying, huh?"

I chuckled.

"It's a given. Without me there'd be no January and without you there'd be no mini us baking."

Her glossed lips lifted higher and I felt now was the perfect time to answer her question from earlier in the day. Asking Couri to open up while I kept my shit bottled inside under the guise of needing time to work through it wouldn't fly, not if I wanted our relationship to work.

I waited until our server took our drink and dinner orders before speaking what was on my heart.

"Earlier, when you asked how I was feeling," I began as she regarded me with keen eyes. "I wanted to tell you that I feel mixed up inside about Shondra being gone but especially about what her mom is doing."

She was silent for a while, a little too long.

"You haven't grieved the loss of Shondra," she said eventually. "I know you want to settle on anger because of how she went about things but it's okay to be a little sad, too."

January had been with me for over a month now and I still

wasn't sure when I'd allow myself to feel the loss of her mother.

Was I even sad?

It was hard to see past my disdain for the woman I'd spent a small part of my life with.

"She was cremated," I told Couri. "I think I would have liked a proper goodbye for me and January."

She nodded and reached across the table, laying her hands atop mine.

"A proper goodbye can happen in many ways. Maybe we can release balloons or lanterns on the beach when you feel ready. The options are endless."

I considered her words for a moment.

"And you'd be part of it?" I asked.

Couri replied without pause, "Absolutely. I'm part of your support system now, August."

She never ceased to amaze me.

Her maturity.

The way she offered support without malice or ill intentions.

Her gentle nature with everyone she loved, including me.

I'd won.

"Thank you for being you."

She smiled but dropped her gaze.

"No need to be shy, baby. Let me see those eyes."

She looked up but there wasn't a shy woman staring back at me. Nah, Couri was turned on and I knew just how to remedy that.

"Go to the bathroom," I murmured after the server dropped off the scallops and mussels we decided to have as an appetizer.

Couri stared at me for a moment then stood, her fingers grazing my arm as she passed.

I waited a few seconds and followed, nodding at the host as I passed her station.

Glancing over my shoulder, I checked for any eyes then slipped into the women's bathroom.

It smelled of vanilla and something else I couldn't quite place.

For a second, I took in the space, liking that it was clean and taken care of properly.

Couri stood in front of the sink, her eyes on me as she washed her hands.

I flipped the lock and said, "We don't have a lot of time. Come here."

She came to me while I worked the button on my jeans, her strides purposeful.

I lifted her by the backs of her thighs after allowing my pants to drop a little and backed her against the wall.

"You're bad," she whispered, cupping my face as she secured her legs around my waist.

"For you," I muttered, taking her lips with mine. "I'll be any and everything you need."

I pulled the thong she wore to the side and buried myself deep inside those slick walls, covering her mouth again to silence the cry of pleasure.

Fuck.

She was so goddamn wet I could barely contain myself as I thrusted in and out of her pussy, enjoying the wild ride to climax. I flicked and pinched her clit a few times to get her there faster and she did not disappoint.

Her body jerked against mine as she gasped for air.

"I got you, just breathe for me," I coached, quickening my strokes to meet her over the edge. "Mmhm. *Fuck*, Couri."

She tightened her arms around my neck as if to give me support while I painted her walls.

"Now we can eat," she concluded, breathless.

I chuckled and slowly disengaged our bodies, setting Couri on her feet.

After wiping her essence from my dick with a few paper towels and helping her do the same, I washed my hands and kissed her lips then slipped out as if I'd never been there.

I arrived at our table and started to plate some of the scallops and mussels for Couri to have the minute she sat down.

She showed face a couple of minutes later and tossed a sultry grin my way.

"Thank you, baby."

I dipped my head and smirked, knowing she was thanking me for the pre-dinner dick.

"Anytime, Angel face."

Any *fucking* place.

* * *

I pushed the door open to my parents' home and stepped into pure beautiful chaos.

Music playing, kids running amuck, loud talking traveling from the kitchen, but most importantly, the smell of food. It was always about the food on days like these.

Couri tugged on my fingers and I glanced down, finding a nervous set of eyes on me.

Last night we'd fucked so much after dinner I could still feel her pulsating around my dick, the taste of her on my tongue, and the feel of her lips on mine.

This morning and up until we stepped inside of my parents' home she'd looked relaxed and happy. But this new expression... I wasn't sure I'd ever seen it on her before.

"Nervous?" I asked, reaching around to touch her face with my free hand.

"A little," she admitted, side stepping a toddler on the run.

"Your family is still coming, right?"

She nodded.

"You'll have some familiar faces to help quell the nerves soon, but until then I won't leave your side unless you give me the go ahead, alright?"

"Thank you."

My family was harmless; she'd see that soon and the nerves would disappear.

Just as I turned to enter the family room, JJ came barreling out and almost knocked Couri over.

"Ay, yo!" I barked, stopping his quick strides halfway down the hall.

He turned, his face balled up in anger and fists clenched.

JJ had bulked up in the last year and grew a beard. He almost looked older than his young twenty-one year old self.

"Don't leave this hallway without apologizing for almost knocking her over."

My cousin narrowed his eyes but when they shifted to Couri, he softened immediately and took one step forward.

"I'm sorry," he said, voice deeper than the last time I'd seen him. "I wasn't paying attention."

He looked at me and I nodded, giving him the permission to leave.

"I hope whatever is troubling you fades away soon," Couri said, smiling at him just as he began to turn.

JJ looked at me with his brows lifted and I shrugged.

This was Couri.

She was caring as fuck, even to people she didn't know.

"I receive that," JJ said, nodding. "Thanks."

He retreated before she could respond but I was certain she'd gotten what she wanted from the encounter. We continued into the family room where most of the younger kids were lounging around watching TV or playing video games.

My dad was one of ten kids his parents had.

Every last one of them had kids. Including my sisters and me, there were twenty of us and out of those twenty about eight had spouses or kids or both. Maybe more but it was hard to keep up.

Our family would never stop growing.

"Finally!" Myiesha yelled from her spot in one of the reclining chairs. "The man of the hour has arrived."

"Don't start," I warned in jest.

The smile spreading her lips widened.

"I heard you got—"

Her brother Mykel covered her mouth before she could finish.

At seventeen, he was a bit more reserved than his older sister who had only just turned eighteen and was about to enter her first year of college.

"Wassup, Aug," Mykel greeted, grinning while Myiesha struggled to get free. "That your girl you holding on to?"

I chucked.

"Yeah, this me."

I made quick introductions and Mykel finally released Myiesha.

"Pleased to meet you, Couri. If he ever gets out of line tell—"

Mykel slapped his hand over her mouth again and I shook my head.

"Go before she powers up on me."

I backed us out of the family room just as Myiesha pounced on Mykel.

The loud howl from his lips brought a smile to my face.

"I love the sound of family coming together," Couri mused wistfully.

I moved through my parents' home toward the kitchen, stopping along the way to kiss Couri behind a wall, away from prying eyes.

"Stop," Couri fussed, her lips against mine. "Your mother will think I'm a harlot."

I chuckled and pulled away.

"My harlot," I corrected, dodging her swat at my arm. "Besides, you're already pregnant."

"Keep it up and—"

She snapped her lips shut as my mother turned the corner and stopped at the sight of us.

"Hey, Ma," I greeted, pulling her into a hug after she stepped close enough for me to grab.

She hugged me back but I knew her attention was on the beauty standing beside me.

"Adrina Hanson, meet Couri Mitchell."

Couri lifted her hand to wave but Mom pulled her into a tight embrace before she could get the hand in the air. Her eyes widened over my mother's shoulder but after a brief second I watched her relax into the embrace.

"It's so nice to meet you," Mom said, pulling away. "August is smitten with you."

"Ma," I complained. "Chill."

"Don't get all cranky." She waved me off. "Something tells me she's well aware of it."

Couri winked in my direction and I shook my head.

"It's really nice to meet you, Mrs. Hanson. Thank you for thinking of my family when inviting me here today."

Mom cut her eyes at me, more than likely wondering why I hadn't told her it was me who requested her family be present.

I shrugged.

She could tell her or not, didn't matter to me.

Couri didn't need to be aware of everything I did because of her on the back end. As long as she knew I had her through whatever, I was satisfied.

"I wish it were me who thought to invite them," Mom said, smiling. "That was all August but I'm happy to host your family today."

"My niece is excited. She loves Sunday dinners."

Mom started toward the swinging doors that blocked the kitchen from everything else and I followed like a little puppy, wanting to keep my promise of not leaving Couri's side.

Upon entry, gazes shot in our direction but mine zeroed in on January, who was being held by Landon.

"No," he all but shouted, backing away as I approached. "I just got her and you will not—"

I cornered him but before I could demand my child, her eyes met mine and a little smile lifted the corners of her mouth. She leaned toward me and I smirked at Landon who looked betrayed but handed her over.

"She'll never pick you over me," I told him, dropping kisses all over January's chunky face.

That's a given." He shrugged. "I'm looking to take that number two spot though."

A throat cleared and we turned.

"I'm sorry to burst your bubble but I'm her number two," Couri declared, making her way over to me.

"You must be the infamous Couri," Landon mused, gaze filled with mischief.

"And you must be Landon the engineer," she quipped, earning a few chuckles from his parents who were also in the kitchen. "Speaking of, how's your trivia skills?"

He frowned and glanced at me for clarification but I lifted a shoulder and waved for him to answer.

"Well... I know things."

Couri leaned in, oblivious to the silence as everyone listened.

"What kind of things exactly? Wow me."

Landon, who liked to be challenged, took on a determined expression.

"The world's smallest radio is the size of a marble."

Couri nodded and glanced at me.

"Told you," I said, chuckling.

"Would you like to join our two-person trivia brigade, making it a three-person group?"

He nodded.

"Sure but we need to think of a better name. That one is giving me a headache."

Couri laughed and I admired how easily she'd won Landon over. He wasn't that hard to please but it proved she'd fit right in no problem.

"Oh, hey, Snowflake," she greeted, stealing her from me. "I missed your pretty face so much."

I glanced at my mom who watched the exchange closely, a hand covering her mouth.

I'd told her I was in love with this woman and she got to see firsthand why it had been so easy for me to fall. Our eyes met and she smiled, giving me a nod of approval before checking something inside the oven.

I took a moment to introduce Couri to Landon's parents and my dad.

Slowly but surely, the house began to fill with cousins.

Lola and Leslie made their separate entrances.

My sisters finally showed face, having rode together.

Mia—Aunt Paula's daughter—who was general manager of the tasting rooms showed face eventually with her mother and daughter Lily in tow.

I was surprised to see my aunt but should've known she'd come to meet January.

Family drama or not, she showed up when it mattered.

"We've met before, haven't we?" Mia said, staring at Couri. "A while back at the tasting room in Royal Oak."

Couri nodded and smiled. "Oh, yes!"

"You were behind the bar. I kinda figured you two were related. It's nice to officially meet you though."

As more family made an appearance, we found ourselves migrating to the family room and taking it over from the younger generation. Not everyone had been able to make it but Couri got to meet a handful of us, some stopping in to grab to-go plates before work.

Eventually, her family showed up and I saw her relax at the sight of them.

Kingston was privy to who most everyone was and took his wife around to make introductions.

Kali found a friend in Lily who was the same age.

I looked around and felt a sense of calm wash over me.

This was exactly what I'd needed.

Family.

"Bea just got here," Couri whispered in my ear. "I'm gonna go meet her outside really quick."

She got up and I watched her leave the room.

The minute she was out of sight, her sister took up a spot beside me.

"So you and my sister, huh?" she mused, giving her finger to January.

"Yeah." I nodded. "Me and her."

"Do right by her. She's special and deserves to be treated as such."

"You're right, she is special and I'll only ever treat her the way she deserves."

Journi nodded, the same dark eyes her sister possessed staring deeply into mine.

"I know you probably worry about her, about how she's doing mentally, but I hope you find peace in knowing that she has me to lean on. Even if she doesn't come to you about it right away, she isn't dealing with anything alone."

"And your word is bond?" she questioned, brows pinched.

I put my hand on top of hers and squeezed.

"My word is bond. Your sister is in good hands, I promise."

"Damn," Landon mumbled from the left of me, drawing my attention to him and then to where his eyes were trained. "Who's that?"

Couri had entered with her friend Bea. I remembered seeing her a while back at the zoo, wearing a security uniform.

She was pretty and Landon's type.

Her and Couri smiled in our direction after she pointed at us and I felt Landon tense up.

What the fuck is happening?

"That's Bea," Journi said, answering Landon's question after I failed to. "Her and Couri have been friends since high school. Nice girl."

"You were in love with your co-worker last I saw you," I reminded him.

He cut his eyes at me, a frown marring his face.

"I said she was in love with me but shit went left this week," he explained, not elaborating enough for me to understand. "I decided she wasn't worth the drama."

He hadn't said that but I nodded.

"Stay clear of Bea," I warned. "You fucking up with her could potentially blow back on me and I'd rather it not."

His frown deepened but he looked away as they began to approach.

"Never said anything about pursuing her."

"Right," I muttered, not believing a word out of his fucking mouth.

Journi hummed, giving me the feeling that she felt the same.

Landon was going to do what he wanted, regardless of what I said.

His sudden change of heart about his coworker felt a little off, like more than just *something* happened. But it wasn't my place to drag it out of him, so I kept my questions to myself.

The day went on, with people stealing Couri and January from me. Luckily before we were called in for dinner, Couri and I were able to sneak off to my childhood bedroom.

"How you feeling?" I asked, backing her into the door.

She looked up and smiled.

"Very overwhelmed but in a good way. Everyone is so nice."

I boxed her in, my hands at either side of her face.

"Would you do this again?"

"Yes..." Her fingers danced along the back of my neck. "I would love nothing more than spending time with you and your family again."

I sighed in relief.

"You were nervous," she surmised, eyes dancing with mine. "Why didn't you say anything?"

"We couldn't both be openly nervous."

"You and I can be whatever we want, August. Sad, happy, nervous... whenever we want at the same or different times, doesn't matter."

I dropped my forehead against hers.

"Thank you for reminding me."

"Of course, that's my—"

Mom's voice carried from wherever she stood in the house

as she yelled, "It's time to eat! I want hands washed and fingernails scrubbed and do it fast, the food is hot!"

I shook my head.

"We better go. We'll never hear the end of it if the food gets cold before everyone is seated."

Couri pushed me and I moved back two steps.

"I refuse to be the new girl and get fussed out by the host," she said, snatching the door open while reaching for my hand. "Come on, baby daddy. We're a team. You can't make me look bad my first day here."

Because we were upstairs, we got our hands washed and were at the table before most everyone else.

"Look at the overachievers beating us to the table," Omar jested, swaggering in quickly to steal the seat beside me. "Heard you got a girlfriend and babies."

"One on the way," Couri chimed in before I could, leaning forward to get a good look at Omar's ugly mug. "Who are you?"

He chuckled and reached for a roll but snatched his hand back when someone cleared their throat from the other side of the room, more than likely his mother or mine.

The "special occasion" dining room had two, large, sixteen-seat tables, splitting us almost evenly. We had a pact between us cousins to fill one table before the parents could find seats near us and dig into our lives.

Now that there were younger kids mixed into the bunch, Mom bought one of those mini tables to fit them near the entryway. If this had been planned in advance we would've used the distillery to fit everyone.

More food slowly began to make it on the tables, double pans of mac and cheese, string beans cooked in bacon fat, and baked beans. The meats consisted of fried chicken, moms famous slow cooked roast, and I smelled ribs but hadn't seen them yet.

"I'm Omar," my cousin finally said, looking past me at Couri. "I see why he got you—"

I slapped the back of his head.

"Don't make me hurt you, O."

Our eyes met and he fucking smiled.

"You wouldn't hurt me, I'm your favorite cousin."

"Bullshit," Landon called, sliding into a chair next to Bea on the other side of the table.

"Watch your mouth, Landon Hanson," my mother chastised.

"Sorry, Auntie," he murmured with a smile only we could see.

He thought he was slick, sitting next to Bea, but I peeped game.

"Landon, let's not start this right now." Omar waved him off playfully. "I'm tryna get to know this beauty beside our beloved cousin here."

Omar was an only child on my mother's side. He'd spent most of his time growing up with the Hanson kids, making him one by heart.

"She's pretty smart," Landon mused, cutting his gaze at Bea. "This is her friend. I think we should get to know her too. What do you think, Omar?"

The two of them exchanged knowing glances and I sighed.

"Don't let them play you into telling your whole life story, Bea," June said, stopping at the entryway to look for a seat. "I don't know how they do it but it's witchcraft."

After spotting one near Kingston and Journi she made her way to it.

"Landon thinks he has charm but we all know the truth," Mia teased from where she sat.

Bea looked more uncomfortable than when she'd arrived and I opened my mouth to tell my people to chill but stopped when her lips curled into a smile.

"I'm not easily swayed into sharing things I never planned to," she said, looking at Landon from the corner of her eye. "I guess you can try though."

"I think he might actually want to know her," Omar surmised, voice low enough for only me to hear.

I nodded.

"What do you do?" Landon asked. "Everyone has a thing. We got some lawyers, a doctor, a judge, some master distillers..." He glanced at Couri and winked before saying, "Ms. Overachiever right there is a zoologist, which I'm sure you know. So, what's your thing?"

Bea shrugged and smiled when my dad came barreling in with a "Master of All" apron on and a large pan filled with his famous ribs.

"First Sunday dinner we've had since the snow melted," he bellowed, silencing the room. "Today is different. We're here to celebrate the newest addition to our family January Marie Hanson. Sometimes life doesn't go as planned and you may not end up where you thought you were going but you will always end up where you were meant to be."

Couri took my hand under the table and laced our fingers together just as September entered the dining room with January tucked in her right arm.

"Dad..." She looked hurt. "I can't believe you started your speech without your favorite daughter here."

"Hey! Not true!" June and July contested in tandem.

September ignored them and made her way over to me, pushing January in my direction with narrowed eyes.

"Your child pissed up my arm, so we're beefing right now."

The room filled with soft chuckles and I took my baby, not

wanting to believe she'd do such a thing but knowing it was true. She'd pissed up my arm a few times but I was grateful we hadn't graduated into blowouts yet.

"You didn't do that, did you?" I asked, kissing her cheeks. "Daddy knows. We won't let Auntie Tem smear your name like that again."

I hadn't been able to really hold her since arriving and got my fill while Dad went back into his spiel.

He went on for a while, proving himself to be long winded like everyone complained about on occasion, but eventually ended with, "Let's eat!"

Pure chaos ensued after that but all I could focus on was Couri picking around the food I'd put on her plate.

"I can get you something else," I offered quietly. "I wasn't thinking—"

She stuffed green beans in her mouth and chewed slowly.

"I'm fine," she mumbled, going for the mac and cheese next. "Promise."

I wasn't sure if I believed her but left it alone.

Mom came over not long after and set a plate of home fries next to Couri's food.

"Just in case," she said, smiling down at the love of my life who looked perplexed by the gesture.

She walked away and took her seat at the other table next to my dad.

"Did you tell her?"

I shook my head.

I hadn't told her shit but when I caught eyes with June, I knew it had been my sister who looked out.

"That was really sweet..." Couri's wide eyes met mine. "I think I'm okay though. Ribs are calling my name."

I grabbed the tongs and waved between the sauced and plain piles.

"Which one?"

She regarded them closely and chose plain, biting into it the second it was in her hands.

"Oh, wow," she moaned a little too loudly.

"Another one bites the dust," Myiesha and Mykel said at once. "Jinx!"

They started to bicker and it riled up the rest of the kids.

Before I knew it, everyone was talking over one another.

"There's nothing like family," Couri whispered, leaning into me.

Especially this family, I thought.

We were all tied together now and I wouldn't have it any other way.

This was meant to be.

"Yeah," I agreed, leaning over to kiss her forehead. "My mom is keeping January until after my meeting with the lawyer tomorrow. Your place or mine?"

I never wanted to spend nights away from her again.

"Mine," she answered. "It's closer."

I nodded and swiped sauce from the rib left on my plate to feed January.

She cleared my finger quickly and gnawed on it afterward, eyes bouncing at the sound of voices.

"That's your family," I murmured to her. "These are some of the best people you'll ever meet."

Hands down.

couri

I FLICKED the light above the stove on and stretched, rolling my arms behind my back until they popped.

"Mmm," I hummed, sifting through my Nespresso coffee pods for the flavor of the day. "Napoli will do."

I filled the machine with enough water for two cups and stuck my favorite *Good Morning, Bitches* mug underneath. While waiting for it to brew, I grabbed another mug from the cabinet with a Hanson Distillery logo across the front.

I eyed the Nespresso machine with impatience, needing my morning dose of caffeine to really get my day started. As I shifted from foot to foot, the dull ache between my legs reminded me of how my night had ended.

Yesterday had been an exciting yet emotional day. August's family treated me and mine like we'd always been part of the crew.

By the time we made it to my place, I was brimming with the need to feel August deep inside me and was selfishly grateful his mom insisted on keeping January until after he met with Shondra's lawyer.

Shaking my head, I brushed my fingers against my lips and closed my eyes, still feeling part of him against my skin.

"What's on your mind?"

I jumped and opened my eyes, gripping the counter to stop myself from falling.

"Nothing," I lied, watching August grab my cup from the machine and extend it to me.

He reached for the mug I'd left out for him and stuck it right where mine had been, before finding which pod he wanted to start his day with.

"Never took you for the lying type," he said, cutting his eyes at me as I sipped my coffee without cream or sugar.

I grimaced but kept sipping, knowing it would be the only cup I drank all week.

Fucking pregnancy.

"I can still feel you all over me," I admitted softly, never wanting to be seen as the lying type. "I was thinking about that."

He hummed while filling his brewed cup with caramel creamer and two sugars.

Once finished, he came to me and switched our cups.

"Drink your coffee how you like it if you're going to have it," he said. "But remember it's the only cup you're allowed."

I rolled my eyes and sipped on the perfectly made cup of joe.

We fell into a comfortable silence.

I'd never shared my favorite pastime with another man, not even my ex who had been in my life for years. But August made being silent with him easy.

I rested my elbows on the counter and leaned in deeper, eyes closed while humming a made up tune.

His gaze lingered on me; I felt it dancing along the exposed parts of my skin and squirmed a little. Soon his body brushed mine and I waited with bated breath to see what he would do.

"You're wearing the shirt you stole," he murmured, slipping his fingers underneath and grazing the skin of my bare ass. "Might be my new favorite thing to see before starting my day."

I shuddered as his hands drifted up my sides and around my waist.

He pulled me away from the counter and into his chest. We swayed slowly from side to side as he peppered kisses along my shoulder, giving me chills.

"August..."

He chuckled against my skin, spun me around, and pinned my back against the counter in one swift motion.

"We should do this more often."

I shook my head.

"We haven't done anythin—"

The tickle of his fingers on the inside of my thigh shut me up faster than I cared to admit.

"That's an easy fix," he said, lifting me on the island and pushing my legs apart.

He reached for something and came back with the Hanson Distillery mug.

"Drink your coffee while I have an early morning snack."

Slowly, he lowered himself until face first with my pussy.

I wrapped my lips around the rim of my mug and sipped the lukewarm concoction, spreading my legs wider.

August buried his head deep, attacking my clit with his tongue and teeth just how I liked.

"Yess," I whimpered, lowering my cup to grip the edge of the counter. "Oh, *fuck.*"

Nothing, not even caffeine, could get better than this.

* * *

"You okay, baby?" August asked, snatching the blanket from over my head a couple of hours later.

He reached out to touch my forehead and I swatted his hand away, upset he'd disturbed me after I found a position that made my head pound less.

"I'm okay," I grumbled, squinting at him. "Just a headache. Probably shouldn't have had that caffeine so early."

He frowned and leaned over me, his fingers caressing my temples.

"You sure? Didn't your aunt say to call her if you got another headache?"

"I haven't had one since that last appointment." I leaned into his touch. "I think this is an isolated event but I promise to call her if it lasts all day."

"I don't know…" He kissed my forehead and nose then my lips. "Maybe call out today and get some rest."

"Stop worrying."

I pushed him away and tugged the blanket up to my neck.

"Go handle your business and we'll see each other tomorrow."

"Nah, I'm seeing you later today. Bring some shit to my place you can leave behind."

I nodded and started to drift off.

"I love you," I whispered.

"I love you more." He pressed another kiss to my temple. "Call if you need me."

I heard him but chose sleep over responding.

What felt like only a few minutes later, my phone rang, pulling me from bed.

"Bea, what's up?"

"Why haven't you been answering your phone?"

I looked around my bedroom and frowned.

"I was asleep. Did something happen?"

"Girl, it's noon. I thought you were here until Lizzie asked if we had talked. Are you okay?"

What?

I pulled my phone away from my ear and checked the time.

"Shit," I cursed, rushing from bed into the bathroom. "I had a headache this morning and laid down thinking I set an alarm to wake me."

"And how are you feeling now?"

I paused my quick movements and took a deep breath.

"No head pain, thank goodness." I reached into the shower and twisted the handle. "I should be there soon and I'll call Lizzie's office so she knows. Thanks, Bea."

"I got you, girl. See you soon."

I set my phone on the counter and removed August's shirt from my otherwise naked body. As I spun around, I caught sight of my stomach in the hanging door mirror and gasped.

"What the fuck?"

Where the hell had all this belly come from?

I had stupidly thought that expecting mothers were overexaggerating about their bellies sometimes growing overnight.

Oh, no.

I poked at the protruding flesh and turned sideways for a second before deciding that I would freak out about it later. Somehow, I managed to get myself showered, dressed, and hair tamed in less than an hour.

When I arrived, I noticed two school buses parked near the entrance, loading kids inside.

"Damnit." I rushed into the conservatory and stopped by the security office to see Bea. "Can't believe I missed talking to the kids."

She turned with a smile on her face.

"I thought that's where you were at first." She checked her watch and whistled. "You got here fast."

"Can't believe it myself. Look at this shit."

I lifted my shirt and her eyes widened.

"I literally just saw you yesterday. Where was that at?"

"Exactly!"

I stretched both hands out in disbelief.

She chuckled a little then glanced at me a little seriously.

"About yesterday..."

I leaned into the doorframe and crossed my arms.

"What about it?"

She tucked pieces of hair behind her ear and avoided my knowing gaze.

"What does August say about Landon?"

I smiled.

"That he's really smart," I told her. "Kind of unserious but I think it's just his way of protecting himself for whatever reason. Oh and he's a button pusher."

She frowned, her nose scrunched in the cutest way.

"Not my type."

"I wish I knew more about him from my own perspective but remember that August wouldn't know what he's like in a relationship."

"Doesn't matter," she said, turning toward the screens. "I'm not in a position to start anything new. Besides, I'm about to enroll in school later today. Men are distractions."

I straightened at her news.

"You're going back?"

Smiling, she glanced over her shoulder.

"I think it's time, don't you?"

She'd dropped out a while back and took this job to take

care of her grandmother and the medical bills that came with her declining health.

Now that some things had changed in the last year, I guess she was ready to try again.

"Oh, Bea! I'm so proud of you!"

I wrapped my arms around her shoulders from behind, pressing the side of my face against hers.

"And I'm sure your granny is excited for you."

She sighed as I pulled away.

"If she remembered me, I'm sure she would be."

"Yeah..." I gripped her shoulder and turned toward the door. "I know that has to be tough for you."

"That's why I appreciated yesterday so much," she confessed. "Hearing Landon name different careers people in their family have gave me the push I needed to act on my long forgotten plans."

I looked over my shoulder and said, "Sometimes all we need is a little push."

I moved to start my day, stopping by my office to put on the proper gear.

Once in the enclosure, my stomach rolled at the smell.

"Hey, girlie," Lizzie greeted, a large bucket with fish hanging off her arm. "Are you okay? You look a little green?"

I plastered on a smile and shook my head.

"I'm good. Got lost in my head for a moment. Have you done afternoon meds yet?"

She regarded me closely but didn't question me further.

"Not yet. I figured you'd get here by then."

"Mmhm," I hummed, stepping away from her and the stinky fish. "I'll handle that now."

Once a distance away, I took a breath and thanked God the need to hurl had passed.

To protect my nose, I grabbed a clean mask and slipped it on.

There were only two penguins who needed meds this week. A gentoo named Mimi and a chinstrap named Nico. Giving them antibiotics through their food was the easy part, but the problem with those two was they liked to fight.

Chinstrap penguins loved being in the water. It was where you'd usually find them but Nico was different. He hung out near the gentoos on rocky terrain and Mimi gave him a run for his money on most days.

They were easy to spot and not just by the flapper bands each had, but the loud shrieking from Mimi.

"No hitting, young lady," I chastised as I approached. "We've talked about this. He likes you."

She stepped her little web feet toward me and I handed her krill over, drawing the attention of penguins nearby.

I moved around them, eyes on Nico.

"You're coming on too strong, my guy," I told him, throwing the krill into his open beak. "Try playing it smooth from now on."

After I watched them flap around, some following my every movement, I left the enclosure and headed into my office to handle paperwork.

The faster you get this done, the faster you get to go home, I thought as my phone vibrated on the desk.

I cut my eyes at the screen, set on ignoring it until I saw August's name.

"Hello," I sang, happy to hear his voice. "How did everything go with the lawyer?"

He took a shuddering breath and I slapped my pen on the desk, confused.

"What's wrong, baby?"

He wouldn't say anything but I could hear what sounded like ragged breaths.

"I-I n-need you," he muttered.

I snatched my desk drawer open and grabbed my bag.

"I'm on my way," I told him, grateful that we'd shared our locations a while back and neither of us stopped. "Stay where you are, okay?"

"D-Don't hang u-up."

Fuck.

He was scaring me.

TWENTY-EIGHT

WITH A FEW HOURS TO spare before my meeting with Shondra's lawyer, I headed to the distillery.

I hadn't been on the grounds since bringing January home and wanted to sneak into a meeting with Mia. Wedding season was approaching and she was set on doing better than last year.

"August!" she greeted with a smile, fucking up my attempt to enter undetected. "Surprised to see you this morning. We're getting started a little late."

I nodded and took a seat in the back against the wall.

"Pretend like I'm not here."

Mia nodded and got right down to business, whipping out her laptop and sharing the screen on the projector.

"We have five spring and ten summer weddings. The fall is filling up as we speak, so I'm happy to announce that we will double profits from last year's wedding season."

I clapped twice and earned a smile from my cousin before she jumped back into the meeting, all business. She was good at her job and efficient as fuck.

"Find out from the quads if there's anything new we can add to the available wine and liquor list."

A couple of gazes glanced where I sat but didn't speak up.

Everyone knew the quads were my sisters and me. People mostly used it to avoid having to say all our names.

"My new blend should be ready by the summer weddings," I tossed out. "We can offer it as a tester option depending on the package couples choose. I'm not ready to have it on the shelves yet but it would be good to get feedback from possible consumers who aren't family."

"We're ready to try when you're ready for us," the head of marketing chimed in, quickly gathering support from the others in low murmurs.

"Find me at the bar all day tomorrow for your sample."

Mia took over, finished the rest of her talking points, then sent everyone on their way. When the last person exited, she dropped down in a chair at the table and rolled it in front of me.

"You look stressed, what's up?"

I forgot I hadn't filled her in on the custody issue and made a mental note to update everyone in the cousin group chat while explaining my dilemma.

"So, she just dropped it on you without any indication that she would?" she asked.

I nodded and Mia's frown deepened.

"Do you know whose court it'll be in?"

"Not your mom's," I said, lifting an eyebrow. "If it did come across her desk she wouldn't take it and I wouldn't want her to."

She nodded.

"Sometimes I wish we could use that to our advantage though," she mused, rolling her eyes.

"Lily's dad still on some bullshit, huh?"

Mia laughed.

"I stopped trying to get him to acknowledge her more when she started putting two and two together."

"What do you mean?"

She leaned forward and shook her head.

"The last time he saw her was about six months ago. He gave her his phone number, told her to call or text any time now that she was 'old enough' to communicate without my help. I think for a while she thought I was keeping him from her but after months of calling and texting and barely getting a reply, she came to her own conclusion."

Damn.

"And I hate it because I never wanted that for her. Been feeling like the worst kind of mother lately."

"Come on, Mia. Don't go down that road."

"I know I shouldn't but it was my decision making skills that has my daughter out here feeling like she's not enough for her father to simply answer the phone and say hello."

"Fuck that. We all made some questionable decisions eleven years ago. Lily is smart, and respectful, and honest. Only a good parent can raise a kid like that. If Will doesn't want to know his own flesh and blood, that's his loss. Be who you've always been to her and hold on to that."

Maybe in ten years when January started asking questions, I'd be able to remember this conversation and take my own advice.

"Shit…" Mia sat up. "I didn't mean to drop that on you this early."

I shook my head and stood, pulling her up with me.

"We are family. You can unload on me any day and I'm sorry I haven't checked in—"

"Aht. Aht," she chastised, pushing me away with a laugh.

"Dude. You became a dad overnight. I would never hold being too busy to check-in against you."

"Alright but if you need me to fuck Will up just call. Landon's been waiting to get hands on him."

Mia scoffed and rolled her eyes before following me to the door.

"I wouldn't waist my 'come beat this nigga ass' coins on my deadbeat ex. He's not worth it."

I chuckled and moved into the hall.

"I feel it." I checked my watch and turned toward the direction of my office. "I'm heading out at noon but I'll be around until then if I'm needed."

"You probably won't be but August?"

I paused halfway up the hall and glanced over my shoulder.

"Yeah?"

"Thanks for always listening and congrats on becoming a dad. You'll do good, don't ever doubt that."

I turned to face her but took steps backward.

"Thanks, cuz."

She nodded and threw her hands up.

"Can I get Journi's number if you have it?" she asked. "I should've asked last night but it slipped my mind. Lily is dying to hang with Kali again. The two of them exchanged numbers but I want to make sure she's cool with them getting close."

I smiled at the thought of my family and Couri's coming together on their own accord.

"I'll give your number to Couri and have her pass it along to her sister."

"Appreciate it!"

She waved me off and slipped back into the conference room.

When my afternoon meeting rolled around, I found myself quickly reminded of all I had going on.

"Mr. Hanson," Barton Brown greeted, standing from his desk as his assistant led me into his office. "I'm glad you could make it. Your lawyer filled me in about your custody dilemma and there was only so much I could reveal to her before speaking to you about Ms. Thomas's will."

He waved toward one of the chairs stationed in front of his desk and I took a seat.

"I apologize for not getting to you in a more timely fashion." He pulled a few pieces of paper from a manila envelope and lifted his gaze to meet mine. "I have to read this in its entirety, so please bear with me."

I frowned, confused by his impersonal cadence, but nodded.

Nothing he said registered though.

I couldn't focus on anything but his monotone voice and the way he dragged his words as if he were from Boston.

"Do you have any questions?"

I blinked and sat back.

"Questions about?"

He shuffled the paper back with a huff.

"Ms. Thomas left fifty-five thousand dollars for you and a blue sapphire diamond ring she'd like passed down to her daughter when she's of age. You'll have to fill out some paperwork for me and I'll handle the transfer of money from there."

"We don't need her money," I said, shaking my head. "I'm only worried about custody. What is it you know that can squash her mother's claim?"

"You have to take the money. After it's in your possession, you can do with it what you will. Donate it to charity, open a trust fund for your daughter..." He sighed and sat back, loosening the only clasped button on his suit jacket. "I have to follow the will."

"And custody?"

It was all I cared about.

"As a 'just in case' she never got around to signing her parental rights away..." He slipped a piece of paper from the back of the pile and slid it to me. "We had this addendum added to her will. It states, in her own words, that if she were to pass on during or after childbirth that the biological father —August Hanson—is to take custody."

"Why didn't she sign the papers?"

He adjusted his tie, tugging it from his neck a little.

"I advised her to wait until she'd given birth. Sometimes all it takes for a mother to have a change of heart is to hold their baby for the first time."

"She wouldn't have changed her mind," I snapped, standing. "Is that all?"

His baby blue eyes widened.

"Ah, well, I need this paperwork filled out and you're good to go."

I took the stapled pages from him and turned toward the door.

"I think I'll go out into the waiting room and get it done."

Being in his office only made this more real.

I couldn't breathe and stepped outside the building for some privacy.

Leaning my back against the cold brick, papers sticking to my damp hand, I called Couri.

"Hello," she sang into the phone. "How did everything go with the lawyer?"

I took a shuddering breath and could hear Couri stop whatever she was doing.

"What's wrong, baby?"

I tried to let air in my lungs but nothing seemed to work. My throat burned as I tried to speak. "I-I n-need you."

"I'm on my way. Stay where you are, okay?"

"D-Don't hang u-up."

I could feel her panicked movements.

"I won't," she said softly. "I'm here. Just keep trying to breathe. Slow breaths. In and out."

I crouched down and listened to the sound of her voice coaching me through whatever was happening to me.

"It hurts," I murmured, blinking tears away.

"I think maybe you're having a panic attack."

"No." I shook my head. "All of it hurts, Couri."

She was silent for a while then in the softest voice, she said, "Let it be."

I did that, let myself feel without stipulation and it was almost too painful to bear alone.

But I wasn't alone, especially after Couri sat next to me on the ground and curled her fingers around my neck.

My heart broke for my child.

January deserved more but so did I.

Not a letter or money or a stupid fucking ring.

Shondra left chaos at my door and I felt like I was drowning in it.

"You came," I murmured, pulling Couri into my lap, papers forgotten on the ground beside me.

"I'll always show up for you, August Hanson. Same as you would for me."

I'd never felt the innate need to cry before, but the tears were rolling before I could stop them and Couri held me like I had done for her.

She didn't let go until I took a deep breath in the crook of her neck and murmured, "Thank you for being my safe space."

In that moment, with us on the ground, I realized she was

more than just the love of my life. Couri was my lifeline, the only person who could put me back together again with the sound of her voice.

She was my everything.

Before I could demand she marry me, my phone rang, stopped, then rang again.

Couri grabbed it from my jacket pocket and swiped the screen.

"Hey, Lola." She brushed lingering tears from my face while nodding. "Yeah. He's here. Just needed a moment to gather himself. Yeah, I got him. Okay, hold on."

She placed the phone on speaker.

"He can hear you."

"Hey, Aug," Lola greeted softly. "I got a hearing date. Anything I need to know about your meeting with Barton?"

"Right now?" I asked, not in the mood to deal with court shit.

"Yeah. Right now is probably best while it's fresh."

"How'd you know I was finished?"

"I—okay, Barton called and said you'd run out without leaving some important paperwork behind. Are you okay?"

"I don't know."

"That's honest. It's okay not to know."

"She put in her will that she wanted January to be with her father, named me specifically."

"Great. The DNA results will be back before the hearing. I'm certain the judge will deny Helen's petition and close the case."

Knowing that hadn't changed my mood.

"There shouldn't have been a fucking case."

"You're right but there is one and we're handling it. I need you to get yourself together and fill out that paperwork so we can end this once and for all."

"Alright, yeah..."

Couri stood and pulled me up.

"I'll do that and thanks for calling, Lo."

I handed the phone off and went back into the building.

It took me twenty minutes to get the paperwork filled out with my banking information for the money. Barton then gave me a key to a safety deposit box with the ring in it.

After I finished with him, I went in search of Couri and found her leaning against my truck.

"You gotta get back to work, right?"

She nodded.

"I was actually late, so I'll probably stay an extra hour or two to catch up on some stuff."

I frowned and brushed my fingers across her forehead, checking her temperature.

"Why were you late? Slept in?"

"Yeah and look..." Couri pulled me toward her and opened the driver side door to conceal us. "Your baby did this to me."

I leaned back, eyes wide at the sudden change in the size of her stomach.

She was still small but it hadn't been like this the night before.

"You think it's two in there?" I asked, smiling at the look of horror on her face. "Afraid of multiples?"

"I refuse," she grumbled, shoving my shoulder.

I knew it was a joke but still found myself asking, "What do you refuse?"

Couri blinked a few times and tipped her head.

"Um... what exactly is the question?"

"I asked if you were afraid of multiples and you replied *I refuse*. What does that mean?"

"Oh..." She shrugged. "It was a joke. I didn't actually mean..."

Her eyes widened a little and she took a step away from me.

"You didn't mean what?"

"If you have to ask then you don't know me at all," she accused, drawing further away. "That doubt in your eyes is hurting my feelings, August."

"I'm not—" She walked away and I went after her. "Couri, don't do that. Please, turn around and talk to me."

I wanted to grab her arm but with us both in our feelings I chose to keep my fingers to myself and moved in front of her instead.

She bumped into my chest and only then did I hold her in place to stop a fall from occurring. Her eyes were wet with tears and I felt like a dick for putting them there.

"Couri—"

"No," she cut in. "I get it. Emotions are high and there's a lot on your mind. My joke was in bad taste but I thought you trusted me. I would never..."

She wiped her eyes and stepped around me.

"I have to get back to work but I'll call you afterward."

"You'll end the night with me."

In my mind it had been a question but the words left my lips in the form of a demand.

"I will call you," she reiterated, widening the space between us.

Instead of upsetting her more by opening my mouth to argue, I watched until she got in her truck and drove away.

Annoyed with myself, I headed toward my parents' place to grab January.

Hopefully, Couri would allow me to make up for how I handled her later tonight.

TWENTY-NINE

couri

"DO YOU THINK I'M TRIPPIN'?"

I propped my phone up on the jug of milk and slid my bowl of Cap'n Crunch in front of me.

"Your feelings are valid," Journi said, half her face out of the screen as she worked while playing therapist.

"But—"

"There aren't any buts. He let what his ex did trickle into your relationship, even if it was only for a brief moment. You can be upset but make sure you verbalize why it upset you. Give him the room to grow from his mistake and you two will be fine."

I shoveled cereal in my mouth, mentally chastising myself for not having more than lunch today.

"You make it sound so easy."

She scoffed but never looked at the camera.

"The only thing remotely easy about not letting the small misunderstandings later become big misunderstandings is a partner who's on the same page as you."

"But how do you know they're on the same page as you?

297

Me and August usually communicate well, but today it was like he'd seen me as Shondra for a minute."

It hurt my feelings way more than I would have liked.

"Maybe, for that minute, he did see you as Shondra."

I frowned and pointed my spoon at the camera.

"You aren't helping his case."

"I'm here to tell my baby sister the truth, not coddle her feelings because that'll ruin a relationship before it ever helps. Plus, I like August for you."

"I like him for me too," I murmured harshly. "The fact that I have to have this conversation with you right now is making me upset with him more. He should know."

"You should tell him that."

I growled and Journi popped the other eye into the camera.

"Don't get angry with me because I'm right. I'll always be a non-judgmental listening ear but you're only talking to me to avoid talking to him."

"I'm not avoiding him."

"Then why are you home?"

"Because I live here," I deadpanned.

"You've been under that man and living in his skin for a while now. I can't believe I missed the signs before."

I rolled my eyes.

"Couri Lee Mitchell, get off my phone and go be with your family."

She hung up and I burst into tears but managed to finish my cereal through the sobs.

No matter how hard I tried to stop myself from crying I couldn't.

Frustrated with my emotions, I climbed the stairs toward my bedroom and crawled beneath the covers. It was so stupid how upset I was, but the more I thought about August and his grief it reminded me that I was supposed to be grieving too.

How could I allow myself to forget?

Burying my face in the closest pillow, I screamed over and over until I physically couldn't anymore.

I realized as a deafening silence filled the space around me that I wasn't angry at August for having insecurities nor myself for finding happiness in a deep sea of grief.

I was angry at God and that wasn't a truth I could bear.

Not when now was the time I needed his guidance the most.

Confused and physically drained, I curled into a ball and let sleep take me under.

A dull ache in my lower belly slowly pulled me from my slumber. I rolled from side to side until the sound of banging from a distance snapped me from my misery.

"Okay! Okay!" I yelled, flipping the blanket back. "Geez."

Halfway down the stairs, I stopped to touch my stomach. Everything hurt, my entire body, but that tick in my belly gave me pause.

"Couri!" August yelled through the door, drawing my attention away from the sense of dread filling me.

I snatched the door open once I reached it, eyeing a concerned August with a car seat clutched between the fingers of his right hand.

"Sorry," I mumbled, blinking the sleep from my eyes. "I didn't hear you knocking."

"Or my calls," he said, moving me back as he stepped inside. "I was worried when it got dark and I hadn't heard from you. Your location said you were home and I thought you were avoiding me."

I leaned against the wall to catch my breath.

"And you decided it was best to show up here?"

He set the carrier next to my feet and leaned his body into mine.

"Yeah, it sounded like the perfect fucking idea."

I grimaced and his eyes moved across my face in shock then worry.

"August..."

He gripped my forearms and stopped me from swaying.

"What's wrong?" he asked, cupping my face. "Couri, baby..."

"I don't..." I tried blinking the haze away. "I can't. Something's not right."

He brushed his fingers all over my body, calling out for me to speak if where he was touching hurt.

"Shit. We need to take you to the ER."

Emergency room?

"No," I whispered, pushing him away. "I'm fine. I'm fine."

But nothing was fine.

My skin buzzed as I turned to walk away.

"Couri!" he bellowed, the bass in his voice stopping me in my tracks and drawing me from the fuzziness inside my head.

What the fuck is wrong with me?

"Baby, look at me," he serenaded softly. "You're right. Something's wrong but you have to let me help you, okay?"

The ache in my belly intensified and I cried out for him.

"Okay." I nodded. "P-please, help."

"I got you." He curled his fingers around my waist and pulled me close. "We're going to get shoes on you and go, alright?"

"O-okay."

"Don't worry, I got you."

He took care of me as I sat dazed and confused, somehow managing to get me out the door with a baby hanging off his arm.

"I'm sorry," I whispered, resting my head against the window as he drove. "I fell asleep and—"

"We don't need to talk about that," he cut in. "And even if we were, you aren't the one who needs to be apologizing."

August took my hand and held it until we made it to the ER.

After forty minutes of being checked in, they put us in an observation room.

"She should be home asleep, not here," I complained.

"She needs to be right where she is," he quipped, rocking the car seat with his foot. "With us."

"What if—"

"Don't go there."

Our eyes met and I knew he'd already been there and back.

"We'll be okay," I said, reaching for his hand. "You and me, right?"

He dropped the foot he used to rock the carrier and leaned forward, bringing our joined fingers to his mouth.

"Yeah, me and you."

The nurse came in and checked my vitals.

"Your blood pressure is low and you have a spiked temperature," she said, writing the numbers down. "Is there pain anywhere?"

"There's an ache in my lower belly..." I rested my hand on my stomach, needing to feel the bump. "I'm almost four months pregnant."

She took notes on her chart.

"She was faint," August added, always the one to be involved no matter what. "And a little lethargic."

"And when you're sitting down, how do you feel?"

"Tired but less wobbly."

She nodded and I tried to get read on her but she was a beacon of professionalism.

"The doctor is doing her rounds now. She should be in soon, so sit tight for me, okay?"

I rolled my head toward August and tried my hardest not to cry but the tears broke free of my resolve.

"I can't stop from crying. They just keep coming and coming and coming."

August chuckled and I glowered in his direction.

"I'm sorry, baby," he said, caressing my fingers with his thumb. "It's just I've never seen you like this before and while I hate it, I think you're cute."

"You find my pain cute?"

It was such a dramatic response that I found myself laughing through the sobs.

"It's the hormones, right? None of this will last forever."

"Maybe. Maybe not," he said softly. "Let's make sure you and the little one are alright first then we'll worry about the long-term effects of pregnancy."

"Okay." I nodded, feeling satisfied with that solution. "Yeah, let's do that."

We sat in silence for a while.

August anxiously checked January more often than necessary.

She was a little squirmy but slept through the chaos and noise of the emergency room.

It was pretty impressive.

"I know I hurt your feelings earlier," August said out of nowhere. "You didn't deserve that."

I took my hand from his and laced my fingers together, resting them over the white knitted blanket.

"August, I would never—"

"I know your heart. That shit had nothing to do with how I see you or the level of trust I have in you."

"But it felt that way," I murmured, staring at the monitor beside me. "I can't say that I understand what you're going

through but I know you're angry and rightfully so. It's just...
maybe you aren't seeing the bigger picture."

"And you see it?" he asked, tone soft.

"I think you are angrier at yourself for believing Shondra
would never do something like this. You loved her, the two of
you moved on, but she shattered your trust and dropped the
pieces on your doorstep."

She had every right to choose the direction of her life. Not
wanting children wasn't the problem and it never would be.

"In the midst of all that brokenness, you've stood strong in
my heart and mind," he avowed. "Untouched and in perfect
shape."

I turned on my side to face him.

"Do you really believe that?"

"I know it with all of my heart." He leaned forward and
rested his palm against my face. "I'm sorry I let doubt seep into
our well-built foundation. Whatever I have to do to fix it, I
will."

"Just be here with me as you are. I'm really scared right
now."

He brushed his lips against mine and sighed. "I'm so
sorry."

"I accept your apology."

The words left my lips as the doctor made herself known
on the other side of the curtain.

When a Black woman stepped in, a sense of relief washed
over me.

Everything would be okay.

THIRTY

"AUGUST! WE NEED TO TALK," Helen demanded from behind us.

My mother spun around before I did.

"He doesn't have anything to say to you, Helen," she warned.

Have you taken your iron pill?

I pushed send on the text to Couri before giving Shondra's mother my attention.

Had my mother not insisted on being here with me, using threats to get her way, I'd have walked away already. We were due in court in thirty minutes and I wasn't in the fucking mood for Helen or my mother's need to punch shit.

"I don't want to fight," Helen said, taking a step back.

The man standing at her side, her lawyer presumably, looked a tad uncomfortable as he laid his hand against her forearm.

"We should—"

"No." Helen snatched away from him. "I only want to talk. We can—"

I took a step forward.

"You had ample opportunity to talk," I snapped. "Before you decided to petition for custody. When I came by your place and the time that has passed since. Now you want to talk and I really don't feel like listening."

She reared back as if I slapped her, but if anyone felt beat up on it was me.

"August—"

"Look." I spotted Lola speed walking toward us and sighed. "This is what you wanted and now we're here. I'm sorry you lost your daughter but you won't be taking mine."

Lola pushed me back. "Whatever this is... We're done. I suggest you escort your client away from mine, Mr. O'Brien. I'm sure the judge would love to hear how she accosted him before court."

Lola led us over to a bench and waved for Mom to sit, her gaze narrowed.

"I love you, Auntie, but I have a full workload today and I'd appreciate you not adding to it by getting locked up."

"I have a perfectly good criminal lawyer on retainer, but I promise not to make your day harder."

Lola chuckled and turned to me.

"What was that about?"

I shrugged and checked my phone for a new text.

"She wanted to talk but there's nothing to talk about. Not this late in the game."

I swiped through my messages with Couri, smiling at the pictures she'd sent of January doing tummy time. She hadn't liked it until she learned to hold her head up.

"Is there something more important than why we're here on that phone?"

Yes, I took them. Just as I have every day for the last two weeks.

I tucked it away after getting the confirmation I needed.

"Besides making sure my girls are alright, nah. Couri's iron levels are just getting back on track since the scare. I worry a little when we're apart."

Lola nodded.

"This should be quick." She waved toward the courtroom door as it opened but then shook her head to stop us. "Before we go inside, check your email."

I grabbed my phone and pulled up the app, pausing after getting a glimpse of why she wanted me to check. It sat right at the top, marked urgent from Lola's work email.

My mom leaned over to get a look at what I was staring at and drew in a breath.

"Well," she mused, resting a hand on my shoulder. "Open it and see."

I tapped the email and once it loaded, zoomed in to read what was there.

Mom caught it first, her little shout of joy telling me everything I needed to know.

It took a second to get there but as my gaze slid over what she'd seen, I sighed in relief.

The alleged father is not excluded as the biological father of the tested child.

The probability of paternity read ninety-nine point nine percent.

She was mine.

I'd known it with all my heart and there it was, big as day, proving me right.

January Marie Hanson was mine.

Thank God.

I had come into this today certain Helen's petition would be denied, but not having the DNA results sooner left me worried it could be prolonged until the court established paternity.

Our docket number was called shortly after we entered the courtroom.

The bailiff called out the infamous *all rise* and we stood.

"The honorable Judge Lawrence is presiding."

Lola stiffened beside me as the man in question entered, his eyes pinned intensely on my cousin.

"Is that—"

Lola shot me a look and I closed my mouth.

"Please be seated," Judge Lawrence instructed, waving off a courtroom norm as if he was annoyed by it.

I glanced at Lola, and she'd secured her poker face for masses, but I knew she was itching to bolt.

Quinten Lawrence was the... *had been* the love of her teenage life.

The last time I'd seen him his father had been stripped of his robe and charged with judicial misconduct. He left town a week later on his eighteenth birthday, leaving behind the one person he promised forever to.

I glanced back at my mom and she widened her eyes before looking away. She was as shocked to see him as I was.

Quinten started to announce what was being brought forth but Lola cut in, standing.

"Was this not assigned to Judge Lenox?" she questioned.

Quinten leaned forward but didn't respond.

Lola was simmering, her fists clenched as she restated her question, "*Your honor,* I was not made aware of the change in judgeship for this hearing."

"Judge Lenox has the flu," he explained. "Now the case belongs to me. Is that okay with you, Ms. Hanson?"

"Yes, your honor. Please, continue."

As she sat down, I flipped open the notepad covered in a leather binding and wrote, *you good?*

Instead of taking the pen, she traced *no* with her finger and started to speak, "Motion to dismiss, your honor. My client was not aware of the deceased being with child. He learned of it after the plaintiff called him to a hospital and broke the news. I have two signed affidavits from a nurse and social worker on shift that day attesting to the plaintiff mentioning my client's name as the father."

Lola flipped through pages as she talked, walking them one by one from the table to the bailiff, who handed them to Quinten.

She'd barely taken a breath but her voice was clear and confident.

"Here is a copy of the letter the plaintiff had delivered to my client by a nurse on shift that same day. It states clear as day what the deceased wanted for her unborn child and who the presumed father is. The deceased has a will and once more stated where and whom she wanted her unborn with. Per the court's order, the question of paternity has been satisfied by a DNA testing facility assigned by the court. My client August Hanson is the father of January Hanson. Each party, along with the court, should have a copy of the results."

She took a step around the table and continued, "Please excuse my tone when I say that the plaintiff and her counsel have wasted not only the court's time but its resources for a half-cocked reach."

Quentin flipped through pages I hadn't even known Lola was collecting.

He got to the last one and lifted his head, eyes starting on Lola but settling on Helen and her lawyer.

"Mr. O'Brien, is there anything you'd like to add on your

client's behalf? Before you speak, I'd like to remind the court that time is taxpayers' money."

He'd agreed with Lola in a not so subtle way.

"My client would like propose a visitation arrangement—"

Lola turned quickly, shaking her head.

"Your honor—"

"Mr. O'Brien, I asked you not to waste the taxpayers' dollars but what you're doing by asking the court to change the nature of the petition filed is the opposite..." His gaze slid to Helen. "The court is sorry for your loss. But we won't be discussing visitation today nor will this court be awarding custody of the child in question to anyone other than her biological father."

He flipped the papers over and picked up his gavel.

"Motion to dismiss, *granted*."

Lola came over and kissed my cheek.

"Told you it would all be good. Let's get out of here."

I knew she needed to put distance between her past and present and blocked Quinten's view of her while she quickly packed up her shit.

Looking over my shoulder, I met his gaze and tipped my head.

Whatever moment he planned to coerce out of her wasn't happening on my watch.

He nodded and called for the next case.

I ushered Lola and Mom out into the hall then down the stairwell to the main floor after Lola fussed about us wanting to take the elevator. Once outside I watched her take a breath then turn to us.

"I need to meet with my next client but I love the both of you. Don't tell anyone about Quinten, please. At least not until after my day has ended."

Lola's request was really for her gossiping auntie. She knew I was a steel trap.

"I won't say anything, Lo Lo," Mom said, giving her a kiss on the cheek. "By the way, you would've made a great criminal lawyer."

Lola chuckled.

"I'm sure I'd be rich off your cases alone. Thank you." She turned and expertly speed walked off in heels. "Gotta go. I'm on a schedule."

"She'll be okay," Mom said as we walked to the other side of the parking lot.

"Have no doubt about that."

"How are you feeling now that this is over?"

"Is it really over?" I asked. "Nothing about this makes me happy. January loses in the end."

"When things settle down you and Helen can work things out. I—"

"I'm not working shit out with that lady," I griped, snatching open the driver's door of her car. "Excuse my language but it'll be a while before she can speak to me."

"And that's fine but because I raised you, I know you won't hold a grudge. Time and another baby will soften you right up. Speaking of..." She slid into her seat and glanced at me. "How is Couri?"

"Worried about me while I'm worrying about her. She's doing better though. I guess I wasn't exactly prepared for low iron being this big of a problem."

She hadn't told me a nurse called after her first prenatal appointment to recommend an additional iron supplement. I almost wanted to be upset with her but how could I be?

The pressure to take care of yourself properly in the middle of grieving felt criminal.

But we had to be better, for ourselves, and the kids that'll depend on us for a lifetime.

"A lot of change happens in a woman's body to accommodate a pregnancy," Mom said, pulling her door shut while rolling the window down simultaneously. "You and Couri have a long way to go and the work won't stop after she has the baby. Be patient with one another."

I nodded and brushed a hand down my face.

"Is that what you and Pop did with four babies?"

She chuckled.

"Your father and I played rock paper scissors in the middle of night on many occasions, but I found peace in knowing that he was equally as tired. He put in the same amount of work and effort as me. I pray that you and Couri find that kind of peace."

"That mean you like her?"

"Like her?" She leaned out the window. "Maybe it's too soon but I love her for you. Never have I seen you look at anyone the way you look at her. I don't think I've seen anyone look at you the way she does."

I took a step back and waved for her to leave.

"I love you, lady. Thanks for always having my back."

She tossed a saucy smile my way as she backed out of the parking lot.

"I love you more. No matter how old you get, you're my baby. Now stop watching me and go home to your family."

My family.

It had a nice ring to it.

And for what it was worth, they were mine.

We were each other's and there weren't any outside forces that could change that.

It didn't take long for me to get home and as I walked through the door the sight before me stopped my world. June was laid across the couch with her feet propped in Couri's lap, eyes barely open from laughing.

"No, I mean, it wasn't funny at first," Couri explained through sputters. "I was terrified of that damn lion but it didn't even blink at me."

She had a sleeping January propped up against her chest and I smiled.

"I love lions," June mused, her eyes meeting mine. "Oh, hey, brother. I didn't realize you were home. Couri was telling me about her wildlife adventures while we waited on you."

She hadn't been here when I left, nor had she let me know she was coming over at all.

But I appreciated her showing up where she was needed the most.

"Don't let me disturb this little bonding moment," I teased, approaching the sofa to squeeze between them. "Move your legs off my woman, Ju."

She rolled her eyes but lifted her legs for me to sit and then dropped them in my lap afterward.

"You sound jealous but there's no need. I like men and even if I did like women yours isn't my type."

"I don't know whether to be offended or intrigued," Couri said, laughing.

"Don't be offended, boo. You're way too pretty. If I were into women I think I'd want one a little less dainty."

She sat up and stretched.

"I take it everything went well in court," June surmised, slipping her feet into a pair of pink Crocs.

"Judge dismissed it after Lola basically told the court Helen was wasting everyone's time."

June snorted.

"One thing about Lo Lo, she hates time wasters. There was no doubt in my mind that things would work out how they were supposed to..." She leaned down and kissed my cheek. "Love you. I'm gonna head to work."

She kissed January's cheek and squeezed Couri's shoulder before what she said set in.

"You never work on Tuesdays," I pointed out, frowning at her retreating frame. "Is there something I need to know?"

"Nope. Just feel like creating some shit."

I didn't believe her but most importantly she knew I wouldn't and refused to turn around and face me.

"Have a good time *creating* shit," Couri called as the front door shut behind June.

I glanced at my woman, frown deepening.

"You know something."

She smiled and turned her body, stretching it and her legs over mine.

"I know nothing. Did court really go fine?"

"Court was interesting. Why does it feel like my sister is hiding something from me?"

"She's not hiding any more than you did when we first started out."

"Touché," I replied, reaching out to steal January.

"Why was court interesting?"

"Judge Quinten Lawrence."

I rested my head back and closed my eyes, hopeful for a couple of minutes of sleep.

"Am I supposed to know who that is?"

I hummed, forgetting she was new to the fold.

"Now that you've been integrated into my family, what we talk about is meant for our ears only."

She laughed and I popped one eye open.

"What's funny?"

"You thinking I'd actually tell anyone the things we talk about in private."

"It's the furthest from what I think," I told her. "We have to seal the bond."

She raised an eyebrow and I smiled.

"Repeat what I said back to me."

"Which part?" she asked, raising up a little.

"What we talk about is for our ears only."

She regarded me closely but repeated my words back to me verbatim.

"Now what?"

"We sealed the bond. Now your secrets are mine and vice versa."

She snorted and let out a bark of laughter that widened the smile on my face.

"Alright…" Her eyes met mine. "Who is Judge Quinten Lawrence?"

I smirked then told all of Lola's business, at least the shit I was privy to.

"Damn," Couri mumbled. "That had to be tough."

She took her feet from my legs and tucked them underneath my thigh.

"Yeah, I don't—"

January farted and wiped the words right out of my mouth as the sound startled her awake. Her big brown eyes met mine and she smiled.

"Don't think I'll ever get used to you—Ah, fuck you're taking a shit aren't you?"

The area where she sat warmed and I sighed.

She was definitely taking a shit and smiling while doing it.

"She's gonna have such a potty mouth," Couri said through her laughter as the farting continued.

I lifted January with both hands and cursed as my fingers grazed something seeping through her onesie.

"Okay, okay." I stood and held her away from my body. "You nasty little…"

Couri's laughter grew louder, got all under my skin, and before I knew it I was laughing.

January's face contorted then she let out a wail that brought me to attention.

"Now you wanna cry after laughing at me," I grumbled, taking her to the nursery.

It took a minute to get her wiped down and a clean diaper under her butt, but we managed. Leaving her locked behind the adjustable side rails on the changing table, I went into the bathroom and loaded her baby tub with water.

I could hear her feet hitting the water resistant pad as she thrust them against it.

A soft melodic hum over my shoulder gathered my attention and I glanced back.

"I'd love to help," Couri said, leaning against the door jamb with January tucked in the crook of her arm. "More than just today or every now and again. I want this and everything that comes with it forever."

I straightened and stepped toward her.

"Is there anything else you want to add to that?"

Our eyes lingered on one another for a long while before she softly whispered, "Yes."

I pressed my hand against the wall connecting to the bathroom's entrance and leaned in her personal space.

"Yes you have something to add or yes you'll marry me?"

"Yes, I'll marry you," she replied without pause.

Finally!

"Size five. Pear-shaped halo diamond, with an encrusted band."

She shifted against me and I smirked.

"Mmhm. Exactly that."

My lips brushed hers as I took January and sat at the edge of the tub to lower her inside the mini version of it. I waved for Couri to join me and she sat at the other end, dropping her hand in the water. She swayed her fingers back and forth as she watched me.

"You and me, right?" I asked, meeting her dark gaze.

"Yeah..." She nodded and slid in close until her knee touched mine. "You and me."

PART FOUR

where we ended up

"You are my sun, my moon, and all of my stars."
– E.E Cummings

THIRTY-ONE

couri

"JANUARY, NO!"

I narrowed my eyes at her fist dangling off the side of the high chair.

She mimicked the expression on my face and unclenched her fingers, dropping a helping of baby cereal on the floor.

As if the acrobat I was carrying felt mischievous behavior going on, they kicked.

"Mm," I grunted, caressing my belly.

This kid loved to kick and sit on my bladder.

They loved to do everything but turn around during an ultrasound to give us the answer we'd been waiting on. Seven and a half months pregnant and nothing. Though, we had decided that whether a boy or girl we were naming them October.

"Da Da," January blurted for the first time as she tossed more cereal.

"August!" I screamed, fumbling with my phone to get the camera up. "Say that one more time, Snowflake."

I padded toward her as August came barreling down the stairs and flew into the kitchen, sans a shirt.

"What's wrong?" he asked, slightly panicked.

Since my scare a few months back, he's been on edge. Especially if I say his name a little too loudly. I'd been good at not doing it but January saying *da da* for the first time got me excited.

"I'm okay. I promise. Snowflake said—"

"Da da da da da," she performed, kicking her chubby legs at the sight of August.

"Oh, shit," he cursed, covering his mouth with a fist. "Did you get that?"

"I got it."

He started to remove her from the chair and she squealed in excitement.

They were twins, those two.

Her skin had darkened to match his hue. She had the cutest button nose that I realized resembled her Aunt June's more than anyone else's.

"Say it one more time," he sang, holding her Lion King style while spinning in circles. "Da Da. Come on, you can do it. Da Da."

She did everything but repeat his words.

Laughing, I pressed record again and caught the moment in real time.

He was such a good fucking dad.

A good man.

A *great* one.

"You probably want to stop spinning, she—"

January spit up right in his face and I covered my mouth to stop from laughing.

"Damnit."

I moved to help him, grabbing a few paper towels to clean his forehead.

"Da da da da," January finally repeated, clapping her little hands.

"I think she likes catching you off guard," I surmised, tossing away the soiled towels as he sat her on the countertop.

"She's a menace," August griped with a smile. "Our menace but one, nonetheless."

She pushed herself up with the help of Daddy and bounced on her chubby feet.

"She's said no, two, and da da. Remind me to write that in her little book."

I nodded and leaned against the counter.

"Do you think she'll..." I shook my head, feeling stupid for wanting to ask. "Never mind. Go finish getting ready. Your ride will be here soon."

He ignored my command and tucked his fingers under my chin, slowly guiding my gaze to his.

"Don't do that," he said softly. "Talk to me. What's up?"

"It's stupid."

"Nothing you've ever purposefully said or asked or blurted randomly has been stupid. Get out of your head and remember that this is me you're talking to."

"Do you think she'll recognize me as a mom? Enough to randomly blurt *ma ma*."

"You worried about that?"

I nodded.

Babies could feel the truth no matter how hard you tried to hide it.

It wasn't that I wanted to hide not being her biological mother; I just wanted her to know that I would try my best to be a good second chance mom.

I wanted her to *feel* that.

It was such an insane thing to want from a six month old.

"I think she already recognizes you as *her* mom because you are, Couri."

He swiped the lone tear from my cheek and leaned over to kiss me.

January protested, sticking her hand between us while shouting, "No. No. No."

For whatever hormonal reason, the tears began to fall in waves.

"This baby has turned me into a stupid, blubbering, emotional mess," I accused, wiping my face.

August secured January under his arm in an airplane position and tugged me into his other side.

"Our baby has only enhanced everything I love about you." He squeezed my ass and nodded. "Especially that."

"You are such a pervert."

"And you love that shit." He led us into the living room, put January in her playpen, then turned to face me. "You are her mother. She is your daughter. When she's old enough to know the truth and talk back, she'll still see you as her mother. Everybody in our household will share the last name Hanson. It's you and me and them."

It wasn't the first time he'd said this to me and it probably wouldn't be the last.

"I still have a bare ring finger and all my important documents have Mitchell etched next to Couri."

He chuckled and backed me into a wall, boxing me in with his hands.

"Patience, Angel face. I have ideas and plans."

The brat in me wanted to pout.

His elaborate proposal plans, whatever they might be, were taking forever.

I wanted so badly to put Hanson next to my first name and

322

he knew it, which meant making it special for me took precedence for him.

"I love you," I whispered into his mouth, my fingers curling around the back of his neck.

"Stop turning me on. We have company."

I grabbed his dick through his shorts and kissed just below his ear.

"Fuck, I love you, woman," he growled, nipping at my shoulder. "Don't wear anything to bed tonight."

I nodded and tried to release him but August wouldn't allow it.

"Stand your pretty ass right here until I can calm myself down."

Feeling proud of how easily I could affect him, I got comfortable against the wall.

Didn't he know I lived for being all up in his personal space?

The doorbell chimed before I could talk my shit, cutting our moment short.

August dropped a kiss on my forehead and lips and excused himself, knowing it was Kingston, Journi, and Kali.

The girls were hanging while the boys drove up north to a little town called Norbank Shores.

August wanted to expand further outside the city and after researching prime locations for Black businesses in Michigan, almost dead last on the list was Norbank with a tiny inscription under the name.

Rich in Black culture.

He'd been set on scoping out the area since.

"Where's the baby?" Kali asked, bypassing me to find the one in question.

"Wow," I said, feigning hurt. "I used to be the highlight of your life and now I can't even get a *hey*."

"Kali Rain," Journi called. "Don't be rude."

Feet hitting the floor sounded then she appeared, a bright smile on her face.

"Sorry, Te. She's just so cute!"

Kali inched closer and kneeled down to kiss my belly.

"Hello, young one. Is your host treating you well? I'm sure she is, so treat her just as good, okay."

She lifted that loving gaze to meet mine and smiled.

"Hi."

"Hey, baby," I greeted, fluffing her curls. "Look at that definition."

"Finally perfected your wash-n-go routine."

She took off before I could respond and Journi chortled.

"She's been chomping at the bit to get over here. Kingston just wasn't moving fast enough for her."

"So, basically..." I chuckled and led us into the living room. "You birthed my built-in babysitter."

"You know, eventually she'll be in high school and will want money for her services."

I shrugged and lowered myself onto the sofa, gaze on Kali as she removed January from the playpen and lifted her little body in the air.

"You are such a cute little thing. I'm your big cousin but maybe we can pretend I'm your auntie instead. Anyway, I vow to never charge for my babysitting services."

Journi snorted. "We'll see about that when you're sixteen."

"I don't want to hear anything about my sweet baby girl becoming a mean teenager," Kingston said, ambling into the living room with a recyclable grocery bag in hand.

"Dad, I could never be mean to you." Kali simpered. "Have some faith."

"I know, Buttercup..." He lifted the bag and turned toward the kitchen. "Saved some breakfast casserole for you, C."

Journi's breakfast casserole was my new obsession.

"You are a godsend and I'll love you even more if you heat it up as well. Spoon no fork."

August made an appearance, making a beeline for Kali and January who were playing on the floor.

"What's up, lil mama," he greeted Kali. "Feeling the curls."

She looked up and smiled.

"Thanks but you can't take her yet."

August chuckled and handed her the pacifier he'd been hiding behind his back.

"Da da da da," January babbled, earning a gasp from Journi and a squeal from Kali.

"That's new," Journi said, sitting up. "Right? She hasn't said that before or did we miss it?"

"It's new," August confirmed, standing proud. "King, we gotta bounce if we want to make it back before six."

"I was wondering..." Kali stood and placed January back in the play pen. "Can I come along and get some content for my YouTube channel?"

August shrugged and walked over to me. "As long as your pop is cool with it, I don't mind."

Kingston wouldn't say no and Kali celebrated without waiting for his response.

"I won't let January do anything exciting while you're away," I said as he leaned in to kiss me. "Be safe. I love you."

"I love you more, Angel face. Don't do too much today, alright?" He kissed me again. "Oh and my sisters are stopping by. Something about last minute baby shower details."

I groaned but my despair about baby shower planning went away as Kingston approached with my food.

August had already fed us so I could take my vitamins and iron pill, but my appetite was endless these days. A far cry from a few months ago when nothing would stay down.

"Be good for Mama, okay, Snowflake?" August murmured as he leaned into the playpen and kissed the top of her head.

Once they were gone, Journi turned to me and said, "He told her to be good for *mama*."

"Mmhm," I hummed, mouth full. "I might've had a little moment before y'all got here."

"What kind of moment?"

I really didn't want to talk about it but my sister knew how to pull information out of a person without much effort on her part. Or maybe deep down, I knew this was exactly what I *needed* to be talking about.

"I guess... I don't know..." I shrugged. "He's her dad, you know. By blood and I'm not her mom, just the—"

"The woman her father loves deeply," she cut in, brows raised. "The woman who's carrying her sibling. The woman who has never once turned her nose up at being present in the life of someone else's child. For all intents and purposes, you are her mother and time will only prove it to be true."

"Yeah, I know."

Journi regarded me closely and sighed.

"This isn't about fear of not being accepted by her, is it?"

Wasn't it?

"Sounds to me like you know more than I do."

January released a guttural cry that startled us into action.

I'd only been standing halfway when Journi returned with the fussy baby in question.

"Girl, sit down," she said, chuckling. "Why would you even think you had to get up if I'm sitting here?"

I plopped down while saying, "Because you aren't good with—"

January screamed, flailing her arms and legs around.

In the midst of her breakdown, she spotted me and started to reach.

Her fingers and body stretched in my direction and Journi chuckled.

"It's okay, I know," she cooed, handing the spoiled little girl over along with the pacifier she'd spit out. "If this wasn't confirmation enough, I don't know what else to tell you."

"What's the matter, Snowflake?"

She dropped her head on my shoulder and sniffed, but the screams were no more.

"I guess it is close to your naptime."

I sat her on my belly and maneuvered her head to my chest.

She moved around a little, gathering the fabric of my shirt between her fingertips before settling with having them inside my shirt.

"I'm afraid of not being here one day," I whispered. "What if the same thing that happened to Shondra, happens to me? January will never even know I was here for her. Maybe that's why I want so badly to hear her say *mama*. It's stupid and selfish."

"It's love," Journi said, sliding close to us.

She rested her head on my shoulder and sighed. "You love her and even though she can't verbally say it back, January loves you too. Stop working yourself into a tizzy over the what ifs. You're alive and well and experiencing a once in a lifetime kinda love. Be in the moment and let the rest come as it may."

I nodded and murmured, "I wish Mommy could be here to see this."

"Mommy is here, but I know what you mean. You wish she was here for you to witness her witnessing this."

I smiled.

"Yeah, exactly that."

We sat with one another in silence, mixed up in our separate thoughts.

A commotion from outside the house came right on time.

There was a limit on how long I could be left to think about my mother before sadness crept in and took over.

"Are they always so loud?" Journi asked as August's sisters argued about if they should knock or use one of their keys. "They don't do this at work."

"Always," I mused wistfully. "Can you let them in, please?"

I loved their perfect mix of chaos and calm.

"Journi, you're just the woman I wanted to see," June said.

And even though I couldn't see her face yet, I knew she was smiling.

"If it has to do with contracts, please spare me."

June laughed as September said, "She doesn't know how to not work these days."

"Mind your business, Tem."

Eventually they were in eyesight and I felt part of the conversation.

"Hey, baby mama," July greeted, plopping down next to me. "I love seeing you in mom mode."

I gathered myself to respond but she moved the conversation back to being in June's business so smoothly that I missed my chance.

"June's been thinking about mergers lately," she said, eyes on Journi. "Investing in smaller, failing distilleries, and making them part of the Hanson brand. Since August wants to expand we can work both his angle and this one."

My sister perked up at that.

She talked a big game but loved brainstorming with them, especially as their in-house counsel. All mergers and acquisitions would fall within her purview.

"This is where I shine," she boasted. "I'll compile a list of potentials."

June nodded and clapped.

"Now that that's out of the way, let's talk baby shower..."

She turned her big brown eyes on me and smiled. "You're literally glowing."

I touched my face.

"Am I?"

Everyone nodded and my cheeks warmed.

"Anyway," she went on, never missing a beat. "Everything is set and ready to go, just need to know what's your favorite flower?"

I blinked.

"That's it? I thought we were gonna be talking about this forever."

"Nah, we didn't want you stressing," Journi mused.

I glanced at my sister, eyes wide.

"You've been helping?"

"Of course," September chimed in as Journi nodded. "It'd be absurd for us to throw you a shower and not include your sister and best friend. Bea had class and couldn't stop by today."

Ugh.

My eyes got all watery and I couldn't stop the tears even if I tried.

"T-that's really sweet," I cried. "Wow. I love you guys."

"We love you too," July said, patting my back. "Please, stop crying though. August made us promise not to make you cry and we've already failed."

I snorted and it woke January.

She looked around but stayed against my chest.

"I need to capture this moment," September declared, pulling out her phone.

As her sister snapped multiple photos, June said, "Even though Bea and Journi know like everything about you, no one knew your favorite flower."

Four sets of eyes waited for my response and oddly enough I didn't have one.

"Oh..." I shrugged. "Uh. Daffodils will do. Yellow or white or a mix."

June blinked.

"Really?" she asked softly. "That's our favorite flower."

The three of them lifted their right hands, showing off the daffodil tattooed on the fleshy part near their thumbs. August shared the same one.

"I know." I nodded. "I guess I've never really had a favorite flower but I like what it stands for."

New beginnings. Rebirth.

It was a reminder that after every storm there was a rainbow out there somewhere trying its best to bring color back into the world.

I guess I officially had a favorite flower now.

THIRTY-TWO

DAFFODILS.

"Are you sure?" I asked Kingston, certain Couri had never mentioned those being her favorite flower. "That doesn't sound right."

"How would you know what sounds right if you didn't know the answer in the first place?" he asked, earning a snicker from our backseat passenger.

"Hey, guys!" Kali started, addressing her camera. "This is the very first vlog on my channel and it's a special one. If you don't know, I'm Kali Rain and I sing and write music. I also play a few instruments, but that isn't what today is about..."

Kingston wore a tiny smirk as he drove us away from the tuxedo rental place and toward our next destination. He was entertained with Kali re-recording her introduction for the tenth time.

She wanted to *perfect* it.

"...I'm with my dad and Uncle August," Kali went on. "Well, he's not my uncle yet but he will be soon. We just finished finalizing the details of the surprise wedding ceremony he planned."

She thrust the camera between the seats and angled it to put us both in frame.

"This is August."

I tipped my head and she rolled her eyes.

"He doesn't talk much but he loves my aunt, right?"

"Yeah," I said, feeling the need to verbally respond. "Very much."

Kali's big eyes brightened as she fell back into her seat.

"See, here's something you should know about August. He speaks when it matters most or when he's talking to my aunt..." She paused and addressed us after cutting the camera off. "Okay, I think that take was much better. Also, Te doesn't have a favorite flower."

Journi and Kingston raised one hell of a kid.

She was also great at changing conversations then bringing them back to the topic at hand without much effort.

"She chose mine then," I murmured as Kingston rolled to a stop near the barn at the distillery.

Workers were moving about the grounds, going in and out of the two large tents set up for me and Couri's wedding—one for the ceremony and the other for the reception.

Kali wedged herself between the seats, sans camera, and asked, "Why is the daffodil your favorite?"

I showed her the tattoo on my right hand.

"One thing I remember most about my childhood are the daffodils at my grandparents house. They sat in vases, grew from flowerbeds, and hung from the porch. My grandmother was kinda obsessed with them." I chuckled thinking of her. "When she..."

I looked to Kingston for the okay to talk about death with Kali and he nodded.

"When she passed my sisters and I wanted something to

remember her by and got the matching tattoos. Because I'm not good at taking care of plants, I don't buy them."

"But, they're still your favorite," she stated.

"Yeah, still my favorite."

Kali lifted her phone and smiled.

"I hope it's okay that I voice recorded that..." She pushed her door open and hopped out. "My wedding video is gonna be awesome."

Kingston sat back, eyes on Kali as she got film near the gazebo.

"She adores Couri," he said, glancing over at me. "The bond between aunt and niece is different and I want to make sure she'll keep that connection."

I frowned.

"Why wouldn't she keep that connection?"

"I'm asking you to make sure that doesn't happen..." Only after Mia and Lily joined Kali did Kingston turn to me. "Not because I don't trust you or your intentions. We're boys, more like brothers, and I trust *you*."

He looked away.

"I won't let it happen," I said, gripping his shoulder. "You know now that I'm here you don't have to carry the weight of being their protectors alone anymore, right?"

"Might take me a while to get used to that." He tipped his head toward the windshield. "Incoming..."

From the corner of my eyes, I could see Mia making her way over and rolled my window down. She leaned her head through it a few seconds later with a smile on her face.

"Those two are gonna be lifelong friends, I can tell," she mused, eyes moving between Kingston and me. "June texted and said Couri chose daffodils, is that right?"

Her brows dipped, knowing the significance to our family.

"Yeah, that's right."

I watched a barrage of emotions cross her face before disappearing as laughter from afar stole her attention.

"Anyway," she went on, turning back. "Mostly everything else is set and ready to go for Saturday. Your only job is to tell the bride-to-be, alright? Leave the stressful shit up to the rest of us."

"We should head out," Kingston said, eyes moving from me to Mia. "You sure it's cool for Kali to hang here until we get back?"

"Isn't that what was planned?" she queried, brows raised. "Kali is family now. She's safe wherever a Hanson is. Plus, from the shrill of giggles I hear, Lily is on a cloud having a cousin her age around."

He nodded and hit the push-to-start.

"We'll be back around five," I said, leaning out the window as she straightened and took a step back. "Kali's getting film for a vlog, so let her explore but with one of the distillers if it's upstairs."

Mia nodded and turned away.

"Send pics of the water up there, I know it's beautiful," she said over her shoulder as I rolled my window up.

"GPS says two and a half hours."

I checked the time on my phone and nodded.

"We're making good time. I hope it's worth the trip."

Norbank Shores would be worth it.

I had a feeling I'd stumbled upon a special community and needed to see how I could contribute. It sat on a shoreline near Lake Michigan, east of Detroit.

The population was eleven thousand as of twenty-twenty, making it small enough for everyone to know just about everyone but big enough that it wasn't considered a small town.

"Grab a few scenery videos for Kali," Kingston said as we

rode down the shore toward the town in question hours later. "She's gonna be upset when she sees them."

I chuckled and grabbed my phone, changing the camera settings to get the best quality possible.

"I might like it already," I murmured, panning my camera in Kingston's direction to get the views from his window. "We could spend summers with the family out here to get away from the hustle of the city."

"You think there's enough real estate in the area to buy?"

I shrugged.

"I wouldn't want to take away from full-time residents."

"There are ways to fix that," he said. "But, getting to know the town first might be best."

He merged into the far left lane and pointed.

Coming up a few feet ahead of us was a *Welcome to Norbank Shores* sign.

It was carved into the wood, giving a 3D effect that had me snapping more than a few pictures.

The only exit leading into town from the highway came up quickly.

"Shit," Kingston cursed, swerving over just before we missed it. "If we hadn't known where we were going already, that would've been an easy miss."

I nodded.

"Definitely," I agreed, leaning forward as flickers of the town came into view.

Kingston slowed and I pulled up a digital map I found on the Norbank Shores official website. I flipped it around a few times and then zoomed in.

"Alright, this is city hall," I told him, pointing to the building sitting in the center of a turnabout. "There's the library, secretary of state, and mayor's office."

We moved deeper into the quaint town, passing an

elementary and high school along the way. The road split into two, left leading into a residential area while the right led us toward downtown.

We went right and everything came to life right before our eyes and just as I imagined this wasn't any ol' ordinary town.

"I think we found our people."

Kingston wasn't wrong and the sea of Black and Brown faces staring at the foreign car entering their domain proved it. They were having some kind of event.

Damn.

"There's an empty spot right there," I told him, pointing to space behind an almost identical G-wagon to the one I had back home.

He parked and I hopped out, sniffing the air as something savory filled my nose.

Kingston joined me and we glanced at one another, both saying simultaneously, "Barbeque."

We started toward the tent with smoke blowing from under it.

"You two new?" the burly man standing behind the table asked, his brows raised.

I nodded. "I'm August and this is Kingston."

He started piling two styrofoam containers with food.

"August and Kingston, I'm Bernie..." His gaze drifted between us. "Where you from?"

"Detroit," Kingston replied, taking the food without question. "I own a construction business and August's family owns a distillery."

Bernie handed me the covered container and I flipped it open, gaze roving over the macaroni and cheese, baked beans, green beans, and ribs.

I filled my fork with a little bit of everything, said a small prayer and stuffed my mouth.

"The fuck," I cursed, stunned at the flavor profiles mixed together.

Bernie smiled and nodded.

"I know about owning a family business. *Bernie's* has been in mine for four generations."

"You're Bernie the fourth?" Kingston asked, barely keeping his laughter in.

"The one and only," Bernie boasted proudly. "Welcome to Norbank Shores. You'll be the talk of town for a week straight. I hope you aren't here to stir up shit."

"Nah," I said, shaking my head. "We want to contribute but had to see for ourselves what we'd be contributing to."

He nodded but I wasn't sure he believed us.

When you've witnessed non-Black faces changing Black neighborhoods all over the country, washing away the culture one luxury high rise at a time, a new face in this slice of heaven deserved to be met with skepticism.

"Never seen you two around here before," an older lady with a small tea hat on spoke as we walked the small pavilion, taking in some of the other businesses from town with tents.

She sat on a bench with her legs crossed and a cane to her left.

It looked as if she were fresh from Sunday service, though it was only Thursday.

"First time," I said, lifting my half eaten platter from Bernie's. "We smelled the barbecue."

She narrowed her raven colored eyes and snorted.

"All the way from the highway?"

Kingston chuckled and took a seat to her right as I filled the one to her left.

"To be honest," he started, leaning back. "We drove down from Detroit to see Norbank Shores specifically."

"Big shot developers, I bet," she grumbled, ready to write us off. "We don't need—"

"My family has owned a distillery in the city for six generations," I told her. "Recently, a new generation took over..." I smiled at the way she squinted in my direction. "We expanded and now we're looking to reach other cities."

"And why'd you pick our little town?" she asked, some of the disgust present before now missing.

"I don't have an exact answer to that..." I shrugged. "Just a feeling that this is where it's meant to be. In a town that will appreciate what a Black man and woman started in their garage."

"You two a couple?" she asked, changing topics.

I chuckled, shaking my head.

"We grew up together," Kingston shared. "I have a wife and eleven year old daughter."

The older woman's keen eyes met mine.

"And you?"

"I have an almost wife, a six month old daughter, and one on the way. We still don't know if it's a boy or girl."

"Mmmm," she hummed, focusing her attention in front of us.

There was a group of teenagers walking down the paved road, talking and laughing over one another. A few spotted us and pointed, whispering to each other as they gawked.

"This is a family town," she said, waving her slender brown fingers. "We look after one another and do a little gossiping on the side."

I smirked and nodded.

"Is that your way of letting us know that by the time we're home everyone will know who the unknown visitors were?"

She grinned, a little mischievous glint shining in her eyes.

338

"Well, if you want to bring your business here it's best they know now."

"Does that mean you approve?" Kingston asked, after we glanced at one another and stood.

She shrugged.

"Only time will tell if you two are good for Norbank or not. God will handle you accordingly if it's the latter." Her gaze landed on me and she tipped her head. "What's the name of your family's business?"

"Hanson Distillery Company."

I could see her mentally storing that information for later.

"On the northside of town is the warehouse district," she informed us. "Or what used to be."

I started to ask what happened to it but she looked away, ending the conversation.

Kingston and I took the hint and drove north of downtown right into the deserted warehouse district. We parked on the street and got out, gazes looking both ways at the real estate sitting empty but surely costing the town money to keep standing.

"I told you," I said, leaning against the hood of his truck. "We were meant to find this place."

"You were right," Kingston agreed, chuckling.

We took in the quietness for a short while and left town on the guise of returning soon.

Real soon.

As planned, by five in the evening we were back in the city.

We stopped by the distillery to pick up Kali then went straight to my place where Journi was waiting for her ride. Once the family of three was on their way home, I went in search of Couri after learning she'd complained of a headache and went to bed early.

My sisters had taken January with them but I still ducked

339

my head into her room and glanced around. I couldn't believe how big she'd gotten or that she could speak; it was all surreal but I enjoyed being a father to her.

I noticed the door to my bedroom was slightly ajar and slipped through it to avoid that little squeak it made when in motion. Even in the dark, the outline of Couri's silhouette was visible to me.

"You're home," she whispered.

Surprised to find her awake, I stripped away everything but my briefs and climbed into bed.

"I'm home," I murmured, molding my body to hers from behind.

We weren't *technically* living together but hadn't spent a night apart in months. Our days would continue to start and end together in the new house after the baby was born.

Couri placed her fingers against mine and guided them to a bulge in her side.

A small kick against my palm brought a smile to my face.

"Our kid knows their daddy," she said.

"How's your head?" I asked, caressing the little foot poking from her skin until it retracted and the skin evened out.

"I slept with my headache cap on for a little and it worked wonders. No fever and my blood pressure is normal, please don't worry."

Instead of reminding her that worrying for her would probably never change, I let us fall into a comfortable silence and drifted off for a short while.

"I have a question but you can only say yes," I murmured as I forced myself awake and walked to the other side of the bed. I tapped the bedside lamp once and it illuminated the room a fraction. "Damn, you look sexy as fuck like that."

Blinking sleep away, Couri smiled.

She rolled on her back with the sheet pulled over her, legs

poking out, and belly sitting high. I grabbed my phone and took a few pictures, wanting to capture a visual memory of this stage of her pregnancy.

"What's the question?" she asked, watching me climb into bed and go straight for her bump.

I snatched the sheet away from her body and kissed down the darkened linea nigra.

Everything that visibly changed about her body, Couri googled. And because of that everyone who was willing to listen knew the actual name of the black line most women got on their stomachs during pregnancy. Especially women of color.

"Will you marry me on Saturday?" I asked, lifting my gaze to meet hers.

"But, the baby shower is Saturday," was the first thing out of her mouth. "And I don't have a dress," she went on, trying to sit up but having a hard time with her bump. "Nothing will fit me."

I admired her persistence to get into a sitting position without my help and only when she reached for me did I assist.

"I have that covered," I averred, lifting her chin with my index finger. "You trust me, right?"

"With all of me," she replied without pause.

"Make me a husband this Saturday and prove it."

The way her eyes sparkled made all the planning worth it.

I reached into the bedside dresser drawer and grabbed the ring box I'd been hiding there all this time. She never opened the one on my side, making it the smartest place to stash it.

Couri eyed the ring box, her gaze widening by the second.

"Let me see it!" she requested excitedly, pulling the sheet over her bare breast.

I flipped the top open and as her eyes settled on the exact ring she'd asked for, she squealed.

"I hope two carats is enough," I murmured, pulling it from the box and slipping it on her finger. "We can always upgrade it and—"

"August, you aren't touching my ring. It's so goddamn beautiful."

She dangled her hand in front of her face.

"I have to get up," she decided, pushing me away. "There's so much I need to do with so little time."

I chuckled and fell back, pulling her with me at an angle that would protect her belly.

"Lay down, woman." I turned the lamp off and climbed over her, molding my body to hers from behind again. "You don't have shit to do but cuddle and sleep with your man."

She huffed a little but I knew she liked being in my arms.

"How long have you had my ring?" she murmured, backing her ass into me.

"Picked it up from being sized a month ago..." I tucked my hand under her belly and closed my eyes. "You said yes and I swiped my card the next day."

Nothing would stop me from making her a Hanson.

THIRTY-THREE

I STARTLED MYSELF AWAKE, sitting up a little too fast for my own good.

"Shit," I cursed, taking a few breaths. "Sorry, little one."

Ugh.

My belly was way too big and made me less agile than usual.

I managed to get out of bed and stretched the minute I was on my feet.

There was a lot of commotion happening downstairs but upon hearing the shower running, I decided to head in that direction first while smiling down at my engagement ring.

"Good morning," August greeted as I entered and began to strip, his gaze slated keenly in my direction.

Before joining him, I shut the bathroom door.

"Morning, handsome," I replied softly, trying to wrap my arms around him from behind. "Never works anymore."

He chuckled and turned, pinning those pretty browns on me the moment he could.

"You'll be back in action in no time."

His fingers gently roamed my bare skin, leaving a trail of goosebumps in their wake.

"Love the way you react to my touch," he mused, kissing down the side of my neck. "And you smell like me. Was your plan to seduce me?"

I giggled like a fucking schoolgirl.

"Not purposely..." I kissed his chest and dropped my head against the wall, eyes on his. "But I think no matter what it'll always feel like I'm seducing you."

There wasn't a soul who could convince me that I wasn't this man's end all to be all.

His *obsession.*

The love of his life.

Not a *fucking* soul.

"You asked me to marry you tomorrow," I whispered, almost scared to repeat it.

How would we even pull something like that off on such short notice?

"I asked and you said yes," he reminded me. "Now let me scrub you down then feed you before the chaos begins."

He spun me toward the showerhead with a smirk plastered on his face.

Chaos?

After showering and dressing in a loose fitting lounge set, I understood what August meant.

"Hi, Couri, I'm Georgina," a petite woman with dark brown skin, a blonde fade, and piercings in her lip, nose, and eyebrow said. "Your fiancé hired my team to assist in finding your wedding dress."

She pointed to the several racks of zipped garment bags.

"I promise there's something here you'll love."

I touched my belly.

"But will it fit?" I asked, concerned.

Her smile widened and I admired her straight teeth.

"That's my specialty," she boasted, earning nods from her three person team. "Find the dress you can't absolutely say no to and let me handle the rest."

I was at a loss for words.

If August had done this for me, what else had he managed to do?

"Give us about thirty minutes, Georgie," August chimed in from the kitchen. "Couri needs to eat then she'll be all yours."

Georgie?

"You know her personally?" I asked, sliding onto a stool at the counter.

He glanced at me as he plated a fried egg and two pieces of bacon.

"Georgina Hanson," he said, chuckling. "Don't think I've ever seen you jealous before."

I scoffed and rolled my eyes but made sure to drop my head and hide the smile forming.

August didn't call people by nicknames unless he *knew* them, but I'd never heard of a Georgina before. His family was so damn big, keeping up with who's who was hard.

"Don't let him pull your card like that, Couri," Georgina said with a smile from the living room. "Besides, my last name is Green now. Please respect my husband."

August snorted.

"Your husband stole you away from us and I'm supposed to respect him."

I could tell it was all in jest and smiled at their banter.

"I live all of five hours away," Georgina said, throwing her hands in the air.

He set breakfast in front of me with sliced pineapples added to the mix, a cup of apple juice, and my vitamins.

"Thank you..." I looked up and poked my lips out for a kiss, to which he obliged. "For everything you do."

"My world revolves around you." He tipped my head back and regarded me closely, eyes soft with adoration. "I hope you've figured it out by now." He pointed to the food and backed away. "Eat."

I obeyed, starving but also eager to try on dresses.

Fuck.

Were we really doing this?

August had disappeared upstairs for a short while and by the time he'd returned, I'd finished breakfast and cleaned up my mess. He stepped in front of me with my phone in hand as I popped my vitamins, grimacing at the lingering taste before the apple juice washed it away.

"Your sister and my mom will be here in about twenty minutes," he informed me before leaning forward to kiss my belly. "Don't do too much, alright?"

I nodded and glanced at the carry-on sized suitcase he'd brought down with him.

"Are you leaving?"

He chuckled a little and extended the handle.

"Did you forget we're getting married tomorrow already? I can't see the bride or her dress until the big day."

"But—"

He silenced me with a passionate kiss that drew me to the tips of my toes, needing more before he left me for the day.

"Allow me to make this easy for you," he muttered into my mouth. "Your dress, hair and makeup, shoes and accessories are all taken care of. All you need to do is pick from the plethora of options available to you and relax."

"I don't know what to do with myself."

"It's a good thing I know exactly what to do with you." He backed away and I wanted to follow but stood my ground. "Let Georgie help, it's what she does best and I trust her."

"Finally something nice out of that mouth of yours," Georgie said, moving around racks to clear space for him to get by. "Don't worry, I got this. Go handle your business."

I watched August leave, following him to the door and standing in it until he pulled away.

"Hey..." Georgie met me in the hall and smiled. "You'll see him tomorrow."

I nodded and followed her into the living room.

"Can we wait until my sister and Adrina get here?"

"Of course." She pointed to the sofa and I took a seat. "Let me officially introduce you to the team."

The three women she'd brought with her were Ena, Cahlia, and Kera—each had different areas of expertise.

Ena was a stylist and jeweler, she brought accessories galore to pair with the dress options Georgie brought. Cahlia did makeup and was already swatching shades to find my perfect match. Kera was a hairstylist who owned the salon next door to Georgie's studio showroom.

I learned after asking a few more questions, that Georgina was a wedding dress designer.

She had a large studio and wedding dress shop in downtown Chicago where she and her husband lived. Ena and Kera were her childhood best friends.

"Which parent of yours is related to August's dad?" I asked.

The look of sadness that zipped through her eyes caught me off guard.

"It's okay if—"

"No..." She shook her head and smiled. "My dad was the youngest and wildest. A rolling stone kinda guy. He passed away when I was fifteen. The same year August and the girls were born."

I blinked, eyes widening.

"Damn, girl..." I whistled. "You look good."

She chuckled and did a little spin.

"My parents had me young, so I'm the oldest of our little gang. They're all my babies and I didn't realize how much I missed being in Chicago."

A knock at the front door and the sound of Kali's voice singing my name got our whirlwind of a day started before I could hug Georgina about her dad.

"Georgie, baby," Adrina greeted with arms wide open and a bright smile. "I've missed your beautiful face."

Georgina lit up at the sight of her.

"Hey, Auntie! You're looking good, girl. Where did these hips come from?"

Kali giggled with her camera out, pointing it every which way to capture as much as she could.

Adrina scoffed but twisted her hips to show off what Georgie spoke of.

She and September had similar body types, thick but slender from their height.

"Alright!" Georgie clapped and moved toward the rack closest to her. "Now, I pulled these pieces based on August's description of your taste."

I stepped forward as she pulled the first garment bag and gave it to Ena to hold up.

As she unzipped, pieces of the dress fell out and a smile formed before I even saw the rest.

"How did August describe my taste?" I asked, following the intricate lace detail with my eyes.

It wasn't the one, but my God, it was beautiful.

"Delicate," Ena said, smiling.

"He said your style was reserved," Georgie added. "Never too revealing but always just enough. And if you are going for a risqué look it's a subtle show off of legs, shoulders, and a sliver of cleavage."

I smiled.

"I take it he knows you well from the smile," Cahlia mused from her accessory table.

"Yeah..." I nodded. "He does. What's this one called?" I asked, taking in the sweetheart neckline stitched to perfection.

"This is Vena from last year's fall collection."

"It's beautiful," I whispered, caressing the fabric.

"But, not the one."

I nodded, feeling a little bad about it.

Georgina squeezed my forearm and smiled.

"This is your day. You can't hurt my feelings, I promise. Besides..." She shrugged and stuffed the dress back into the garment bag. "I know you'll find the one."

We went through a few more options; all were equally beautiful but didn't call to me.

For a second I thought all hope was lost but then Ena came over and whispered something to Georgie that had her lips curling deviously.

"They're up to something," Journi said softly from beside me.

Cahlia had set up her makeup chair to avoid me lowering myself on the sofa over and over when I got tired.

"I brought something no one has seen yet," Georgina explained, waving for Kali to follow. "It's for this year's fall collection."

I sat up a little, intrigued.

"Is it runway size?"

She sifted through garment bags until finding the one she'd been looking for.

"I would never bring a runway size dress for a seven month pregnant woman," she griped, no real malice in her cadence.

"When I designed this dress it was with the idea that I'd have a pregnant model wear it. Inspiration sparked one night and this..." Kali helped her unzip the dress. "...is what I came up with."

"Oh my God," Journi murmured as Adrina pulled in an audible breath.

This dress was *breathtakingly* beautiful.

It wasn't quite white, more on the ivory side with a hint of blush pink showing through when the light hit it at the right angle. The fabrics were a mix of tulle, lace, and satin.

I stood and moved closer, ignoring the camera Kali shoved in my face.

"This embroidery is insane, Georgie," I murmured, enjoying the feel of it on my fingertips. "And the stitched flowers... I don't have words."

The embroidered flowers and veins were weaved in with a freestyle design that curled around the floral satin arrangements extending from the dress. It was a mix of roses and daffodils, running from the top of the skirt through the seams of the deep V-neck, and over the shoulders.

"What's this one called?" I asked, breaking the silence.

"Couri, meet Regina."

I allowed my fingers to get lost in the layered tulle skirt and smiled.

"That is a perfect name for a perfect dress. I want to try it on."

Kali squealed.

"I can't believe I caught all of that!" she exclaimed, lowering the camera. "August is going to love th—"

"What are you up to, Kali Rain?" I questioned, my gaze narrowed.

She took a few steps back and raced around me to get to Journi.

I followed her movements and eventually met eyes with my sister.

"You two were in on this, weren't you?" I asked, finally putting the pieces together. "The baby shower was never a damn baby shower. Excuse my language, Ms. Adrina."

Did this child have my brain so muddled that my ability to read the room disappeared?

"In their defense," Adrina chimed in, drawing my attention to her. "August wanted this to be perfect. He knew the only way to do that was with the help of your family."

I wasn't upset, just overwhelmed with how much everyone loved me.

"I don't get it," I whispered, looking at Adrina.

She closed the distance between us and wrapped her fingers gently around my biceps to hold me in place.

"What is it you don't get?" she asked, her gaze peering through my soul. "Is it that my family has not only welcomed you with open arms but grew to love you on their own accord?"

I found it hard to look away from her.

"Yes," I admitted.

"I know what it's like to be thrust into the Hanson fold, but once you're in, that's it. They'll love and protect you for life even after you slap them around a little, but only if they deserve it."

Georgie snorted and said, "Don't take that advice, Couri. She's trouble."

Adrina smirked and pulled me into a tight embrace.

"This is my promise to your mother," she whispered in my ear. "I got you now."

I sobbed, the tears pooling from my eyes harder than ever.

It wasn't sadness I felt but relief.

The guilt of moving on with my life and finding happiness

in the midst of my grief lifted from my shoulders. Everything was okay; I was okay.

More arms and bodies wrapped around us and a sense of security filled me.

"Oh!" Adrina squealed, tossing her arms out to break up the bunch. "A kick!"

I grimaced.

"Whew," I touched my stomach, trying my best to soothe their little kicks and punches. "I know you're excited about Nana hugging us..." I smiled at Adrina, so grateful to be accepted by her. "Me too."

"Alright!" Georgie clapped. "Let's get this dress on you and figure out what type of adjustments it'll need."

Ena and Georgie helped me into it and circled me like vultures while tossing out where and what needed to be taken in or out. Kera brought over veils and pieces of jewelry that Ena left out.

Eventually, Cahlia made her way over and showed me makeup palettes.

"I'm thinking we'll go blush pink and gold with the eyeshadow. You have lash extensions but if you trust me I'd like to put a strip set on top of it with magnetic liner. It'll give a smoky eye effect without the dark makeup."

I nodded.

"If Georgie trusts you, then so do I."

She smiled and I knew the creative inside of her was excited for tomorrow.

"Hear me out," Ena started as she made her way over with a weird headpiece in hand. "The details in this dress can't be covered by an ordinary veil."

"And you have this thick curly hair that I think should be showcased," Kera chimed in, bringing her phone over to show me an inspiration picture. "The headpiece she has is made of the embroidery detail on the dress. I'd have to weave in it like the picture but your hair is dense enough to hold it well."

"Let us show you," Ena said as they started to work around me in unison.

After a minute or two of being fussed over, Georgie led me to the wall mirror.

"Wow," I murmured, rolling fingers over the tulle that covered my bump. "I can't believe this part fits."

"We actually need to take more in than not. Probably because you're naturally small."

"I want this," I declared, feeling whole. "This is it."

It had been all they needed to hear and everyone got to work.

Ena and Georgie on the alterations.

Kera on washing and doing a two-strand twist set on my hair that would be unraveled tomorrow.

Journi and Adrina found themselves in the kitchen cooking, while Kali walked around asking everyone questions with the camera in their face.

"This is the bride to be," she said, approaching where I sat. "How did you and August meet?"

I shifted and smiled.

"In the driveway of your parents' home," I said truthfully, even though I was thinking of what followed afterward.

"Nice," she said. "Now tell the people what you love most about August."

She'd put me on the spot but the words flowed effortlessly out of me.

"I love the way he speaks to me with his eyes," I explained, thinking of those whiskey browns. "The way he respects and adores the women in his family. I love how free he is with me, his honesty and loyalty. I love that he's a dedicated father. I..."

Realizing that I'd gone well over my time and all eyes were on me, I closed my mouth.

"Sorry, I got carried away."

"Don't apologize," Georgie said from the sewing station she'd set up. "That was beautiful and it's good to know that August is being seen and loved for who he is. We all deserve that kind of love."

"Mom laughs at Dad's corny jokes, does that count as loving him for who he is?" Kali asked, earning a few snickers and a half-hearted threat from Journi.

"Trust me there's a lifetime of that to come," Adrina mused, gathering support from the married girls.

"August is actually pretty funny," I said, shrugging.

"Show off," Georgina accused through a fake cough.

"*August is actually pretty funny*," Journi and Adrina mocked before bursting into laughter.

I couldn't believe those two were ganging up on me or why I was smiling because of it.

"Haters," I mumbled under my breath, sticking my tongue out at Kali's camera.

She giggled and lowered it before crawling on the sofa and resting her head in my lap.

"I'm glad you're happy," she said softly as I massaged her scalp. "Nana must've made sure we'd be okay."

"Yeah, Buttercup," I agreed, blinking back tears. "I think so, too."

She was all around us, preening at her handiwork.

I could feel it.

Thank you, Mommy.

Later that night, the townhome bustled with August's sisters in the mix.

I laid stretched out on the couch with my bonnet on, eyes

drooping as June fussed over January's hair. Adrina had put a blanket over me after finding me nodding off a few times.

"She's still bald like we were," she said, brushing down barely there pieces that stood up.

January fought to get away, her eyes taking in all the things to get into around the living room. I watched her while trying to relax my mind in preparation for the big day.

"Hey, June," I called, losing that battle.

"Mmm," she hummed, glancing over.

"Can you do something for me?"

She nodded.

"Sure, whatcha need?"

I took a long second to sit up, suddenly wide awake with inspiration.

"I've been working on something for August for y'all birthday but I think I want to give it to him before the ceremony tomorrow. Do you think you could bring it to life?"

I called for Kali to bring my phone and showed her what I meant.

June's lips parted in shock and slowly her eyes met mine.

"You did that for him?"

I nibbled on my lip and nodded.

"I know you guys have—"

"No..." She shook her head, eyes filled with tears. "This is so... I can't put into words how much I know this will mean to him."

For a moment, I thought maybe I'd gone too far and stepped on someone's toes but the way June was forcing herself not to shed a tear said otherwise.

"Does that mean you'll help?" I asked, hopeful that it could be done.

"Absolutely. Is it here?"

"I stashed it at my place since we spend more time here."

She nodded, gaze wandering as she worked something out in her head.

"Okay," she determined aloud, smiling. "Give me the key to your place and I'll handle the rest."

I regarded her closely, worried she might be overextending herself.

"I was mentally working out when to deliver it to him," she explained, somehow reading my expression. "All is good, Couri. I promise."

"Okay, yeah. I'll get Journi to give you her spare key. And if you know anyone that's looking to rent let me know; I haven't gotten around to listing my place yet but I should probably do that before we move into the house since I'm never there."

August and I both owned our spots and decided to rent them after we moved into our forever home.

"Actually one of our bartenders is looking for a new place..." She tapped her chin. "She has a kid, I think he's three or four. I'll check to be sure she's still looking and get back to you."

I nodded.

"If she asks how much the rent is, tell her it's whatever her budget will allow."

"Getting to know you is understanding why my brother fell in love with you." She stood with a half-sleep January clutching her chest. "I could feel his happiness, his adoration for you, but now I get it."

She shook her head and walked away, leaving me confused but appreciative of her words.

I couldn't investigate longer because Kali came running in.

"Can I stay with you instead of coming back in the morning with everyone else?" she asked, batting her thick lashes. "Mom is about to leave."

"Yup..." I patted her cheeks. "But you knew that already."

Kali took off without acknowledging that she had me wrapped around her finger just as my phone vibrated with a text from August.

> Strawberry full-moon tonight. Watch it with me?

I slowly lifted from the sofa and climbed the stairs to his bedroom.

His room had a large window with a treeless view of the sky, and as I expected, the moon sat clear as day from this angle.

I took a picture and sent it to him with the message, **Here with you,** attached.

As I lowered myself on the windowsill bench to watch the moon with my man from a distance, I smiled. No matter where we are, together or apart, August Hanson was always thinking of me.

THIRTY-FOUR

"THERE'S STAFF FOR THAT, you know?"

I turned to find Landon ambling toward me dressed for the ceremony already, his brows lifted. Ignoring him, I placed the picture of Couri's mom on the seat reserved for her and next to it one of her father.

They couldn't physically be here but they'd *be here*. I wanted Couri to not only feel them on this day but see them as well.

"I know," I finally said, walking toward the groom's suite with Landon in tow. "Just needed to do that one thing."

Landon caught up and pulled the door open, allowing me to walk in before him.

"Found the groom," he announced, gathering the attention of my dad, Owen, and two uncles.

"Now that you're done checking behind Mia's work, have a seat and breathe for a moment," Dad said from the barber's chair. "You're moving too much when you need to be reflecting. Preparing yourself."

I shrugged and kicked one leg up on the coffee table.

"I've reflected enough and I'm prepared."

Owen dropped down next to me and said, "Come on, Unc. I know you've seen the way he looks at that girl. August is probably anxious to see her again."

I nodded, agreeing with Owen for once.

"All I care about is this being special for her after everything she's been through."

Landon's pop—Lincoln—hummed from the second barber's chair.

The bride and groom suites Mia oversaw the design of were top of line and equipped with everything a wedding party would need. In the six hundred square foot room we occupied there was a mini barbershop with vanity and equipment—included in all packages—and fully stocked bar with only premium selections.

Though I didn't have a wedding party, I'd invited the men in my family to get dressed with me or stop by before the ceremony.

"You've also been through a lot," Uncle Lincoln said, his gaze on me through the mirror at his station. "Don't forget that it should be special for you too. A chapter is closing and another one is opening."

"Listen to Mr. Know-it-all," Landon joked, earning a hard stare from his dad that didn't faze him. "Not saying you're wrong but two things can be true at once. It's special for him because he made it special for her and that's it. Doesn't need to be more complicated than that."

I eyed Landon closely, wondering where that had come from.

Before I could question him, JJ walked in with a surprise guest looming at his back.

"Look who made it to town in enough time," he said, waving to his brother Saeed.

"Wouldn't miss this for the world," Saeed said, pulling me

into a snug embrace after I stood to greet him. "Besides, I think I'll be back home for good soon."

Saeed had been living and working in Minnesota for about five years. He'd left right after he and JJ's mother passed from kidney failure. Out of my father's ten siblings, two weren't with us anymore.

"That right?" I asked, tipping my head.

He nodded and moved around the room to greet everyone else.

"Why the change of heart?" Uncle Lincoln asked, squinting at him suspiciously. "You running from something?"

Lincoln had been their mother's twin brother; he took losing her hard.

Saeed chuckled.

"More like running toward something but today ain't about me…" He leaned against the wall near the door and crossed his arms, eyes now on me. "So, you got a baby. A soon-to-be wife in the next hour and a half, and a little one on the way."

I nodded. "Sounds 'bout right."

"You look happy," he surmised, gaze narrowing a little. "Yeah, definitely happy."

I opened my mouth to confirm but JJ cursed and jumped up from his seat, phone clutched tightly in hand.

"What's the problem?" Saeed asked, grabbing him by the arm as he tried to leave.

JJ snatched himself free and opened the door.

"Nothing for you to worry about. I'll be back before the ceremony."

The door slammed behind him as he retreated and Saeed sighed.

"Why didn't anyone tell me how bad he'd been spiraling?"

No one could respond to that.

JJ had been spiraling for a while and it didn't really make sense, at least not to me.

It started well before Aunt Luna passed, though her death seemed to have sent him over the edge.

None of us knew what he'd gotten himself into but I wasn't in the business of dictating another man's life. When JJ was ready to seek our help, he would, and all any of us could do was pray he did it before shit went left.

"You have to let him find his way," my dad said, checking his watch. "Alright, you need to dress August. It's almost that time."

Knowing she was already here, because of the car I'd scheduled to pick her and her entourage up, didn't stop me from glancing at my phone to check Couri's location.

Our little pictured icons were sitting right on top of one another and I stood.

"Alright, let me make another round and I'll—"

Landon grabbed me before I could take a step.

"Everything is good," he said, giving me a wide eyed look before schooling his features. "You're anxious and about to go looking for her without even realizing it."

If I hadn't known it, how the hell had he?

Kingston entered the suite and glanced between us while shaking his head.

"Something told me I needed to make my way here," he said, shutting and locking the door. "I'll stand guard while you dress."

I glanced around the room to find all eyes on me.

They were dressed and ready while I was still in my gray joggers and white t-shirt.

"I'm trippin'," I said as Landon released me. "Good looking out."

It didn't take long for me to get my classic tux on with the help of my pop.

He stood in front of me after I shrugged into my jacket and did a hand sweep down my arms a few times.

Our eyes met and I could see what he was feeling.

"I'm proud of you," he said before turning to grab what looked like a watch box from Uncle Lincoln. "This watch was a gift from your grandfather when I married your mom. He told me it was a reminder to use the time I have with the ones I love wisely."

He flipped it open and Landon whistled.

"A vintage Rolex," I said, more to myself than anyone else. "Damn, Pop."

I flipped my wrist and unlatched the Movado Couri had bought as a just because gift. After handing it off to Landon, I let the man I loved and respected deeply put the vintage time-piece on my wrist.

"Got it!" Owen blurted, turning his phone for us to see a picture of the exact watch. "It's a Tudor Royal from the fifties. Wow. Gramps probably got it from his father."

"He did," Dad confirmed, squeezing my shoulders. "I love you."

He pulled me in and I murmured the sentiment back, getting a little choked up.

Luckily a knock at the door had us pulling it together quickly.

Kingston pushed it open to reveal June and Kali, who was holding January.

"Da Da Da," my little munchkin called, kicked her socked feet.

She was in a blush pink dress with a mountain of tulle and bows everywhere.

Kali brought her over and I lifted January in the air but only once this time, not wanting either of us covered in baby spit-up.

It wasn't until June started to speak that I noticed the tray cart they'd brought along.

"Your bride-to-be wanted to gift you with something before the ceremony," June explained, rolling the cart closer. "Read this first."

I eyed the ribbon covered box and handed January to Landon before flipping open the notecard. Couri's perfect cursive greeted me and I smirked, obsessed with everything about her.

August,

This was supposed to be part of your birthday gift, but I couldn't allow this momentous day to pass without you receiving it. Life took us on a journey neither expected, but we made it.

Our lives, before and after the storm, deserve to be watered equally.

When we met, you were in the beginning stages of launching your very own whiskey.

You were so proud of the product you'd produced with your own hands.

I'll never stop thanking you for allowing me to be part of your exclusive tasting club.

As your biggest fan and supporter, I hope this gift is what you need to finish what you started.

Always yours,
- Couri

I tucked the card inside my jacket as June lifted the box.

Underneath sat a classic shaped whiskey bottle with deep ridges down the sides and what looked to be a daffodil flower etched into the front. Inside an amber liquid swished as I tipped it from side to side.

It was sealed, the top shaped like a diamond.

"This isn't one of ours," I said, brushing my fingers down it. "Perfect bottle though..." I lifted it. "And sturdy."

June nodded.

"I thought so too," she said, smiling. "Couri had that made for you and I got it sealed this morning by the grace of God. It pays to have connections."

Everyone moved in after June explained but I found myself taking one step back.

She did this for me?

It wasn't that I had forgotten about my whiskey; I'd just been focused on other shit, like making sure Couri didn't have another pregnancy scare. The idea of that alone made it hard for me to focus on anything else but my family. Lately, my whiskey had been on my mind though and Couri's gesture felt like a sign I needed to listen to.

Noticing Kali recording, I looked right in the camera and said, "You and me, Mrs. Hanson."

Clutching the bottle in my hands, I cracked the seal.

"Grab a few glasses," I said to no one in particular. "Let's have a toast."

Kingston had been the one to oblige.

He set them on the cart and I poured a finger of whiskey in each.

Once everyone had their glasses lifted, sans Kali who was walking around the group getting her footage, I made my toast, "To love and using our time wisely."

Landon clapped and gripped my shoulders after knocking his back. "Whew! Let's do this!"

Kingston opened the door and everyone filed out one by one, leaving me to step into the late-summer heat last. As the door shut behind me, I closed my eyes and took a deep breath.

This next chapter of my life was called... *happiness.*

epilogue one

COURI

JANUARY 1; OCTOBER 6 MONTHS

"OUCH, MAMA," January whined, showing me her finger. "Hurts."

She stood at the edge of the couch, lip poked out, while I rocked a grumpy October to sleep.

I smiled and shook my head at the dramatic display before me.

"Let's see..." I took her finger and examined it closely. "Ah," I mused, pretending to see the issue. "There are only two things that can make this better. A lot of kisses from Mommy or...."

August crept up on her from behind, ready to attack.

"Or a whole lot of kisses from Daddy," he roared into her neck before tossing her little body in the air.

"Daddyy," she screeched, happy to see her main man.

We'd perfected getting in and out of our forever home undetected, especially with both girls hating when either of us had to leave.

"Hey, beautiful," August greeted, dropping a kiss on my forehead and lips.

After getting his fill, he firmly kissed Ms. Grumpy's forehead.

October Lee Hanson made her debut one month after our wedding. It was a rainy day in September, and though she'd come a little early, she was healthy as an ox with a fierce attitude, especially now that she was teething.

"The cake got delivered today," I told him, laying my head back. "She won't remember it, but the pictures will be nice."

Yesterday was January's official first birthday, but we were celebrating with a party at her Nana and Pop Pop's house tomorrow.

August went to check it out with the birthday girl hanging sideways in his arm while I managed to escape the death grip of our youngest. With her resting safely in the pack-n-play, I stretched my limbs and met him in the kitchen.

"I wanted to talk to you about something..." I opened the drawer and pulled out the letters Shondra's mother had been sending for months. "We have to do something about this."

She wanted to reconnect and apologized profusely in every letter, including the newest one. Motherhood had softened me already because I felt for the woman.

Yesterday made a year since her daughter passed away during childbirth.

A year since life and death rocked two families.

It had to be hard for her, and while I was still team whatever August wanted to do, I secretly had hoped he would give her a chance at redemption.

We'd been certain that when August began to allow Monique visits with January, Helen would eventually learn of them. The letters started to show up soon after.

"I've been thinking about it," he said, setting a wiggly

January on the counter. "She fucked with me when I was at my most vulnerable, and it has been hard to forgive, but deep down, I know January could benefit from that connection to her mom's side in the long run."

I nodded and stepped toward him, wanting to be all in his space.

"You can start slow; maybe extend an invite to the party tomorrow through Monique," I suggested, bumping my shoulder with his. "Whatever you need to do to be comfortable, that's what we'll do, and now that I'm not pregnant, I can slap the taste out her mouth if she tries that bullshit again."

"Shit," January cursed, clapping.

"No cursing," August chastised half-heartedly.

She tipped her head and I knew what was coming next.

"Shit, Dad-dy..." Her little brown eyes widened, then she smiled. "Shit, Mommy. Shit, Shit, Shit."

I tried my hardest not to laugh, but she was such a funny kid and always testing the limits.

Kali had been a mild-mannered baby, even in the infamous terrible twos stage.

I wasn't sure either of the girls would let us off the hook.

August tossed January in the air, his eyes brightening at her laughter.

Through her giggles, I could hear a soft whine from her sister and I turned to get her.

"Always a short napper, huh?" I accused, picking my twin up.

She had her father's eyes but resembled me the most, though I had a feeling she'd grow up and suddenly begin to take after him.

"Da Da," she murmured, eyes over my shoulder.

I turned to find him standing behind us with January weaving in and out of his legs.

October reached for him, and he obliged, smiling down at her.

"Hey, babygirl," he muttered as she dropped her head against his chest.

I scoffed and August beamed at me.

"She's a little terrorizer when you aren't here," I snitched, frowning as his smile enlarged. "You can't just come here and get her to act like a little princess for you."

I folded my arms and pouted.

August chuckled and tugged me into him, his lips brushing my temple several times before he said, "I'll make it up to you later, Angel face."

Our eyes met, and immediately, I ducked away, feeling shy.

"I love it when you get all shy on me," he called as I left them to warm dinner up.

Later that night, we managed to get both girls down without too much fuss.

October usually conked out after a bottle with cereal mixed in; she devoured those and, like most Black people, was ready to sleep the night away on a full stomach.

Now that January was mobile, she was harder to get down, but tonight, she'd fallen asleep with ease, and I was feeling a little smug because it had been me she wanted to cuddle until she was down.

"I love you," I whispered, my lips against August's ear as I straddled him. "So much."

"I love you," he returned, fingers tracing the darkened stretch marks along my sides. "I love these. My very own tiger."

I giggled and fell forward, grateful for a man who loved my old body but adored the new one just as much. Even when my insecurities wouldn't allow me to, he did it for the both of us.

"How quiet do you think you can be?" August asked, flipping us until I was on my back and he was between my thighs.

I raked my fingernails down his chest and admired the new ink with our daughters' names and birthdates.

"Depends on how deep you go," I replied, hooking a leg around his waist to draw him closer. "I need deep, baby."

He smiled against the skin of my neck and ripped my thong off, exposing my pussy to the chilly room. I sank deeper into the mattress, pushing my hands between us to stroke him until he slapped them away.

"Deep…" He kissed me fiercely, biting my bottom lip as he thrust into me. "I can do deep."

"Shit," I cried, digging my fingernails in his back. "Baby…"

He shook his head, forehead against mine, as he worked me good and hard.

I struggled to keep my whimpers at bay, needing so badly to scream his name but knowing it would wake the whole house.

"Take what you asked for like I know you can," he murmured, slowing his deep strokes to passionately devour my mouth. "That's my good girl."

I clawed at his skin, breathless.

Goddamn, this man for fucking me like it was our first time.

He flicked my clit, pinching the nub with enough pressure that it sent me over the edge far quicker than I'd wanted.

Fuck.

"Mine," August growled, raining kisses all over my face.

"Yours," I confirmed through laughter.

Always his.

epilogue two
AUGUST

JANUARY 6; OCTOBER 5

"LIKE THIS, TOBER," January said, snatching the marker away from her sister to demonstrate how to properly draw Princess Peach from Super Mario Bros.

Couri and I had taken them to see the movie and both were suddenly obsessed with the badass princess.

"Don't snatch, Snowflake," October retorted, stealing the marker back. "I know how."

A little too bossy for her own good, January looked away and crossed her arms.

When she spotted me staring in their direction, she walked over—a pout marring her pretty face. She looked more and more like Shondra as the years passed, though no one seemed to see what I did.

Maybe it was her mannerisms or how she loved prancing around the house like a ballerina. Couri eventually talked me into signing her up for lessons.

"Dad, Tober isn't listening," she complained, big brown

371

eyes filled with contempt. "Can you and Mom have another baby that will listen?"

I lifted an eyebrow at her request.

"Who put you up to that?" I questioned, lifting her onto my knee.

Couri and I had decided against more kids. A newborn among two toddlers wasn't on our list of things to accomplish, besides that we liked our family of four.

"I don't know."

She shrugged and watched her sister.

"Why don't you try helping her without taking the marker she's already using? And after you're finished, go get your bookbag and shoes."

She hopped off my knee and rushed over to her sister, who hid the marker she was using but returned to her masterpiece after January reached for her own.

It didn't take long for them to come together and draw something that didn't exactly look like Princess Peach, but I saw the vision, nonetheless.

"When does Grandma come?" January asked as she rounded the corner with the bag Couri packed before she left for work.

"Soon..." I checked my watch and stood. "What do you two want for a snack?"

"Peanut butter and jelly," they yelled in tandem.

I'd expected it to be that but found myself asking them each time in case it changed.

"Dad, how soon is soon?" January questioned impatiently. "Grandma promised to take me to Target. I can get anything I want for my birthday."

I tensed at the mention of her birthday.

March had come and gone, but Helen was making up for lost time today with an overnight sleepover.

She and January were well acquainted and had spent time together with supervision in the beginning stages but alone over the last three years. I trusted that she was sincerely apologetic for her antics six years ago, but lately, she'd been missing more and more time with January without a real explanation.

Her life was hers, but it was starting to affect my kid, and I took issue with that.

I knew she might get a little slower with time and age, but the last I'd seen her, something seemed off.

"She'll be here by the time you finish this sandwich."

I placed two plates on the table and waved for them both to sit.

Once settled, I returned with apple juice for October and milk for January.

"I want milk too, Daddy," October declared after noticing her sister had it.

She typically didn't want milk, but I switched them out without questioning her motives.

While they were preoccupied, I called June—away from their bionic ears—for advice.

"Hey, brother," she greeted breathlessly. "Sorry, this kid is driving me wild today."

I chuckled; June as a mom was fucking hilarious.

"If you're busy—"

"No!" she shouted, startling the fuck out of me. "Don't hang up. I need adult conversation."

"Couri talked to you about Helen, right?"

June sighed.

"Yeah, and I think something's off like the both of you. Maybe she's sick and hiding it? That's what your other sisters think."

"It crossed my mind. Should I talk to her? I don't want to pry, but Snowflake is starting to notice her absence. When we say Helen is coming, she questions us until the woman shows face."

June chuckled a little.

"She's so much like September when we were that age," she mused wistfully. "I think you should have the conversation but be gentle, August. I know your mind is working up all kinds of theories because of her past actions, but this more than likely isn't that."

"Alright," I agreed as the doorbell rang, playing Bowser's love song to Peach.

"Is that—"

I hung up before she could inquire about the stupid shit Couri and I did for our kids.

January and October sang from the kitchen, their little voices carrying a nice tune together. Everything we did was for their happiness and always would be.

I ambled toward the door and pulled it open, revealing Monique on the other side, not Helen.

"Wassup, Mo," I greeted, frowning. "I thought Helen was—"

"Can you step out here?" she cut in, tucking her hair behind her ear. "We need to talk."

Reluctant to do so, I regarded her closely.

"Why?"

"Because—"

"Monie!" January screeched, rushing past me to get to her aunt. "Where's Grandma?"

"She's meeting us at Target, Snowflake," Monique explained. "I'm here to take you."

I frowned and directed January to clean her face and lace her shoes while I talked to her aunt. After she darted inside, I stepped out on the porch and shut the door behind me.

"What's going on?"

Our eyes met and she sighed.

"Helen is sick and refusing to tell you because she thinks you'll keep January from her."

"After accepting her back into our lives, she—"

"She's just afraid of dying," she murmured, lifting and dropping her hands. "I know you still feel a way about what she did all those years ago, but I was hoping you'd have a conversation and reassure her."

"How sick is she, Monique?"

"It's Leukemia. She's in the chronic phase, so they caught it early, but her treatments can be brutal."

I nodded, the pieces finally coming together.

"Is that where she was last month?"

"She wanted so badly to make the theme park outing, but the day after treatments are always the hardest for her."

I closed my eyes and took a deep breath, pushing my feelings aside for my daughter.

"I'll talk to her when she drops January off tomorrow. Make sure it's her, even if you have to drive her here."

Monique nodded and I turned to open the door.

"I'm ready," January announced with the biggest smile on her face.

"Me too!" October declared, running toward us with shoes and a half-packed bag in hand. "I'm ready."

I shook my head.

"Baby, you—" `

"If it's alright with you, she can come," Monique cut in. "The more, the merrier."

I wasn't so sure; October had spent time with them before but never overnight.

"Let's take a second to check this bag first," I told her, forcing the duo back into the house with Monique in tow. "Be right back."

I took the bag and jogged up the steps, my phone in hand as I dialed Couri.

She picked up my FaceTime call after the third ring, hair flying wild before her eyes met the camera.

"Hey, baby, what's that look on your face?" she asked, regarding me closely.

I lifted the bag October called herself packing and said, "Your child would like to spend the night with her sister and Helen."

"Oh..." Her eyes widened a little as she leaned back in her desk chair. "I don't think we ever saw that coming."

"Me either, but I'm not against sending her if you aren't."

Couri nodded then frowned.

"Do we know why she's been missing in action lately?"

I propped my phone up on the dresser in October's room and started to repack her bag.

"She has Leukemia and is afraid that I won't want January around her."

"But—"

"I know..." I sighed. "I get it, but I wish she'd have said something sooner instead of leaving us to deal with the fallout of her not showing up. She ain't even here to pick them up, Monique is."

"She just needs a little reassurance, that's all," Couri mused, picking up on what I hadn't told her. "You'll give that to her, right? No one deserves to deal with cancer alone."

She looked away briefly, and I wished I could hold her, knowing thoughts of her mother's battle with the disease crossed her mind.

"I will reassure her," I avowed. "Now, tell me you love me and I'll let you get back to work."

Couri smiled and dropped her gaze.

"I love you, August Hanson."

"I love you to the moon, Couri Hanson."

We mutually ended the call after I finished with October's bag.

As I entered the living room, the kid in question came running to me with her arms out.

"Stand with us, Snowflake." I pointed to the spot next to her sister and kneeled before them. "I love the both of you with all my heart."

After securing their backpacks, I pulled them into me.

"I love you, Dad," January murmured into my chest, holding me tightly.

"I wuv you, too, Daddy," October said, her hold equally firm.

"Be good for Grandma and Auntie Monie, okay?"

They nodded, both bouncing on their toes in excitement.

Chuckling, I stood and glanced at Monique.

"They're all yours, and here's some money for both." I handed her a couple hundred. "Don't let Helen spend a bunch. They already have too much shit between the two of them."

Laughing, she ushered the pair toward the door but turned before leaving.

"Thank you, August," she said softly. "This is going to really brighten her week."

"It's nothing; just remind her that life is way too short to hide. I'm not her enemy."

"She knows, but I'm sure it'll be nice to hear, regardless."

I followed them out, grabbed a spare seat from the garage for October, and helped strap them in. Taking a step back, I watched from the driveway as Monique drove away, honking her horn as a final goodbye.

Damn.

Now what the fuck was I supposed to do without my girls?

epilogue three

COURI

JANUARY 10; OCTOBER 9

"FAMILY ROAD TRIP!" I cheered, earning groans from the girls. "Aren't you girls excited? We haven't spent the summer in Norbank in two years."

Norbank Shores had become like a second home to the lot of us.

After August successfully launched Hanson Black, his whiskey line, he and his sisters jumped headfirst in opening Hanson Distillery 2.0.

"Mom, please," Snowflake groused, rubbing her eyes. "It's way too early."

October nodded but stopped in her tracks after spotting Kali sitting at the counter.

"Auntie Kali!" she screeched, rushing her favorite person in the world these days.

Though she was their cousin, Kali had always wanted to be an aunt but as an only child that wouldn't come. So, she'd declared herself the girl's *auntie* at an early age and neither had questioned it as they got older.

Kali stood and lifted October off the floor, spinning her slender body in a full circle before doing the same with January.

"Mom didn't say you were coming," January said, feigning betrayal. "We thought we'd have to deal with her and Dad's singing the whole way to the shore."

I chuckled at her dramatics.

My child was a lowkey hater, but I loved her regardless.

"Don't come for my auntie," Kali said, smiling brightly. "Besides, it's her melodic voice on my earlier tracks."

Goodness.

I couldn't believe my first baby was a junior in college—a music major.

She'd grown into her large brown eyes, grew to a tall five-foot-nine, and chopped her big curly hair into a pixie cut like the one September wore before she married and had children.

"Wait..." October stared at me as if she had no clue who I was before turning to an amused Kali. "Mom sang on your records? On 'Imperfect Harmony'?"

I smirked.

"*Mom* also helped your auntie write that one and a few others," I bragged, enjoying the shocked expression on her and January's faces. "She was only eleven when she started her YouTube journey."

As the years passed, she'd grown her channel to three point five million subscribers.

"Wow," January murmured, her gaze far away. "I want to start a YouTube about ballet."

"You should do whatever your heart desires, Snowflake," Kali encouraged, winking at me. "That's what your mom told me when I expressed interest in starting a channel."

I understood that being the cool aunt to my niece wouldn't

automatically transfer to my children and their faces proved that theory right.

"When you get a little older, you'll understand," I told them. "Now! The both of you go put your bags in the car."

They took off, both stopping to hug me first.

Once they were gone, Kali laughed.

"I can't believe they don't see how cool you are."

"It's all good..." I smiled. "I'm good with just being a mom."

She rounded the island and wrapped her arms around me.

"I love you, Te."

"I love you more, Buttercup. Glad you decided to spend the summer with us last minute, but I do wonder what caused the change of heart."

She pulled away and returned to her stool with a shrug.

"Eh, I don't know. I wanted to stay on campus, but that didn't work out."

I placed drinks in the cooler while contemplating her half-truth.

Kali didn't keep much from me, but I had a feeling this was a subject she preferred not to visit yet. And while I respected her privacy, the sadness in her eyes was breaking my heart.

"Whenever you're ready to talk about it, I'll be here," I said softly. "All ears. No judgment."

She nodded and I continued to pack snacks for the road.

August came down shortly after I finished, his gaze lingering on Kali for a short moment before I got the kiss I'd been waiting on.

"Wassup, Kali?" August greeted, picking up on her gloominess. "You alright?"

She smiled and shook her head, standing to hug him.

"Hey, Uncle August. I'm okay, just sleepy. It's so early."

He tossed a knowing look my way after she mumbled something about going to check on the girls and I nodded.

Someone had broken my baby's heart and we could do nothing about it.

"You think Kingston knows?" August asked, phone already in hand as he typed a message.

"Baby..."

"He should know that she's hurting before he sees her face tomorrow."

I scoffed.

"So you aren't texting him about finding who the boy is and roughing him up?"

He shrugged and kissed my forehead.

"Both things can be true, Angel face."

His lips grazed the tip of my nose before he devoured my mouth.

Fuck me.

Ten years with this man and I still couldn't get enough.

"Oh, come on!" January groaned.

"Not this again," October complained. "Auntie, do you see what we have to deal with?"

Kali's laughter was what forced us apart.

Her eyes had brightened and the stiffness in her shoulders disappeared.

All she needed was to witness the girls' disgust of the love August and I shared to come back to life.

"This is going to be a great summer," Kali declared, eyes meeting mine. "When is everyone else coming down?"

When the Hansons started to settle down one by one and create little versions of themselves, Norbank became their second home too.

After all these years, we'd managed to purchase a row of homes that sat off the shoreline. The townspeople had started calling it Hanson Row.

"June, July, September, and their families are coming down

next weekend. I think Landon and Leslie and their crews are heading in at the same time, but Lola and her family are rolling in late because of open cases. Your parents are coming down tomorrow. The rest will pop in sporadically."

She hummed.

"What's for breakfast?" October asked, already over the topic. "Snowflake and I think we should stop at the Bluetop."

"Auntie Kali also thinks we should have breakfast at the Bluetop," Kali chimed in, pulling the girls into her. "Look at these faces..." They pouted in unison. "You can't deny them, can you?"

We couldn't and probably never would.

They were good, respectful kids with good grades and high remarks from their teachers to prove it. And as long as they continued to do the few things we asked of them, our girls could have the world.

"Bluetop it is," August decided after we exchanged nods.

The girls screeched in excitement and took off to grab their iPads and phones charging upstairs. I reminded January to call Helen, so we could stop by and see her before hitting the road.

She'd been in remission for two years now and the girls really enjoyed having her in their lives. With us spending the entire summer away from the city, she wanted to see them off and we couldn't deny her that.

I would be forever grateful for August's forgiving heart.

"This is going to be the best summer ever, Tobs," I heard January say before they got too far.

I had a feeling this summer would be one for the books.

epilogue four
AUGUST

JANUARY 15; OCTOBER 14

"Hey, Dad, can we talk?"

January first poked her head through the door and entered after I waved her inside.

"What's up, Snowflake?"

She dropped down on the sofa, track uniform rumpled from the last meet of the season. Her gaze bounced around the room before she settled her pretty browns on me.

"Um... Well, I was wondering..." She shifted and dropped her gaze. "Can you tell me about Shondra? Like in the way you knew her?"

I observed my daughter, noting the way she dug her fingernails into the sofa, something she'd been doing since high school started.

This was a long time coming, but I'd foolishly thought having Helen and Monique in her life to talk about Shondra would let me off the hook.

January knew that Couri wasn't her biological mother all her life.

Once she began to spend time with Helen, I couldn't bring myself to forbid the woman from talking about her daughter and lying to January had always been out of the question.

"I knew her as kind," I said, finally finding the words. "And stubborn but smart as a whip. She loved to dance, especially ballet."

I spotted the little smile curling her lips.

She had taken after her in that respect, ballet and jazz being her top two genres of dance.

"But like..." Her curious eyes met mine. "Did you love her? I-I know you have Mom, but I guess I want to know if you ever loved someone else before her."

I nodded and moved to sit beside her.

"I loved Shondra very much, but we didn't want the same things."

Her eyes took on a thoughtful expression before she asked, "Did you not want me?"

"I wanted you from the moment I learned of you. Loved you from the very moment I saw your chubby face."

She smiled and pushed my shoulder.

"Dad, I saw my baby pictures. I wasn't chubby until after I came home."

"Yeah, you eventually grew into this head." I ruffled her loose curls before she could duck away. "If there's something else on your mind, we can talk about it, Snowflake."

She turned to face me, dragging one leg on the sofa to hold.

"Why do you always look so uncomfortable when her name comes up?"

My body tensed without my permission.

Fuck!

"Like that..." She pointed. "You go all ramrod straight, then I think that I did something wrong, but I know I didn't."

She sounded so frustrated and I hated that it was because of me.

"To be honest, I am a little uncomfortable with the topic of your... of Shondra."

"Okay, can we talk about that? Dad, I feel like people are hiding things from me and it's making me feel crazy. So please tell me what I'm missing."

I sighed and walked over to my desk.

After grabbing the letter Shondra left me fifteen years ago, I returned to the sofa.

I'd told myself long ago that she'd never see it but over time my stance on the matter changed.

"When your bio mom was pregnant with you, we'd already broken up," I said, staring at the slightly tattered envelope. "I only learned that I would be a father after you were born."

I glanced over as her facial expression changed from curious to confused.

"I knew you two weren't together anymore or else that'd make you a cheater."

I lifted an eyebrow and she shrugged.

"My sister is only six months younger than me, Dad," she elaborated with a huff. "Why didn't you know?"

"She didn't tell me."

January nodded.

"But—"

"I never got to ask why." I took her hands and placed the letter in her palm. "She was already gone by then, but she wrote this to me. I'm going to let you read it, but you have to understand that it's nothing like what you're probably hoping. It might break your heart, but I promise to be here and help mend it."

She clutched the envelope while squeezing my fingers.

"I don't want to have a broken heart," she whispered before pulling away. "What do you think I should do?"

"Unfortunately, Snowflake, I can't make this decision for you." I stood. "Do you want to know the truth and find a way to accept it or do you want to cherish what you already know and leave the past in the past?"

"I—"

"No one but you needs to know the answer." I opened the door and sighed. "I'll be a room away whenever you're ready to talk about what's in there."

I knew what she would decide to do.

January couldn't go through life without knowing the whole truth.

Feeling sick about it, I went in search of Couri.

The sweet sound of soft humming drew me to the living room.

October was knocked out in the reclining chair, mouth wide open, with her track uniform on. She fell asleep after every meet in that exact spot.

"What's wrong, baby?" Couri asked, patting the spot next to her on the sofa.

I stretched out on my back and rested my head against her legs.

"She finally asked," I said, staring up at her. "For the truth, all of it."

"I don't know why I thought we had more time when so much of it has passed."

I nodded.

"Fifteen years, but it'll feel brand new to her. Not sure what to do with myself."

She walked the center of my face with her fingers, going back and forth until I stopped her.

"You and me, remember?"

Her eyes were watery, but she held it together.

"I don't want her to hurt," she whispered. "I hope she talks to us."

"Me too." I kissed the inside of her palm. "We'll be here whenever that time comes," I affirmed.

"Must you guys be all over one another all the time?" October asked, sitting up but somehow still half asleep.

She stretched before officially opening her eyes.

"What's wrong?" she asked, looking between the two of us. "Where's Snowflake?"

I sat up.

"Upstairs. You should go check on her."

She narrowed her eyes but jumped up as I expected and headed upstairs.

"I have never been happier about them being the best of friends until now," Couri mused as she stood.

She reached for me and I let her pull me up and into a hug.

"You are a great father," she whispered, chin on my chest and eyes on me. "Our girls adore you just as I do."

"You don't think she'll be upset with me?"

Couri frowned.

"Upset about what?"

I had no fucking idea, but as her father, I felt somehow responsible.

"You did your part, August. No move you've made since you brought our baby home has been wrong. It's been about making life easy for her from day one and you've done that."

"We did that," I corrected.

"I know we did and she'll always know that."

"I will," January said from behind us.

I turned and the look in her eyes broke my heart.

October stood beside her as support and I looked between them, suddenly realizing my girls weren't so little anymore.

The silence ate me up inside, but we waited for January to make the first move, and eventually, she did.

"Mommy," she cried, rushing to Couri. "I love you so much and I hope I never made you feel taken for granted. Everything you've done for me, I-I..."

"Hey..." Couri wiped her face and smiled. "You've never once in your life made me feel anything but loved and proud and a little emotional at how big you've gotten. What I did for you, choosing to be your second-chance mom, was and will always be one of the best decisions I've ever made. My greatest accomplishment is this family with you and your sister and dad."

October, who had been trying to make herself smaller, inched closer to me. I draped an arm over her shoulder and tugged her into my side.

"Whenever you're ready, she left you a couple of things that I've been saving," I said, not wanting us to stand in sadness anymore.

January threw herself at me and we ended up in a group hug.

"I'm sorry, D-Dad," she murmured, choking on her words. "You didn't deserve that, but I'm glad you came for me and stayed."

I bundled my girls close, pulling Couri into the fold before falling back onto the sofa.

"My hair!" October complained.

"Oh my goodness, you two really smell like you've been running for your lives," Couri threw out, holding her nose.

"Way to mess up the moment, you two," January fussed as they removed themselves from me.

I regarded her red-rimmed eyes closely until she smiled and said, "I'm not sure how I feel about what I learned, just mostly sad right now. But I have you guys, so I'll be okay. Anyway, I'm gonna go shower. Can we have pizza for dinner?"

She walked away before either of us could respond and October followed her movements until she couldn't anymore.

"Don't worry; I'll make sure she's okay."

Couri straddled me once October took off after her sister.

"Another year, another chapter written," she said, cupping my face.

I chuckled.

"And still fucking happy..."

Even with this new obstacle to overcome, I felt relief that we would get through it as a family.

"How about another fifteen years?"

Couri's eyes went soft.

"You and me, August Hanson..." She kissed me gently and I savored the moment. "You and me."

Always and forever.

bonus chapters

january (18)

"ARE you sure you guys don't want to go to school closer to home, Snowflake?" Mom asked as she repacked my bags.

My folding hadn't been up to her standard but I didn't mind the intrusion. She only wanted to sneak more solo time in before we drove to Tennessee in the morning.

"We already accepted the scholarships, Mommy," I said, kissing her cheek. "Besides, it isn't that far away and we'll be home for Thanksgiving."

The holidays were big in my family; so big that we used the distillery to fit everyone.

"I can't believe how much time has passed. Now you and your sister are off to college. Maybe it's time for a new baby."

My eyes bucked and she laughed.

"Don't give me those big eyes. It was a joke."

I regarded her closely, wondering if she was telling the truth or not.

My parents never stopped touching one another. It was gross but endearing.

I knew what genuine love looked like because of them.

Deep down, I hoped to one day experience a love like theirs.

October and I talked about that a lot growing up.

"You two almost ready?" Dad asked from the doorway with one of October's bags clutched in his hand. "We're gonna be late to the party Nana and Pop Pop insisted on throwing."

I groaned, not wanting a party, but also not wanting to miss an opportunity to celebrate with our family.

October and I collectively decided on Tennessee State University. Having a sister who was only six months younger than me meant we got to do everything together and that included being college roommates.

I was grateful to have my best friend and confidant with me on this new journey, it made it less scary.

Dad's gaze moved slowly from Mom to me.

"Has she been crying?"

Mom slapped my suitcase closed and huffed.

"I need a second," she murmured, trying her best to push past Dad who wasn't allowing it.

"Look at me," he murmured, tucking his fingers under her chin. "You and me, remember?"

I ducked my head to hide my smile.

Ugh.

They were so cute but I refused to ever admit that aloud.

"I'm sure she remembers, Dad," October said, making herself known from behind them. "How come January and I are never included in this saying? What are we, chopped meat?"

I chuckled and she beamed from her tired joke. We knew it was just their thing and had nothing to do with us not being part of their unit.

"Because you both decided to forgo being close to home and leave us," Dad mused with a smirk as we followed him downstairs where the rest of our things were piled by the front door, ready to be packed in the car tomorrow.

"It's only eight hours away," I defended with a nod of support from my ace.

"That's an entire shift to get to you," Mom argued, hands on her hips. "Nonetheless, I'm proud of you girls for keeping up your grades, excelling in sports, and dance, and every other extracurricular activity you committed to..." She tossed a watery smile at both of us. "Very proud."

Tober and I glanced at one another and rushed her, knocking us to the floor on purpose.

She screeched with laughter as we attacked her with kisses.

It was all she'd needed, some love from us before we flipped the last page on this chapter and started anew.

My mom was the best, most loving and caring and selfless person ever. She wanted everyone to be happy and safe, to feel loved and adored.

I couldn't have asked for a better woman to step up and help raise me.

Feeling a little emotional, I sat up and closed my eyes briefly.

"I've been thinking," I said, bringing my knees to my chest as Mom and October sat up with me.

Dad kneeled and smiled, knowing where I was going with this conversation.

It had been our plan for a long time to present this to her but I was admittedly afraid.

Finding out two years ago that my biological mother hadn't wanted me was a hard pill to swallow but my family pulled me through that with grace and love.

If it hadn't been for my *real* mom being a staple in my life before learning the truth, I wasn't so sure the hurt would've subsided as easily.

"What's on your mind, Snowflake?" Mom asked softly, her hand caressing my back in support.

"We should make this union official," I declared, turning to stare into her dark eyes.

She nodded slowly, her interest piqued.

"Okay but first you gotta tell me what we're making official."

I glanced at Dad for help and he stood to grab the papers we'd had drawn up eight months ago.

He came back with the manila envelope and handed it to Mom.

She looked between us then opened it, pulling the stapled pages from inside.

Her gaze moved rapidly as she read what we'd given her then the tears came.

"Oh, Snowflake," she cried as Dad swiped the droplets from her face. "Do you mean it?"

I nodded and squeezed my legs tighter.

Of course I meant it, didn't she know what she meant to me?

"We should've done it a long time ago," Dad said, his gaze moving between the three of us. "It's always been us four and it always will be."

Though we had a big family and a lot of cousins thanks to Dad's three sisters and first cousins, it had always been us four against the world.

I smiled and rested my head on Mom's shoulder.

She wrapped one arm around me and lifted the petition for adoption.

"Wow," she murmured wistfully. "You know, I've always been your mom, even when I was afraid you wouldn't see it that way. Didn't matter if it was by blood or not, but this…" She shook her head and smiled. "It means the world to me."

She meant the world to me.

My *mom*.

From day one, always *mine*.

october (18)

"HEY, ARE YOU—"

"Did Mom or Dad say anything about them buying new cars?" I asked, grateful our Uber pulled into the driveway before January could inquire about how I was doing for the thirtieth time.

Two Range Rovers sat side by side near the garage, one in dark blue and the other in midnight black.

"No..." She tsked as we got out. "I thought they said no new purchases until after the holiday."

We'd both been begging for a car, one to share or two if they were feeling generous.

Our parents moved at their own speed when it came to giving in to our requests, but mostly they always said yes.

Dad appeared in the doorway with two big boxes in his hands and a stupid smile on his face.

"What's going on?" I asked, waving toward the trucks.

"And why does it have you smiling like a goof?" January added.

Mom appeared seconds later wearing the same silly smile as she grabbed one of the boxes to hold.

I glanced between them, eyes narrowed.

After a few seconds, it hit me what was happening.

"Oh my god. The trucks are ours, aren't they?"

It suddenly made sense.

"Wait..." January released the handle on her suitcase and took a step forward. "Did you get those for us?"

"You asked, didn't you?" Dad quipped, an eyebrow raised.

We screeched in unison and ran toward the Ranges, bags forgotten.

"But you said—"

"I only said it to get you two off our backs," he cut in, laughing.

January and I circled our new trucks, easily figuring out which belonged to who by the license plates. Hers had a little snowflake emblem, while mine had a pumpkin.

Halloween was my favorite holiday.

"You're like little hyenas when you want something," Mom added.

I bounced on my tiptoes, excited to get the key.

"What's in the boxes?" I asked just as a soft whine came from one.

"Is there an animal in there?" January questioned as we approached them.

"Take the tops off and see," Mom instructed.

I reached for the one in Dad's hands and lifted it.

Sure enough, underneath was a sleeping chocolate Labrador.

January's dog was also a Labrador but with a black coat, just like she'd been asking for since we were kids. It whined until she lifted it into her arms.

"What did we do to deserve all of this before Christmas?" she asked as I gently picked my sleeping puppy up and cradled him in my neck.

Mom had wanted a hoard of pets but for whatever reason never acted on the urge.

I guess now that January and I were off at college they needed the company and chaos two puppies would bring.

"You finished your first semester of college," Mom explained, eyes filled with pride.

"Also, Landon bought the boys cars and we couldn't let him outdo us," Dad added. "Those were supposed to be your Christmas gifts. The dogs were for finishing your first semester."

I rolled my eyes and laughed.

Our cousuncle Landon was competitive for no reason at all. But we used it to help our cousins get things faster.

During our weekly cousin Zoom, we'd told them that our parents were thinking of getting us cars after Christmas.

All they had to do was tell their dad to get the ball rolling in their favor and it had clearly worked.

January and I shared victory nods as Dad stacked the over-sized boxes on the ground and pulled two sets of keys from his pocket.

"For now, these stay home," he said, looking between us sternly. "You don't have permits for campus and it's too late to get them."

We nodded, neither of us caring.

There were plenty of people to ride around and see in the city.

"I don't trust that they won't get stolen or broken into either," Mom added. "We'll figure something out, but you'll have full access while home for now."

Dad handed each of us a set and smiled.

"Merry early Christmas; you won't be getting anything else."

We handed our pups over and raced to open the doors of our trucks.

"You customized it!" I screamed, brushing a hand over my name stitched into the driver's seat.

The genuine leather was smooth as butter and smelled of lavender, somehow soothing my broken heart.

I turned abruptly, needing to show my appreciation a little more.

"Hey, Dad," I called after noticing Mom talking to January.

He made his way over, clutching my pup, his gaze curious.

"What's up, Tob—"

I wrapped my arms around him, angling myself to his right to avoid the pup I still needed to name.

"Thank you for being the best dad in the world," I murmured, squeezing him tightly. "I don't know if I've told you this recently, but I appreciate you."

He grumbled about me making him emotional and I smiled.

Everyone I knew outside my family didn't understand how I could wear my emotions on my sleeve without fear of being hurt.

It was because of my parents and family I felt comfortable doing so.

They raised us to not only speak up for ourselves but to show love to the people we cared about unconditionally.

I knew firsthand that not everyone in the world would protect my heart like my family did, but I wouldn't change who I was for anyone.

Being a Hanson just made me different.

"You show me every chance you get that you're appreciative," Dad said, dropping a kiss on my forehead.

"Thanks, Dad."

He shifted to the left and I released him.

"Looks like someone wants to talk," he said, eyeing January and me closely as he took Mom's hand. "We'll be inside."

They left us alone and I turned to my sister, already knowing where this conversation was going.

"I hope this made you feel better," she whispered, looking me over. "You know you won't be able to hide that you're hurting from them for long."

I rolled my eyes but nodded.

Mom and Dad were too in sync with our emotions to miss it.

"I'm not hurting, just disappointed."

I shrugged.

"Feeling disappointed because of someone else's actions is a much worse feeling than being outright hurt. You know I know."

I twirled my key fob around my finger to avoid thinking about how right she was.

"He could've just told me he didn't want to do the long-distance thing anymore," I whispered, thinking of my childhood love. "It took one semester and now it's just... *over*."

I had been a little naive to think I could maintain a long-distance relationship with someone at our young age while in college, but I figured nothing could beat a failure but a try.

I tried.

I failed.

But that was part of life, right?

"Forget him, Tobs. You are worthy of so much more, and when we take over Norbank this summer, he'll wish he never broke your heart."

I smiled at the thought, more than grateful to always have my sister and best friend by my side.

"I love you, Snowflake."

"I love you more," she whispered, pulling me into a tight embrace. "You and me, remember? I've got your back through thick and thin."

I nodded, knowing that to be true.

"And I've got yours. It's you and me. *Always.*"

author notes

Thank you for reading.

I hope you enjoyed the first book in the Hanson family series.

Please leave me a review on Amazon and/or Goodreads.

Interested in viewing a Pinterest board with visuals from the book?

Link: https://pin.it/2v0PYJC

Would you like to read bonus content from the book? Join my Patreon for chapters from January and October's POV here:

patreon.com/asiamonique

Here are a few other ways to stay connected with me:

Website: www.asiamonique.com

Like me on Facebook: http://bit.ly/AuthorAsiaMonique

Join my readers group on

Facebook: http://bit.ly/ForTheLoveOfAsiaMonique

Follow me on TikTok: https://vm.tiktok.com/TTPdkpVDvK/

Follow me on Instagram: www.instagram.com/_ayemonique

Made in the USA
Columbia, SC
15 June 2025

59433756R00248